Dance Away with Me

Dance Away with Me

A Novel

Susan Elizabeth Phillips

HARPER LARGE PRINT

An Imprint of HarperCollinsPublishers

DANCE AWAY WITH ME. Copyright © 2020 by Susan E. Phillips, LLC. All rights reserved. Printed in the United States of America. No part of this book may be used or reproduced in any manner whatsoever without written permission except in the case of brief quotations embodied in critical articles and reviews. For information, address HarperCollins Publishers, 195 Broadway, New York, NY 10007.

HarperCollins books may be purchased for educational, business, or sales promotional use. For information, please e-mail the Special Markets Department at SPsales@harpercollins.com.

FIRST HARPER LARGE PRINT EDITION

ISBN: 978-0-06-300596-9

Library of Congress Cataloging-in-Publication Data is available upon request.

20 21 22 23 24 LSC 10 9 8 7 6 5 4 3 2 1

To the beloved "bonuses" in my life: first Nickie, the dancing queen, appeared. And then Leah, Andy, and Anya came along. Families are built in the most amazing ways.

Dance Away with Me

Prologue

The boy held the spray can perfectly straight. Kept it close to the ribbed stainless steel. Squeezed the nozzle and watched the brilliant slipstream of red paint form the letter *I*.

He'd done it. He'd hit a train. Anybody could tag a wall or the roll-down security gate in front of some stupid-ass pawnshop, but only the outlaws, only the best graffiti artists, could tag a New York City subway train. And he was only ten years old.

Getting here from the Upper East Side was as dangerous as being in freaking Bosnia or Iraq or someplace like that. Walking across Central Park in the dark. Taking the 1 train north with four spray cans of Krylon in his backpack. He'd pulled his black sweatshirt hood over his head, trying to make himself invisible to the

2 · SUSAN ELIZABETH PHILLIPS

drunks and the junkies traveling with him all the way to 207th Street. Freaking Inwood, like one of the worst places in Manhattan, with everybody getting murdered and robbed and stuff.

Staying in the shadows. That was how he'd managed to slip past the security guards at the 207th Street Train Yard, ducking and weaving his way into the night jungle of rail and metal to tag his first subway car.

He sprayed some blades of orange and purple grass at the bottom of the car. He added cool demonic creatures peeking through. And now, before they spotted him, the rest of his tag. *IHN4*.

It wasn't a made-up tag like everybody else used. Not for him. These were his real initials, the first three letters the same as his old man's, his grandfather's, his great-grandfather's. Only the 4 was his alone.

Painting all the letters the same size was for amateurs, so he'd made the 4 big. Last year, he hadn't known better when he'd tagged his first building, the Central Park West co-op where he lived. That had kicked up a shit storm with the co-op board. Nobody had suspected it was him.

Almost nobody.

If he didn't get out of here soon, they'd spot him. He added black cracks across the letters, like they were falling apart. If only he had a brush and the time to do it right. But he didn't.

Now all he had left was to take the photo. The freaking MTA had this new policy. Any car that got tagged, they'd take out of service until the graffiti was wiped clean. The only way an artist could prove he'd done the work was with a photo. If you didn't get a photo, the tag didn't exist.

He fumbled for his backpack and grabbed the Olympus Stylus camera their housekeeper had given him for his birthday. He stepped back from the car and aimed, getting in as much as he could. The flash might give him away, but he had to take the risk. Without the photo, he couldn't claim the tag.

"Hold it right there!"

He pressed the shutter. The flash exploded at the same time the guard grabbed his arm, ruining the shot.

His father picked him up at the police station. His dad was a big shot in the city, and he was all nice guy, can-we-talk-about-this-in-private with the cops. But after they were out of the station, crossing the crumbling parking lot, his dad body-slammed him against the side of his new Porsche 911.

"You fucking loser!" He drew back his arm and

slapped him hard. On the right side of his head. The left. A punch.

Inside the car, the diamonds in his mother's earlobes glittered as she turned and looked the other way.

His father threw him in the tiny backseat. But as Ian wiped the blood from his nose on the sleeve of his sweatshirt, all he could think about was that he didn't get the photo. He was used to his father's violence. He'd live through it like he always did. But the photo . . .

The photo would have made him a god.

Chapter One

Tess danced in the rain. She danced in her underpants and an old tank top with her feet tucked into a sad pair of once-silver ballet flats. She stomped her feet on the slippery, moss-covered flagstones under the dripping hickory tree that had sheltered the mountain cabin for so many years. Today she danced to hip-hop, yesterday it was reggae, the day before that— maybe grunge, maybe not, as long as it was loud, loud enough to be an accomplice to her anger, to sanctify the grief that would never, ever go away. The kind of loud that wasn't possible in Milwaukee, but here on Runaway Mountain, where her nearest neighbors were deer and raccoons, she could blast her music as loud as she needed.

The cold, wet wind of an East Tennessee February carried the scent of decaying leaves and skunk. This wasn't the right weather to be outside in only a tank top and underpants, but unlike a dead husband, being wet and cold was something Tess could fix.

A broken flagstone caught the toe of her ballet flat, sending it flopping into the weeds. One shoe on, one shoe off. Sending all her emotions into her feet. A sharp stone dug at her heel, but if she stopped, her anger would burn her up. She forced her hips to move, tossed her head so that her wet, tangled hair flew. Faster and faster. *Don't stop. Don't ever stop. Once you stop—*

"Are you *deaf?*"

She froze as a man charged across the rickety wooden bridge that spanned Poorhouse Creek. A mountain man with shaggy dark hair, a fierce nose, and a jackhammer jaw. A bear of a man—sycamore tall and oblivious to the rain—wearing an untucked red-and-black-checked flannel shirt, paint-splattered boots, and jeans designed for hard work. She'd read about these mountain men—hermits who holed up in the wilderness with a pack of feral dogs and an arsenal of military rifles. They went without human contact for months—for years—until they forgot their origins.

She stood there immobilized in her old bikini underpants and a wet, white cotton tank top that strained over her breasts. Braless, furious, half-wild herself, and very much alone.

He charged toward her, oblivious to the rain, the wobbly, wooden bridge swaying behind him. "I put up with this crap yesterday afternoon, and yesterday evening, and at *two* frigging o'clock this *morning*, but I'm not putting up with it any longer!"

She took him in with a series of quick impressions. Defiant waves in the unruly, too-long hair that curled wet against his neck. His workman's clothes were rumpled, and a dozen different colors of paint spattered his cracked leather boots. His beard stubble wasn't long enough for a crazed hermit, but he looked crazed nonetheless.

She wouldn't apologize. She'd done enough apologizing back home for the burden her grief had put on her friends and her co-workers, and she wouldn't do it here. She'd chosen Runaway Mountain, not only for its name, but also for its isolation—a place where she could be as impolite, as grief-stricken, as angry at the universe as she wanted to be. "Stop yelling at me!"

"How else are you going to hear me?" He snatched up her Bluetooth speaker from its dry spot underneath the splintered remains of a picnic table.

"Put that down!"

He jabbed at the power switch with a big, blunt-fingered paw, shutting off the music. "How about a little common courtesy?"

"*Courtesy?*" She relished having an outlet for the injustice life had thrown at her. "That's what you call storming down here like a wild man?"

"If you had any respect for all this . . ." He made a slashing gesture toward the trees and Poorhouse Creek, the harsh lines of his face so rough-hewn they could have been carved with a chain saw. "If you had any respect, I wouldn't have had to storm down here!"

And then she saw it. The moment he became aware of her dress—or undress. Eyes the color of slate grazed her disparagingly. But disparaging of what? Of her wet, tangled hair? Of her body, heavier than it should be from trying to suffocate herself with food? Her legs? Her ratty underwear? Or maybe just her audacity for taking up space on his planet?

Who was she kidding? With her breasts straining against a wet tank top, she must look like a grotesque cliché of a drunken college girl on a Cancun spring break. Her head swam, high on the rush of her anger. "All you had to do was ask politely!"

His gaze cut through her, his voice a low, deep growl. "Yeah, I'm sure that would have worked."

She was clearly in the wrong, but she didn't care. "Who *are* you?"

"Someone who'd like a little peace and quiet. Two words you don't seem to comprehend."

No one had reprimanded her since her husband had died. Instead, they all acted as if they were still standing in the funeral parlor with its overstuffed furniture and nauseating smell of Stargazer lilies. Having a target for her anger was sickly intoxicating. "Are you this rude to everybody?" she exclaimed. "Because if you are—"

Just then, a wood sprite flew across the narrow creek bridge, effortlessly skipping over the missing planks, her steps so light the structure barely moved. "Ian!" The fairy creature's long blond hair floated behind her from beneath a big red umbrella. A gauzy, ankle-length cotton gown better suited to July than early February swirled around her calves. She was tall and lithe, except for the mound of her pregnancy.

"Ian, stop yelling at her," the ethereal creature said. "I could hear you from the schoolhouse."

So that's where he'd come from—the renovated, white wooden schoolhouse on the ridge above the cabin. In January, when Tess had first moved here, she'd trudged up the trail to see what was there. When she'd looked through the windows, she could tell the place had been turned into a residence, but no one appeared to be living there. Until now.

"Don't pay any attention to him." The sprite was a blue-eyed Disney fairy, maybe in her thirties like Tess. Just past prime fairyhood. She breezed through the undergrowth bordering the cabin, oblivious to the wet grass brushing her calves. "He's always like this when he's having trouble with a painting."

A painting. Not painting in general. The mountain man must be an artist. A temperamental one.

The fairy laughed, a laugh that didn't quite make its way to those storybook blue eyes. Something about her seemed familiar, although Tess knew they'd never met. "He's more bark than bite," the fairy said, "although, he's been known to do that, too." She held out a slim, warm hand from beneath the red umbrella. "I'm Bianca."

"Tess Hartsong."

"Your hands are freezing," the woman said. "They feel good. I've been so hot."

Tess's professional midwife's eye took over. Bianca was short of breath, the way many women were as they neared their third trimester. Maybe around seven months. She was carrying high and to the front. Her complexion was pale, but not washed out enough to be worrisome.

"Ian, you've done enough damage," the sprite said. "Go home."

He was holding Tess's Bluetooth speaker as if he intended to walk off with it. But he gifted her with another growl and set it down hard on the picnic bench. "Don't make me come down here again."

"Ian!"

Ignoring the sprite, he strode across the narrow bridge, his steps rattling the wet, wooden planks so ferociously Tess expected the whole thing to crash into Poorhouse Creek.

"Don't mind him," Bianca said. "He's being a prick."

Next to the stormy mountain man, the sprite underneath the red umbrella was a dewy rainbow, and Tess twisted the lock on her internal Pandora's box, the place where she stored her emotions when she needed to get through the day. "It was my fault," she confessed. "I didn't know anyone was living up there."

"We moved in three days ago. Not my choice, but my husband thought the mountain air would be good for me. At least that's what he said." Bianca handed Tess the umbrella and whipped her gauzy cotton gown over her head. She was naked underneath except for a tiny champagne-colored thong. "Oh, god, I've been wanting to do that all morning. It's like I have a furnace running inside me."

The rain had become a light drizzle, and Bianca gazed into the dripping trees. She was thin, with slender thighs and light blue veins tracing small, porcelain breasts. Comfortable in her nudity, she stretched, going up on the toes of her sandals and letting her long hair cascade down her back in a silky waterfall. "It's so peaceful here. But boring." She glanced toward the cabin. "Do you have coffee? Ian freaks out if I even look at a coffee mug, and I have another two months."

Tess had come to these Tennessee mountains to get away from people, but the novelty of talking with someone who didn't view her as a tragic widow drew her in. Besides, she didn't have anything better to do other than stomp her feet or stare out the window. "Sure." She gathered up the ballet flat she'd kicked off. "Fair warning. It's still a mess."

Bianca shrugged and closed the umbrella. "Organized people freak me out."

Tess managed one of those smiles she feigned to convince everyone she was fine. "No worries about that."

Back in the old days, it had been different. She'd been organized. She'd believed in structure, logic, predictability. In the old days, she'd believed in following the rules. If you did your homework, stopped at stop signs, paid your taxes, everything would be fine.

The cabin's rough-hewn log exterior was solid, but ugly. Moss grew on the roof, and two thin tree trunks, long ago stripped of their bark, supported the over-hang above the back door. The still-bare branches of the hickory, maple, and black walnut hovered above the old house, their branches scratching the roof like witches' fingernails.

The main room held both the kitchen and living area, with a wooden staircase leading up to the two bedrooms. The walls were technically whitewashed pine but had yellowed with age. The dusty curtains had fallen apart when Tess tried to take them down to wash, so she'd had to replace them with plain white ones. A big front window offered a glimpse of the valley below and the small town of Tempest, Tennessee. The back windows looked out over Poorhouse Creek.

Bianca draped her cotton gown across the armchair and used the back to steady herself as she pulled off the sandals pinching her feet. Straightening, she gazed from the soot-blackened stone fireplace at one end of the cabin to the old-fashioned kitchen at the other.

The cast iron farmhouse sink was original, as was the fifties gas stove. Open shelving, now divested of the crumbling paper that had lined it, held the sparse collection of dishes and canned goods Tess had brought with her from Milwaukee. "This is a fixer-upper's dream," Bianca said.

Only as Tess's teeth started to chatter did she realize how cold she was. She stuffed her damp legs into the jeans she'd abandoned next to the back door and pulled Trav's ancient University of Wisconsin sweatshirt over her wet tank top. "I'm not much of a fixer-upper."

Trav hadn't been, either. He was the one who'd held the flashlight while she crawled under the sink to fix a leaky pipe.

"Did I ever tell you how hot you look with a pipe wrench?" he'd say.

"Tell me again."

Tess rubbed the finger that had once held her wedding ring. Taking if off had ripped out her heart, but if she'd worn it here, she would have had to endure too many questions. Even worse, she'd have had to listen to others' stories of loss.

"I know how you feel. I lost my grandmother last year."

". . . my uncle."

". . . my cat."

No, you don't know how I feel! Tess wanted to scream

at all of her well-meaning friends and co-workers. *You only know how* you *feel!*

She unclenched her fingers. "The best I can say is that the place is clean."

She'd scrubbed the kitchen from top to bottom, taking steel wool to the stove and scouring powder to the sink. She'd mopped the old pine floors, dragged the threadbare Turkish rug outside to beat the grime from it, and fallen into a sneezing fit when she'd done the same with the couch cushions, which were slipcovered in a monumentally inappropriate English foxhunting scene. Her only significant purchase was a new mattress for the double bed upstairs.

Bianca glanced over her shoulder and wrinkled her small, perfect nose. "Do you have to use an outhouse?"

"God was merciful. Indoor plumbing upstairs." She zipped up Trav's sweatshirt. She'd worn it for months after he died until it had gotten so filthy she'd had to launder it. Now, it no longer held his familiar scent, the combination of warm skin, soap, and Right Guard deodorant.

What the hell, Trav? How many thirty-five-year-olds die from pneumococcal pneumonia these days?

She tugged her long, tangled hair from the neck of the sweatshirt. "I bought the place sight unseen. The price was right, but the photos were misleading."

Bianca waddled toward the kitchen table. "It could be really cute with some paint and new furniture."

Once Tess would have risen to the challenge, but not now. Not only couldn't she afford new furniture, but she also didn't care enough to buy any. "Someday."

As Tess made coffee, Bianca chatted about a biography of one of Picasso's mistresses she'd just read and about how much she already missed Thai food. Tess learned that Bianca and her husband lived in Manhattan, where she worked as a visual merchandiser in the fashion industry. "I design windows and pop-up stores," she explained. "It's a lot more fun than modeling used to be, although not as lucrative."

"Modeling?" Tess turned from the stove to stare at her as she finally put it all together. "That's why you seem so familiar. Bianca Jensen! We all wanted to be you." She hadn't made the connection between Bianca's name and Tess's own college days, when that face had been on the cover of every fashion magazine.

"I had a good career," Bianca said modestly.

"More than good. You were everywhere." As Tess poured two mugs of coffee and carried them to the table, she remembered how dissatisfied those magazine covers had made her feel with her own big breasts, disobedient hair, and olive complexion.

Bianca took a sip from her mug and released a long,

delicious sigh. "So good. You'd think it was heroin the way Ian acts."

As a midwife, this was hardly the first time Tess had sat across the kitchen table from an almost nude woman, but unlike Bianca, those women had been in labor. Bianca curled her free hand around her belly in the protective, self-satisfied way of pregnant women. "How long have you lived in Tempest?"

"Exactly twenty-four days." Being too evasive made people inquisitive, and it was better to volunteer a little information so it didn't look as though she had anything to hide, because once people knew she was a widow, everything would change. She braced her heels on the chair rung. "I got tired of Milwaukee."

"But why here?"

Because she'd seen the name Runaway Mountain on a map. "I got restless."

Not true. Trav was the restless one. In the eleven years they'd been married, they'd lived in California, Colorado, and Arizona before moving back to Milwaukee, where they'd grown up. He'd been ready to move again when he'd died. She traced the handle of the mug with her thumb. "What about you? How did you end up in these mountains?"

"Not my choice. There can't be more than eight hundred people living in this godforsaken place."

Nine hundred sixty-eight, according to the sign on the highway.

"It's all Ian's fault," she said. "Too many people were bothering him in the city—dealers, the press, wannabe artists—so he decided to move us here."

"Dealers? The press?"

"That man who was yelling at you is Ian Hamilton North the Fourth. The artist."

Even if Tess hadn't loved art museums, she would have recognized his name. Ian Hamilton North IV was one of the world's most famous street artists, second only to the mysterious Banksy. He was also, she seemed to remember, the black sheep of the blue-blooded North family financial dynasty. Although she didn't know a lot about street artists—or graffiti crapologists, as Trav had called them—she'd been fascinated by North's work.

"Give me a can of spray paint, and I can do the same thing," Trav had said. But the critics didn't share Trav's opinion.

She remembered what she'd read about North. His reputation had grown from urban street corner tags as a kid to the stenciled posters he'd plastered on bus stops and utility boxes. From there, he'd started producing larger pieces, which had begun showing up on the sides of buildings all over the world—outlaw works at first and finally commissioned murals. Now sold-out gallery shows and museum exhibitions, like the one she'd seen, displayed his posters and paintings, all of which bore the tag he'd adopted as a kid—IHN4, Ian Hamilton North IV.

Street artists, by nature, had little regard for law and order, so it shouldn't surprise her that this particular artist, however brilliant, lacked the unselfishness gene. Witness the fact that he'd dragged his heavily pregnant wife away from her home to the middle of nowhere two months before her due date.

"I saw the MoMA exhibition." She and Trav had gone to Manhattan not long before he'd gotten sick. At the time, she'd loved the explosive images she'd seen on the museum's walls, but now that she'd met the artist, not so much.

"I'm his muse." Bianca touched her collarbone. "I drive him crazy, but he needs me. Two years ago we broke up. He was paralyzed for almost three months. Couldn't paint a thing." She smiled, not bothering to hide her satisfaction.

Tess wasn't sure how an ethereal creature like Bianca could inspire such a mythic body of work. In the exhibit she'd seen, the video game–like creatures of North's early work had transitioned into grotesque, mythological creatures he placed in everyday surroundings—the family breakfast table, a backyard barbecue, an office cubicle. The calligraphy in his paintings had grown more intricate, too, until finally his letters lost themselves in abstract design.

Bianca's smile turned dreamy as she cupped her hands over her abdomen. "I have a doctor in Knoxville now, and we're moving into a hotel near the hospital a couple of weeks before my due date. I can't wait for it to be over."

She didn't look as though she couldn't wait. She looked as though she were reveling in every moment of her pregnancy. An ache tugged at Tess's heart. *You should have left me with a baby, Trav. It was the least you could do.*

"I've wanted a baby for so long, but Ian—" She planted both hands on the table and hoisted herself from the chair. "I'd better get back before he comes looking for me. He's overprotective." She crossed the floor to retrieve her dress and sandals. "Modeling turned me into a nudist. I hope I didn't freak you out." She struggled with the sandals. "I shouldn't have taken these off. Now I'll never get them back on."

Her edema wasn't alarming, but it looked uncomfortable. "Try drinking more water," Tess said. "It seems counterintuitive, but it'll help your body retain less fluid. And put your feet up as often as you can."

"You sound like you're speaking from experience. How many kids have you had?"

"No kids. I used to be a labor and delivery nurse." Only part of the truth. She was a certified nurse midwife whose joy from delivering babies had been sucked out of her, along with everything else.

"That's so great!" Bianca exclaimed. "I've heard how hard it is to get good medical care out here in the boonies."

"I'm . . . taking some time off." If she was careful with the money from the sale of their condo, she could get by for a few more months before she'd have to pull herself together enough to look for a practice and get back to work.

"Come up to our place tomorrow," Bianca said. "Ian will be out hiking or locked in his studio—he's having one of his artistic crises—and I can show you the house. I'm craving company that doesn't growl at me."

Tess needed the novelty of being with someone who didn't know about Trav's death, who didn't see her as the broken woman she was.

When Bianca left, Tess carried their mugs over to the farmhouse sink, with its old-fashioned, built-in drain board, chipped porcelain finish, and rusty stains that refused to surrender to scrubbing. As she dried her hands, she noticed her ragged cuticles and broken fingernails. Unlike Bianca, Tess would never be anyone's muse, not unless the artist had a passion for unkempt, sloe-eyed brunettes with wildly curly hair and twenty extra pounds.

Trav said her dark, bluish-purple eyes, olive complexion, and almost-black hair made her look earthy and exotic, like she belonged in one of the Italian movies from the sixties that he'd loved. She'd reminded him more than once that her almost-black hair had come from some Greek ancestor who had never once sashayed through the streets of Naples in a tight cotton dress like Sophia Loren with Marcello Mastroianni chasing after her, but that hadn't discouraged him from teasing her with made-up Italian words.

Tess used to be funny herself. She could make even the most nervous pregnant mother laugh. Now she couldn't remember what laughter felt like.

She wandered over to the front windows, trying to decide how to fill the rest of her day. A gravel switchback snaked up the side of Runaway Mountain from the town, curling past her cabin, then the schoolhouse, and ending at what was left of an old Pentecostal church. At her side, a rickety table held a paperback copy of

Elisabeth Kübler-Ross's *On Death and Dying*. As Tess stared at it, a blistering rage overcame her. She snatched up the book and threw it across the room. *Fuck you, Liz, and your five stages of grief! How about a hundred and five stages? A thousand and five?*

But then Elisabeth Kübler-Ross had never met Travis Hartsong with his floppy, auburn hair and laughing eyes, his beautiful hands and unending optimism. Elisabeth Kübler-Ross had never eaten pizza in bed with him or had him chase her around the house in a Chewbacca mask. And now Tess was living in a dilapidated cabin on an aptly named mountain in the middle of nowhere. But instead of pressing the reset button on her life, she felt only anger, despair, and shame at her weakness. It had been nearly two years. Other people recovered from tragedy. Why couldn't she?

Ian Hamilton North IV was having a bad day. A particularly bad day in what had been a series of bad days. Bad weeks. Who the hell was he kidding? Nothing had been right for months.

He'd bought a place in Tempest, Tennessee, because of its isolation. The main street sat on a treacherous, two-lane highway with a gas station, a bar named The Rooster, a drive-in barbecue joint, a Dollar General, and a redbrick building that housed city hall, the police station, and the post office. There were three churches, a suspect establishment that called itself a coffee shop, and more churches tucked away in the hills.

At the end of the highway, a newer, one-story building declared itself the Brad Winchester Recreation Center. Ian had already learned that State Senator Brad Winchester was the town's wealthiest and most powerful citizen. In the old days, Ian would have tagged that building first chance he got—*IHN4* in yellow Krylon spray paint with one of his gargoyles weaving in and out of the letters. He'd probably have gotten arrested for it, too. The public had narrow tastes when it came to public art, especially in small towns. They all wanted their murals, but they hated the tags, not understanding you couldn't have one without the other. But the line between vandalism and genius was open to interpretation, and he'd long ago abandoned the role of misunderstood artist.

The town was too small to disturb the region's natural beauty: the hills and mountains that looked as though they'd been drizzled in watercolors, the wispy morning mists, extravagant sunsets, and clean air. Unfortunately, there were also people. Some came from families that had lived here for generations, but retirees, artisans, homesteaders, and survivalists had also settled in the mountains. He intended to have minimal contact with all of them, and he'd only come into town on the slim chance that the Dollar General might have the English muffins Bianca craved. The muffins had been missing from the order he paid a fortune to have delivered every week from the closest decent grocery store twenty miles away. But English muffins were too exotic for the Dollar General, and he was in no mood to make the drive to get them.

As he reached his car, he stopped.

The Dancing Dervish.

She was gazing into the window of the Broken Chimney, the town's so-called coffee shop, a place that also sold ice cream, books, cigarettes, and who knew what else. It was odd. Despite how furious he'd been, he'd noticed the complete absence of joy in her dancing. Her fierce, percussive movements had been tribal, more combat than art. But now she stood still, suspended in a dapple of sunlight, and that quickly, he wanted to paint her.

He could see it. An explosion of color in every brushstroke, every press of the nozzle. Cobalt blue in that fierce gypsy hair, with a touch of viridian green near the temples. Cadmium red brushing her olive skin at the cheekbones, a dab of chrome yellow at their highest point. A streak of ocher shadowing that long nose. Everything in a full palette of colors. And her eyes. The color of ripe August plums. How could he capture the darkness there?

How could he capture anything these days? He was trapped. Imprisoned in his youthful reputation as surely as if he'd been fossilized in amber. His father had failed at "beating the artist out of him," and now Ian was doing the job for himself. Street artists like Banksy might be able to carry their careers into middle age, but not Ian. Street art was the art of rebellion, and with his father dead and more money in his bank account than he knew how to spend, what the hell did he have to rebel against? Sure, he could cut more stencils, make more posters, paint more canvases, but it would all feel phony. Because it would be.

But if not that, then what?

A question he couldn't answer, so he turned his attention back to the Dervish. She wore nondescript jeans and a bulky maroon sweatshirt, but he had an excellent visual memory. What he'd seen of her body as she'd danced her primitive dance had been too thin, but with a few more pounds, she'd be magnificent. He thought of Rembrandt's luscious *Bathsheba at Her Bath*, Goya's *Naked Maja*, Titian's sensual *Venus of Urbino*. The

Dervish would have to eat up to match those immortals, but he still wanted to paint her. It was the first creative impulse he'd experienced in months.

He pushed the idea out of his head. What he had to do was get rid of her. And quickly. Before she caught Bianca's attention more than she already had.

He set off toward the coffee shop.

Chapter Two

Tess knew he was close by even before she saw him. It was a stir in the air. A scent. A vibration. And then the surly growl she remembered. "Bianca told me I was incredibly rude this morning."

"She had to tell you this?"

Tess had been studying the sign in the window of the Broken Chimney when he approached. Close up, he was even more formidable—the opposite of the whippet-thin, garret-living stereotype of an artist sporting a scraggly goatee, nicotine-stained fingers, and deep-socketed eyes. His shoulders were broad, his jaw rock solid. A long scar ran down the side of his neck, and the small holes in his earlobes suggested they'd once held earrings. Probably a skull and crossbones. He was an outlaw, the grown-up version of the teenage punk who'd holstered a spray paint can instead of a handgun—the young thug who'd spent years in and out of jail for trespassing and felony vandalism. Despite worn jeans and a flannel shirt, this was a man at the top of his game and accustomed to everyone kowtowing to him. Yes, she was intimidated, both by the man himself and by his fame. No, she wouldn't let him see that.

"I tend to be self-absorbed . . ." he said, stating the obvious, ". . . except as it affects Bianca." His words had slowed so that each one carried extra weight.

"Really?" This was so none of her business, but from the moment he'd stormed into her yard, he'd raised her hackles. Or maybe she was simply enjoying the freedom of someone glaring at her instead of regarding her with pity. "Dragging a pregnant woman away from her home to a town that doesn't even have a doctor?"

His ego was too big to be put on the defensive, and he brushed that aside. "She's not due for another two months, and she'll have the best care. What she needs most right now is rest and quiet." His eyes, the unfriendly gray of a winter sky just before a snowstorm, met hers. "I know she invited you to the house, but I'm withdrawing the invitation."

Instead of backing away as any normal person would, she pressed. "Why is that?"

"I told you. She needs rest."

"These days healthy pregnant women are advised to stay active. Isn't that what her doctor recommended?"

His slight hesitation might have been imperceptible to someone who hadn't been trained to observe, but not to her. "Bianca's doctor wants the best for her, and I'm making sure she gets it." With a curt nod, he walked away, his strong musculature and purposeful stride giving him the look of a man who'd been designed by God to weld girders or pump petroleum instead of creating some of the twenty-first century's most memorable art.

Bianca had said he was "overprotective," but this seemed more like smothering. Something felt wrong between these two.

A muddy pickup sped past, blowing exhaust. She'd come to town for doughnuts, not to become enmeshed in other peoples' lives, and she returned her attention to the sign in the window.

HELP WANTED

She was a midwife. Any day now, her anger, her despair, would fade into resignation. It had to. And as soon as that happened, she'd be ready to look for work in her field. She'd find a job that would let her recapture the satisfaction of helping vulnerable mothers give birth.

HELP WANTED

She didn't need to go back to work yet, so why was she staring at the sign, as if her whole messy world had been reduced to this backwater coffee shop?

Because she was scared. The solitude on Runaway Mountain that she'd thought would heal her wasn't working out. It had become too tempting to stay in bed. To eat doughnuts and dance in the rain. Last week, she'd gone four days before she'd remembered to take a shower.

The bitter swell of self-disgust ballooning inside her forced her through the door. She could either ask about the job, or—a better idea—she could buy a doughnut and leave.

A counter to her right held cookies and doughnuts, but this was no funky urban coffee shop. A compact freezer showcased eight tubs of ice cream. Open shelves offered up cigarettes, candy bars, batteries, and other oddities not normally found in either a doughnut, ice cream, or coffee shop. A pair of spinning wire racks for paperback books were tucked in a corner, and a rock song she vaguely recognized but couldn't name played in the background.

An espresso machine hissed. Her reflection stared back at her from the mirrored wall behind the counter. Puffy face, purple shadows under her eyes, a thick tangle of hair that hadn't seen a brush since . . . maybe yesterday, maybe the day before, and Trav's worn maroon Wisconsin sweatshirt.

The man operating the espresso machine passed the finished drink across the counter to an elderly customer with a cane. The old man hobbled to a table, and the espresso operator turned his attention to her. A thin, graying ponytail snaked down his back. He regarded her with small eyes folded into a leathery road map of a face. "Doughnuts or pie?"

"How do you know I want either one?"

He tucked his thumbs through the tie of the red apron he'd knotted in the front. "Reading people's minds is my business. You're new around here. My name's Phish. With a *p.h.*"

"I'm Tess. You must be a big fan."

"Of the band? Hey-ll, no. I'm a Deadhead. Greatest band that ever lived. I got 'Ripple' playing now. . . . It's the only song most people know." His grimace telegraphed his opinion of such unaccountable human ignorance. "Phisher is my last name."

"And your first?"

"Elwood. Forget I told you." He tilted his head toward the three-tiered acrylic display case on the counter. Next to it, a small, erasable whiteboard read PIE OF THE DAY. "Dutch apple," he said. "One of my bestsellers."

"I'm more into doughnuts." There wasn't much

variety. Glazed or powdered, which she could never think of as real doughnuts, more as cake masquerading as a doughnut. She tipped her head toward the door. "Broken Chimney is a strange name."

"You shoulda seen the place when I bought it. Cost me twenty grand to fix it up."

"I noticed you didn't fix the chimney."

"The fireplace is bricked up, so there wasn't much point. Good way for people to find us."

She scraped the side seam of her jeans with her fingernail. "I . . . saw your sign in the window. You're looking for help?"

"You want the job? It's yours."

She blinked. "Just like that? I could be an escaped felon, for all you know."

He shouted to the old man across the store. "Hey, Orland! Tess here look like an escaped felon to you?"

The old man turned his attention from his newspaper. "She looks 'talian to me, so you never can tell. She's got some meat on her bones, though. I like that. Wouldn't mind looking at her when I come in."

"There you go." Phish's grin revealed a set of crooked teeth. "If Orland likes you, that's good enough for me."

"I'm not Italian." She ignored the whole "meat on her bones" thing.

"As long as you're willing to work for minimum

wage and take the shifts nobody else wants—plus put up with my niece and my sister-in-law—I don't much care what you are."

"I only came in here for a couple of doughnuts."

"Then why did you ask about the job?"

"Because . . ." She dug her fingers into her hair and caught a tangle. "I don't know. Forget it."

"You know how to make espresso?"

"No."

"You have any experience working a cash register?"

"No."

"You got anything better to do right now?"

"Better than—?"

"Grabbing an apron."

She thought about it. "Not really."

"Then let's get to it."

For the next few hours, Phish showed her the ropes as he waited on customers. She went along with it, not sure how she'd let this happen but too aimless to do anything about it. Before long, she felt as if she'd been introduced to half the town, including a local micro-brewer, some retirees from up north, the head of the local women's alliance, and two members of the school board. Everyone was curious about her—exactly what she'd been wary of—but it was the normal curiosity of people meeting someone new, and the evasive answers she'd given Bianca seemed to satisfy them.

At four o'clock, she waited on her first customer. Two scoops of butter pecan ice cream and a copy of the *National Enquirer.* At five o'clock, as the Grateful Dead finished the final chorus of "Bertha," Phish pulled his apron over his head and headed for the door. "Savannah'll be in at seven to take over."

"Wait! I don't—"

"If you have questions, hold 'em till tomorrow. Or ask one of the customers to help you out. We don't get a lot of strangers around here."

As quickly as that, she was on her own. A barista, ice cream scooper, pie server, candy bar purveyor, and cigarette vendor . . .

She sold two slices of pie—one à la mode—a pack of AA batteries, a cup of hot chocolate, and some breath mints. She made her first cappuccino, only to have to remake it because she screwed up the proportions. The store was finally between customers when he came in, a trucker's cap growing from his head, a rusty mustache growing down his chin. He took his time checking out the swell of her breasts under her apron bib. "Pack of Marlboros."

She should have anticipated this, but she didn't anticipate much of anything these days, and she played for time by rearranging the bananas in the bowl on the counter. "Do you have any idea what those things do to your body?"

He scratched his chest. "You serious?"

"Smoking increases your risk of coronary heart disease, lung cancer, stroke. It also gives you bad breath."

"Just hand me the damn cigarettes."

"I . . . I . . . can't do that."

"You *what?*"

"I'm kind of a . . . a conscientious objector."

"A what?"

"My conscience objects to selling something that I know is toxic to the human body."

"You for real?"

Excellent question. "I guess."

"I'm callin' Phish!"

"I understand." It wasn't as if she had a personal investment in her new career, and getting fired was fine with her.

He stood right there at the counter as he made his call, giving her the stink eye the whole time. "Phish, it's Artie. This new lady won't sell me my Marlboros. . . . Uh-huh. Uh-huh. Uh-huh. Okay." He thrust his cell at her. "Phish wants to talk to you."

His phone reeked of tobacco. She held it slightly away from her face. "Hello."

"What the hey-ll, Tess!" Phish exclaimed. "Artie says you won't sell him his cigarettes."

"It's . . . against my belief system."

"It's part of your job, damn it."

"I understand. But I can't do it."

"It's your job," he repeated.

"Yes, I know. I should have thought about that, but I didn't."

His grumble rumbled through the odoriferous phone. "Well, okay. Let me talk to Artie again."

Dazed, she handed the phone back.

Artie snatched it from her. "Yeah . . . Yeah . . . You shittin' me, Phish? This place is goin' to hell." He shoved the phone in his pocket and glared at her. "You're as bad as my girlfriend."

"She must care about you." She studied his T-shirt. The front read WILL BUY DRINKS FOR followed by a picture of a cat. It took her a few moments to get it. "What does she think about your shirt?"

"You don't like it?"

"Not so much."

"Shows what you know. My girlfriend's the one gave it to me."

"I guess nobody's perfect."

"She is. And I ain't coming back in here when you're workin'."

"I understand."

"You are crazy, lady." And he stomped out the door.

She'd won some kind of victory, and she thought about how much Trav would love this story. But there was no Trav waiting for her. No Trav to throw back his head and give that big, loud, shake-all-over laugh she'd loved so much. She had a new town, a new house, a new mountain, and a new job, but none of it mattered. She'd lost the love of her life, and it would never get better.

Phish's niece Savannah arrived and took an immediate dislike to her. The girl was a belligerent nineteen-year-old with choppy magenta hair, cat-eye glasses, ear expanders, and an armload of tats. She was also pregnant, although Tess didn't have a chance to ask how far along she was because Savannah immediately insisted Tess clean the toilet.

"Phish cleaned it a couple of hours ago," Tess said, not adding that Savannah had shown up late, and Tess's shift had been over half an hour ago.

"Clean it again. When he's not here, I'm in charge."

Unlike the cigarettes, this was wasn't a fight worth having, at least not on her first day. She found the cleaning supplies, gave the bathroom a quick once-over, and left by the back door before her unpleasant co-worker could stop her.

When she got back to the cabin, she shed her sweatshirt, stuck in some earbuds, and went outside to dance. She danced through a stubbed toe, through the first drops of rain, through the evening chill. Danced and danced. But no matter how fast she moved, how hard she pounded her feet, she couldn't dance through to the other side.

The cupola atop the schoolhouse's peaked roof still held an iron bell, but the three steps that led to the shiny black double doors were new. She remembered Ian North's warning from the day before but knocked anyway. The door flew open almost immediately, and a beaming Bianca stood on the other side, a single blond braid falling over her shoulder, like Elsa in *Frozen*.

"I knew you'd come!" She grabbed Tess by the wrist and pulled her into the hallway where long ago students must once have stripped off their coats and doffed their muddy boots. Bianca was barefoot in a gauzy, off-the-shoulder summer dress that caressed her abdomen. "Wait till you see this place." She tossed Tess's jacket on one of the old brass coat hooks and directed her into the main living area. "Ian bought it from these friends of mine, Ben and Mark. They're both decorators, and they did the renovation. They planned to use it as a studio and vacation house, but they got bored after the first year."

Watery morning sunshine streamed through the big, deep-silled schoolhouse windows. The ceilings were high, maybe eighteen feet, the walls chalk-white beadboard at the bottom with dusty, cornflower-blue paint at the top. White glass schoolhouse globes hung from the ceiling, and the original floors—scars, gouges, and all—had been thickly varnished to a high, dark sheen.

The furnishings in the large, open room were low and comfortable. Couches upholstered in white canvas, a long, industrial-style wooden dining table with metal legs, and a big coffee table in the same style, but with wheels. Under one wall of windows, bookshelves displayed rocks, animal bones, a few twisted tree roots, and a generous collection of hardback books. A schoolhouse globe perched on top of an old upright piano. A Seth Thomas pendulum clock hung near an old potbelly stove, and a bell rope dangled from a rectangular opening in the ceiling.

Bianca pointed to a staircase with open wooden treads and railings made from fat pieces of gray-painted iron pipe. "Ian's studio is upstairs, but we can't go in. Not that he seems to be doing anything in there. Totally paralyzed. The master bedroom's up there, too. There's a smaller one on this floor. Ben and Mark loved to cook, so the kitchen is great, but neither of us is much of a cook. Are you?"

Tess used to cook but hadn't for a long time. Roasted pork loin, asparagus, ricotta dumplings with pancetta and crispy sage. . . . That was the last great meal she'd fixed. The dumplings had been perfect, but Trav hadn't eaten much. *"I'm sorry, babe. No appetite. It's this damned cold. I can't seem to shake it."*

It hadn't been a cold. He'd had pneumococcal pneumonia, a disease that should have responded to treatment, but hadn't. Ten days later, he was dead.

"Are you okay?" Bianca was looking at her with concern.

Tess remembered to smile. "Yes. Fine. I was . . . I like to cook, but I haven't done much of it lately."

"And I like to eat. Maybe you can give me some ideas."

Bianca showed her the galley kitchen: white subway tiles behind the sink; one long schoolhouse window at the narrow end; white beadboard; cupboards painted a lighter shade of the same blue as the rest of the downstairs. An outside door led to the rear of the house. An eggplant sat on the soapstone counter next to a couple of withering tomatoes and half a loaf of French bread.

Bianca perched on the low windowsill, hands resting on her belly, and gleefully listed some of her favorite foods, the restaurants she loved and hated, the missing items from their weekly grocery delivery, and her pregnancy cravings. Her conversation, Tess was discovering, tended to swirl around herself, which suited Tess perfectly.

"Make something!" Bianca demanded, with girlish enthusiasm. "Something healthy and delicious that neither of us has ever eaten. Something to feed my baby."

Tess had no appetite, but she pulled a bunch of wilting Swiss chard from the refrigerator, a bulb of garlic, and a bottle of balsamic vinegar for an improvised bruschetta.

Bianca exclaimed over everything Tess did, as if she'd never seen an eggplant being diced or a garlic clove peeled. "It's like watching the supreme earth mother at work."

"I don't know about that."

"Look at you. Your hair, your body. Next to you, I'm all pale and feeble."

"Those pregnancy hormones have done a job on you. You're one of the most beautiful women I've ever seen."

Bianca sighed, as if her appearance was a burden to bear. "That's what everybody says." She turned away to gaze out the window at the dry, winter grasses in the glade that stretched beyond the schoolhouse. "I want this baby so bad. Something of my very own."

Tess swept the eggplant peelings into the trash. "Your husband might have a few thoughts about that."

Bianca went on as if she hadn't heard. "I lost my parents when I was six. My grandmother raised me."

Tess had lost her own mother almost ten years ago. Her father had deserted them when she was five, and she had only a few memories of him.

"For a long time, I didn't care about having kids," Bianca said. "But then I kind of got obsessed with getting pregnant."

Tess wondered how her husband had felt about that. For all of Bianca's chatter, she hadn't said much about her marriage.

Delicious smells began to fill the kitchen as Tess sautéed the garlic and chopped Swiss chard in olive oil, throwing in some butter to cut down on the vegetable's bitterness. She toasted the French bread and diced the aging tomatoes, along with some finely chopped olives. After mixing it all together, she adjusted the seasonings, splashed on a little more olive oil, and spooned it on top of the toasted bread. With the finished pieces set on a pair of ironstone plates, she and Bianca settled at the long dining table.

The bruschetta was perfect, the bread crisp, the topping meaty and full of flavor.

There was something restorative about being in this beautiful, sun-splashed room with a woman who was so vital and alive. Tess surprised herself by realizing she was hungry. For the first time in forever, she could taste her food.

The front door opened, and North came in, a backpack slung over one shoulder of his heavy jacket. He stopped inside the door and gazed at Tess, not saying anything, not needing to. *I told you to stay away, and yet here you are.*

Her last bite of bruschetta lost its taste. "I was invited," she said.

"And we've been having the best time!" Bianca's lively chirp hit a flat note.

"Glad to hear it."

He didn't sound glad.

"You have to taste this," Bianca said.

"Not hungry." He shrugged off his backpack and set it on a long wooden bench.

"Don't be such a grouch. We haven't had anything this good since we got here."

He shucked his jacket and advanced toward them. The closer he came, the stronger Tess's urge grew to protect Bianca.

"I'll get you some." Bianca hopped up—or as near to hopping as she could manage—and went to the kitchen.

North stopped at the head of the table, the place where Bianca had been sitting, and gazed down at Tess. The February light coming through the windows fell on the long scar that ran down the side of his neck. "This isn't good for her."

Tess deliberately chose to misunderstand his words. "Vegetables and olives are highly nutritious."

His wife reappeared with a plate. He took it, but didn't sit. "You need to rest, Bianca."

"I need to walk," she said, showing a defiance she hadn't previously exhibited. "Come on, Tess. You promised you'd go out with me."

Tess had promised no such thing, but she was happy to comply. What she hadn't counted on was Ian North's insistence on accompanying them.

Bianca directed all her conversation toward Tess, an awkward process, since North had positioned himself at his wife's side on the narrow trail, forcing Tess to lag behind. Whenever the ground was uneven, he took Bianca's arm only to release it as soon as they reached steadier footing. As soon as she could, Tess made an excuse to leave.

Bianca stopped walking. "I'll see you tomorrow."

"That won't work," North said. "We have plans."

"We can change them."

"No, we can't."

Bianca shrugged, then rested her head against his arm while she smiled at Tess. "We'll work it out. I know the two of us are going to be besties."

Tess was less sure of that. The last thing she needed was to be pulled into the odd dynamics between these two.

A week passed. Tess danced at midnight when she couldn't sleep, at three in the morning when a nightmare awakened her. She danced at sunrise, at sunset, and whenever she had trouble finding her next breath.

Bianca popped in unannounced—sometimes several times a day. Mostly Tess didn't mind the visits, despite the one-sided nature of Bianca's conversation. Far more annoying were Ian North's intrusions. He invariably showed up with one excuse or another to pull his wife away.

"I can't find my wallet. . . . We need to call in an order for groceries. . . . Let's drive into Knoxville. . . ."

He acted as though Tess posed some kind of threat.

A week passed. Then another. Tess checked in with Trav's parents, who were recovering from his loss better than she was. She texted her friends—cheery lighthearted lies.

Doing gr8. Mountains beautiful.

The structure of having a job forced her out of bed and reminded her to take a shower and comb her hair. She didn't love her job, but she didn't really hate it, either. Working at the Broken Chimney helped fill the hours, and Phish's laid-back nature, combined with his marijuana habit, made him a genial boss.

One day when there was a lag between customers, Tess used the Broken Chimney's intermittent WiFi to check out Bianca's husband.

Ian Hamilton North IV, known by his street tag, IHN4, is the most well known of American street artists. The last member of the powerful North family, he is the only son of the deceased financier Ian Hamilton North III and socialite Celeste Brinkman North. Although graffiti artists customarily hide their identity, North has flaunted his by using his real initials in his tags—a practice generally ascribed to his troubled relationship with his parents. He gained notoriety as he abandoned street graffiti for more thoughtful work beginning—

She closed the computer as Mr. Felter banged on the counter, demanding an extra pump of hazelnut syrup in his coffee.

Phish's pregnant niece Savannah was only slightly less rude to the customers than she was to Tess, and it became evident that Phish only kept her on out of loyalty to her father, his brother Dave. "Savannah didn't use to be this bad," Phish confided to Tess, "but then her ex-boyfriend knocked her up and left town. I knew he was a loser first time I met him. He never even heard of The Dead!"

In Phish's eyes, no sin was greater than lack of reverence for the Grateful Dead.

Phish's other employee was Savannah's mother, Michelle, a deep-bosomed blonde who, at forty-two, also happened to be pregnant. "I thought it was perimenopause," she announced to anyone who'd listen. "Ha!"

Michelle was just as difficult to work with as her daughter. Her grudge against Tess had its roots in Phish hiring Tess instead of Michelle's younger sister. "All that money you spent to go to college, and you end up working for Phish." Michelle had smirked the first time she'd seen Tess in Trav's Wisconsin sweatshirt.

Savannah and Michelle had their own problems, and after three weeks on the job, Tess had learned not to get in the middle of them. "It's like she did it to get back at me," Savannah hissed at Tess. "Having her pregnant at the same time as me makes me feel like a freak." She took a swipe at cleaning off the steamer wand from the latte she'd made. "She's like always doing things like this."

"Getting pregnant?" Tess tipped the used coffee grounds from the dump box into the trash.

"No. Like trying to show me up."

Tess was happy when two of the bartenders from The Rooster appeared at the counter. They chatted with her longer than was absolutely necessary, but they were more pleasant to talk to than either of her co-workers.

Eventually Tess made her way to the back room where she could continue the argument she'd been having with Phish for the past week. She was right. She knew she was right. "Just a small, out-of-the-way display," she said. "So customers know they're there."

He pulled a burlap bag of coffee beans from the shelf. "Hey-ll, Tess, how many times have I gotta tell you I'm not puttin' out rubbers. People who need 'em know I keep 'em in the back room."

It felt good to try to do something positive, instead of being a drain on humanity, and she pressed him. "The men in hard hats might know, but what about the women who come in here wanting condoms? What about the teenagers who really need them?"

"And there you go. I put out rubbers for teenagers, and there'll be a rumpus kicked up in this town like you never seen."

"Give people a little more credit than that."

"You're an outsider, Tess. Rubbers stay in the back room, and that's all there is to it."

Instead of arguing, she waited until Phish wasn't around and sneaked a small display of condoms onto a stand near the unisex bathroom. She set them between a stack of handmade soap, emery boards imprinted with Bible verses, and a two-page pamphlet aimed at teens that she'd driven fifteen miles to have printed out. At the end of her shift, she hid the condoms and pamphlets in the storeroom. Taking action, however small, felt like a small step forward, and what Phish didn't know wouldn't hurt him.

Ian hadn't been to town since Tess Hartsong had started working at the Broken Chimney. He wouldn't be here now except they'd run out of coffee. As he walked in, he saw Tess behind the counter. She'd tied a red apron around her waist and pulled her hair into a ponytail, but rebel strands curled around her face and down the back of her neck.

A man in jeans and a suede bomber jacket stood at the counter. Ian had overheard enough to know the guy operated a microbrewery nearby, and he'd seen enough to realize Mr. IPA was more interested in Tess Hartsong's curves than in the pie he'd ordered.

"Let me take you out for barbecue after you get off work."

"Thanks, but I'm a vegetarian."

The hell she was. She'd made a BLT for Bianca and eaten one herself.

"How about drinks, then, at The Rooster?"

"It's nice of you to ask, but I have a boyfriend."

She was lying about that, too. He'd observed enough by now to know that Tess was a loner.

"If you change your mind, let me know." The guy took his pie and a mug of coffee over to the community table but continued to watch her out of the corners of his eyes. No surprise that he seemed especially drawn to her hips.

The place was busy with a motley collection of the town's citizens, too many of whom he'd heard about from Bianca.

"Tess is getting to know everybody. She says a lot of

people in town owe their jobs to Brad Winchester. He's the big shot around here. . . .

"Tess says the townies secretly look down on the re-tirees who've moved in from out of state, but they don't show it because of the money they bring in. . . .

"Tess says she's met some of the artists: a guy who works with iron, and she says there's a woman who makes mandolins. We should have a party."

Over his dead body. And he was getting more than a little sick of hearing *"Tess says."* Apparently Tess hadn't mentioned any of the homesteaders and surviv-alists hanging out in the mountains. He'd met a few of them when he'd been hiking, including some with kids. They were an interesting lot—earnest environmental-ists who wanted to reduce their carbon footprint, con-spiracy theorists hiding from the apocalypse, a couple of religious zealots.

Ian approached the counter. The dusting of pow-dered sugar on Tess's apron must have come from the cake doughnuts. He'd never understood why those dense, powdery lug nuts were even considered dough-nuts. Except for their shape, they had nothing in common with a light-as-a-feather glazed doughnut.

He knew what he wanted, but he glanced at the menu board anyway. "A cup of house blend, plus a pound of your darkest roast, and a couple of doughnuts. Glazed."

Without asking whether the doughnuts were for here or to go, she slipped them into a white paper bag, rang up his purchases, and handed him the coffee in a paper cup instead of a mug. "Are you going to let Bianca drink any?"

"I guess that's up to her."

Her hands stilled on the register drawer as she looked up at him. "Is it?"

He didn't like subtlety. "What are you getting at?"

"A cup of coffee won't do her any harm."

"I'll remember that."

"Where did you get that scar on your neck?"

Most people were too polite to ask, but she didn't seem to care about everyday courtesies. Neither did he. "Trying to squeeze under a chain-link fence when I was eighteen and the cops were chasing me. Do you want to know about the others?"

One on his arm from a nasty encounter with a New Orleans guard dog. Another on his leg from falling off the roof of an apartment building in Berlin. When you spent so much of your life climbing ladders and sneaking around dark city streets, shit was bound to happen.

The one he prized the most was the jagged mark across the back of his hand. He'd earned that after he'd tagged his father's Porsche. It served as a reminder of a beating he'd never forget, along with the evidence that he'd fought back.

"No. That's okay." She dismissed his question and also dismissed him.

He grabbed the coffee, along with his change. Instead of leaving, as she seemed to expect, he took a seat at the opposite end of the community table from the horny brewer and opened the doughnut sack.

A woman came in. He didn't know for a fact that she'd once been a homecoming queen, but her diamond-shaped face and faded-blond prettiness bore the hallmarks. Now, however, her blond bob had lost its fluff and her facial bones had sharpened. Twenty years earlier she might have been succulent, but the juice had been sucked out of her.

"Tess, can I talk to you?"

"Hello, Mrs. Winchester."

Winchester. Even he'd heard about the local boy who'd made good with some kind of start-up involving Internet domain name trading. Apparently, he'd sold the business for a fortune and used the money to finance his political career.

Tess nodded at the teenager who'd accompanied the woman. "Hi, Ava."

And here was the current homecoming queen. Blond like her mother, but fleshed out. Round cheeks, rosy lips, in the full bloom of prettiness. She smiled at Tess, then left her mother to join two other teens at a table by the window.

"Can we talk privately?" Mrs. Winchester nodded toward the back of the store.

Tess was the only one working, but she made her way toward the minuscule hallway by the bathroom. He could see them but not hear what they were saying.

The Winchester woman did all the talking, her gestures as sharp as the rest of her. When Tess finally spoke, she appeared calm in the face of the onslaught. Winchester shook her head, clearly dismissing whatever Tess said. Meanwhile, her daughter, Ava, was making a concerted effort not to look at her mother.

His curiosity annoyed him. Whatever human drama was unfolding had nothing to do with him. He picked up his remaining doughnut along with the coffee and dropped a dollar tip on the table. He didn't like leaving Bianca alone.

Chapter Three

The storm started on a Friday, the first day of March, a month after Tess had begun working at the Broken Chimney. It rained all that day and the next. By Sunday morning, the temperature had dipped below freezing, with the rain changing to sleet and Poorhouse Creek racing like a river. Instead of going to work, she wanted to curl up in a blanket by the windows and watch the rushing water creep closer to her back door.

Last night, her Honda CR-V had barely made it through the flooded low spots on the road up from the highway, and there was no way her car could make it to town today with the water rising even higher. She'd have to walk to work—over a mile down Runaway

Mountain, which wouldn't be nearly as bad as the hike back up. For a job she'd taken on a whim.

Cell service was spotty up here, but she had just enough signal to reach Phish, who was in Nashville, hungover from a rock concert. When she told him she couldn't get to work, he wasn't having it. ". . . get down there . . ." His voice cracked over the bad connection. ". . . count on. . . . Women's Alliance . . . monthly meeting . . ."

"The road's flooded. I can't get my car out."

". . . walked to work before. You said . . . exercise."

"I've walked when the weather's been decent."

". . . mountain girl now, not some city puss . . ."

"Go away and put my nice guy boss on the phone," she grumbled.

But she'd lost the connection.

Muttering, she shoved dry jeans, a pair of flats, and a flashlight into a plastic bag, which she stuffed in her backpack. Wearing her oldest sneakers, she flipped her rain jacket hood over her head and let herself out into the sleet and gloom.

The trek down the mountain was cold and miserable, but not as miserable as the trek back up would be. With the road buried in nearly three feet of water in spots, she stuck to the narrow track that served as a trail.

When she finally reached town, the sidewalk was an ice rink, and she nearly fell as she approached the Broken Chimney. Light showed brightly through the steamed-up front windows. Despite the weather, or maybe because of it, at least ten people were gathered inside. Savannah, wearing leggings and an oversize T-shirt, stood impatiently behind the counter. "You're late."

"And good afternoon to you." Tess hung her rain jacket in the back room and exchanged her sodden sneakers and wet jeans for the dry clothes she'd brought with her. An old Campari advertising mirror indicated that her hair was as wild as the weather. She snagged it back in a ponytail and retrieved the condom display from behind a broken table to put out.

"You're going to get in trouble if Phish sees that," Savannah said as she collected her coat to leave.

"Are you going to tell him?"

"Maybe." She absentmindedly scratched her swelling abdomen. "Guys don't like condoms."

Tess suppressed half a dozen snarky responses. She'd been setting out the condom display for a week now, and the only person who'd protested had been Kelly Winchester. That had happened the same day Ian North had come into the shop. Kelly was the town's social leader and the wife of Brad Winchester, the area's state senator. Phish hadn't yet said anything to Tess about the condoms she'd set out, so Mrs. Winchester must not have gotten to him, but from what Tess had learned about the power of the Winchester family, once Mrs. Winchester talked to Phish, the condoms would be gone.

For now, she counted the sale she'd made yesterday to the teenage boy—a boy she'd discovered was Savannah's younger brother—as a major victory.

Phish was right about their customers. A steady stream came through the door with reports of the worsening weather, as well as news that the highway had flooded and the town was officially cut off. Everyone seemed philosophical about it.

"Happens a couple of times a year," Artie, her cigarette-denied customer, said. "Usually in the spring, but not always." Despite his vow not to return to the Broken Chimney when she was working, Artie kept showing up.

Fiona Lester, the owner of Purple Periwinkle Bed and Breakfast, shook out her down coat. "Remember when we had that big rockslide out by Ledbedder farm?"

The other customers chimed in. "Worst was that snowstorm back in two thousand fifteen."

"Took the plows two days to clear us out. It would have taken longer if Brad hadn't gotten on it."

Tess hadn't yet met Mr. Winchester, but she knew the town was proud to have one of their own holding such a lofty position at the state level. She'd also heard occasional rumblings from Phish about the control Winchester exerted over both the town's budget and its jobs.

Even Courtney Hoover made it into the Broken Chimney later that afternoon. Courtney was Tess's least favorite customer. In her early twenties, Courtney lived in Tempest with her family but worked as a front desk clerk at a budget hotel thirty miles away. Her greatest ambition was to become an Instagram star, so she spent vast amounts of time taking provocative selfies.

"Hey, Tess." Her accent was all bruised magnolia petals.

"Hi, Courtney."

Today Courtney had squeezed her enviable figure into a short V-necked tube dress with boots up to her thighs. Her thickly applied glimmer powder gave her complexion an odd iridescent glow. She studied the menu painted on the mirror behind the counter, even though she always ordered a medium mocha.

Tess wiped her hands on her apron. "What can I

get you?" Tess made Courtney's mocha exactly like Phish, Michelle, and Savannah made it, but Courtney only complained about Tess's—too much espresso, not enough whipped cream, "old" chocolate, whatever that was.

"I'll have a medium mocha." Courtney's toffee lip gloss was as hard as marine varnish. She regarded Tess critically. "Have you been sick, Tess? You don't look too good."

"Healthy as a horse," Tess said. "Just not naturally beautiful."

While Courtney tried to figure out if Tess was serious or not, Tess reached for the milk. "How many followers do you have now?" Courtney liked to be asked, and maybe it would keep her from complaining about the mocha.

"Almost three hundred. I picked up four more last week."

"That's impressive."

"It's harder work than you'd think." She tossed her blond hair extensions. "Move over by the banana bowl. Let's do a selfie."

The only reason Courtney wanted a selfie with Tess was so she could hashtag it *#BeautyandtheBeast*, but Tess propped her elbow on the counter while Courtney adjusted her own pose half a dozen times. Nothing she saw, however, satisfied her. "Oh, well. I'll try again sometime when you've had a chance to do your hair."

"Good idea." Tess produced the mocha. Courtney took a delicate sip and pronounced it too salty.

"The ingredients haven't changed," Tess said.

"Something's changed. It's salty."

"How about a cappuccino instead?"

"Never mind." She turned away in a huff.

By three o'clock, the Tempest Women's Alliance had canceled their meeting, and the place was emptied out. By four o'clock, the *rat-a-tat-tat* of sleet against the windows had turned into a full-fledged ice storm. Tess was supposed to stay open until five, but as four-thirty approached and no more customers appeared, she flipped the sign to CLOSED.

She briefly considered spending the night in the back room rather than tackling the storm-battered mountain after dark, but the prospect of making a bed from broken-down cardboard boxes and the moth-eaten quilt Phish's old lab had died on was even less appealing than venturing out. She had a flashlight, relatively warm clothes, and common sense. She could make it.

She'd thrown salt on the sidewalk in front of the shop, but the pavement beyond was pure ice, and she hugged the sides of the buildings. The highway was eerily quiet. No eighteen-wheelers blasting through, no motorcycles or junkers missing a muffler. The sidewalk ended at The Rooster. She could barely make out the flooded gravel road, let alone the trail that led up the mountain, but with the aid of her flashlight, she eventually found it and began her climb. Ice coated everything, and even with the light, it was hard to keep her footing.

The hood of her rain jacket blew off. Sleet slithered down her neck and icy slivers cut at her cheeks. The locals had assured her the weather wouldn't last long, but that was no help now.

Her sneakers slipped in the weeds, and she fell for the third time, getting even colder and wetter. All this for a minimum-wage job at a coffee shop that wasn't really a coffee shop in a town that led to nowhere. Her hands throbbed and her toes were going numb. By the time she reached the cottage, she was a shivering, sodden mess.

Naturally, the propane furnace had gone out, so she wrapped herself in blankets until she stopped shivering. Why had she ever thought coming here would be a good idea? *This is your fault, Trav! You're the one who wanted to move to Tennessee, not me.*

She was too worn out to cry and too cold to dance.

Something awakened her in the middle of the night. The storm still pounded the cabin, but it was another sound, loud enough to be heard over the rain and the sleet.

A church bell. Ringing again and again. Deep, loud bongs. She rolled to her back, slowly orienting herself to the ugly room with its strips of floral wallpaper curling at the seams instead of the sunny yellow bedroom she and Trav had painted together.

She closed her eyes. The bell continued to sound. Loud. Persistent.

She huddled deeper into the covers. The church high on the mountain had fallen into ruins long ago. It must be the school bell. And after Ian North had made a big frickin' deal out of her loud music. Yet now it was one o'clock in the morning, and he thought it was perfectly acceptable to—

Her eyes shot open. With a groan, she climbed out of bed and grabbed her nearest dry clothes. Minutes later, she was out the door.

The light shining through the long windows testified that the schoolhouse generator was working. She let herself in without knocking and took off her rain jacket. "Bianca! Where are you?"

North answered from the downstairs bedroom. "Back here. Hurry!"

Let this be a false alarm. Bianca was only around thirty-four weeks. Tess had delivered preemies before, but she'd had access to fetal monitors and a neonatal intensive care unit. Here, she had no equipment: no stethoscope, instrument packs, syringes, or suture kits. Most of all, she had no heart for it. And yet here she was.

She forced herself toward the downstairs bedroom and stepped over the threshold.

The room was a soothing amalgam of soft gray walls, brushed nickel lamps, and filmy white curtains. Bianca lay uncovered on a low, platform bed; a pewter-colored nightgown twisted around her body, her face contorted with panic. "Tess! It's too early! My water broke, and I'm having contractions. It—it wasn't supposed to happen yet."

Tess's heart sank. This didn't look like false labor, and Tempest had no doctor. Even if they could have reached the nearest hospital in this weather, it was fifty miles away.

She fumbled in her jeans pocket for a tie to twist up her hair. "Babies are little dickheads. They have a will of their own."

Her irreverence made the corners of Bianca's mouth

temporarily ease. Tess secured her hair and crossed to the bed. Bianca grabbed her hand in a fierce grip. "I'm scared."

"You'll be fine," Tess said with false certainty. "I've delivered more babies than I can remember, and we've got this. How far apart are the contractions?"

"About six minutes," North said from behind her.

She gently disengaged from Bianca's grip. "I'm going to go wash up."

Bianca's hand tightened into a fist. "Hurry!"

North led her to the adjoining bathroom, but instead of leaving her there, he followed her inside. As she stood at the sink, the mirror reflected his hard jaw and too-long hair. "Bianca said you used to be a labor and delivery nurse. Is that right?"

His intensity made the small room claustrophobic. She pushed her sleeves above her elbows and turned on the water. "That's right."

"Exactly what does that mean? Have you ever delivered a baby by yourself?"

What would he do if she said no? She reached for the soap and began to scrub. No matter how famous, how talented, how wealthy this man was, she didn't like him. Didn't like the way he was so uptight with his wife. Didn't like watching Bianca cling to him one minute and snipe at him the other. "I'm a certified nurse midwife. I've delivered preemies before."

But not without backup.

In the mirror, she saw his shoulders slump so that he no longer looked so aggressive. "I—I can't get a cell connection," he said. "I thought maybe a helicopter could get through. We were leaving for Knoxville in a couple of days. There should have been plenty of time."

"Your baby didn't get the memo."

He winced, and she regretted her sharpness. She'd dealt with a lot of difficult fathers, and she knew better. "I need you to gather up some things." She reeled off a list: clean towels, hand sanitizer, sterilized scissors, string, any gauze pads he could find, a big pitcher of ice water. "Do you have receiving blankets? Anything for the baby?"

"No. Bianca was going to have everything shipped from Manhattan."

"Cut some up, then. From the softest, cleanest material you can find. Two or three."

He didn't ask her to repeat the list but set off.

Tess propped Bianca up with pillows and felt her abdomen as she timed the contractions. "It'll be a while. Would you like to walk around?"

Bianca gazed up from the bed, her blue eyes as large and questioning as a child's. "I can do that?"

"Sure. Walking's good. You can labor in the shower or rock on your hands and knees. Whatever feels right to you. There aren't any rules."

What felt right, it turned out, was to labor in the bath.

Ian reappeared as Tess was helping Bianca, still clad in her nightgown, into the warm water. He dropped the supplies on the bathroom counter with a thud. "What are you doing? She should be in bed!"

Tess had heard more than enough from unlicensed Doctor North. "Women labor differently now than they did in the fifties."

"But—"

"Staying in bed is the least productive way to labor, but put some fresh sheets on in case she decides to deliver there."

"In case?"

Tess had delivered babies at the birthing center from mothers crouched on the floor or curled up in tight spaces. A surprising number of women wanted to wedge themselves between the bed and a wall. "If you have clean plastic, put it under the sheet to save the mattress."

"Screw the mattress!" He hurried out.

The filmy material of Bianca's nightgown floated in a smoky cloud around her body. Tess rubbed her shoulders, kept the water warm, and breathed with her through the contractions. Fortunately, Bianca's self-centered nature kept her from picking up on Tess's tension.

"I wanted drugs!" Bianca cried at the end of one strong contraction.

Not an option with this birth. "Drugs are over-rated," Tess said, giving her a gentle head massage. "Your body will know exactly what to do." She prayed that was true.

"Where's Ian? I want Ian!"

"I'm here."

He appeared inside the bathroom door, but he didn't look at her.

"You don't care!" Bianca snarled at him. "You couldn't even pretend to be happy when I got pregnant!"

"You were happy enough for both of us," he said quietly.

Tess had seen more than a few women turn on their husbands while they were in labor, and she reached for the taps. "The water's getting chilly. Let me warm it up."

Eventually Bianca wanted out of the tub. Tess took

off her wet nightgown and gave her a robe. "Let's walk a little."

They moved into the main living area. North stood by the windows, staring out into the night. Now that he'd gathered the birth supplies, he didn't seem to know what to do with himself, but Tess believed fathers should be actively involved, especially when there was so much marital tension. "Walk with her," she said. "Let her lean against you when she has a contraction."

"No!" Bianca exclaimed. "I want you! I want you to walk with me, Tess."

North seemed relieved, another black mark against him.

Tess walked with her. When the contractions hit, Bianca braced herself on Tess's body. Twenty minutes ticked by . . . thirty. . . . The contractions were closer together, each one lasting longer.

Bianca wanted Ian, who held her as Tess had. Bianca leaned against him. "You know I love you."

"I know," he said.

Bianca was tiring and finally wanted to lie down. Tess made her as comfortable as she could, but hard labor had taken over. Bianca would reach out for her husband, crush his hand, and then abruptly let him go.

As her contractions peaked, her low, guttural groans grew louder. North repositioned himself at the head of the bed, out of sight of the action. Tess slipped a clean towel under Bianca's hips.

Bianca threw back her head and screamed as her next contraction crested. "Take care of my baby!" Her fingernails gripped the sheets. "If something happens . . . promise me, Tess. . . . He doesn't care! Promise me you'll take care of my baby."

Tess stroked her leg. "You're strong and healthy. You'll be taking care of your own baby."

The contraction had eased, but Bianca's eyes were frantic. She grabbed for Tess's hand with supernatural strength. Tess winced. "I want you!" Bianca cried. "Promise me!" Tess glanced up at Ian, who stood tight-lipped and grim. Bianca's fingers dug into Tess's hand. "If something happens to me, promise you'll take care of my baby."

"Oh, honey . . . I—I can't promise that. I—"

Another contraction. Another scream ripped from her throat. *"You have to."*

"Promise her!" North exclaimed. "For God's sake, promise her!"

The very top of a tiny head appeared, wrinkled like a prune from the pressure. "The baby's crowning,"

Tess said soothingly. "You're doing great. Turn on your side now. Here. Let me help you." Lying this way would get more oxygen to the baby and might reduce tearing.

She ordered North to brace Bianca's top leg. From his reaction, she might have been asking him to hold a cobra, but he did as she said. "That's good. Perfect." North looked everywhere except at the place where his offspring would emerge.

The cord was wrapped around the baby's neck. Tess eased it over the baby's head without difficulty.

With the next contraction, a tiny shoulder emerged. She gently lifted it and waited, murmuring words of encouragement.

The other shoulder appeared, and with the following contraction, the baby slipped into her hands.

Tess took a long breath of relief. "You have a girl." Tess kept the baby's head down to drain the fluids then settled her on Bianca's bare chest. The baby was so utterly defenseless. A sea creature suddenly washed to shore.

"A girl," Bianca said weakly. "Look, Ian . . . a girl."

"I see." His voice was hoarse.

Breathe, baby girl. Tess gently rubbed the small body with a towel. She stroked along the slopes of her minuscule nose to get rid of any more fluid trapped there. *I know those fragile little lungs don't want to work yet, but they're going to have to.*

Bianca's voice sounded as if it were coming from the next room. "She's not crying. Isn't she supposed to cry?"

"Give her time. It's a big adjustment. The placenta's still attached, so she's getting oxygen."

The seconds ticked by. And then the tiny baby drew one shallow breath. . . . Another . . . A tiny birdlike wail . . .

Tess smiled. "That's the way, sweetheart."

Bianca made cooing sounds as she stroked the infant's back. Tess delivered the placenta. The cord stopped throbbing, no longer a lifeline. She tied it off. Cut it.

And then everything went to hell.

"I'm cold. I'm so cold."

Tess's head shot up. Bianca's complexion was developing a blue tinge. Tess's own skin began to prickle.

"Take off your shirt," she ordered Ian.

He stared at her dumbly.

"Take off your shirt!" she exclaimed, picking up the baby. "Hold her against your skin. Keep her warm!" She thrust the baby into his arms.

Bianca gagged and then vomited.

A gush of blood between her legs . . .

She was having a stroke.

"What's wrong?" North cried. "What's happening to her? Why is she choking?"

Tess struggled to comprehend what was happening. She'd never seen anything like this. But she knew what it was.

Amniotic fluid embolism.

With frightening clarity, the words from that long-ago lecture rushed through her head as if she'd heard them yesterday.

One of the rarest complications of pregnancy . . . Cells have managed to enter the mother's bloodstream and trigger an allergic reaction. . . . Amniotic fluid, fetal skin, even a fragment of an infant's fingernail . . . Bronchial tubes constrict. . . . Airways shut down. . . .

The last part she remembered exactly. *It often results in the death of the mother.*

This was a condition so rare, so calamitous, that most midwives retired from long careers without ever having witnessed it. A condition with an 80 percent mortality rate . . .

Tess grabbed a towel and stuffed it against the rush of blood. Her mind raced as she struggled to come up with something—anything—she could do to stop the inevitable. She was dizzy, nauseated.

"What's wrong with her?"

The sweet, cloying scent of blood filled her nostrils. She pulled herself together enough to speak. "Anaphylactic shock. She's having an allergic reaction to the baby's cells." A *fatal* allergic reaction. "It's rare . . . random." As if that were some comfort.

Bianca screamed in pain, blotting out whatever else she was saying. Even as Tess applied pressure to the blood gushing from her body, Bianca's blood pressure was dropping. Soon she wouldn't be able to breathe. She needed arterial catheters, a breathing tube, a ventilator. And even with all the intervention of modern medicine, women still died from this.

Without that surgical intervention . . . Tess fought against her panic.

"I don't understand!" he cried. "Why aren't you doing anything?"

Because there was nothing she could do. *Your wife is dying, and I'm powerless to save her.* She couldn't say it aloud. Couldn't tell him that, in the space of minutes, Bianca's life was being snuffed out by a condition so rare, so catastrophic, that it was nearly incomprehensible.

She was helpless. As helpless as she'd been when Trav was dying. Her heart was pounding so hard she felt it in her throat. All her experience, all her years of training, counted for nothing.

Bianca had begun making horrible choking sounds. Her throat was closing. Tess had to make an impossible decision. She could do a tracheotomy without anesthesia, using whatever tools were in the house. The most brutal, barbaric tracheotomy imaginable. The pain would be excruciating. And for what purpose? It wouldn't save her, only make her death more agonizing.

"She can't breathe! Do something!"

She gazed up at Ian North. Saw his fear and his bewilderment as the baby lay forgotten against his chest. One moment his wife was cooing over their new daughter, and the next moment his wife was dying. Tess shook her head, wordlessly telling him what she couldn't speak out loud.

His mouth twisted. His snarl, so primal it was barely human, cut through her. "You can't let this happen!"

Tess turned away, hating her impotence, hating herself. As Bianca gasped for air, Tess stroked her hair, fought her tears, trying to calm, to comfort.

Bianca's eyes darted frantically around the room, looking for her baby—the baby held forgotten against her father's chest. She cried out again from the pain.

Her gaze found Tess's. They were barely focused, and yet they spoke.

"I promise," Tess whispered as Bianca faded into unconsciousness. "I promise."

Twenty minutes later, Bianca was dead.

Chapter Four

Bianca's still, bloody body.

North. Frozen like a gravestone.

The baby.

Tess made herself get up from the bedside. She took the baby from him. Swallowed a scream. It was too much. It was all too much. This should never have happened.

But so much in her life shouldn't have happened, and yet it had.

He moved. Seconds later the front door slammed. She was alone. Alone with a dead woman and a helpless infant.

Moving numbly, she cocooned the baby's torso in Saran Wrap and then in the piece of blanket North had cut out. She opened her sweatshirt and cradled the tiny body against her skin. Sitting on the couch in the darkened living room, she kept her back to the closed bedroom door where Bianca lay still and cold. Her chatty, self-absorbed friend. The friend she'd been helpless to save. For the first time in her career, Tess had lost a mother, and nothing could ever make that right.

The hours ticked by. She couldn't scream. Couldn't cry. Tess's anger had made this happen. It had seared the placental membrane, boiled Bianca's blood until it couldn't coagulate. Tess willed her breath into the frail baby, no bigger than a bird. She'd lost the mother. She couldn't lose this child.

She counted the seconds between the infant's breaths, listened for the tiny mews and watched for the faint flutters that indicated she was still alive. Pink light began seeping through the windows. The longest night of her life. She covered the baby's eyes to protect them.

It was full morning when she heard the chop of a helicopter. The baby's absent father must have found a way to make a call. Needles and pins shot through her legs as she got up. The baby, nested against her, still breathing on her own. Still alive.

Through the window, she watched the helicopter land in the grassy area between the schoolhouse and the gully that dipped behind it. Where there had only been quiet, there was now commotion. Two medics burst through the unlocked front door. "National Guard, ma'am."

Tess's voice croaked from disuse. "The mother's in the bedroom."

One of the medics disappeared. The second, barely more than a kid, approached her. Tess knew she looked like a wild woman in her blood-spattered clothes, and she tried to summon the authority of the profession she would never again practice. "I'm a nurse. The baby is about a month premature. She's breathing on her own, but she needs to get to a hospital. The mother . . ." She could barely speak the words. "An amniotic fluid embolism." The simplest answer, even if it couldn't be proven without an autopsy. The scientific answer. But she knew better. Her own anger had done this.

They wheeled Bianca's lifeless body out on a stretcher. The younger medic approached. "I'll take the baby."

"No. You have to take us both."

She wasn't the mother, and she expected resistance, but he nodded.

On the helicopter ride, she saw nothing but the baby in the portable Isolette and the covered body across from her. When they reached the hospital, Ian North was nowhere to be seen.

Despite Tess's gruesome appearance, the head nurse in the Neonatal Intensive Care Unit let her stay while they hooked the baby up to a monitor and started an IV. "She's had a rough beginning," the nurse said, "but you did everything right, and she's holding her own."

Not everything, Tess thought. *I lost her mother.*

The baby was four pounds and three ounces, a decent weight for a preemie, but the ID band looked like a tire around her ankle. When the baby was safely cocooned in the NICU Isolette, the nurse sent Tess away. "Get cleaned up," she said gently. "We're watching her."

Tess was filthy, exhausted, defeated. She saw Ian North slumped in one of the vinyl chairs in the lounge, his forearms braced on his thighs, head hanging. An abandoned parka lay across the chair next to him. The dried mud crusting his boots and jeans suggested that he'd hiked out of Tempest, which must have been how he'd been able to call for help. She made herself approach him. "I'm sorry." Her voice was flat, devoid of emotion, uttering the most inadequate apology imaginable.

He looked up at her with dead eyes. She didn't explain that she couldn't have saved Bianca. How did she know that was true? No explanation would bring his wife back, and she didn't deserve absolution.

"Have you talked to the doctor about the baby?" she asked.

The curtest of nods.

"Have you . . . seen her?"

"No."

"You should see her."

He snatched up his parka and came to his feet. "You make the medical decisions. I signed the paperwork." He pulled a wad of bills from his pocket, thrust it at her, and strode to the elevator. "Don't fuck this up, too."

The elevator doors slid shut. Ian leaned against the wall. When had he turned into such a bastard? As mean as his father had been.

Bianca was gone. His beautiful, fragile Bianca . . . His inspiration, his burden, his touchstone, his punishment . . .

He rubbed his eyes. Tried to ease the ropes strangling his chest. He'd hiked for miles in the dark, slogging through the trees and the frozen underbrush, barely staying above the flooding as he searched for an elusive cell signal. He had to get help. Had to make this end differently.

His flashlight battery had failed, but he'd kept moving, sometimes managing to avoid the fallen logs and tangled roots, sometimes not. When he'd finally cleared the flooded highway, he'd tried to hitch a ride, but there weren't many cars on the road, and those that passed weren't eager to pick up a filthy wanderer.

It was dawn before he'd managed to get a call through. The state police picked him up not much later and took him to the hospital, where the staff put him in a small consultation room. Finally, a social worker appeared to tell him his daughter had arrived and he could see her. He'd sent the woman away.

A doctor showed up and explained it to him. "We can't be sure yet, but all signs point to an amniotic fluid embolism. The condition is fatal without surgical intervention."

Putting a name to what had happened didn't change the outcome. Bianca was gone.

The elevator hadn't moved. He'd forgotten to press the button.

The doctor had talked to him about the baby. He didn't remember much of what she'd said. Didn't care. But Tess Hartsong cared, and since he had no heart, he'd dumped everything on her—the unhappy Dancing Dervish—and now here he was.

The elevator doors opened. A woman on the other side took one look at him and quickly stepped back. His eyes itched. His throat felt as if it had been rubbed with sandpaper.

Bianca was dead, and it was his fault.

———

The wad of cash North had thrust at her before he'd stalked off burned her palm. She didn't want his money. Walking out on his daughter, trusting someone he hardly knew to make life and death decisions, was wrong. But Tess recognized grief all too well, and she almost understood.

One of the nurses found her a sanitary kit and a set of scrubs. She could never look at her bloody clothes again, and she tossed them in the trash. She hesitated only over Trav's sweatshirt, but it now smelled of blood and death. She shoved it in the bin along with her jeans, then locked herself in a cubicle and threw up.

She fell asleep in one of the NICU recliners.

Bianca's tortured face. "Help me! Why won't you help me?"

Blood pooled around Tess's ankles. An ocean of blood pulling her into its depths. Leadened arms. Missing legs . . .

She jolted awake from her nightmare. The skin between her breasts was damp with sweat. She blinked her eyes. Tried to get her bearings.

It was evening. The baby lay in the Isolette, cradled in a horseshoe-shaped nest of blankets with an IV, a pediatric cannula in her tiny nostrils, and electrodes fastened to her chest. In the way of preemies, she looked like a frog. "Let's give her twenty-four hours," the nurse said, "and then you can hold her."

Tess didn't want to hold her. Didn't want to contaminate her more than she already had. But she knew hospital protocol. All babies needed skin-to-skin contact with their mothers—none more so than preemies. Except Tess wasn't her mother. This little one had no mother, and right now, no father. Tess's skin was the only skin the little one could count on.

She fled the NICU. The corridor was deserted. She leaned against the wall and made herself breathe. Made herself do the right thing

The volunteers at the information desk steered her to a B and B only a few blocks away. From there, she walked to the closest store to pick up a couple of changes of clothes and some toiletries with Ian North's money.

She set the bedside alarm clock for exactly one hour but she couldn't fall asleep for fear the nightmare would return. Eventually, she got up, took a shower, and walked back to the hospital, where she once again settled in a lounger near the baby.

Toward morning, a nurse took the baby from the Isolette and asked Tess to unbutton her top so the infant could feel her skin. Tess had made the same request of dozens of new mothers, but she wasn't this baby's mother, and her fingers trembled on her buttons.

Tess put the infant in the proper position, holding her upright against her breast, the head turned so she could breathe. The nurse placed a blanket over them both for warmth.

Bianca should be holding her baby. Or North. But there was only Tess.

The infant nestled against her breast. *Nothing there for you, little one. Nothing there.*

The next few days passed in a blur. Tess learned from the nurses that North had checked in by phone, but he didn't contact Tess. She called Phish. The town grapevine had been at work, and everyone knew about the baby and Bianca's death. Tess didn't ask what people thought, but Phish wasn't one for subtlety.

"Hey-ll, Tess. It's all anybody's talkin' about. Nobody knew you was a nurse, and now all kinds of stories 're floatin' around. People are sayin'—"

"I can imagine. Is the road open?"

"Yep. You want me to come and get you?"

"No. I . . . I need to stay here for a while."

Tess began feeding the baby. Each day, she held her longer, the little bird clad only in a diaper as she rested against Tess's bare skin, both of them wrapped warmly in a blanket. The infant had a fuzz of dark hair underneath her newborn's cap. Tess counted the baby's breaths and listened to the little protests she made.

Tess would have to hire a lawyer. She wasn't certified to practice midwifery in Tennessee, and Ian North would almost certainly sue her. Maybe the state's Good Samaritan laws would protect her. Maybe not. Either way, the legal fees would ruin her, but she couldn't bring herself to care.

One day passed into another. Phish called. He was making Savannah and Michelle fill in for her, which was certain to make them dislike her even more. She spoke to the nurses when she needed to and exchanged a few necessary words with the couple who ran the B and B she only visited to shower and change clothes. Otherwise, she held the baby and thought about Bianca.

A week after they'd arrived, the doctor informed her that the baby would be released the next morning. Tess felt only dread. She still hadn't seen North. Would he even show up? And what would happen to this helpless baby bird if he didn't?

All the doilies, peacock feathers, and china cupids in the Victorian B and B suffocated him. Ian liked big, clear spaces: high cement walls, vast canvases, empty horizons.

He reached into his pocket for a tissue. The head cold he was just getting over hadn't bothered him much. A head cold had boundaries. Sooner or later it went away, unlike other disasters.

He'd spent the last few days in Manhattan. Bianca had no family left, but she had business acquaintances. He'd fended off their questions about the baby and arranged a memorial service.

The front door opened.

Tess stopped inside the archway that led to the parlor. She wore jeans and a bulky white sweater, her dark hair curling in a free-for-all around her face. No makeup. She was tired and drawn. But alive. Functional. Despite the shadows under her eyes, she was solid and practical. Everything Bianca hadn't been. Tess Hartsong was a creature of the earth instead of the sky. Ready to strip down to her underwear and dance her furious dirge. He wanted to make her dance for him, dance all the emotions he couldn't voice. Her dark eyes—the color of manganese violet paint—took him in. Seeing right through him. Judging. And why shouldn't she?

A single, awkward move in this overstuffed room

could unleash a domino chain of Victorian clutter. He had to get on with it. Get out of here.

He gazed at her forehead instead of into those eyes. He had to absolve her. It was only fair. "About what I said at the hospital . . ." *Don't fuck this up, too.*

But if he absolved her, he'd lose his advantage.

Was he really going to try using her guilt against her? The doctor had confirmed what Tess had told him about the cause of Bianca's death, but there had to be an autopsy. That meant cutting into Bianca's perfect body. And Ian was responsible. Not Tess. Ian himself. But he needed something from her. And guilt was a powerful tool.

He gazed at the fireplace with its glass cloches and enameled urns, its gilded mirror and marble clock. His eyes fastened on a badly executed seascape of roiling water and misshapen headlands.

He couldn't do it.

He cleared his throat. "What I said at the hospital . . . It was unfair. I know you couldn't have done more."

"Do you?"

He couldn't deal with her guilt. He had enough of his own. He should never have given in to Bianca's pleas to come to Tempest with him. He should have stayed with her in the city, but she'd been so adamant.

He bumbled on. "About this baby . . ."

"Your daughter."

"There are some complications."

Complications? **Tess** tried to calm herself, but there he stood. Hard and distant. No longer haggard the way she was. He looked almost respectable in dark pants and a blue dress shirt. Clean-shaven. Hair still long, but trimmed.

She beat back the panic that kicked in her chest. "Yes, there are complications. Preemies are fragile, and they need special care."

"That's what I want to talk to you about." He came closer. "I want to hire you to take care of her."

"Hire me?" He had to be crazy.

"Until I get everything sorted out. A couple of days. A week at the most."

"That's impossible." She hadn't been sleeping or eating. She was living on adrenaline, and she had to get away from them both. "There are nannies specifically trained to care for preemies."

"I don't want a stranger. I'll pay whatever you ask."

"This isn't about money." She'd stayed with the baby at the hospital. She couldn't put herself in any more emotional jeopardy. This man. This baby. They were living reminders of her own failure. "I'll get some recommendations from the nurses and make a few phone calls."

"I don't want anyone else. You're smart. You're competent. And you're no bullshit."

"I appreciate your trust in light of what happened, but I don't want to do it."

He regarded her with steady eyes and struck his lowest blow. "I guess you've forgotten."

"Forgotten?"

"The promise you made to Bianca. Right before she died."

The hospital made certain his immunizations were up-to-date and gave him instructions on infant CPR that caused him to break out in a cold sweat. They told him about car seats and something called kangaroo care, which he hoped Tess knew all about because he sure as hell wasn't going to provide it. He tried to focus on the birth certificate worksheet they'd given him. His handwriting was barely legible.

Tess sat on the other side of the lounge. She didn't look at him. Didn't speak. He stopped writing. "They want the baby's name."

Tess got up from her chair and walked toward him.

She took the clipboard. Took his pen. Wrote something, then handed everything back to him.

Wren Bianca North.

Not right, but good enough.

The nurse came to get them, but he stayed where he was while Tess followed her. Minutes ticked by. He shifted in his seat. He was a hard man. Not sentimental. He put his identity into his work. Only there. That was the way he lived. The way he wanted to live. And now this.

Tess appeared with the baby. He tried not to look at either one of them.

They were silent in the elevator

Eventually, the doors opened. As they passed through the lobby, people smiled, seeing them as loving parents bringing their precious newborn home. He wanted to run. Get away from everyone. He wanted things the way they used to be when he could block out the world with his brushes and spray cans, his posters, stencils, and murals. When a new commission, a new gallery exhibition, a new army of critics praising his work meant something.

When he still knew who he was and what his work meant.

He left Tess long enough to pull her car up to the hospital entrance. Yesterday he'd retrieved her keys from her cabin and hired a kid who worked at the gas station to take care of the rest—installing a car seat and getting her car from Tempest to the hospital. He had his own car here. Tess would have to take the baby with her.

Anything else was unthinkable.

Chapter Five

Tess white-knuckled it all the way to Tempest. She'd never been a nervous driver, but then she'd never had a newborn strapped in her backseat. Fortunately, a newborn who was asleep, but that could change at any moment.

More than her deathbed promise to Bianca had made her agree to do this. There was something else. Something selfish she was only beginning to understand. Because Wren needed all her attention, Tess could go for an hour or more without thinking about Trav. This fragile infant had brought her a sliver of respite.

She glanced into the rearview mirror for a fruitless view of the baby. Nothing. She understood why it was best for infant car seats to face the rear, but she'd already pulled off the road twice to make certain Wren was still breathing. She fought the urge to pull over a third time.

The battered sign for the TEMPEST WOMEN'S ALLI-ANCE slipped by. She drove carefully up the bumpy mountain road to the cabin. North had left first, and he was supposed to meet her here, but there was no sign of his dirty white Land Cruiser.

The baby had slumped into the very corner of the car seat, her lavender beanie askew on her doll-size head. She awakened as Tess took her out. She didn't look happy, and by the time Tess had them both inside, she'd begun to cry, an unnaturally piercing sound coming from such a small body. "Shhh . . . Give me a chance, will you?"

The cabin was cold. Cold and damp. North was sup-posed to have turned on the small furnace and unloaded the things she'd asked him to order, but he hadn't done it. She only had the starter kit of the supplies the hospi-tal had sent her off with, along with a handmade dark green baby sling that her favorite of the NICU nurses had given her as a gift. She was furious with him for not following through. Wren, in the meantime, had ratcheted up her crying.

Tess set her down long enough to take off her jacket, unbutton her blouse, and slip into the preemie sling. She repositioned the baby against her bare skin, Wren's cheek to her breast, and draped them both in the shawl she retrieved from the back of the couch. It wasn't yet time for another bottle, so she walked the perimeters of the cabin until the motion lulled the baby back to sleep. All the time, she fumed about North's absence. Only after Wren quieted did she go into the closet behind the kitchen to investigate the furnace.

It wasn't working, and she couldn't exactly crawl around on the floor to investigate with a baby on her body. The lack of heat in the cabin worried her. How could she keep Wren warm? Where was North? Caring for Wren was supposed to be a two-way street, but all the traffic was running in one direction. Was it possible he'd intended all along to dump the baby on her and take off?

Wren awakened and began to fuss. Tess dug out one of the preemie bottles. As she poured in an ounce of formula, she thought of her own breasts. "Sorry," she whispered. "You'll have to make do with this."

Feeding was hard work for Wren, who tended to fall back to sleep after a few tugs. Tess gave her the time she needed, burping her gently and keeping her elevated. When it was finally over, they were both exhausted. Tess propped herself up and settled on the couch, tucking the shawl more tightly around them.

She felt Wren's heartbeat against her skin. Saw the quiver in her tiny, seashell eyelids. Heard her soft, sweet breaths. Maybe North had a flat tire. More likely, he'd fled back to Manhattan. She drifted off to sleep

The blood tugged at her calves, rose to her waist. Bianca screamed.

Tess had to get to her. Had to save her. But the blood wouldn't let her move. She struggled against its force. Her legs were gone. Her arms. Bianca slipped into the red pool.

She awakened with a gasp. She rubbed her eyes, trying to shake off the ugly nightmare, and heard a car pull up outside. She looked at her phone. Two hours had passed.

But instead of North, Phish came through the cabin door. He wore an ancient boho hippie pullover and carried a white pastry bag, his scraggly gray pony-tail hanging down his back. "Hey, Tess." He wiped his sneakers on the rug inside the door and gestured toward the baby. "This sure is screwin' up the work schedule. Michelle is all over me to hire her sister."

"I told Ian North I'd look after the baby for another week or so. I think you'd better hire her."

"No way in hell. You've never met her." He set down the pastry bag and came over to look at the baby. "Dude, she's little."

He sounded critical, and Tess took umbrage. "She's a lot stronger than she looks."

"I'll take your word for it."

"She is."

He threw up his hands. "Chill, all right?"

"I need coffee." She eased her legs over the edge of the couch so she didn't wake Wren. "Are those doughnuts?"

"Your favorite."

"You're a saint. Have you seen Ian North in town?"

"Nope." He headed for the kitchen to make coffee.

"Bastard." She eased the kinks from her legs. "Would you check the furnace? There's no heat."

He shrugged and went to look. Moments later, he reappeared. "It's not working."

"Really? I hadn't noticed."

He was immune to her sarcasm. "Maybe you ran out of propane."

"I just had a delivery."

Tires crunched on the gravel outside. Cradling the cocooned infant, she went to the window and saw the battered Land Cruiser pull up. She backed away to keep from exposing the baby to a draft as North ducked through the doorway. Yelling would scare Wren, so she had to be satisfied with a fierce whisper. "Where have you been?"

"I had some things to do." He filled up the space

with his body—making the ceiling too low, the walls too close.

"Yeah, well, so do I. You were supposed to be here hours ago." She reached under the shawl to unfasten the sling. "Hold her while I look at the furnace."

He stepped back. "I already looked at it. That's why I'm late. You need a new one."

"Want some coffee?" Phish said from the kitchen.

North eyed the pastry bag. "No, thanks."

Tess withdrew her hands from the sling's straps and lowered her voice to a hiss. "What do you mean I need a new furnace?"

"The one you have is older than you are. Apparently you didn't get my message."

"What message?"

"The message I left on your cell telling you I was tracking down somebody to replace your furnace."

She'd forgotten that she'd muted her phone to keep from waking Wren, but considering his general attitude, how was she supposed to know he hadn't run out on them?

"I ordered a new one for you," he said. "Bad news is, the model you need is hard to get, and it'll take time."

"How long?"

"A few weeks."

"*Weeks?* I can't keep a newborn here with no heat!"

"Right. You'll have to stay at the schoolhouse."

She grappled with two thoughts at once. The expense of a new furnace and the idea of staying at the schoolhouse. Somehow she'd deal with the first, but as for the schoolhouse— Not with the memories it held. "That's the last place I'll ever go."

"There's no decent alternative. I'll move whatever you need to take up there, and then I'm leaving for the city. You'll have the place to yourself."

"The city? Are you out of your mind? Do you really think I'm going to let you run off to Manhattan and leave me alone with your child?"

Phish, still standing by the coffeepot, watched their exchange with interest. Phish was unpredictable. He might keep their argument to himself, or he might blab it to every customer who came into the Broken Chimney.

"That is not going to work," she said.

"It has to." North seemed to decide the coffee shop owner had heard enough because he dropped the subject and picked up the doughnut bag. "Mind if I have one of these?"

"Don't ask me," Phish said.

"They're mine," she retorted.

"I got more in the car." Phish turned to North. "They're a dollar each. She's an employee is the only reason she gets 'em free."

North gazed at her. "He doesn't like me much, does he?"

She gritted her teeth. "Nobody does. They think you're arrogant."

He nodded. "Fair enough."

Phish suddenly looked embarrassed. "I forgot about your loss. I never met her, but I'm sure she was a good person." He hurried toward the front door. "I've got more in the car. They're on the house."

Not long after retrieving a bag of day-old dough-nuts, Phish took off. The small reprieve had given Tess a chance to get her mental house in order, and as soon as Phish was out the door, she rounded on North. "You're not running out on your daughter. She's your respon-sibility. You even think about abandoning her, and—"

"I'm not abandoning her. You'll have whatever you need."

"It's not what *I* need that counts. It's what she needs."

His stony expression told her everything.

She retrieved the baby from the sling. "Never mind. I quit."

She'd finally rattled him. "You can't do that."

She reached for a baby blanket with her free hand. "Take her. I won't be any part of this."

He stepped back. "All right! You win. What do you want?"

She wanted him to be a father to this tiny speck of a human, but that would take a while. "Don't leave her."

"You want me to stay at the schoolhouse?"

The last thing she wanted. She wrapped up the baby. "If that's where she is, that's where you are."

And where Tess would have to be, too. Tess had been so fixated on the importance of keeping father and daughter together that she hadn't thought about the misery of sharing space with him, but she couldn't see an alternative. "You even think about leaving her, and you're on your own. Am I clear enough?"

His lips barely moved. "More than clear."

Wren had begun to stir again. "I need to change clothes, and you can't put it off forever. Sooner or later you'll have to hold her."

"Later. I have a cold, remember."

"You seem to be over it." She stopped herself before she said more. If she had to coexist with him, she needed to broker some kind of peace. She knew how many disguises grief could wear, and she had to do what she'd sworn she wouldn't do when she came to

Tempest. She kept her voice steady. Her eyes dry. "I understand mourning better than you might think. I lost my husband. He was young, and he shouldn't have died." She sounded strong, as if it had happened long ago, and she'd recovered. So far from the truth.

"I'm sorry to hear that." No pity. A direct statement.

"I'm only telling you this so you won't think I'm unsympathetic, but you have a daughter, and she needs a father. Right now, that might not seem like much consolation for losing a wife, but maybe it will before long." The words sounded hollow, but at the same time they might be true. If she and Trav had had a child . . . But Trav hadn't been ready.

North set his unfinished doughnut on top of the paper sack. "You still haven't figured it out, have you?"

"Figured what out?"

He rubbed the scar on the back of his hand. "Bianca wasn't my wife."

Wren let out a tiny mew of protest. Tess stared at him. "But—" Bianca had repeatedly referred to him as her "husband," and since Bianca had hardly been a slave to convention, Tess couldn't imagine her being ashamed of an unmarried pregnancy. "Why would she say that you were her husband?"

He grabbed his car keys. "I have some things I need to do at the house. I'll come back for you."

"Wait! You can't walk out like—"
But it seemed he could.

Ian shrugged off his jacket and flung it on the school-house couch. His shirt was stuck to his chest with sweat. He'd lied about having things to do here. Lied because Tess would want an explanation, and when it came to Bianca and himself, explanations were complicated.

He gazed around the open room. This house on top of Runaway Mountain should have been a perfect retreat. No sycophantic gallery owners or wannabe apostles banging on his door. In Manhattan, everybody in the art world wanted something from him: his approval, his mentorship, his money. He'd thought he could escape here. Figure out who he was as a thirty-six-year-old artist instead of a rebellious kid. Find a new direction that made sense. But then he'd given in to Bianca's entreaties to come with him. Now she was dead, and he had to deal with the aftershocks, including the disturbance that clung to Tess Hartsong as tightly as that baby.

He gazed toward the back of the room and the closed door that shut off the place where Bianca had died. Leave it to her to tell Tess they were married.

Even though Bianca was gone, he kept waiting for the phone to ring, as it had rung so many times.

"*Ian! I booked a new job. A pop-up store for this fantastic new menswear designer. He's amazing! I can't wait for you to meet him.*"

"*I'm flying to Aruba for the weekend with Jake. . . . He's incredible. You'll see. I've never felt this way about anyone before.*"

"*Ethan wants me to move in with him. Oh, God . . . He is so amazing. I don't care if he's an actor. He's different.*"

"*Ian, I've had a shitty day. Can I come over?*"

"*Ian, life sucks. I'm bringing wine.*"

"*Ian, why do people have to be such shits? Come get me, will you?*"

Now she'd made one more mess for him to clean up. And he'd do it. He always did.

The schoolhouse was warm, but without Bianca rushing to the door to welcome her, it felt empty to Tess. Ian headed toward the open staircase with her suitcase in one hand and the things she'd asked him to order for the baby in the other. "The two of you can take my bedroom upstairs." He sounded as unfriendly as a winter ice storm.

The schoolhouse had only two bedrooms, which meant he'd be left with the one down here. The room where . . .

The shadow of Bianca's death hung everywhere. Tess instinctively curled Wren closer. Living in the same house with him, if only for a few days, was impossible, and yet, how else could he bond with this child he'd so far rejected?

"You won't see much of me," he said as he disappeared up the stairs. "I'll be in my studio."

Tess gazed around at the light-filled room. It was as if Bianca had never been here. No flip-flops abandoned by the front door. No fashion magazines, half-empty water bottles, or discarded granola bar wrappers scattered around. Her gaze landed on the closed bedroom door.

Sooner or later she'd have to go in there. If she didn't get it over with now, she wouldn't be able to think of anything else. As Wren snoozed in the sling, Tess approached the room. She took a long, shaky breath, then turned the knob.

The bed was gone. The curtains ripped from the windows. The carpet had disappeared, leaving the wooden floors bare. And the rest . . . It was as if he'd painted his feelings all over those once light-gray walls.

Swirling shapes covered the surfaces in a pallet of

sooty white and muddy gray, smoky taupe and bleached bone. He'd painted twists and coils, loops and arches. Some of the shapes curled onto the ceiling. Others draped the baseboards and spilled onto the floor. A muted landscape of grief with all the snares and tangles she knew so well.

"Everything is here." She whispered the words to herself, to Wren— "Every emotion . . ." Her throat caught. "Every . . . feeling."

He spoke from behind her, his voice hoarse. "Get out."

Pulling herself together, she turned away.

Unlike the chaos in the room downstairs, the master bedroom was subdued and orderly, with masculine charcoal walls and contrasting chalk-white trim. Its simple furnishings included a boldly striped gray-and-white rug, a big bed with a sturdy headboard, a dresser, and a set of bedside tables. A curved chrome reading lamp looped over an easy chair and matching ottoman.

She'd explained kangaroo care to North, the importance of skin-to-skin contact for preemies. She'd told him how it regulated a baby's body temperature, stabilized respiration, reduced infant mortality, etc. etc. etc., but she wasn't sure he'd been listening. What she hadn't mentioned was how exhausting it could be.

Fortunately, Wren didn't cry when Tess set her in the portable infant bed North had carried upstairs—a little yellow snuggle nest. She'd keep her there just long enough to work the kinks out of her back and set up a changing area on top of the dresser.

She opened the drawers, hoping North had cleared one out for Wren's things. Instead, she found lumberjack socks and solid-color boxers in black and navy, everything simple and masculine with none of the boldness of his art. Plain T-shirts, jeans, a couple of serviceable sweaters. Only the subtle scent of wood moss and cedar suggested anything more exotic.

He'd ordered everything for Wren from a high-end Manhattan boutique. Luxury onesies, pricey swaddles, pastel baby hats, and socks more expensive than any Tess had ever owned.

She left Wren's things on top of the dresser, checked to make sure the baby was still breathing, and wandered toward the room's two front windows. Grief was familiar. So was anger. They had both reshaped her. Now, staring out at this unfamiliar view, she wondered who she might be without the heavy weight of either.

So much had happened today that she'd barely thought of Trav. Despite the strain of caring for Wren, despite her guilt and grief over Bianca's death, she was beginning to experience an odd sense of pliability. Its newness made her feel off balance.

A pair of wooden garden chairs and an iron bench sat near a small garden below. It was mid-March, and the trees were still bare, but a Tennessee spring should begin to arrive any day now. Would the garden come back to life, or would something new need to be planted there? Planted inside her?

Straws of golden light from an Appalachian sunset stretched above the trees into a peach and purple sky. She drank in its beauty. "Would you look at that, Wren?" she whispered. "Would you just look at that?"

"I doubt she's paying attention," North said.

He occupied the doorway, his appearance sudden and unsettling. What did he see when he looked out at the world? Looked at her?

"I thought she was supposed to be in your marsupial pouch," he said, his voice rough.

So he'd been listening to her after all. "She got bored." Her response reminded her that she used to be funny. All her friends had thought so. And she could make Trav laugh so hard he'd snort.

North didn't laugh. He glanced at the changing pad and baby supplies on top of his dresser. "I'll get my things out of here."

Since the downstairs bedroom had no furniture, she wondered where he'd put everything. His studio took up most of the back of the second floor. Maybe he'd move in there. She watched him cross to the dresser. "How old are you?"

"Thirty-six. Why do you want to know?"

He was a year older than she was. "I saw one of your black-and-white graphics a few years ago, a self-portrait. I still remember it. You didn't flatter yourself."

"No need to." He opened the middle drawer. The one with the monochromatic briefs.

"Why did you depict yourself that way?" she asked. "More skeleton than flesh."

"Why do I do anything?" He grabbed the stack of clothes he'd piled on the changing pad and left her alone.

Ian dumped his things on the long, purple couch in his studio. The room smelled of fresh lumber from the open shelves he'd built. Bianca's friends had designed this space, with its big skylights and exposed brick, as a second studio, a place to come when they needed inspiration for their decorating business. But the isolation had proven more romantic in their imaginations than in reality, while the isolation here was all he craved.

He'd added additional lighting, shelving, and a big purple velvet couch. He'd set up the computer work-station he'd used for digital art projects, which ranged from creating wall-size stencils to designing giant light shows he'd splashed on skyscrapers. But the graphic manipulation that used to engross him had lost its allure. He needed to do something else. Something—

How the hell was he supposed to figure that out with all this chaos? He might as well be back in Manhattan.

He thought of Bianca's bedroom downstairs. The Widow Hartsong didn't strike him as a fanciful person, yet she'd understood. He wasn't sure he liked that. No, he *was* sure.

He didn't.

Morning came too early. Tess stumbled downstairs, Wren in the crook of her arm. Ian emerged from the back bedroom as she finished giving Wren her bottle. With his untidy flannel shirt and jeans, he looked as though he belonged in these mountains—as big and rugged as the landscape around them.

"Coffee," she croaked, before he could say a word. "And don't speak to me. I was up with her three times last night. I hate her."

"That would explain why you're kissing the top of her head."

"Stockholm syndrome. I've fallen under the spell of my captor. It's a survival strategy."

His grunt might be his version of amusement, but she doubted it. "Sit down," he said. "I'll make coffee."

She'd never heard a more begrudging offer. "I hate you, too. You've had a full night's sleep, it's not even seven o'clock, and you've already been outside."

"Somebody has to keep the country safe for democracy."

Had he made a joke? He'd left for the kitchen, and she couldn't tell.

The long dining table occupied the north side of the open living area. Its heavy, rough-hewn top had been thickly varnished to guard against splinters. The contrast between the white beadboard on the walls and all the dark wood—the table; the shiny, wide-planked floors; the bookcases set under the windows—made it a cozy winter space, but it would also be a cool retreat on the hottest summer days.

He carried two coffee mugs in from the kitchen, set hers down, and seated himself at the far end of the table, a good eight feet away. If she weren't so cranky from her rotten night's sleep, it would have been funny. "Oh, right," she drawled. "You still believe girls have cooties. Once you're in sixth grade, you won't mind us so much."

His mouth ticked. "I'll move closer as long as you promise not to talk." He slid his mug to the middle of the table.

"Don't do me any favors." She pushed her hair out of her eyes. "I need to borrow one of your flannel shirts. Mine aren't big enough for both Wren and me." Trav's sweatshirt would have been big enough to drape around them both—the sweatshirt saturated with Bianca's blood and dumped so unceremoniously in the hospital trash can. She pulled herself together. "And FYI, you're going to have to start taking over at least one of the nighttime shifts."

"I wouldn't know what to do."

"I'll show you."

"Not necessary."

"Very necessary. You can touch her, you know. None of this is her fault."

"I didn't say it was." He carried his mug back to the kitchen.

She followed in his path, coming up behind him. "Catch!"

He whipped around, his hands instinctively reaching out. She gently set the tightly wrapped baby in his arms.

"What the—"

She backed off. "I need to brush my teeth, take a

shower, and I'd like to use the toilet without a baby on my lap. You'll have to cope."

"But—"

"Deal with it."

As she marched away, Wren began to cry. Tess hesitated and then forced herself to keep going. Wren had just eaten. There was nothing Tess could do for her that North couldn't.

"I hired you!" he called after her.

"Consider this a government-regulated rest break."

Chapter Six

Half an hour later, showered and shampooed, Tess returned downstairs. Ian had barely moved. He stood by the kitchen window only a few steps from where she'd left him. Wren was crying, and instead of walking her, he held her as if she were a grenade about to detonate. Any hopes she'd had that leaving them alone would break the ice around his heart disappeared.

"I'm not doing this," he said stonily.

"I see." She went over to the counter to pour herself another cup of coffee. Wren looked like a mouse in his big hands. His frown became a thunderstorm as Wren worked herself into a full frenzy. He thrust the baby toward her. "I have to get to work."

She tucked the baby in the crook of her arm and

began to readjust the blanket only to stop, her hand stilling on the soft fabric as she was struck by the possibility that she'd gotten it all wrong, right from the beginning. She went after him. "Wren isn't yours, is she?"

He paused in his path from the kitchen. "What makes you say that?"

"If she were your baby, I don't think you'd ignore her the way you have." She followed him into the living area. "Although, considering your generally unpleasant disposition, I could be wrong."

"Yes, you could be." He headed for the front door and grabbed his jacket. "I've hardly ignored her. You're here, aren't you?" The door closed behind him.

She gazed into Wren's unhappy face—wrinkled forehead, nose flattened, tiny tongue curled like a potato chip as she howled. Was Tess's intuition right? But if Ian weren't Wren's father, why had he allowed himself to be listed that way on her birth certificate? And if he were her father . . . ?

Too many unanswered questions. Cradling Wren's fragile spine, she hesitated and then made her way to Bianca's bedroom. She opened the door and stepped inside.

The room was a womb of sorrow. She couldn't believe a man who painted with this much emotion was capable of so coldly rejecting his own child. Unless she was thinking about it the wrong way. Maybe all that emotion explained why he refused to get close to her.

Wren had begun to quiet. Tess gazed down at her little frog-face. "I'm not your mother, sweetheart." But right now, this orphaned baby knew Tess's touch the best. Tess drew her closer. She had years of practice at professional detachment, and she was too clear-eyed to get attached to this child who wasn't hers. But whose was she?

"I'm doing my best, Bianca," she whispered to the empty room. "I promise. I'm doing my best."

Ian needed to get away from this house, from her. The Widow Hartsong saw too much. He strode toward the trail that led up the mountain. For someone who'd grown up in the city, he was most at home outdoors. He'd hiked part of the Appalachian Trail, climbed Mount Whitney in a winter snowstorm, and thru-hiked the John Muir. He'd hiked in Europe, too, with nothing much in his backpack but a change of underwear and whatever drugs he'd been able to get his hands on at the time.

A gust of raw March wind made him wish he'd

grabbed a heavier jacket, but he wasn't ready to turn back. The old fire tower rose off to the east. He'd climbed it a couple of times, but today he needed his feet planted firmly on the ground.

A white-tailed deer loped across the path in front of him. He veered off the trail to follow it toward the creek. As he got nearer he heard a different sound from the usual noise of rushing water. Something like a wail coming from what was left of an old moonshine still.

He quickened his step. He'd discovered the still on one of his first hikes, identifying it for what it was by the telltale U-shaped arrangement of creek rocks that marked the location of an abandoned furnace. A corroded fifty-five-gallon drum lay on its side, along with an old galvanized bucket missing a bottom and some broken mason jars cloudy with dirt. But it was the remains of the old boiler that caught his attention, the rusty slabs of sheet metal etched with ax marks left by long-ago revenuers. Now a kid was trapped underneath.

"It hurts!"

The boy's leg was caught under the heaviest section of the deteriorated boiler. Ian hurried over. "Hold still, Eli."

The kid looked up at him, tears, dirt, and snot

smearing his face. He had brown eyes the size of buckeyes and thick, dark hair with straight bangs that covered his eyebrows. "It fell on me."

"I see that." Ian had run across Eli before. In modern parlance, Eli was a free-range kid, roaming the woods with a lack of supervision urban eight-year-olds couldn't imagine.

Eight and a *half,* Eli had told him.

Despite his perpetually dirty face and homegrown haircut the kid seemed to be well cared for, with a sturdy body and no more bruises than the average boy. "This isn't the best place for you to be poking around." The jagged metal piece was heavier than it looked with murderously sharp edges, and Ian took care lifting it. As he moved it aside, the long gash visible through a rip in the leg of Eli's jeans gushed fresh blood. Too much of it. Ian threw off his jacket and unbuttoned his flannel shirt. "That's got to hurt."

"I'm—I'm tough." Another tear made a fresh road in the dirt map of his face.

"Sure you are." He stripped off his shirt, leaving himself in only a T-shirt, and tightened one long sleeve around the wound to stanch the flow of blood. "Promise me you'll stay away from here from now on."

"I guess."

He bunched the rest of the shirt on Eli's chest and carefully picked him up. Eli whimpered. "Hurts."

"Sure it does. Let's get you home."

Eli leaned into Ian's chest. "You don't have to carry me like I'm a baby."

"I know that. But I'm training for the Ironman. I need to work on my endurance."

"You're training for the Ironman?"

"I might." Or might not. Running and swimming were one thing, but 112 miles on a bike was a deal breaker for someone who liked to have direct contact with the earth.

Eli's parents were homesteaders. Ian had seen the tin roof of their house below the ridgeline off to the west. He slowed his pace as the boy's face contorted with pain. "How's your mother doing?" he said to distract him.

"She's still sad."

"I'm sorry to hear that." In their last conversation, Eli had revealed that his mother was going to have a baby but that "something went wrong and now she cries a lot."

Eli gripped Ian's neck tighter. "My dad says she'll get better soon."

Ian nodded. "That's good." He carefully stepped over a sapling that had fallen across the trail. "What have you been eating lately? You weigh a ton." In truth, the eight-year-old didn't weigh much at all.

Eli made a face. "Beans. We ate most of what Mom put up last summer, but the onions and mustard greens'll be comin' in soon."

Eli sounded like a seasoned farmer. Ian kept the conversation going as he climbed toward the ridge. He asked him what new birds he'd identified, if he'd spotted any bear, how his homeschooling project on beekeeping was progressing. Finally, the bare-bones farm came into view.

The utilitarian house had unpainted wood siding and a couple of solar panels on the tin roof. The freshly plowed ground off to the left marked the vegetable garden. The outbuildings included an old tobacco barn, a goat pen, and a coop with a rudimentary wire chicken run. All of it was surrounded by a crude barbed wire fence guarded by a pair of barking dogs and a rangy man coming toward them with a rifle. "Stop right there!"

Ian wasn't big on firearms, but he knew enough to recognize an AR-15.

"Dad!"

"Eli?" The man squinted into the morning sun.

"Eli ran into some trouble," Ian called out.

"Rebecca!" The man rushed toward them across

the rutted dirt yard, still carrying the assault rifle, but no longer pointing it at Ian's chest. He fumbled with the gate one-handed as a slender, brown-haired woman came out the front door. "What's wrong?"

"It's Eli!" The man set the rifle against the gatepost and hurried toward them. "What happened?"

"Eli cut his leg on a piece of sheet metal at the old moonshine still," Ian explained.

"Damn it, Eli! You should have known better."

Eli's mother raced to her son's side, her hand pressed to her mouth.

"It wasn't my fault!" Eli declared from his father's arms.

His mother soothed him, worry etched in every line of her tired face. "Nobody said it was."

"I say it was," his father snapped. "You gotta be smarter, Eli."

Ian stepped back. "He might need some stitches."

"No stitches!" Eli howled.

"Let me see." His mother's hand shook as she started to unwrap the shirt binding her son's leg.

Ian stopped her. "You need to leave that on until you get him to a doctor. The cut's pretty deep."

"Oh, baby . . ." The woman brushed Eli's bangs from his eyes. She was probably in her late twenties or early thirties, with a long nose and sad eyes that turned down a bit at the corners. She and Eli shared the same straight dark hair and almost identically cut bangs. Her hair, however, hung lank and needed washing.

The man nodded at Ian. "Appreciate what you've done. We'll take it from here."

Something about the stiffness in his phrasing told Ian there'd be no doctor. "He needs medical attention."

"We're good at taking care of ourselves," the man said firmly.

Unlike his wife, Paul had a stocky build and light, wiry hair. He wasn't tall—maybe five foot eight—but his wide shoulders and bulky biceps testified to his strength.

From the look of the farm, the family was living off-the-grid, probably at a subsistence level, without the spare cash to pay for a doctor's visit. This wasn't his business, but he couldn't walk away. "There's a nurse down at the old schoolhouse," he said reluctantly. "I'm sure she'd take a look at Eli in exchange for some fresh eggs. She's one of those natural food fanatics." A flat-out lie, but people had their pride.

"We need to take him, Paul." The pleading note in the woman's voice suggested her husband was a tough man to sway.

It was clear from Paul's expression that he didn't want to give in, but either because he knew his wife was right or he didn't want a showdown in front of a stranger, he gave a curt nod.

The ancient Dodge Ram pickup's dents and cracked windshield testified to years of hard use. Rebecca rode in the backseat, holding Eli, while Ian sat in front.

The family didn't meet the popular stereotype of Tennessee mountain folk. Their accents were Southern, but not backwoods. They'd been homesteading for five years. Rebecca told Ian she and Paul had met during their freshman year at UT but didn't reveal anything else other than their last name—Eldridge.

Tess was walking the floor with the baby as they came inside. The protective movement she made was slight—cupping her hand on the baby's head, pulling her closer—but Ian didn't miss it. As she saw the boy in his father's arms, however, she was all business.

"Put him on the table." She tilted her head toward the dining table and, predictably, handed the baby over to Ian. After carrying Eli, the baby was as light as sea foam in his arms, but that didn't make holding her any more welcome.

"Hey, kiddo. I'm Tess. Ian, would you get the first aid kit? It's above the stove."

The last time he'd looked, there hadn't been anything above the stove but a Christmas cookie tin that had come with the house. Now he found a bright yellow, tackle-size box Tess must have brought with her. Judging from its size, she wasn't risking ever being caught again unprepared for an emergency.

He heard Tess order Rebecca into the kitchen to scrub her hands. They passed each other in the doorway. Eli was stretched out on the dining room table, one of the couch pillows under his head. Tess had cut away his jeans, leaving him in a T-shirt and a pair of superhero briefs she was telling him she envied. Paul paced across the room by the bookcase windows.

Ian set the first aid kit next to her and, making sure Eli couldn't hear, let Tess know Eli's medical care would end with her. "They weren't going to take him to a doctor."

She gave a quick nod. The baby moved in his arms and screwed up her face until she looked demented. Predictably, she started to cry. Tess's head momentarily lifted in response, but she immediately returned her attention to Eli. "Let's see what's going on here." She spoke soothingly as she began untangling the shirtsleeve tourniquet. "I love adventurous kids. What was it that got you? A bear? Or . . . don't tell me. . . . A zombie squirrel?"

Eli offered a teary smile. "It wasn't either one." He began telling her about the moonshine still and Ian's rescue. Tess appeared to be fascinated, but Ian could see her true focus was on what she needed to do. As he repositioned the baby, Rebecca came back from the kitchen, and Tess asked her to unwrap one of the gauze pads from the first aid kit. "I'm going to take a look now," she told Eli. "I hope I don't barf."

Eli gave another teary smile. "I don't think you will."

"I'd better not." She dropped the blood-soaked shirt to the floor, made a quick survey of the wound, and pressed the pad to stanch the fresh flow of blood. "I thought you said this was serious."

"It's not?"

"Serious is when your leg's hanging off. This is a lot easier to fix."

"The metal that cut him was rusty," Ian told her.

"And it's been two years since he had a tetanus booster." Rebecca glanced toward her husband, who was still pacing by the windows. "We'll have to get him another shot."

"I don't want a shot!" Eli cried.

Tess gave him a reassuring smile. "I don't think you'll need one." She glanced at Rebecca. "It's not the rust that causes trouble so much as the type of bacteria that forms on it. But if he had a booster two years ago, he should be fine once we get this cleaned up. The bad thing, Eli, is that I have to get all the cruddy stuff out of the cut. I'll be super gentle, but I'm afraid it's still going to hurt. Crying is okay. Ian cries all the time, and look how big he is."

Ian suppressed the urge to contradict her.

"My dad doesn't cry," Eli said earnestly, "but my mom does."

"Miss Tess isn't interested in hearing about that," Rebecca said quickly.

Ian knew Miss Tess well enough by now to suspect she was very interested, but she hid it well.

Tess had Paul carry Eli to the kitchen sink, where she began cleaning the wound under gently running water and rinsing it with a Betadine solution. Eli did remarkably well, considering how painful it must be. Even the baby quieted, only to kick up again. He remembered what Tess had said about skin-to-skin contact, but he damn sure wasn't taking off his T-shirt.

When the wound was cleaned to Tess's satisfaction, she had Paul move Eli back to the dining room table. There, she smeared it with antibiotic ointment and closed it up with a large, unusual-looking surgical bandage made up of hinge-like strips of adhesive. "This is a relatively new type of wound dressing some doctors are using instead of stitches," she explained, as she helped Eli sit up. "I've heard good things about it, but I've never used it, and I'd feel better if you had a doctor look at this. I suspect he'll end up with a smaller scar if he has stitches."

"Scars don't matter," Paul said. "As long as he's going to be all right."

Tess didn't press. She instructed them on wound care and the signs of infection to look for. "Bring Eli back in a couple of days so I can check on him, will you?"

"Thank you!" Rebecca impulsively threw her arms around Tess. "I don't know how we can ever thank you enough."

"You tell us what we owe you," Paul said stiffly.

Ian stepped in. "I already negotiated for you, Tess. I know how you like to keep your food natural, so I figured you'd appreciate having Eli bring you some of their fresh eggs when he feels better."

She shot Eli a comically incredulous look. "Seriously? You'd do that?"

Eli nodded vigorously, then looked at his father. "Is that okay, Dad?"

Paul gave them a stiff nod. "Sure."

After they'd left, Tess began cleaning up. "I'll do it," Ian said, thrusting the baby at her as if she were contagious.

Tess put her back in her sling. She repacked the first aid kit she'd assembled while Wren was in the hospital, but all the time, she was conscious of Ian working efficiently to bundle up the bloody shirt and gauze, then wiping down the table. She looked over at him scrubbing the sink. "It was a nice thing you did for Eli."

"Did you think I'd leave him there?"

"Hard to tell." She readjusted the sling, watching the economical way he moved and puzzling over who this man really was. "I still don't get it," she said. "You could have hired any of a dozen competent nannies. Why didn't you pick someone else? You don't even like me."

He turned. "Who said I don't like you?"

His words didn't exactly sound confrontational, but close enough. "*You* said you don't like me."

"I never did."

"Your face did. Your words do. You can barely resist sneering at me whenever you see me."

"I never sneer."

"You're sneering right now."

"That's the way my face looks. I can't help it."

She planted one hand on her hip. "How about this, then? I might not like you."

"Understandable. I'm not long on charm."

"I've noticed."

But he was long on talent. A talent he didn't seem to want to use. And she was beginning to suspect he

might—just might—have more humanity than he
wanted anyone to see.

She was draped in a shawl and naked from the waist
up when someone knocked at the front door. Worried
that Eli's wound had reopened, she wrapped herself
and Wren tighter and went to open it.

Three teenage girls—two white and one black—
stood on the other side. She recognized Ava, daughter of the unpleasant Kelly Winchester, but she didn't
know the other two. One had braces, light brown hair,
and a scatter of pimples across her forehead. The other
had an uncertain smile and a bright pink plastic head-
band holding her curly hair away from a heart-shaped
face. Tess waited for one of them to say something, but
they weren't making eye contact. Tess eventually broke
the silence. "What can I do for you?"

Ava licked her lips nervously. "Is that the baby?"

"Yes. Why don't you step in? I don't want her to get
chilled."

Ava was one of those rare teens with straight, shiny
blond hair; a creamy complexion; and perfect, metal-
free white teeth. "It's sad about her mother dying."

"It's been difficult."

Ava nodded toward the other girls. "This is Jordan

and that's Imani. If you ever need a babysitter, all of us are good with kids."

"It'll be a while before Wren can have a babysitter."

"Is that her name?" Ava reached out to touch the baby's head, but Tess moved back before there was any contact. "She's still frail, so I'm not letting too many people touch her. You might have a cold you don't know about."

"Women should have babies in the hospital with a real doctor," Ava said, so firmly that Tess knew she was parroting something she'd heard, probably from her uptight mother.

"That's not always possible."

Jordan, the girl with the braces, had been looking around the room and interrupted. "My mom and dad went to school here."

"So did mine," Ava said. "And my grandma and papa."

"My parents had to go to school at Jackson," Imani said.

The other two girls nodded. "That's because black kids couldn't go to the same school as white kids back then," Ava said. "Some of the white people around here still don't like that we have black friends."

Imani rolled her eyes. "You have *one* black friend.

Don't make it sound like you have more." And then, to Tess, "I'm like their token BFF so they don't look like as big of racists as their parents."

"My parents aren't racists," Ava protested.

"We'd like Imani even if she wasn't black," Jordan said earnestly.

Imani looked more indulgent than offended. Tess smiled. She decided she liked all three of these girls, even perfect Ava, whose flawlessness she would have hated when she was their age.

The other two were starting to look twitchy. Ava finally pulled a folded piece of yellow paper from the pocket of her jacket. "We heard you wrote this."

Tess recognized the pamphlet she'd tucked next to the condom display that had raised Kelly Winchester's ire. *What You Need to Know about Safe Sex.*

"We're in tenth grade," Jordan said. "But they don't teach us this stuff in health class."

"All they teach is don't do it," Imani explained. "It's like an abstinence-only class."

"Mandated by the state," Ava said.

Her terminology reminded Tess that the teen's father was in the legislature. "And we're not doing it!" Ava added so quickly that Tess wondered if she were lying. "We're all virgins. But the thing is . . ."

"Ava and I both have boyfriends," Imani said. "And . . ." She trailed off. The room fell silent.

"And," Tess said, "you're thinking about having sex?"

"No!" Ava and Imani shook their heads too vigorously. "We only have some questions. Things we might need to know for, like, when we're older."

"I mean, we tried to find stuff on the Internet . . . ," Ava said, "but, like . . ." Air quotes. "Parental controls."

"Have you talked to them?" Tess asked. "Your parents?"

They looked at her as if she'd descended from the planet Neptune.

"My father's pastor at Angels of Fire Apostolic," Imani said in explanation. "He's really strict, and he's on the school board."

"And my dad's Brad Winchester. You probably heard of him."

Tess nodded.

"I don't have a boyfriend yet," Jordan said. "But I might. And my mom says that any girls who have sex when they aren't married get AIDS."

"That isn't true," Tess said. "But it's easy to catch an STD or to get pregnant, which is why you have to take care of yourselves."

Wren had begun to fuss, and it was time for her to eat. Tess had all she could cope with right now, and she didn't need three inquisitive teenagers staring at her as if she held the secrets to the sexual universe. She had to send them home to their parents.

But what if their parents shut them out? That happened too frequently. "Let me get her a bottle, and we can talk. Why don't you all have a seat?"

A few minutes later, as Wren tugged sleepily at the bottle and the girls settled on the couch, Tess reminded herself how frequently Trav had warned her about sticking her nose in where it didn't belong. He'd also said she was too judgmental, but that was mainly when she criticized his taste in music.

She brought Wren closer to her body. "Let me tell you up front that I don't think it's a great idea for kids your age to have sex."

They all spoke at once.

"We're not going to . . ."

"I would never . . ."

"I'm not . . ."

Tess held up her free hand. "You have enough to cope with right now—school, parents, peer pressure— and no matter how nice a boy is, having sex too early can make life difficult. In too many cases, the girl ends up being the loser."

"Like, if she has sex and some of the other kids hear about it," Ava volunteered. "And then everybody would say she's a slut."

"I hate hearing that word used against women," Tess said. "If she's a slut, that means he is, too."

Jordan nodded. "That's what I think."

"Maybe he's not any more ready than she is," Tess said. "And maybe she's the one pressuring him. Or maybe he's not as nice as she thinks he is."

"Connor is super nice," Ava said earnestly.

"And so is Anthony," Imani said.

The shawl slipped down over Tess's bare shoulder, and she readjusted it. "But from what you're telling me about your health class, they might not know any more than you do."

Imani fiddled with the arm of the couch. "A lot of boys say it's not that big a deal."

"And if you have cramps, it'll make them go away," Ava said.

Jordan tugged on a lock of her hair. "I heard you can't get pregnant the first time. But I don't believe that. It's not true, is it?"

"It's definitely not true," Tess said.

Ava caught her pink bottom lip between her teeth. "What if a boy says—if you don't have sex with him, he'll like break up with you?"

Tess took a calming breath. "That would be your lucky day because, if a boy ever says that to you, you know for a fact that he's a complete jerk and you absolutely have to break up with him first."

Jordan looked pointedly at Ava, who said, "But you can't get pregnant if you do it in the pool or hot tub, right? Or standing up."

"Stop!" Wren twitched against Tess's outburst. "Sorry, little one." Tess brushed her cheek and returned her attention to the girls. "You can get pregnant in any position, sitting, standing up, lying down, in a car, on a trampoline—although that might be tough to pull off—but the point is, where there's sperm and a vagina, you can get pregnant. And if sex isn't a big deal, why do we spend so much time thinking about it?"

She caught a movement out of the corner of her eye and realized North had returned and was standing inside the front door. From the expression on his face—incredulity mixed with general pissed-offness—it seemed he'd been standing there for a while.

She gave the girls a big smile and stood. "If you have more questions, please talk to your parents."

"But . . ."

"Promise me you'll at least think about talking to them."

Three sets of betrayed puppy dog eyes met hers.

Ava flipped her enviable hair. "Yeah, like I really want to be locked in my room for the rest of my life."

Tess started to tell her to have more faith in her parents, but from what she'd seen of Kelly Winchester, Ava might be right to have misgivings. Tess felt an all too familiar frustration with unrealistic parents and with schools that clung to a curriculum that left teens achingly vulnerable. If she didn't step up, was she any better? "If you have more questions, come back in a couple of days." Even as she said it, she suspected she was making a mistake. "And don't get pregnant before then!"

They giggled, chirped their thanks, and turned to leave, only to falter in embarrassment as they finally noticed North standing in the doorway.

"Don't worry about him," Tess said. "He only cares about himself."

Ian stepped aside to let the girls hurry past. The door closed behind them, and he shot her one of his incredulous looks. "Just to make sure I understand . . . We're not only running a clinic here, but you're now teaching sex education classes in my house?"

"Write down any questions you have. It's important for boys to be as well informed as girls. And I didn't invite them. They showed up. And before you go into your whole Prince of Darkness routine, you should know that two of those girls are teenage pregnancies waiting to happen."

"That's not your problem."

She touched Wren's cheek. "Don't worry about that bad man, sweetheart. I'll slip some garlic in your blankie."

A snort and then he pulled the black-and-red flannel shirt he'd worn the morning of their first meeting from a hook. He delivered it to her. But instead of moving away, he stayed where he was, his eyes lingering.

Only then did she realize her shawl had once again slipped off her shoulder. Far off. Revealing most of the top of one breast. She jerked it back up as if she were some kind of outraged virgin.

"Think about what you're doing, Tess," he said. "Think about how you'd feel if you were a parent and a stranger started talking to your kid about sex."

"I'm right." She sounded self-righteous even to herself.

He tilted his head ever-so-slightly and then headed upstairs.

She heard the studio door close above her and gazed at his flannel shirt for several seconds before she remembered she'd asked him for it. She discarded the shawl and buttoned herself and all of Wren, except her face, inside. The shirt felt wrong. It didn't smell like

Trav's sweatshirt. Instead, it smelled of the outdoors. Most disturbing, it had no hood she could hide inside.

Wren uttered one of her baby coos. North's shirt was fine with her. She had no memories of Trav spilling coffee down the front of it, and she'd never snatched it up from wherever he'd abandoned it and asked him to please, just once, throw the damn thing in the closet instead of leaving it around.

Was it a betrayal that Bianca's death was more on Tess's mind these days than Trav's? What if there was something more she could have done for her? Between Bianca, taking care of Wren, and Eli's emergency, the anger that had been fueling her for so many months had shifted to a new target. Ian North.

She gazed toward the staircase. She needed some answers, and she wouldn't let him stonewall her any longer.

Chapter Seven

A generous pair of skylights brightened the spacious studio. The floors were new, a cool blond hardwood instead of the darker finish everywhere else. No brightly colored paintings hung on the wall—no incendiary posters of missiles sprouting from party hats, no twelve-foot stencils waiting to be taped against brick or canvas and brought to life with spray paint. He sat at a computer with his back to the door.

"I didn't hear you knock."

"Weird." She came farther into the room, Wren the barest weight in her arms. "You're quite the man of mystery. I'm curious. Do you have any personality—other than the dark and mysterious part?"

He turned to her. "I have lots of personality."

"Aloof? Foreboding?"

He rose from the desk, not appearing to be put off by her insult. His height, stevedore's jaw, and long-muscled arms seemed wasted on someone who didn't need to lift anything heavier than a paint roller. "Refusing to telegraph every emotion that flits through my brain doesn't make me aloof."

She caught the implied insult. "I don't flit. And if Wren's not your baby, whose is she?"

"I don't like being interrupted when I'm working."

"You were probably playing solitaire online. And if you were a female artist, you'd get interrupted all the time. Kids, husbands, girlfriends, UPS. That's the way it is with us. And Wren comes first. Even before your work. Whose is she?"

He shoved a hand in the pocket of his scruffy jeans. "What if I told you she's mine? Would that make you go away?"

She gave him the same "you're a moron" look the teens had given her. "Do I look like I'm stupid?"

"What you look like is a pain in the ass!"

"Is it possible for us to have a straightforward conversation?"

"I don't like conversation—straightforward or not. I can't work with you popping up all over the place."

"Tough. You've hauled me into your mess, and I need to know what I'm in for."

"Do your job," he said brusquely. "I'll handle the rest."

She wasn't backing off. "I promise not to make eye contact while you talk. I know that makes you nervous."

"I am not afraid to make eye contact with you." He proved it. His eyes, dark as sin, locked with hers until she felt as if he could see into everything she wanted to keep hidden—her anger, her guilt over Bianca's death, and her shame at not being able to move on from the loss of the only man she'd ever loved. She looked away first, shifting her focus to Wren. "One of us has to care about her."

"Do you think I don't care?" He jabbed a hand toward the window. "Sit over there. In that chair."

She glanced toward the straight-back chair he'd indicated. "Why?"

"Because you don't have anything better to do right now."

She was curious enough to sit where he indicated. He rolled the sleeves of his denim shirt to his elbows, revealing long-muscled forearms all ready to chop wood. But instead of grabbing an ax, he picked up a sketchbook. She stared at him. "You're going to draw me?"

"Don't expect anything flattering."

She wiggled self-consciously. "I'm surprised you can

actually draw. I thought it was all paint rollers, stencils, and spray cans."

"I didn't say I was good at it. Move your legs to the left."

She felt big and awkward, but she did as he asked. "If you give me purple horns or a word balloon, I'm suing."

"I'll remember that."

"Can I have it afterward so I can sell it on eBay?"

He cocked his head at her, a shaggy curl falling over his forehead, but didn't reply.

"How much money do you think it'd bring?"

He moved a second straight-back chair under a skylight and sat. "Turn your torso so you're facing me."

"I've never imagined you using a sketch pad. Maybe a blowtorch, but . . ."

He set an ankle on his opposite knee, propped the sketchbook on his thigh, and studied her. She gazed uncomfortably at the wall behind his head. "I'm serious about eBay. I could use a new car. A yacht would be okay, too."

His pencil began moving over the paper.

She crossed and uncrossed her legs. "Or a house in Tuscany. Maybe in an olive orchard. Or a vineyard."

More long strokes of the pencil. A pause.

He ripped the paper from his sketchbook, crumpled

it into a ball, and tossed it on the floor. She watched it roll toward the purple couch. "Bianca said you weren't working. That you were blocked."

"Did she?" He flipped the sketchbook to a fresh page and began to draw again.

"You could at least have let me comb my hair first. The great Ian North wants to draw me, and my hair's a rat's nest. You're going to put a mustache on me, aren't you?"

"Uncross your legs."

She wasn't aware she'd crossed them.

She couldn't stand the tension any longer, and she gazed down at Wren. She took in her tiny movements— the twitches and sighs. Once again, she heard the rip of paper and watched another crumpled wad hit the floor. She refocused on the baby's little frog-face. Matched her breath . . .

She jerked as his fingers touched her cheekbone. She hadn't heard him move. He gently tipped her chin. His touch was light, merely a brush, but something inside her prickled, like an unhatched chick pecking the tiniest hole in its shell. No one had touched her face in so long. Not since . . .

Her throat constricted. The shawl slipped down on her breast. She drew it back.

He dropped his hand and turned away from her. "Wren's father is a man named Simon Denning. He's a photojournalist. Specializes in covering the world's hot spots."

The pressure in her throat eased. "I'm glad."

"About what?"

"That you're not her father."

He began drawing again, his attention on the sketch pad. "Bianca and I were never lovers."

She mulled that over. "That's hard to believe. She loved you."

"Yes. And hated me, too."

"Because you didn't love her back."

"No more talking. I'm concentrating."

"You were so protective of her. Overprotective. Trying to keep her away from me. What were you afraid I'd do to her?" The moment the words were out, her throat constricted. "I'm sorry, I—"

"Quiet. I'm trying to focus here." He'd cut her off. Given her a reprieve.

She turned her head. "I don't understand why it's so hard for you to hold Wren."

She didn't expect him to answer, but he did, speaking so quietly she barely heard him. "Being around fragile things isn't good for me."

The way he said it . . . So stoically. It almost made her feel sorry for him. Almost. "If you didn't love her, why was she with you?"

His hand stabbed at the sketch pad. "Because *I* was all she could count on. Enough questions."

She rearranged Wren's dark hair into a baby Mohawk. "So here we are, the two of us, taking care of a child who doesn't belong to either one."

He flipped to a fresh page. "My lawyer's trying to find Denning. I should know more in a couple of days."

Wren mewed. Tess brushed the tip of the baby's earlobe sticking out from beneath her cap. "I'm getting a cramp."

He grunted. "Great art requires sacrifice."

"That's not great art. It's a sketch of an ordinary person with a mustache, and you need to change Wren's diaper."

That actually made him laugh. For the first time. She sighed and stood. "Come on, Wren. Off to the ladies' room we go."

"I'm not done."

"I am."

"Do you have any idea how many women want me to draw them?"

"Zillions?"

"Maybe not that many. But a solid half a dozen, at least."

She laughed, then realized she didn't like seeing this easier side of him. It made him more human than she wanted him to be.

As she began to shut the door behind her, she heard the sound of paper being torn in two . . . three . . . four pieces.

On the drive back home from Knoxville the next day, after Wren's first well-baby checkup, she skittered around remembering that moment he'd touched her face. The feeling she'd had . . . A hyperawareness of her own body—a startling reminder that she was still a sexual being. Remarkable, considering how tired she was from lack of sleep. She'd felt—not exactly strong, but . . . strong-ish. Not so much like a wounded animal. It was as if she'd dipped her toe into a fresh version of her old self—tougher and a tad cynical.

She'd liked matching wits with him. It made her want to go up against him again and badger him for answers to the questions he seemed determined to dodge. What hold did Bianca have over him? Or did he have a hold over Bianca? And why had he tried to isolate Bianca?

For the next few days, she barely saw her housemate. His car disappeared and reappeared. She heard his steady footsteps overhead in the studio where he might or might not be working. She heard him behind the closed doors of Bianca's almost bare bedroom when she got up at night to feed Wren. She'd see evidence that he'd eaten—a dirty plate, an apple core in the trash, but she never saw him do it. He disappeared into the woods for hours, and once she suspected he stayed out all night.

The Eldridges hadn't brought Eli back, and that made her uneasy. What if the wound had become infected? She looked out the rear window and saw Ian clearing brush from behind the schoolhouse. He attacked the larger branches with a hatchet and stacked them for firewood.

She bundled Wren and ventured out the back door. The day was overcast with the smell of snow in the air, but he'd discarded his jacket and rolled up the sleeves of his denim shirt. A pale white scar formed a half-moon above his wrist.

"Where did a city boy like you learn to chop wood?" she asked.

He wiped his shirtsleeve over his sweaty forehead. "I might have spent too much time at various schools for recalcitrant youths. They're great places to pick up basic skills."

"Wilderness survival?"

"Along with hot-wiring cars and making a shiv out of a toothbrush. Most people don't know this, but there's a right and wrong way to mug an innocent citizen."

"The scope of your knowledge leaves me breathless."

"It's nice to be appreciated."

"Except you never mugged anyone."

"But I could have if I'd wanted to." He shifted his view toward a stand of trees that edged a gully behind the house. "I'm thinking about building a tree house in that oak over there. Kind of an open-air studio."

She didn't know much about artists, but she did know something about human psychology. Building a tree house studio might be productive or it might simply be another form of procrastination—a way he could make himself feel as though he was working without actually doing it.

"I'm concerned about Eli," she said. "The Eldridges were supposed to bring him back. Have you seen him?"

"No. But I can hike up there and check on him."

"I'd feel better if I saw him myself, but my Honda might not be up to the climb. Can I borrow your Land Cruiser?"

"I'll go. Paul tends to greet visitors with an assault rifle."

"Why would he do that?"

"The Eldridges are what's known as preppers or survivalists. They want to be self-sufficient, so they're prepared for disaster: pandemics, nuclear attack, economic collapse, World War III, a meteor strike, whatever. In fairness, some of what they do is common sense—having extra food, batteries, water. Most of all, taking care of the land. But too many of them are paranoia propagandists. Tell me what to look for, and I'll stop in."

"No. I need to see him. It won't kill you to watch Wren for an hour."

"You don't know that for a fact."

She sighed. "Fine. We'll go together."

He wasn't happy about that, but he seemed to recognize a losing argument when he was caught up in one.

The interior of Ian's ancient Land Cruiser with its faded leather seats, missing radio knob, and dinged-up dashboard wasn't quite as beat up as the exterior, but that was the best she could say for it. She settled in the backseat next to Wren, with one hand clutching the armrest. "Did you ever think about using some of your millions to put new springs in this thing?"

"Wouldn't feel the same."

"That's kind of the point."

Wren, however, didn't mind the bouncing and jostling. She'd fallen asleep.

The Eldridge farm looked as hardscrabble as Ian had described it. With the exception of the solar panels on the roof and the antediluvian Dodge Ram truck, it could have been a homestead from the early twentieth century. As Ian pulled up outside the fence, a pair of furiously barking fecal-brown dogs charged toward them.

Rebecca appeared unarmed at the front door. Not so for Paul Eldridge. He emerged from the weathered barn holding the assault rifle Ian had warned her about. Eli scampered after him, showing no ill effects from his accident.

"Stay here," Ian ordered as he got out of the car and walked toward Paul and Eli.

Rebecca approached the fence, moving slowly, as if each step were an effort. Ignoring Ian's order, Tess got out of the car. She reached the gate at the same time as Rebecca.

"I'm sorry you had to come all the way up here." Rebecca's dull complexion, unwashed hair, and fingernails bitten to the quick testified to a hard life. "Eli's leg is healing fine. I should have let you know. Would you like to come in? It'd be nice to have a woman in the house for a change."

Tess extracted Wren from the car seat and followed Rebecca inside.

Unlike the unpainted exterior, the interior had soft green walls and a few feminine touches: a handmade throw pillow in brightly colored chintz and a string of pastel paper lanterns over the serviceable family dining table. A smaller table stacked with textbooks and pens marked the site of Eli's homeschooling. His artwork hung next to it, mounted in simple frames decorated with painted twigs and pebbles.

Rebecca cast a yearning look toward Wren. "How old is she?"

"Almost two weeks. She's a preemie, but she's doing well."

With no warning and an almost inaudible choking sound, Rebecca turned away.

"Are you all right?" A stupid question. She obviously wasn't.

"I have to stop crying. It upsets Paul and Eli." She slowly turned back, tears tracking her cheeks. The way her eyes naturally turned down at the outer corners made her look even more vulnerable. "I had a miscarriage two months ago."

Tess curled her hand over Rebecca's arm. "I'm so sorry."

"I was almost four months along." She gazed at Wren. "I'll get over it."

The very words Tess had told herself so many times. "Grief seems to have its own timetable."

"I've wanted another baby for years." Rebecca tried to pull herself back together, but she couldn't draw her eyes away from Wren. "You're so lucky to have her."

"She's not mine. I'm only her temporary caretaker."

"What do you mean?" Rebecca gestured toward the kitchen table, and after they were seated, Tess offered a much-abbreviated summary of what had happened. She did her best to be factual and steer clear of the emotional undercurrents, but by the time she was finished, Rebecca had once again begun to weep. "I'm so embarrassed to keep falling apart like this.

"I've fallen apart more than a few times myself."

"What's going to happen to that sweet baby?"

"She'll be taken care of," Tess said more firmly than she felt.

Rebecca tore her eyes from Wren and rose from the table. "Would you like some tea? I grow my own herbs."

Tess wasn't a big fan of herbal teas, but she accepted.

Eli came in while the tea was brewing. Tess checked his wound and saw it was healing well. He rushed back out to join the men. "Dad's showing Ian the wind turbine."

"It's Paul's newest project," Rebecca said as the door slammed behind her son. She set a pair of matching mugs on the table and settled across from Tess. Behind her, bottles of various sizes and colors caught the light on the kitchen windowsill. "We're not crazy, you know. We just want to be prepared."

The tea smelled of lavender, rose hips, and lemongrass, all fragrances Tess loved but didn't necessarily want to drink. She took a sip anyway. It was surprisingly delicious. Maybe she should stop prejudging. "Prepared for what?"

Rebecca gazed at Wren. "Once Eli was born, all I could think about was how precarious our existence is on this planet. Not only the litter and waste, the plastic clogging up our oceans, but crazy men with nuclear bombs, germs we can't even identify, cyberattacks wiping out the country's power grid. We decided that we had to take care of ourselves."

Tess thought Rebecca's palpable anxiety might be better handled by medication than this difficult lifestyle, but that was the judgmental part of her kicking in, and she said nothing.

"**What do** you think of them?" Tess asked Ian on the way back.

"Eli's a great kid, and that speaks well of his parents. But Paul's too much into government conspiracies for my taste. I don't know how anybody with a brain can think our government is well organized enough to hide aliens or fake moon landings, let alone confiscate everyone's guns. I'll say this for the guy, though. He has an amazing skill set."

They got back to the schoolhouse sooner than she would have liked. Being confined was making her stir-crazy. Despite the lousy pay and her obnoxious co-workers, she missed the Broken Chimney. She also hated leaving Phish short-staffed, even though he kept telling her to take the time she needed.

Ian had returned to clearing out the brush in the back. She wished she could curl up in bed and take a nap, but Wren wasn't having it. As Tess bounced her in the sling, she investigated the bookcases. Not even the most fast-paced novel could hold her attention, but she discovered a splashy volume devoted to international street artists, another on the work of the British street artist Banksy, and a third titled *IHN4: A Rebel's Story*. Beneath the title were the words, "How the son of one of America's wealthiest families abandoned his heritage and elevated street art from gutters to galleries."

Wren cried when Tess tried to sit, so she propped the book on the kitchen counter and read.

North spent his teen years as a conventional graffiti artist, vandalizing trains and subways. But as he matured, so did his vision. His youthful video game–inspired graphics gave way to more detailed, socially conscious work, some of it even whimsical, such as turning the iron grid on the side of a grocery into a zoo cage by pasting a herd of escaping wildebeests around it, or transforming the irregular bricks on a city wall into the missing front teeth of a child's mouth.

More recently, he's shown signs of disillusionment as art speculators purchase the actual walls where his work has shown up—buying them from the property owners, paying to have the buildings repaired, and then selling the works for vast profits, all without his permission.

She read about Ian's family—his hostile, driven father, who'd died in a small plane crash, and his mother, a beautiful socialite with a pattern of self-destruction. Nothing was mentioned about her death, so she must have been alive at the time of publication.

"Street art," Ian was quoted as saying, *"stole art from the elitist museum crowd and put it cleanly in the path of everyday people."*

Tess was still thinking about what she'd read as she gave Wren a quick bath in the upstairs bathroom sink. Ian poked his head in. Unlike her, his complexion wasn't pasty, and no dark shadows from interrupted sleep lurked under his eyes. She wanted to snap his head off. "What do you want?" she snarled.

"You have company."

"Company?"

"Oh, yes." The words dripped with sarcasm.

She wrapped up Wren, elbowed past him, and made her way downstairs.

Eight teenage girls stood inside the front door. Ava, Imani, and Jordan, along with five of their curious girl-friends.

Ninety minutes later, when the girls finally left, Ian stormed downstairs, looking as if a grenade had detonated too close to his head. "They asked about *anal sex!*"

Tess shifted uncomfortably. "Kids these days."

"And you answered them!"

"You could have spared yourself by not listening."

"Do you have any idea how far teenage girls' voices *carry?*"

He stalked across the room toward a pair of old wooden lockers. "Look, Tess, I know you're trying to do a good thing, but this has 'bad idea' written all over it."

She didn't exactly disagree. Wren nuzzled at her breast. "What do you suggest?"

He opened both locker doors and pulled out a whiskey bottle from behind one. "I suggest you tell them to stay home and talk to their parents."

"Don't you think I've tried? But most of those girls have parents who seem to be living in an alternate reality. As for their health classes . . . They have an abstinence-only curriculum. It's *illegal* for their public schools or teachers to offer anything else."

He twisted off the cap and splashed whiskey into a heavy-bottomed tumbler. "This isn't your problem."

She sank into the sofa cushions with a sigh. "I know. You're right."

"Of course, I'm right. But . . . Wait. Did you say I was right? Give me a second to recover." He took a slug of whiskey, then gazed at her. "Go ahead. Say whatever it is you don't want to say."

He could read her thoughts too easily. She fiddled with the bottom button on her borrowed flannel shirt. "I've seen the way sexual ignorance can destroy kids' lives. For me, giving them information is . . ." She trailed off, feeling too exposed.

"It's an act of conscience." He said it bluntly, but not exactly unkindly. How could someone so self-centered have figured this out about her?

He set down his glass and took a bottle of wine from the locker. "This is like the way you refuse to sell cigarettes at the Broken Chimney, isn't it?" With a twist of the corkscrew, the cork released.

"How do you know about that?"

"Even a hermit like myself couldn't escape that juicy piece of town gossip."

He filled a wineglass and brought it to her. It was nearly five o'clock, so why not? "I want the girls to respect themselves," she said. "I don't want them having sex because they think it's the only way they can find a boyfriend. I also don't want girls pressuring boys to have sex before the boys are ready." She took a long sip. "God, this wine is good."

"Enjoy." He took another swig of whiskey. "And you need to butt out."

"I know." She set down her glass. The sling was hurting her shoulder, and as he wandered over to the window, she extracted both the sling and Wren from under his flannel shirt. She wrapped the baby, naked except for a diaper, in the receiving blanket she'd draped over the arm of the couch. "What do you do when you go out in the woods?"

"Hike. What did you think?"

He was hedging. She lay the swaddled baby on the cushion next to her. As she stretched her stiff shoulders, the tips of her breasts brushed against the soft flannel. Even though Ian had his back to her, she felt unarmed without a bra, and she crossed her arms over her chest. "Do you think about Bianca?"

"Of course."

"I think about her, too. How she trusted me." She had relived those moments when Bianca had begun to hemorrhage a thousand times, looking for something she'd missed, finding nothing, but still unable to accept her own helplessness. She resisted the urge to polish off her wine in one long slug. "Why did she lead me to believe you were married?"

"Bianca could be flexible with the truth."

"I thought you were smothering her."

He turned from the window with a rough, unmerry laugh. "If you mean you saw me trying to control as much of her life as I could, you're right." His grip on the tumbler tightened, and his voice was bitter. "And look how well that turned out."

She ran her thumb around the rim of her glass. "You were trying to keep her safe."

"Only to have her end up dead."

"Oh, no, you don't!" She shot up from the couch. "You weren't the person in charge of her delivery. Only one of us has that on her shoulders."

He pointed the tumbler at her. "Stop right there. The doctors I talked to were clear about why she died."

"It's only their best guess. Nobody can say for sure until the autopsy results are in. And even then . . ."

"Don't do this to yourself," he said gruffly. "This is on me. I should never have let her come here."

"That was on her, I think. She could have left anytime."

"She was pregnant. Pregnant women don't always think clearly."

"You know this from your vast experience with pregnant women?"

He shrugged.

She eased onto the arm of the couch and glanced down at Wren to make sure she hadn't decided to stop breathing. "I still don't get why were you trying to keep me away from her."

"Did you ever read *The Great Gatsby*?"

"Of course."

"Bianca was like Daisy Buchanan. One of the careless people. Impulsive." He tucked a thumb in the pocket of his jeans. "She'd latch on to someone—form an intense relationship—exactly the kind I could see her forming with you. Then she'd blow it up over some imagined slight. Afterward, she'd spiral into a depression."

"You were trying to keep that from happening." She thought of Wren. "Bianca told me you weren't happy about her pregnancy."

"She tended to act impulsively and then lose interest."

So much of what she'd believed about Ian North was proving untrue. "Did she blow things up with you?"

"Countless times, but it didn't last long."

"Why is that?"

He wandered toward the piano. "It's a long, boring story. Save yourself."

"Are you kidding? Wren and I live for this kind of thing. Tell me."

Chapter Eight

"I'm not telling you," he said.

The baby was beginning to stir. Tess slid off the couch arm and picked her up. "We won't whisper a word. Right, buttercup? Is there a murder weapon involved?"

"Does self-destruction count?"

"Disappointingly mundane, but we'll take what we can get." She cuddled Wren to her breast.

He smiled. Only a shadow of the genuine article, but a smile nonetheless. "I was twenty-five, just out of jail for trespassing, and flat broke." To her surprise, he sat down. "I'd spent a year in Europe, and I had a good reputation with other artists, but that was it. I wasn't a kid anymore, and I was tired of being broke, which is ironic, considering how contemptuous I was of my family's money, even before I was disinherited."

"Being disinherited sounds so cool. Like something from a Regency novel."

He cocked an amused eyebrow. "It's what happens to us black sheep." He polished off his whiskey, the scar on the back of his hand catching the light. "My work stopped meaning anything. The same with my life. I was drowning in self-pity and punishing myself with drugs. Uppers, downers, coke when I could get it, vodka chasers. I squatted on friends' couches until I ran out of friends. I kept getting fired from whatever menial job I could find because I overslept after being up all night stenciling electrical boxes or wheat-pasting posters. My father had always said I was a failure, and I proved him right. Are you bored yet?"

"No way." If she showed any sympathy, he'd clam up. "I love this tortured artist crap. Keep going."

The corner of his mouth twitched. "I didn't expect this kind of heartlessness from a woman whose conscience won't let her sell cigarettes."

"I have a split personality. And your father sounds like a real shit. Tell me more."

"All I wanted to do—all I knew how to do—was paste up subversive posters and paint murals nobody had commissioned. But sitting in jail was getting old.

There's a thin line between art and vandalism, and I'd lost the stomach for tagging buildings that weren't already abandoned. I wanted real commissions, and I wasn't getting any." He set down his whiskey tumbler and rose to wander toward the old upright piano. "When Bianca found me, it was the middle of winter, and I was passed out in a doorway next to a club on East Thirteenth. I'd hit bottom. But instead of walking by, she loaded me into a taxi and got her doorman to drag me inside her apartment. She shoved me in her shower—clothes and all—turned on the cold water, and left me there until I staggered out."

Tess held Wren closer. "You could have been dangerous. Why would she take that kind of risk?"

"She was wild, impulsive. She was only nineteen, at the height of her career, and she thought she was invincible." He rested his elbow on top of the piano, not far from the bell rope that dangled through a small opening in the ceiling. "She had money, an expensive apartment, and the city at her feet. Everything I didn't have. She was a kid. I, on the other hand, was twenty-five, six years older, and a grown man. But she took me in and saved my life."

He spun the schoolhouse globe on top of the piano with his index finger. "She rented a warehouse space for me and told me I had two months to get ready for an underground art show. I argued with her, but she wouldn't back off." He stopped the spinning globe with his palm. "She bought me paint, paper, canvas, big sheets of acetate for stencils. I had no pride left. I took everything she offered."

"A smart move on your part."

He shrugged that off. "She hired a construction crew and created buzz about the show with all her celebrity friends. It cost her over a hundred thousand dollars."

"Wow. Why would she put herself out like that?"

"She had so many people controlling her career—agents, photographers, clients. I think she needed to be in control of something herself, and I was it." He looked directly at her, making no effort to avoid eye contact. "I sold over a million dollars' worth of work in three weeks. That quickly, I was the new hot commodity in the art world. Everything took off for me. She made my career."

"It was your talent that made your career."

"That's not really true. I'd hit rock bottom. If it hadn't been for her, I'd be dead by now."

Tess thought about what it would feel like to owe so much to another person. He lit the fire he'd laid inside the potbelly stove. "And Bianca fell in love with you."

He didn't deny it. "She fell in love easily."

"But you didn't love her back."

He closed the door of the stove. The flames highlighted his strong cheekbones and cast hollows beneath. "You saw how she was. Seductive. Charismatic. I owed her everything, and I was enchanted by her. Yes, I loved her. But like a brother for a kid sister."

"And she wanted more."

He moved away from the fire. "She kicked me out when she realized that wasn't going to happen. It was right around the time I got my first big mural commission. I didn't need her anymore."

"And yet you stayed in her life."

"For a couple of months, she refused to see me—wouldn't take my calls. Then she fell into a bad relationship. . . ."

"And you were there for her."

"Always. She'd been my caretaker. I became hers. She made messes. I cleaned them up."

Tess rubbed a rough spot on her thumb. "When did you start to resent her?"

"How could I resent her? She saved my life. I would have done anything for her."

"You did." She gazed down at Wren in her arms. "And now, you have one more of her messes to deal with."

"The biggest one yet." He sank back into the couch. "For all the poking around you're doing in my life, you haven't told me anything about your own."

She couldn't imagine telling Ian North about Travis Hartsong. "A former nurse midwife. Currently employed as a nanny by an enigmatic street artist with a semisour personality that, I admit, I'm gradually warming up to. On temporary leave from a side job at a decidedly untrendy coffee shop in backwater Tennessee. No solid plan for the future. How's that?"

"Now who's dodging?"

She scooped up the baby. "Come on, Wren. Let's get you a dry diaper."

She'd been at the schoolhouse for ten days. Paul Eldridge had shown up once to help Ian sink the support posts for his studio tree house. If Ian wasn't working on the tree house, he was out on one of his woodland excursions, bringing the smell of fresh air with him when he returned. He did everything but paint.

With the exception of another trip to Wren's pediatrician and their brief visit to the Eldridge farm, Tess hadn't been out of the house, and the outdoors beckoned her as enticingly as the smell of Cinnabons in a shopping mall. If only the third week of March hadn't brought such raw, dreary weather, she'd have taken Wren outside for a walk, but it was too chilly for a newborn.

When she couldn't stand the confinement any longer, she set Wren's sleeping nest on the couch, and as Ian returned from wherever he'd been hiking, she tucked the drowsy baby inside and grabbed her coat. "See you later."

He stood in the entryway, the scent of pine drifting off him in the same way other men smelled of expensive cologne. "Where are you going?"

"Out! I can't stand being cooped up inside another minute."

"You can't—"

"Oh, yes I can!" She spun toward him, one finger pointed toward his head. "And she'd better be *alive* when I get back!"

Short of tackling her, there was nothing he could do to keep her inside.

Dirty snow still lay in shady spots and the wind stung her cheeks, but she was outside, and she didn't care. A crust of ice clung to the banks of Poorhouse Creek, and the filaments of algae growing on the rocks trailed in the fast-moving current like witches' hair. Another plank in the wooden bridge had come loose. She remembered the way the bridge had swayed the morning North had charged into her life.

Without the perpetual pressure of the sling, her shoulders eased. But as she stepped off the bridge, an unsettling anxiety ruffled the pit of her stomach.

"Being around fragile things isn't good for me," he'd said.

But being around fragile things had been Tess's life. The babies she'd delivered. The frightened new moms she'd cared for. What if Wren woke up and started to cry? Would North pick her up? Would he check on her to make sure she was still breathing? Wren had been glued to Tess's body from the day she'd been born. And that's where she belonged. Against Tess's body.

She turned to rush back to the schoolhouse, only to make herself stop. She was behaving like a frightened new mother. Something she wasn't.

She took a few deep breaths. Wren would be fine. Ian wasn't going to let her die. And Wren needed more than one person watching out for her until her father showed up.

What if Wren's father was an unreliable jerk like Tess's father had been? Or a drunk? If she thought like this, she'd tumble into a whole new realm of craziness. She forced herself to go on.

The back door stuck, and she shoved her shoulder against it. Inside, the cabin was cold and musty. A place so sad she couldn't imagine bringing Wren here. She'd have to get new rugs. Buy decent furniture. Except Wren would never come here. By the time the new furnace arrived, the baby would be gone. Tess could leave things exactly as they were. Gloomy and unwelcoming.

The schoolhouse was spoiling her. She wanted something nicer for herself. Clean white walls, a sofa that wasn't slipcovered in an English hunting print. Before, she hadn't cared, but now she did.

Trav . . . I'm think I'm finally getting better.

That made her sad in a whole new way.

She tossed out a wilted bag of salad greens and a moldy cucumber. She ate an apple she didn't remember having bought and filled a shopping bag with more clothes. She glanced at the pile of professional journals that had been forwarded to her post office box in town. *Journal of Midwifery, International Journal of Women's Health.* None of them had anything to do with her new life, but she put them in the shopping bag with her clothes.

Her anxiety got the best of her, and she raced back to the schoolhouse.

She found North pacing the floor with Wren in the

crook of his arm as if she were a football. But she was alive.

He stalked toward her, speaking in a whispering hiss. "She started to cry," he said, as if it were Tess's fault.

"No kidding? That's odd." She gritted her teeth. "And it isn't even *three o'clock in the morning.*"

He got her point and tucked the baby against his chest, but only until Tess got her coat off, when he passed her back over. "My attorney isn't getting anywhere locating Wren's father, so I'm going to fly up to Manhattan tomorrow and do some investigating of my own. I'll probably be gone a few days. Are you okay with that?"

The way he said it told her he didn't much care whether she was or not. "You aren't exactly a big help when you're here."

"When I get back, I have to work. I mean it, Tess . . . I can't be distracted with you and the baby any longer."

"I'll discuss it with her."

His gaze became critical. "Are you losing weight?"

He'd thrown her off balance. "I don't know. Why?"

"Your face is thinner." He sounded as if that were a bad thing.

"So what?"

"Nothing. Only that you don't need to lose weight."

"Thanks for your input. I'll make sure I forget it."

He had the nerve to look hurt.

The nightmare returned that night, worse than ever. Would she ever stop having this dream of blood and fear, or would it plague her sleep for the rest of her life?

By the time she and Wren got downstairs the next morning, Ian was gone. As she drank her morning coffee, she thought about the nightmare and then about the photos she'd uncovered when she was doing her Internet stalking. Photos of Ian with one exotic-looking woman after another. She kicked aside the sneakers she'd abandoned by the stairs. She didn't want him hooking up with one of his lovers. She wanted—

She didn't know what she wanted. Maybe a lover for herself? Even a few weeks ago, the idea would have been unthinkable. She blamed Ian. Living around his overly potent masculinity was messing her up.

She'd thought her sexuality had died along with Trav, and it was unsettling that a man who couldn't be more different from Trav seemed to have resurrected it. But maybe that was the point. Maybe the fact that Ian was

Trav's opposite had given her subconscious permission to get turned on without feeling disloyal. Despite the wayward path of her thoughts, she'd never go to bed with North. If . . . when . . . she had sex again, it would be with someone like Trav. Except sexually aggressive in a way Trav hadn't been.

Always the seducer. Never the seduced.

She was glad she'd never told Trav that she needed him to be more aggressive. Now her sexual greediness seemed petty. Considering how much he'd loved her, she couldn't imagine having that conversation with him. He would have been so hurt.

She rearranged Wren's baby Mohawk. "Distract me from my wicked thoughts, sweetheart. How about a little conversation?"

Wren blinked her sleepy eyes and screwed up her mouth.

"Don't cry, okay? You did enough of that last night."

Tess fed her and poured some Cheerios into a bowl for herself. As she ate, she faced the dismal prospect of being holed up alone with Miss Crabby Pants while Ian dined in fine restaurants and rumpled the sheets with a beautiful woman. Maybe more than one.

She heard a car and peered out the window in time to see a woman she didn't recognize emerge from a muddy SUV and head toward the house. Tess opened the door.

The woman looked like a sixty-year-old fashion model for the alternative, boho, yoga crowd. She had shiny gray hair in a single braid, a glowing complexion, and bright hazel eyes with delicate lines at the corners that bespoke character. Her lithe frame was packaged in an embroidered tunic top, skinny jeans, and ankle boots. Long turquoise earrings dangled from her earlobes, and a mala bead necklace completed her outfit. "You must be Tess," she said. "I'm Heather."

Tess didn't recognize her from the Broken Chimney, but any company was welcome. "Come in."

Heather stepped inside and opened her arms like a preacher embracing his congregation. "What a magnificent space! I wanted to buy the schoolhouse for myself as a home studio. I'm supposed to be a potter." She dropped her arms. "Unfortunately, I've never been good with money." She gazed at Wren. "You're a little miracle, aren't you? Let me wash my hands so I can hold her." She saw Tess's hesitation. "Don't worry. All my immunizations are up-to-date, and I haven't been sick in years."

"That's good to know, but . . . Who are you, and why are you here?"

"Ian didn't tell you? I'm Heather Lightfield. Your backup babysitter. He's concerned about you being alone while he's gone, and he knows Phish needs you."

"My backup—"

"Phish told him about me. And Phish wants you back at the Broken Chimney right away."

"I know. But Ian didn't say anything to me about a backup babysitter."

"Maybe he thought you'd object. I can see the two of you have bonded."

For a moment, Tess thought she was talking about bonding with Ian, but then she realized Heather meant Wren.

Heather headed for the kitchen, talking the whole time. "Ian checked all my credentials, called half a dozen references, and made a general pain in the ass of himself. You can ask Phish." Water began to run in the kitchen sink. "I was a preschool teacher," she said from the other room. "After I retired, I wanted to make pottery full-time. Instead, I started taking care of kids. I throw pots, too, but not as much as I'd planned." She emerged from the kitchen, drying her hands on a paper towel. "Try stroking her instead of patting her like that, Tess. Preemies don't like being patted."

Something Tess knew very well, but she'd been so caught up in her visitor's narrative that she'd been patting Wren's little bottom without realizing it. "You have experience with preemies," she said.

"Twins, not long after I moved to Tempest. I learned fast." She ducked back inside the kitchen.

Tess moved to the door. "Why have I never seen you at the Broken Chimney?"

Heather tossed the paper towel in the trash. "I've been in Kentucky for nearly two months clearing out my mother's house. She died just shy of her one-hundredth birthday."

"I'm sorry to hear that."

"Don't be. She was a terrible human being." Heather reached out for the baby. "Come here, little angel. Why don't you take a bath, Tess? Or go for a walk. I'm sure you could use some time to yourself."

And with no more conversation than that, Tess did what Heather suggested. Handed Wren over to a strange woman, who could have been a demented kidnapper, but wasn't. Everything about Heather exuded energy, competence, and hippie kindness. Even so, as soon as she was upstairs, she called Ian.

"A woman named Heather Lightfield showed up."

"She's great, isn't she?"

"Is there a reason you didn't talk to me about getting more help with Wren?"

"I didn't want to argue with you."

"Why would I argue?"

"Are you serious? As protective as you are?"

He was right.

"I figured once you met Heather," he said, "she'd win you over."

"She's okay."

He laughed.

"All right, she's more than okay, but I can't afford to pay a babysitter. She probably charges more than I make."

"Why would you pay her? I've taken care of it."

"But—"

"I told you I'd make this arrangement as easy on you as I could, and that's what I'm doing."

He'd told her no such thing.

"Also, Phish was starting to get nasty. And don't ask me how much I'm paying her because I've forgotten. I'm not good with money. Never have been. As long as I can buy paint, I'm happy. Besides, this was about self-preservation. Mine."

"What do you mean?"

"Let's just say all the confinement was making you— I'll go with a 'cranky shrew.'"

"Good choice."

She heard a short, low-pitched laugh. As she hung up, she realized Ian had found an efficient way to get Tess and Wren out of the house so he could have the place to himself when he got back.

She soaked in the tub, but even before she finished drying her hair, she was anxious to get back to Wren. When she returned downstairs, she found Heather wandering around the room—Wren in her sling—and reciting *Goodnight Moon* from memory.

She nodded at Tess but didn't otherwise acknowledge her until she'd completed "Goodnight noises everywhere." She smiled. "It's never too early to start them on great literature." She cradled Wren's head in her palm. "My house isn't far from the Broken Chimney. You can drop her off on your way."

This was happening too fast. She wanted to go back to her job, but how could she leave Wren?

Heather regarded her sympathetically. "Write down her schedule—everything I need to know. Why don't you go for a walk and think it over?"

Once again, Tess followed Heather's orders.

The cold, bracing air energized her, but she'd barely walked a mile before her need to check on Wren forced her back inside.

Heather was sitting in a crossed-legged meditation

pose on the floor, Wren nestled comfortably in her lap. Heather looked up, then touched the tip of her finger to the tiny place between Wren's eyebrows. "It's amazing how open her chakras are. You're taking wonderful care of her. Her third eye is already clearing. It's a sign that she'll be wise."

Wren cooed in response to Heather's touch, and Tess felt an irrational sense of pride in knowing her newborn's third eye was already so well developed. Which officially made her one more crazy, doting mother.

Foster mother, she reminded herself. That's what she was. A temporary caretaker until Wren found her real family.

Leaving Wren for the first time was excruciating, something Heather understood, because all morning Tess's cell pinged with photos: Wren sleeping, Wren eating, Wren pooping. Ian texted her saying he'd be gone longer than he'd expected, but offered no explanation. He probably wanted to spend more time in bed with some alluring figure model.

Knowing Wren was in good hands should have relaxed Tess, but the mood at the Broken Chimney seemed to have changed. Maybe it was only in her imagination, but customers who had once taken time to chat were now in a rush. It took a visit from Courtney Hoover for her to understand.

The would-be Instagram queen appeared at the counter, her face freshly polished with her trademark opalescent glimmer powder; eye makeup applied in a kaleidoscope of vanilla, rose, and plum anchored with a perfect smoky liner. "I heard you were back."

"We're out of mocha," Tess lied. "Cocoa bean shortage in Brazil."

"Bummer." She curled her fingers around her ever-present cell phone displaying maroon hard nails with tiny crystals embedded in the tips. "I'll just have a doughnut then. I haven't posted a food shot in a while."

Tess picked up the tongs. Phish had added a new doughnut choice in the almost three weeks Tess had been gone, and Courtney pointed toward the chocolate-frosted Long Johns. "Let me have one of those."

Tess wondered if Ian knew about the Broken Chimney's Long Johns. "How's your Instagram feed going?" she said, to deflect her thoughts.

"I've been posting more videos. Video's the way to go." She tapped the top of the display case. "Not that one. The one on the left has a shinier glaze." As Tess put the more photogenic Long John doughnut on a plate, Courtney dropped her voice and leaned forward. "You should know, Tess, that everybody's talking about you."

"Oh?"

"I'm just being honest."

During the hours Tess had spent after Trav's death numbing herself with reality TV, she'd learned one thing. Whenever someone said they were "just being honest," they really meant they intended to be cruel.

Courtney pulled out her wallet. "A lot of people think what happened to Ian North's wife is suspicious."

Tess's breath hung in her chest. She should have been prepared for this. "Bianca wasn't his wife," she said carefully. "She was his friend. And an amniotic fluid embolism is a lot of things, but it's not suspicious."

In the background, The Dead began singing "Brokedown Palace." Courtney's nails looked like crampon tips as she spread her hand on the countertops. "I'm only being honest, Tess. As soon as she dies, you and Ian North move in together. People notice something like that."

Tess slapped Courtney's five-dollar bill in the cash drawer and counted out her change. "I'm taking care of the baby. That's all."

"Right. That's why you're here now." Courtney deposited her cash in her wallet, shouldered her purse,

and slithered off to the front window with her doughnut, where she posed, neck tilted, hair extensions snak-
ing down her back, Long John dangling above her
parted lips. *#DoughnutBlowJob.*

Tess plunged a pair of dirty mugs into the sink,
berating herself for getting sucked into Courtney's
venom. Phish must have known a lot of people in town
had turned against her, but he'd been afraid she'd quit
if she found out ahead of time.

Her phone pinged. She gazed at the screen. Wren
lay curled adorably in her nest on Heather's yoga mat,
a tiny red bindi painted between her eyebrows. *Don't
worry.* The text read. *Organic ketchup.*

Tess was falling in love with Heather. At the same
time, her arms felt empty. She couldn't wait to throw
off her apron, get away from the condemning stares,
and reclaim her baby bird.

A few of the after-school crowd tumbled through the
door. Unlike the adults, they were happy to see her. Ava
Winchester was the last to arrive. "Tess! You're back!"
She grabbed a girl Tess hadn't yet met and pulled her
toward the counter. "Tess, this is Gabi." Gabi had a
chubby round face, curly red hair, and green, assessing
eyes. Leaning closer to the counter, Ava lowered her
voice. "Gabi's on the spectrum."

"You didn't have to tell her that," Gabi protested.

"How else is she going to help you if she doesn't know all the facts?" the ever-practical Ava said. One day, Tess decided, Ava would make a kick-ass social worker. If she didn't get pregnant first.

"Gabi needs to talk to you about you-know-what."

Tess didn't ask what Ava wanted her to talk to Gabi about. She already knew. "I'll be happy to talk to you, Gabi. But only if you want to."

"She does."

"Don't push her, Ava."

"You want to talk to her, Gabi," Ava said earnestly. "Really. Tess is cool."

Tess didn't feel cool. She felt as if she were in over her head.

Tess distracted Ava from the uncomfortable Gabi by asking her what she would name her future children, if she had any.

"Not 'Wren.' Honestly, Tess, that's lame."

"I was under pressure."

Ava headed off to be with her friends. Gabi, with a look over her shoulder at Tess, went to join her.

Michelle arrived half an hour later. Her pregnant belly had grown in the three and a half weeks since Tess had last seen her. "I'm working with you because I have to," she said as she knotted her apron above her swollen abdomen, "but I'm not going to pretend everything's okay. That poor woman. Her body's not even cold, and you move in with her husband."

Until today, Tess hadn't considered how this would look to the town.

Heather's quirky little house was eclectically furnished with gauzy drapes, fairy lights, and mirrored pillows. Tess curled Wren against her and gazed into her sweet, elfin face. "I swear she's gained weight since this morning."

"She downed that bag of potato chips I gave her like a pro," Heather said.

Wren's rosebud mouth formed a soft oval, and Tess kissed her forehead. "The lady thinks she's funny, but we know better, don't we?"

Heather had a big laugh for a small lady.

Tess wasn't anxious to get back to the schoolhouse, so she eagerly accepted Heather's dinner invitation. The spicy mixture of quinoa, chickpeas, broccoli, and avocado tasted a lot better than it looked. As they finished eating, Tess decided to be upfront. "I'm sure you've heard the gossip, and so you know . . . I didn't kill Wren's mother so I could move in with Ian." She'd spoken more vehemently than she'd intended. "The two of us can barely tolerate each other."

Heather tapped the excess quinoa off the serving

spoon. "Here's what I've learned about people. . . . Life gets boring, and inventing conspiracy theories makes everyday existence more exciting." She touched Tess's hand. "This'll blow over. The more people get to know you, the quicker the gossip will die off."

Tess wanted to believe Heather was right, but she was too much of a realist.

She stopped at her cabin on the way back to the schoolhouse to retrieve some earrings she hadn't felt like wearing until now. As she got ready to leave, she spotted specks of dried mud by the back door that she must have tracked in the last time she was here.

She grabbed the broom and swept it up.

Ian returned home as it was getting dark. Wren had finally settled down after a long crying jag that left Tess counting the hours until she could dump the little hellion back on Heather. As Ian set his backpack inside the door, his shoulders tested the seams of a worn brown leather jacket—shoulders that should have been hauling bundles of roofing shingles instead of cutting stencils and wielding spray cans. He took in her tangled hair, saggy jeans, and formula-stained shirt. As usual, he seemed displeased with what he saw. But not for the reason she thought.

"Did you eat at all while I was gone?"

"A simple bowl of gruel. Your absence left me bereft."

The corner of his mouth kicked up, then settled back into its customary spot at the corner of that hard mouth. "I found Wren's father," he said. "But there's a problem."

Chapter Nine

I an had been trapped in Bianca's crises for so long that he'd forgotten what it was like to be with a woman who could stand on her own. Tess had tied up her hair in a messy bun. No makeup. The neckline of her rumpled white blouse slightly askew—just like her. Her straight dark eyebrows drew together over those brilliant plum-blue eyes—not all that happy to see him. "I want to hear everything," she whispered, "but if you wake her, I *will* kill you."

He wanted to wake Tess up. He couldn't remember when he'd last experienced so much . . . unbridled lust. Bridled lust, sure. He'd felt that lots of times. But not this primitive urge to tumble her right here by the front door. It made him furious. Sex was one thing, but this was total overload. He'd never once produced decent work when he'd been entangled in a relation-ship. It wasn't the women's fault. He was the one with the fragile, emotional fault line.

As he watched Tess carry Wren upstairs, he thought of Bianca. Even without the complication of sex, their connection had sucked the creative juices right out of him. He'd never get back the days, the weeks, the months of productivity he'd lost whenever she was in crisis. And yet, if he had to do it again, nothing would change. She'd been there for him when no one else had.

Tess's footsteps tapped overhead. He reverted to the surliness that kept him comfortable when she was in his vicinity and headed for the refrigerator and a cold beer. At this rate, he'd be an alcoholic before she moved out.

Tess managed to transfer the little beastie to the sleeping nest next to her own bed without waking her. Wren was gaining weight and breathing well, which made Tess less anxious about taking these brief respites from carrying her in the sling. She picked up the baby monitor and hurried back downstairs to cross-examine Ian.

His leather jacket was gone, and he'd rolled up his denim shirtsleeves to his elbows, revealing those long-muscled forearms.

"You should be doing manual labor," she muttered. "I'll bet you've dug ditches."

"I've hung drywall, too, and driven a forklift, but I'm hoping those days are behind me." He sat on the couch. "Why are we having this conversation?"

"No reason." Other than the distraction of those forearms, plus a coward's desire to postpone hearing about Wren's father. She sank into the matching couch across from him, the monitor by her side, and drew her feet underneath one hip. "What did you find out? How did he react?"

"I didn't talk to him." He propped his ankles on the coffee table. Unlike hers, his socks had no holes in the toe. "The guy's a photojournalist, and he's in some kind of foreign combat zone now. But I did locate his parents. They live in New Jersey. Princeton. That's why it took me so long to get back."

"Did they know about Bianca? That she was pregnant?"

"No. But he's their only son, and once they got over their shock, they were happy to know they have a grandchild."

She sank lower into the couch cushions. "What now?"

"They're trying to contact him, but whether they

talk to him or not, they plan to fly down next week to meet Wren."

"I see." She picked at a loose thread on the couch arm. "Did you tell them she's a preemie?"

"I did. I also told them she's being looked after by a trained nurse." He took a sip of beer and carefully set the bottle on the table, watching her the whole time. "Wren isn't yours, Tess."

She bristled against the gruff gentleness in his voice. "Why would you say such a thing?"

"Because I know you better than you might think."

He didn't know her at all. He didn't know how dead she'd been for so long or how much she used to love to laugh. He didn't know that she had a career she could never practice again and no idea what she would do with her future. "I've barely been separated from her since she was born. Of course, I'm getting attached." She came up off the couch. "I also know this is a temporary arrangement, but that doesn't mean I'm willing to simply hand her over to a set of elderly grandparents who don't know the first thing about taking care of an infant."

"They're barely in their sixties, and Mrs. Denning was coming back from tennis when I got to their house. He seems to be into mountain biking."

Deflated, she sank back into the couch cushions.

He regarded her with an expression that, on anyone else, would have been compassion. "They appear to be decent people."

"Great."

He uncrossed his ankles and gave her some time to think it over by changing the subject. "I realized while I was gone that I haven't paid you yet."

She picked up the monitor and held it close enough to her ear so she could hear Wren breathing. "There's no hurry."

"Wren's three weeks old."

"In less than a week, it'll be what would have been her official birthday," she said.

He shifted his weight to his right hip and pulled a check from his left pocket. She instinctively recoiled as he stood. "You can give it to me later. Or not at all. You're paying Heather."

"This is yours."

He was standing in front of her, the check outstretched in his hand. She'd never been more deserving of such a hard-earned paycheck. All the hours of lost sleep, her aching shoulders from the miles she'd walked trying to quiet a crying baby, the formula-stained clothes, the worry, the stress. She stared at the check and then closed her eyes. "I can't take it."

"Sure you can."

"We'll talk about it later." She toyed with the baby monitor, not wanting him to see how stricken she was inside.

The couch cushion sagged next to her. "You're tired now. We'll settle this when you've had a couple of decent nights' sleep."

His rough kindness didn't surprise her as it once would have. She'd sensed this softness inside him, a sensitivity he worked hard to keep buried. She made the mistake of looking up.

He was sitting so close. . . . Her fingers curled involuntarily into the chair arm. Their gazes locked. At first, she saw only his concern for her, but as the schoolhouse wall clock ticked into the heavy silence, something changed. A pulse leaped at the base of his throat, and her own breath quickened. His palm settled on her knee like a caress, and the warmth of his body filtered through her clothes. It was as if her refusal to take the paycheck had shifted the landscape, built a bridge where before there had only been a valley.

The schoolhouse rafters groaned. A gust of wind rattled the windows, and his eyes grew half-lidded. The periphery of the room began to fade into the shadows—the walls and windows, ceilings and doors, melting away.

Her skin prickled as a flame came to life inside her, skittering here and there, creeping toward the borders of what had been frozen. She couldn't look away, and neither, it seemed, could he.

His lips moved. He spoke one word in a husky voice. *Bedroom.*

She stood. With no thought at all. Brought to her feet by the rush of blood in her veins.

Bedroom.

Now he was the one holding the baby monitor. The old schoolhouse clock ticked away as she followed him— not to the back bedroom—but upstairs. *Bed. Room. Bed. Room.*

The clock's rhythm matched the syllables that played in her head but not what he'd said, because the word he'd spoken so softly had been, *"Studio."*

Dazed, she moved inside.

The room was dark, but he didn't turn on the ceiling lights. Instead, he flicked on a lamp that did little more than cast a watery glow. She stood by the studio door and watched as he set down the baby monitor and began pulling fat white candles from the wooden shelves. One after another, he placed them on the floor in a half-circle around the purple velvet couch.

Only a single candle remained. He set it on a shelf

above the couch, turned to her, and gestured. She knew what he wanted. Didn't know. She stepped between the candles and took a seat on the cushion at the end beneath the outlaw candle on the shelf.

He struck a match and began lighting the wicks of the floor candles. When the match grew too short, he blew it out and lit another. Flicking shadows danced up the walls, and the air grew heavy with the scent of sulfur.

Her breath quickened as he stood before her. His hand went to her hair. He tugged on the tie that held it up, and a messy waterfall tumbled to her shoulders. His hand lingered. Tunneled into the tangle.

She tried to find a wisecrack—something—anything— that would dispel the charged air crackling between them. His hand moved from her hair to the top button of her blouse. His knuckles brushed her skin as he slipped it open. That smell of sulfur filled her nostrils.

He unfastened the next button, the one after that. Her blouse parted in a deep V. With the tip of his index finger, he drew the V down over one shoulder, exposing the swell of her breast above the worn lace of her bra.

He gently pressed her against the arm of the couch. Her legs automatically extended on the cushions. He took off her sneakers and set them outside the circle of candlelight. He removed one sock—only one—from her top foot. His hand gently encircled her bare ankle. One thumb pressed into the hollow there and stroked that small sensitive place.

It wasn't like her to be passive. She had no experience with impassiveness. *Always the seductress. Never the seduced.* Yet here she was, letting him do it all.

He brushed his thumb against her cheek as he rearranged a lock of hair. Her blouse fell lower on her shoulder, but he wasn't satisfied. He hooked her bra strap with his finger and slipped it down, too.

She saw herself as he did. The naked curve of her shoulder, swell of her breast. The drape of her blouse at her elbow and the thin white bra strap across her arm.

He barely took his eyes from her as he propped a giant pad of paper on an H-frame easel. With a fat pencil, he began drawing with broad, aggressive strokes. Nothing secretive or contained. No pages ripped off and crumpled on the floor.

She lay against the arm of the couch, her blouse half off, legs crooked along the couch cushions. One sock on, one sock missing, gazing toward him. Watching him.

The candles sputtered. Burned lower. His free hand went to his own shirt. The studio was cool, but he unbuttoned the top buttons. Perspiration glimmered at the nape of his neck as his pencil attacked the paper.

As the minutes ticked away, she grew more and more aroused. She wanted to pull off her blouse, strip away her bra. Get rid of her jeans, her underpants. But she would do none of that. If he wanted more of her, he would have to take it for himself. She wouldn't make it easy for him. Not the way she'd done for Trav.

Always the seducer. Never the seduced.

The light was dim, but not so dim that she couldn't see he was hard. She kept waiting for him to destroy what he'd created. For him to step from behind the easel and come to her. But his drawing arm kept moving. A curve. A slash. A dance. *Pop and lock. Quick step, break step. Adagio, allegro.*

She wouldn't make the first move. Not again. In this new chapter of her life—however chaotic it was—she'd never again be the sexual beggar. She needed to be desired—to be wanted as much as she wanted him.

Work for it. You have to work for it.

A lock of hair had fallen over his forehead, but he was too absorbed in his task to notice. He existed in perfect, tortured union with pencil and paper. She was watching a genius struggle with his work.

And that's when she understood.

He had a hard-on, all right. A hard-on for his art. For creation. Not for her. She was a means to an end. The great artist attempting to use her to break through whatever was holding him back. This seduction wasn't carnal. It was only about his work.

She dropped her feet to the floor. The candle flames shuddered. He looked up at her and blinked, as if he'd been very far away.

She stepped between the candles and left him alone in the studio.

Ian dropped his pencil and shoved his thumbs against his eye sockets. He didn't know exactly how he'd fucked up; he only knew he had. Despite mustering every ounce of his willpower to keep himself in check, he'd somehow offended her.

Tess Hartsong wasn't a woman you could take against a wall. But he'd wanted to. His every base instinct urged him to do exactly that.

Which would have made him a complete bastard. He was guilty of a lot of things, but riding roughshod over women wasn't one of them. And hadn't he proven that by walking away from the sight of Tess stretched out on the couch? By going to his easel?

He finally let himself look at what he'd done. An intricate detail of her bare foot. A delicate sketch of her shoulder. The curve of her neck.

It was crap. The worst kind of formulaic, sentimental crap.

He ripped the paper from the easel. This wasn't what he did! He created huge, bold pieces. He cut giant stencils with X-Acto knives. Shaped his murals with acids and bleach, nozzles and rollers. He worked big, with no room for the old and refined, the musty and mundane.

He went to the window and threw it open to cool off. He'd come here looking for reinvention—a new path that would let him breathe fresh life into his work. But all he'd done was exactly nothing. First, it was Bianca, and now it was Tess. One distraction after another.

The candles sputtered in the draft from the window. Tess's fierceness and determination, that sarcastic mouth, the strength she didn't seem to know she possessed . . . All of it distracted him, and now here he was, producing bullshit greeting card art. He was a cliché. An artist who had to live a selfish life. Picasso might have been able to whip up masterpieces with all those wives and mistresses in his life, but Ian was cut from a different cloth. If he wanted to work through whatever was blocking him, he had to keep his emotions and his sex drive locked up. That's the way it had always been. The way it would always be.

A frozen band of loneliness wrapped itself around him. He leaned down to blow out the candles. One by one their flames flickered and died.

Wren woke at five in the morning with no intention of falling back to sleep. "Would it kill you, just once, to sleep in, you little butthead? Huh? Would it?"

Apparently, it would.

On the other side of the window, the sun shone. Tess lifted the sash. The air was cool and fresh. It was as if spring had arrived overnight. Last night in the studio seemed like a dream. The couch. The candles. What had she thought would happen? More upsetting, what had she wanted to happen?

It was too soon. She wasn't ready to deal with this newly awakened part of herself. Her skin itched. Her body ached to move. To dance. It had been weeks since she'd danced.

Instead, she changed Wren and fed her. "Now would you please go back to sleep?"

Wren stuck out her little pink tongue.

"Did you really do what I saw you do?" Tess pushed her feet into her sneakers. "All right, young lady. It's warmed up outside, and if you're strong enough to give me attitude, you're strong enough to get used to the great outdoors."

She bundled the baby in a fleece onesie and a warmer hat, tucked her in the sling, and headed out.

The birds were celebrating the extra kiss of warmth in the air with a noisy cantata. Instead of going to the cabin, she chose the trail leading up the mountain to the abandoned Pentecostal church. A pair of squirrels searched for the nuts they and their pals had hidden in the fall. The old fire tower rose in the distance. Wren's cap slipped over one eyebrow, but she was wide-awake and attentive, her gaze fixed on the shifting patterns of light and shadow as they passed beneath the trees. Tess heard the distant barking of a dog. One of the Eldridges'?

The trail opened onto a rutted road that had once carried the faithful to worship. What was left of the church sagged on its foundation. Weeds encroached on the rotting wooden siding, and a tree grew through an opening by a chimney. Where the front doors had once been, a hole gaped. Through it, Tess could see the broken altar window.

Despite the decay, the church was a friendly sight, alive with birdsong and speckled sunlight. Off to the east, the last tendrils of mist uncurled in the low spots of a small clearing. Among those tendrils, a figure moved in a slow, methodical choreography.

Defying the morning chill, Ian was shirtless, the muscles of his chest perfectly delineated as he extended one arm and then the other in a slow-motion pantomime punch, both measured and powerful. Mesmerized, she watched him turn his arm. Change the position of his hand. Every movement deliberate.

A knee came up. He raised a leg to the side with absolute control. He pulled the knee back and thrust it out again. Twice, three times, four . . . His torso remained perfectly upright, his resting foot as steady as if it had sunk roots deep into the ground. He brought the other knee up. Once again, that perfect balance.

His movements quickened in a beautiful martial arts ballet of slow squats and meticulous kicks. She'd wondered how he stayed so muscular. Now she knew.

He hadn't seen her, and she didn't want him to. This was a private ritual. Wren squeaked, but he was too far away to hear. Seeing this private part of him discomfited her. She'd been aware of his physicality from the beginning, but witnessing this was something else entirely.

The more she knew about Ian North, the more complicated he became.

After what had happened in the studio last night and what she'd just witnessed, she wasn't looking forward to the awkwardness of seeing him right away, but as it turned out, they didn't encounter each other again until that afternoon. As she bundled Wren in a warm towel from her bath at the kitchen sink, she heard voices coming from the other room. Adult voices, not teenage girls.

Ian came into the kitchen. "You have more company."

She regarded him quizzically. To her surprise, he reached for Wren. She gave him the damp, towel-wrapped baby and followed him out.

Two people waited in the living area, neither of whom she wanted to see. Kelly Winchester, Ava's mother, stood next to a tall, thickly built man, dressed in suit and tie, who could only be her husband, the man Tess had heard so much about.

State Senator Brad Winchester's broad face held angular eyebrows that nearly met in the middle. He had handsome, even features, and a full head of gray hair that was definitely premature, since she knew he was only in his thirties. Both he and Ian were imposing figures, but Winchester had the bulkier build. Next to him, his thin, blond wife, who'd been so daunting at the Broken Chimney, seemed somehow diminished.

"Miss Hartsong," he said, in the sonorous voice of a radio announcer or a career politician. "I'm sure you're more than aware of why we're here."

The time of reckoning had arrived. Tess reluctantly gestured toward the couch. "Have a seat."

Kelly sat, but when her husband didn't, she came back to her feet. Kelly didn't possess her daughter Ava's zest. Instead, there was a brittleness about her, from the sharpness of her features to the prominent bones in her neck.

"You've been meeting with some of our local children," Winchester said.

"Without the consent of their parents." Kelly clasped her hands in front of her, the diamonds on her left hand catching shards of afternoon light. "Ava has told us everything."

Tess highly doubted that. "What specifically has she told you?"

"That you're instructing them in sex and in birth control methods." Considering the animosity in his voice, Winchester might as well have said Tess was teaching them how to build pipe bombs. "Are you going to deny it?"

Tess reminded herself that she had the moral high ground, or at least she thought she did. "The girls came to me with specific questions. I answered them."

"You had no right," Kelly exclaimed. "That's a parent's responsibility."

"Yes, it is."

Brad Winchester visibly bristled. "Are you insinuating that we don't know how to raise our own child?"

She struggled against the sense of righteousness that a woman who'd lost her last patient had no right to possess. "Ava's a lovely girl. You should be very proud of her."

If she'd hoped her words would appease Winchester, his grim expression told her otherwise. "We're a tight-knit family. And we have a close community here with high moral standards. We don't believe in encouraging our fifteen-year-olds to have sex."

"Of course, you don't."

His angular eyebrows crept closer together. "Yet you've been giving them all the information they need to sneak around behind their parents' backs."

"Our schools have a strong health curriculum in place," Kelly said. "A curriculum that's in line with our community values."

Tess tried to bite her tongue but couldn't. "Then how do you explain Tempest's high rate of teen pregnancy?" It was a bluff. She had no idea what the town's pregnancy rate was, but based on every available statistic tracking the effectiveness of abstinence-only education programs, she could guess.

Kelly flinched but quickly recovered. "Statistics show abstinence education in middle school significantly reduces sexual activity."

"Your daughter isn't in middle school."

"Abstinent girls aren't exposed to STDs." Kelly crossed her arms over her chest in a gesture that seemed more self-protective than aggressive. "If you've seen the studies, Miss Hartsong, you'd know these girls are in less danger of being caught in abusive relationships or being exposed to STDs. And you'd understand that these same girls have higher self-esteem than girls who are sexually active when they're too young. When my daughter practices abstinence, she knows a boy likes her for herself instead of using her for sex."

Tess was getting hot under the collar. "I'm well aware of the studies, Mrs. Winchester, but those studies also point out the programs' weaknesses. Teens in abstinence-only programs still have sex at the same rate as other teens, but the teens in programs like yours get pregnant at a higher rate because they're less likely to use contraception." She tried to soften her tone. "I know parents want to believe talking to their children about abstinence will make it happen, but teenagers have never done a great job of keeping their pants on, and all the talking in the world doesn't seem to change that."

Winchester puffed up as if he'd been shot full of helium. "Which is where parental influence comes in. We're not the ignorant Southern hillbillies you seem to think we are."

"I don't think—"

He pushed his finger toward her face. "You're an outsider. You're not part of this community, yet you think you can come in here and tell us how to run our schools."

"I don't want to run anything, Mr. Winchester. Your kids came to me."

"They wouldn't have come to you if it weren't for that display you put up at the Broken Chimney," Kelly said. "I talked to you about it. I asked you very respectfully to take it down, but you refused."

Winchester cut in. "And now we discover you've been filling our daughter's head with filth."

"Define *filth*," North said, from behind her.

Tess had forgotten he was there. He stepped forward, a wide-awake, towel-wrapped Wren in his arms. Unlike Wren, Ian looked pissed.

"I know it when I see it," Winchester shot back.

"And filth is what you see when you look at your daughter?" North countered.

The situation was difficult enough without Ian

making it worse, and Winchester took a threatening step forward. "I can't believe you said that."

Tess shot between them. She would have loved to see North take a swing at the pompous Brad Winchester, but not with Wren in his arms. "Mr. Winchester, I have years of experience in women's health, and I can tell you that simply ordering kids not to do it isn't the most effective form of sex education. If you don't want Ava coming here, tell her that. But I'm a nurse." I *was* a nurse. "It would be ethically irresponsible for me to deny anyone information that keeps them healthy, and if those kids show up at my door with questions, I'll answer them." Even to her own ears, she sounded overbearing, but she was also right.

A muscle in the corner of Ian's jaw twitched. "I strongly advise you not to get caught between this woman and her ethics. She isn't very flexible."

Winchester didn't like being challenged. "What about your ethics, Mr. North? Living with the woman who killed your wife."

"I think it's time for you to leave," Ian said with a cold dignity.

Ian might not be rattled, but Tess was. And so, it seemed, was Kelly. "Brad . . ."

She took her husband's arm, but he shook her off.

"That baby's mother hasn't even been dead for a month, yet the two of you are already shacking up. Maybe the sheriff needs to look a little more closely into exactly what happened here."

Tess caught her breath, but Ian didn't flinch. "He's welcome to."

"You've been warned." He grabbed his wife and pulled her toward the door. Kelly's stiletto turned under her, and she would have fallen if he hadn't had such a tight grip on her arm.

The slam of the door startled Wren, and her arms flailed.

"Well," Ian said, "that was fun."

She waited for his "I told you so." When he didn't deliver it, she did it for herself. "I know this is exactly what you warned me about."

"Forget it. He's an ass."

"A powerful one. Just because I'm right about this doesn't mean I should be telling anyone how to raise their kids."

"Which is why you need to take a big step back."

"The rumors about Bianca . . . About us."

"A bunch of stupid people. Do you know what I'm really concerned about?"

"No idea."

"The fact that your little bundle of joy has peed all over me." He held Wren out to her. Sure enough, there was a damp blotch on his shirt.

She took the towel-wrapped baby from him. "Way to go, Wren."

One corner of his mouth curled. He moved to the stairs but paused halfway up and gazed back down at her. "Posing for me last night . . . You're a good subject."

A jumble of feelings churned inside her. She reached for a wisecrack to diffuse them. "Yeah, Da Vinci told me the same thing, but he paid better."

She thought that was pretty darned cute, but he didn't smile. Instead, he said, "You have an interesting face."

"And the body to go with it." *Shut up. If you can't do better than that, keep your stupid mouth shut!*

"It's a good body," he said, matter-of-factly.

"It would be a lot better if there were less of it."

"Amazing how misguided you women continue to be." He disappeared up the steps.

Tess needed to think about her future. Get away from the schoolhouse. Find a new career. She focused on the simplest of her problems and called the man who was supposed to be dealing with her furnace. "Hasn't shipped yet, ma'am," he told her. "There's a labor strike. I'll let you know when it arrives."

For the next few days, she worked morning shifts at the Broken Chimney while Heather took care of Wren. With the exception of a group of men who seemed to enjoy talking to her, the atmosphere had grown even chillier. Only a few customers openly asked about Bianca's death, but she could sense others talking about her behind her back. One of the customers who didn't shun her was Artie, the nicotine addict. Wearing a new trucker's cap, he wandered in at the end of her shift. "Damn, Tess. When did you start working again?"

"This morning. But Michelle will be here in half an hour if you want cigarettes. Which I hope you don't. Seriously, Artie. You've got to give those things up."

"Maybe. I don't know." He leaned against the counter. "Me and my girlfriend broke up."

"Sorry to hear that."

"Yeah. She decided I wasn't good enough for her."

"Then I guess breaking up wasn't such a bad thing."

"That's what I keep tellin' myself. Still . . . Man, she was hot." He rested an elbow on the glass top, directly above the Long Johns. "So you want to go out tonight?"

"I can't. I don't go out with men who smoke."

"Maybe I'll give it up."

"You do that, and then we'll talk."

"Damn, Tess. Why you gotta be like that?"

Savannah shot Tess a dirty look from the blender station, where she was taking forever to unwrap a stack of cups. "It must be nice having time to flirt with the customers while I'm working my ass off."

Tess appreciated having an excuse to end her conversation with Artie, so she didn't point out that Savannah had spent most of the morning chatting on her cell phone.

Tess returned to the schoolhouse shortly before noon, at the same time Ian emerged from the ridge trail. He took Wren from her car seat without waiting for Tess to do it. Although he didn't interact with Wren the way Tess did—no baby talk or funny faces—he no longer seemed to avoid touching her.

"Tough day at the office?" he asked.

"Courtney Hoover—she works at one of the budget hotels, but her real job is wannabe Instagram Queen. She still hates me. I'm not sure why. And people who used to be friendly look at me as though I'm a serial killer. I do know why. Fortunately, Ava Winchester and her crowd have been in school during my shifts, so nobody's asking me questions about flavored condoms or blow jobs."

He gave her a lazy smile that made her wish she hadn't mentioned blow jobs, then closed the car door with his free hand. "I heard from Wren's grandparents. They'll be here in an hour."

"Crap." She raced upstairs.

Chapter Ten

Tess should never have put off doing laundry for so long. Her jeans and mocha-stained T-shirt didn't exactly project confidence, and she needed to present herself as the most competent professional nanny ever. Trying to quell her panic, she dug out Wren's last clean outfit and hurried downstairs.

Ian was coming in from the kitchen with a sandwich in his hand. "Change her!" She shoved Wren at him and, not bothering with a jacket, took off at a run for the cabin.

Sunlight streamed through the front curtains as she let herself inside. She'd thought she'd left the curtains closed to keep any random strangers from peering into the empty cabin. She was *sure* she'd left them closed. Almost sure. Not sure.

She rushed upstairs and grabbed her best pair of dark slacks, along with a plain white pullover and hip-length gray cardigan. Simple. Professional. She snared her hair into a ponytail and secured as many of the loose ends as she could into something approximating a bun. Like Mary fricking Poppins. The book version, not the movie.

She arrived back at the schoolhouse out of breath. No strange car was parked outside, so she still had time to pick up all the baby detritus strewn around, but as soon as she got inside, Ian appeared from the kitchen with the announcement that Wren had thrown up.

She dashed over to get her. "Come on, Wren! Work with me here."

"She doesn't seem to be a people pleaser."

Tess grabbed the baby from him and started up the stairs again only to hear a car pull up in front. "Shit."

"*Tsk. Tsk.* Not in front of the child."

Ignoring him, she spun around and raced back downstairs to get to the paper towels in the kitchen.

"You kind of look like a prison guard in that outfit," he called after her.

"You're not helping!" she shot back.

"Relax, will you?"

"Don't you tell me to relax!" she shouted.

A knock sounded. The wolves were at the door.

"Shit, shit, shit." She hurried toward the sink.

He stuck his head in the kitchen. "Stay here until you calm down enough to stop acting like an idiot. That's an order."

She grabbed the edge of the counter with one hand and made herself breathe. Wren smelled like sour milk. She snatched a paper towel, wetted it, and did her best to clean her up.

Wren gazed at her with those big navy eyes. Her mouth quivered. Her forehead wrinkled. "No!" Tess whispered. "No, sweetie, no. Please. No crying."

Tess put the baby to her shoulder and jiggled her, using the two-in-the-morning move that sometimes soothed her. "Have I ever asked anything of you? Have I?" she whispered into the top of her fuzzy, dark hair. "Anytime other than in the middle of the night?" She heard voices in the living room. Ian had let them in.

Wren's legs and spine stiffened, and her whimper grew louder. "Not now. Please, not now . . ."

The baby let out a window-rattling wail.

A woman shot into the kitchen. She had to be in her sixties, but she looked younger. Warm, blond highlights shone in her jaw-length bob. Her makeup was perfect—neither too little nor too much. She wore precisely tailored white slacks with a crisp black shell, a chunky silver and jet necklace, and a youthful denim jacket. Although she wasn't a tall woman, the three-inch heels on her strappy nude booties brought her to a respectable height.

"Is that her?" The question was rhetorical because the woman was already reaching forward, arms outstretched, ready to snatch the squalling baby from Tess's arms. "Oh, sweetheart . . ."

Tess was allowed to call Wren "sweetheart," but not this slender, Chicos-wearing, pathetic excuse for a grandmother. Where was the curly gray hair, the pillowy breasts, the scent of cookies baking? This sleek, new operating system was an insult to cozy grandmothers everywhere.

"May I hold her?" the woman asked.

No, you may not! "She's a little upset right now." Tess clutched her tighter.

"Of course."

Wren took in this new face and immediately stopped crying. *You little traitor.*

The woman's eyes filled. "She looks just like Simon's baby pictures." A tear made a miniwaterfall over the bottom edge of her mascaraed lashes. "Same eyes. Same mouth."

A man appeared. With his smooth-shaven jaw, curly salt-and-pepper hair, and preppy clothes, he looked as though he'd come straight from the golf course. "Jeff

Denning," he said to Tess with an obnoxiously friendly nod. "You've met my wife, Diane. And who do we have here?"

"Her name is Wren," Tess said, although neither of them seemed to be listening.

Another tear slipped down the Stepford Grandmother's cheek. "Look at her, Jeff. She looks like Simon. And her nose. That's your nose."

"Don't wish my nose on her," he said with a smile.

"You have a great nose." His wife didn't take her eyes off the baby.

Only the most despicable human being would refuse to hand Wren over to these two youthful, athletic, smitten grandparents. Tess clutched the baby more tightly.

A set of familiar arms swept in and scooped up the baby. "I'm sure you'd like to hold her." Ian set Wren in Diane's arms.

Tess hated them. Hated him. All he'd wanted to do from the beginning was get rid of Wren. These two could have been human traffickers, and he'd have handed her over. Okay, maybe not human traffickers, but the point was, he didn't care. Not like Tess did. Not even close.

Wren nestled in her grandmother's arms, her fussiness gone, totally content. Diane sniffed, the end of her nose beginning to turn red. "We never expected this.

Simon's our only child, and he's been so adamant about never marrying or having children."

"He got one out of two right," Tess muttered.

Ian grabbed her by the arm and steered her toward the door. "Why don't we go in the living room where we can be more comfortable?"

"I'm not turning her over to them," Tess hissed so only he could hear.

Ian gave her arm a warning squeeze.

Behind them, Jeff was glued to his wife's side. "Are you going to hog that baby all day?"

"Yes, I am. You know how long I've dreamed of having a grandchild. You're not getting a turn until I say."

It was the kind of fond exchange that long-married couples did best.

Diane walked toward the windows. Wren was mesmerized by the glittering silver in her grandmother's chunky necklace. "Look at her arms," Diane said. "I'll bet she's going to be a swimmer like Simon."

Tess heard one of Wren's baby coos, as if she couldn't wait to jump in the pool. *What a suck-up.*

Jeff had gone to the windows with his wife but glanced over at them to explain. "Simon was on a very competitive swim team in high school."

Bully for him.

Ian must be reading her thoughts because he *pinched* her. Fricking pinched her!

"We haven't been able to reach Simon yet," Diane said, "but now that we've seen her, there's no doubt she's ours."

Tess bristled. "It's going to be very complicated. Extremely complicated. Legally, Mr. North is Wren's father. His name is on her birth certificate."

Mister North frowned. "We'll get it untangled."

They hadn't said a word about Bianca, and Tess was furious on her behalf. They seem to have forgotten that Wren had a mother who'd died giving birth to her. A mother who would have loved her. Cared for her . . . But the image of Bianca sitting for hours holding a sleeping baby wouldn't take hold. It was easier to imagine Bianca running off to eat sushi and misplacing her daughter along the way.

"I'm sure you've heard that Wren was a month premature," Tess said. "It's vital for her to have the best of care." She launched into an extended description of every complication preemies faced, none of which actually applied to Wren at this point. When she'd sufficiently terrified them, she began embroidering her professional credentials by emphasizing the post-delivery care she'd provided for newborns, as opposed to what she mainly did, which was usher them into the world. "I know we all agree that it's best to leave things as they are for the foreseeable future."

Ian was giving her the stink eye.

"As to that . . ." Jeff said. "We need to talk with Simon, but his career is itinerant, and we know he's not in any position to care for her."

Tess held her breath.

"As much as we love our son," Diane said, "I doubt he'll ever settle down, so naturally, we'll take her."

Of course they would. Tess quickly found her tongue. "Aren't you a little old for that?" Even she knew when she'd gone too far. "Not that either of you looks old," she said hastily. "You're amazingly fit. But taking in a newborn . . . You'll be—what? In your late eighties when she's a teenager."

"Mid-seventies," Diane corrected.

"Yes, but surely this will interfere with your lifestyle. I can see that you're very active. I imagine you love to travel. Take bike trips. Tennis matches. Shuffleboard tournaments. So many things I'm sure you love to do that you'll be forced to give up."

"We know we'll have to make sacrifices," Diane said, "but she deserves a stable upbringing, and we're the only ones who can provide it."

"You have other options. You could—"

"Tess." Ian came to his feet and brought her right along with him. "Let's take a walk and give them some time alone with Wren."

He practically dragged her outside.

"Stop pulling me!"

He didn't. Instead, he force-marched her away from the house and across the clearing where, less than a month ago, the rescue helicopter had landed. When they were in the trees, out of sight of the house, he turned on her. "What the hell do you think you're doing?"

"I'm . . . concerned. That's all."

His hand gripped her shoulder. "You can't have her, Tess. She's not yours."

"I know that. Don't you think I know that? But . . . I made a promise. A deathbed promise to watch out for her."

"Those people are smitten with her. They're dream grandparents. What more could you want?"

Her heart rebelled against his cold logic. "They're only grandparents. She deserves . . . She deserves more."

She knew how foolish that sounded. Wren wasn't going to get more. Her mother was dead; her father a nonentity. Wren was lucky to have grandparents who were already falling in love with her and who were willing to make sacrifices to raise her.

"I know you want what's best for her," he said as she began to walk away from her. "But she needs to be with her family."

I'm her family. I was the first person to touch her. The one who's fed her, changed her, held her against my body . . .

She had to stop thinking like this and start thinking like a foster mother—one of the legions of good women who lovingly cared for newborns until they could be reunited with their families.

He fell into step next to her, his tone softening almost imperceptibly. "You're going to be okay."

"Of course I am." She shivered. She'd come outside without a jacket, only her gray cardigan. "And I know I'm being awful."

"Not awful," he said gruffly. "You have a big heart. That's who you are."

She managed a wobbly smile. "Well, it sucks."

"I can only imagine."

They walked for a while without speaking, her sneakers scuffing the leaves on the trail, his silent. They neared the old fire tower. She stopped. Dug a heel into the dirt. Gazed up at him. "Do you love her? Wren? Even a little?"

He looked past her into the woods, speaking slowly, choosing his words. "I care what happens to her."

"But you don't love her," she said flatly.

"The kind of love you're talking about isn't possible for me."

"Sure, it is."

He shook his head, finally meeting her gaze. "No, Tess. I'm not like most people. I'm selfish. Big emotions get in the way of my work, and my work always comes first. That's why I need my space."

"Bianca must have been a real trial for you." Something she already knew. He started to walk again, and she followed. "So you've never been in love?"

"I didn't say that. There was the typical teenage stuff when I was at boarding school."

"With a girl?"

He cocked an eyebrow at her. "Yes. With a girl."

She'd known from *IHN4: A Rebel's Story* that his parents had stuck him in a boarding school half a continent away, but it still sounded strange when she contrasted it with how he must have looked when Bianca found him passed out in a doorway.

"The important relationships didn't happen until I was in my mid-twenties," he said, "and that's when things went bad."

"They broke your heart." She delivered the right amount of mockery to keep him comfortable.

"No," he said quietly. "I broke theirs. And neither of them deserved it."

"Oh." She tried to process what he'd told her. "You don't strike me as a callous heartbreaker. You're fairly decent. When you're not being a jerk."

"I appreciate the twisted compliment, but I have enough sins without adding to the list. No more breaking hearts."

"Jeez. You're not that irresistible." As long as she discounted the macho that clung to him like woodsmoke. Or those rugged good looks . . . One of her hairpins dangled at her neck. She tucked it in the pocket of her cardigan. "So you've only been with hookers since?"

"Nice try."

"Meaning you've had sex with real women?"

"Yes, Tess. Real women. Now could we talk about something else?"

"Not till I'm done processing. Sex with real women normally involves all kinds of *biiiiig* emotions. Doesn't that scare you?"

"It doesn't need to involve *biiiig* emotions if you find the right partners. It can just be fun."

"Back to the hookers, right?"

"Now you're really baiting me."

226 • SUSAN ELIZABETH PHILLIPS

She took a quick detour. "I thought love was supposed to make creative people more productive."

"Some of them maybe. But not this one."

"So what dire things happened to you when you fell in love?"

"I told you I'm a solitary creature. I stopped working. Prepare yourself for more mockery."

"Because . . . ?"

He stuffed his hands into the pockets of his jeans. "Because my work is who I am. Melodramatic, I know, but there it is. I live a life of dedicated selfishness."

"Not a fun way to live."

"Maybe not to you, but great street art isn't like other art forms. It's rooted in anger, and it's larger than the person creating it."

"I'm not sure what distinguishes great street art from random gang tags."

"You know it when you see it. Great street art isn't about thugs spraying their initials on any surface they can find. There's no thought behind that. Remember the guys in the California garage—Jobs and Wozniak?"

"The beginning of Apple."

He nodded. "Power to the people. That was their motto, and it's ours, too. We bring art to people who've never stepped in a museum. Art to entertain. Art with a social message. Art that exists only to be beautiful."

"That's what you do."

"It sure didn't start out that way. When I was a kid, every time I hit the nozzle on a can of Krylon it was a 'fuck you' to my father. That was therapy. The real art came later. Good street art should make you feel something—anger, curiosity, laughter, recognition."

She pulled out another dangling hairpin. "A giant rat on the side of a building?"

"You're talking about Banksy. What's that rat feeding on? Why is it there? Is it the last survivor? Does it represent us or what we've lost? And how do you feel about having that giant rat looming over you?"

Any desire she'd had to mock him faded as she thought of her own all-consuming grief. "But how do you live life without those big emotions?"

"You just do."

"By making sure you never care too much about anyone else?"

"You're a widow, Tess. As much as you try to hide it, I know you've suffered. So tell me . . . How well did love serve you?"

He didn't say it bitterly or unkindly. Instead, he spoke with a thoughtfulness that made her feel as if he really wanted to understand.

"You didn't know him," she said.

"So tell me."

She'd never imagined talking about Trav to Ian. And yet . . . "We met in kindergarten. Trav deliberately broke my crayons—for no reason. Yet I was the one who had to go to the principal."

"How's come?"

"I might have punched him."

"Love at first sight."

"When I came back to the classroom from the principal's office, he stuck his tongue out at me behind Miss Rawling's back."

He smiled. "It still stings."

She smiled back. "We turned that classroom into a battlefield. I'd draw something, and Trav would tear it up. He'd build a LEGO car, and I'd smash it."

"Mortal combat."

"His mother made the school separate us for first grade."

"Wise mother."

"But we'd find each other at recess. He'd chase me, and I'd go after him with a stick. He'd call me names, and I'd call him worse ones. One day he blocked the slide so I couldn't get up, so I waited until he got on the monkey bars and pulled him off."

"Never underestimate the power of a pissed-off woman."

"I broke his tooth. Fortunately, it was a starter tooth."

"Small mercies."

"Don't laugh. It was serious stuff."

He grinned. "I'm not laughing. I'm counting my blessings that I didn't know you then. So when did the warfare end?"

"Not until we were twelve."

"It's a miracle you both survived that long. What was the magic turnaround?"

"I broke his leg."

"Tooth. Leg. No wonder you went into medicine."

"It was an accident, but my mother made me go to his house and apologize." Her Mary Poppins bun had come undone. She pulled out the last of the pins and the hair tie. "He was in bed, and he looked so sad. The sixth-grade camping trip was that weekend. It was all any of us had been talking about, and now he was going to miss it. He yelled at me, but all the time he was trying not to cry, and I felt so bad that I told him I wouldn't go either."

"Your brutal heart melted."

"Not exactly. The school had already banned me from the trip because of the leg incident."

"But you didn't tell him that."

"Eventually." She slipped the hair tie over her wrist. "We ended up spending the camping weekend watching Jim Carrey movies in his bedroom. After that, we were best friends. He even fought a boy in eighth grade who snapped my bra strap."

"I'm guessing you could have taken care of him by yourself, but still—valiant on his part."

"I made him break up with Lorrie Wilkins. Between us, she was only using him to make Charlie Dobbs jealous."

"My lips are sealed. So it was all friendship and no romance. Until . . . ?"

"Senior year. We didn't have prom dates, so we decided to go as friends. By the time the night was over, we were more than friends."

"You with your lectures on teenage sex . . ."

"We waited a little longer, but not much. And unlike the kids here, we'd had decent sex education." She stepped over a tree root. "We got married two weeks after I graduated from college. He changed majors a couple of times, so it took him longer."

"The two of you were together since your senior year in high school?"

"A couple of times, we dated other people. But it never took with either of us." She stopped walking and looked up at him. "You're right, Ian. If you never love, then love will never hurt you. But I can't imagine never having loved Trav."

"You've suffered for it."

She had. But somehow the suffering she'd carried around for so long had eased.

"We're hoping it won't take longer than two weeks," Diane told them when they returned.

The Dennings planned to fly back home to New Jersey that night, but as soon as they had the preliminary legal work in place, they intended to come back and get Wren. "We'll have talked to Simon by then," Diane said as she gazed at Wren.

Jeff slipped his arm around his wife's shoulders. "We're canceling the river cruise we'd planned. Prague to Budapest. We've been looking forward to it. Celebrating our fortieth wedding anniversary."

"Nothing is more important than family," Diane said firmly.

Finally, after taking dozens of cell phone photos and Diane wiping away tears, they drove off.

Ian shut himself in his studio. Tess banged around the schoolhouse, then packed up Wren and trekked back to the cabin to fetch the clothes she'd tossed aside. Wren picked up on her foul mood and began to fuss. Tess made herself take a long series of calming breaths and began straightening the place. As she finished, she went over to the front windows. With a frown, she tugged the curtains closed.

At the Broken Chimney, Artie told Tess he hadn't had a cigarette for two days and hit on her again.

"You always liked 'em with big knockers," Mr. Felder commented from his post at the corner table.

Artie choked on his coffee, and Tess pointed the metal frothing pitcher toward the rear table. "I don't care how old you are, Mr. Felder. That kind of comment is inappropriate and offensive."

"I'm ninety years old, Miss Hot Pants, and that means I get to say any damned fool thing I please."

"Not while I'm working," she retorted. "One more crack like that, and you're out of here."

"You can't kick me out." He smirked at her. "I'll set the law on you."

Tess slammed down the frothing pitcher. "Somebody had better grab his cane, because I am seriously going to whack him over the head with it."

"I'll do it." Artie went for the cane. "What's wrong with you, Orland? You can't go around saying shit like that in front of a lady."

Mrs. Watkins, the head of the Tempest Women's Alliance, looked up from her copy of *The Omnivore's*

Dilemma. "It's no wonder Northerners think we're a bunch of hayseeds down here."

The male half of a couple who'd retired in Tempest set aside his mug of Americano. "We just tell our old Boston neighbors that you're colorful."

Tess liked the retired couple. Unlike the locals, they didn't know about Bianca's death and weren't spreading the rumor that she'd let Bianca die so she could have Ian.

With the exception of Mr. Felder, her current customers were a blessedly congenial bunch, but it hadn't been like that most of the past two days. Imani's father, the Reverend Mr. Peoples, had shown up, and although he'd been more polite than the Winchesters, his message was equally clear. *Stop corrupting our daughters.*

A heavily pregnant woman Tess didn't recognize— but who obviously recognized her—left without ordering, as if she were afraid Tess would slip some kind of baby-killing poison into her iced green tea. And Tess's relationship with her co-workers had deteriorated even further. Michelle had a habit of covering her belly with her hands when she had to get close to Tess. Savannah looked at her as if she were the devil. Michelle's husband, Dave, was the only one in the family who seemed to enjoy Tess's company.

The after-school crowd began to arrive, but there

was no sign of Ava. Tess suspected her parents had declared the Broken Chimney off-limits whenever Tess was behind the counter.

At the end of her shift, she walked to her car. Written in the dust along one fender was a single word. *Slut.*

Chapter Eleven

Freddy Davis, the town's only police officer, showed up at the Broken Chimney the next morning. He was big and slow, with bushy eyebrows, a thin upper lip, and a preference for caramel macchiatos. "What time do you get off today, Tess?"

Was Freddy asking her out, too? Even with half the town shunning her, she'd been getting hit on, and she couldn't understand it. What did the men of Tempest find so intriguing about a slightly overweight thirty-five-year-old widow with impossible hair?

Slut . . . The dusty inscription on her car . . . She was a slut only in her thoughts, which wouldn't be so intrusive if she didn't keep bumping into Ian at night when she went downstairs to heat up a bottle, or if she didn't have to listen to the sound of his footsteps in the studio as he did god-only-knew what, since he apparently wasn't working.

"My shift's over at noon." Wren had kept her up again last night, and she suppressed a yawn.

"Mind stopping by the police station?"

He had his official face on, so this wasn't a social invitation, and she was suddenly wide-awake. "Uh . . . sure."

"I'll see you then." He left with no caramel macchiato and no explanation.

The Tempest police station took up a couple of rooms in the town's small city hall. An American flag hung on one wall, a whiteboard on the other, along with framed certificates and a photo of the groundbreaking ceremony for the Winchester Recreation Center. She fidgeted with the strap on her purse as she took a seat in an orange molded-plastic chair.

Freddy picked up a blue dry-erase marker and tapped the top of an empty snack bag. "I have a couple of questions about that artist's wife. The one who died."

Her fingers constricted around her purse strap. "Bianca and Ian North weren't married."

"Unusual these days for a woman to die having a baby."

She tried to project a calmness she didn't feel.

"Bianca had an amniotic fluid embolism. It's rare and nearly always fatal. The hospital has my full report."

"I'd like to hear about it in your own words."

She straightened in the wobbly plastic chair, reminding herself she had nothing to hide. She described what had happened, keeping everything factual.

He listened, not taking notes, slung back in his chair and twisting the dry-erase marker between his fingers. "Ian North," he said, when she finished. "The artist. You're living with him now?"

"I'm his employee." She sounded defensive, and she made herself speak more calmly. "I'm temporarily taking care of the baby until he can make other arrangements."

"A lot of people are talking about that. The two of you."

She couldn't ignore the implication, and she felt herself flush. "I wasn't aware malicious gossip was a police matter."

"Hard to tell the difference sometimes between gossip and the truth."

She'd had enough, and she got up from the chair. "I don't have anything more to say."

He dropped the marker into an empty coffee mug. "The thing is, we only have your word for it. The autopsy seems to be inconclusive."

"Inconclusive? What do you mean?"

"I heard from the coroner's office." He rose from behind the desk, dismissing her. "Appreciate you coming in. I'll let you know if I hear anything more."

She'd known this could happen—an amniotic fluid embolism was difficult to confirm, even with an autopsy—but she still felt like throwing up. With a hand pressed to her stomach, she hurried back to her car.

There it was again. Another message. This time written on the dusty hood. *Whore.*

Tess knew she'd eventually tell Ian about the writing on her car, the autopsy report, and her visit to the police station, but right now, her emotions were too raw. Wren's fussiness didn't help. The baby didn't seem to be in pain, and she wasn't running a fever. She was just generally foul-tempered in the way of infants.

At work the next day, Tess nearly nodded off while she went over some receipts Phish wanted her to check. If only she could have four hours of uninterrupted sleep.

But it wasn't to be. That night, not long after Tess had settled Wren for the second time in the sleeping nest by her bed, the baby once again began to whimper. Tess didn't move. Maybe if Tess stayed completely quiet, Wren would go back to sleep.

Wren was way too smart for that con and began crying for real.

"Wren, please. Shut the hell up." Tess buried her face in the pillow.

Wren took offense and wailed louder.

With a groan, Tess reached over to take the baby from her nest. Maybe she could calm her without getting up.

Wren wasn't having it. She wanted the full-on walking-the-floor routine.

Tess got up, tucked the baby under her chin, and sniffed Wren's head. As she took in the warm baby smell, she contemplated what a powerful survival mechanism that scent was in protecting this ill-tempered, self-centered, pooping, vomiting species known as the human newborn from extinction. Would Jeff and Diane walk the floor with her like this when she got cranky?

Tess paced from one corner of the bedroom to the next. Her eyes itched with exhaustion.

The door opened and a shaft of light from the hallway silhouetted a tall, familiar figure wearing only a T-shirt and boxers. He looked as cranky as Wren.

"Don't yell at her," Tess said. "She can't help it."

"I'm not in the habit of yelling at infants. No matter how much I want to."

She was enveloped in the intoxicating scent of warm male as he came closer. First Wren's, and now Ian's smell. She needed nose plugs.

"Give her to me," he said. "You need to get some sleep."

She couldn't believe she'd heard him right. He never willingly volunteered to hold Wren, and yet here he was. She should be grateful, but she didn't entirely trust him. Unlike Heather, Ian had no idea how to distinguish one of Wren's cries from another or how to bicycle her legs if she had gas.

Tess stopped herself. She needed to let go of the idea that she was Wren's only competent caretaker. "You're on." She made herself hand over the baby and climbed back into bed.

He didn't leave the room right away, and she was too tired to ask why. Eventually, however, she heard the bedroom door close behind them both.

It's going to be okay. She'll be fine.

Tess had the nightmare again that night. It was always the same. The blood. Bianca's cries. Tess's inability to get to her. A little before six, she gave up trying to fall back to sleep.

As she got out of bed, the remnants of the nightmare curdled her stomach. She needed to make certain Wren was safe. She padded into the quiet hallway and looked in the studio. No one was there. The living room was empty and the house quiet. He must have taken Wren outside. But his jacket hung on the hook. That left only one other place they could be.

Bianca's bedroom.

Tess hadn't been inside since the afternoon three weeks ago when she and Wren had come to live here. The door was always closed, so it had been easy to avoid the room. She hesitated, then turned the knob.

Dashes of pearly light brightened the sooty swirls of color tangling the walls. When she'd last seen the room, it had been unfurnished. Now it held a simple double bed—a different bed from the one where Bianca had died. This one had no headboard or footboard, only a mattress and box springs on a metal frame. Ian lay on his back, his shoulders propped high on a pile of pillows, a set of black sheets twisted around him. He'd taken off his T-shirt, and Wren was curled sound asleep on his bare chest, her knees under her, butt in the air, cheek against his skin, and his hand curled protectively around her.

The baby was sleeping on her stomach, verboten in modern pediatrics, but at no risk with her head higher than the rest of her. Some would quibble at her perch on his chest, but Wren looked perfectly safe.

A jumble of tenderness, sorrow, and longing snagged in her throat. How she'd wanted to see Trav like this— with their baby—but Trav had been too much a boy at heart to be a father.

Trav . . . A wistful sadness settled over her. Sadness, but not grief. It was time. Time to let Trav go.

She closed the door softly and slipped into her sneakers and Ian's jacket. Still in her pajama bottoms with the long jacket sleeves hanging past her fingertips, she stepped out into a new day saturated with the scents of dew, earth, and leaf mold. So much that hadn't been clear during her marriage was clear now. She'd been the grown-up in their relationship, the responsible one, a burden she hadn't wanted to acknowledge.

She wrapped her arms around herself. Trav was the love of her girlhood—the love of the young woman she'd once been—but grief, time, this new life—this baby—had changed her.

She crossed the yard. Off to her left, Ian's tree house now had a platform. The feelings she held for Ian North were nothing like her love for Trav, but she would no longer deny how strongly she was drawn to him. When she was with him, she felt steady. Her own person. She didn't have to take care of him. She didn't have to raise him, corral him, or chide him. Ian North was a man who knew exactly who he was, a man with a clear picture of his place in the world.

The hems of her pajama bottoms dragged in the dewy grass as she made her way down the trail. He was complex, troubled, and mysterious. A man who'd come to terms with how he needed to live his life. Closed off. Maybe that emotional disengagement explained his powerful sexual allure. Because she wanted him. No more lying to herself. She wanted frantic, dirty, over-the-top sex with him. Earthy, bawdy—maybe even kinky—sex. The kind of sex she'd fantasized about long before Trav had died. The kind of sex she imagined Ian—with his commitment to emotional detachment—would offer.

She could have it, too. All she had to do was ask.

The one thing she wouldn't do.

If Ian wanted her, he'd have to take the first steps. The aggressive female sexual vixen might be a powerful fantasy, but it wasn't her fantasy. She needed to be the object of lust—the pursued, not the pursuer.

Trav's sex drive had never been as strong as her own. He always got into it—she couldn't fault him for that—but she had to make the first move.

"Turn me on, sexy lady. I love the way you turn me on."

"How 'bout you turn me on for a change?" She'd sometimes say to him, only to have him respond, *"Show me how."*

Trav liked things easy. His easy laughter, easy compliments, easy, laid-back nature were as much a part of him as his floppy auburn hair and eternal optimism. Trav didn't judge or criticize. He enjoyed people for who they were. It was why so many sought his company. It was why she'd loved him. Why she'd overlooked his flaws: his unsteady employment and his casual attitude toward the necessary business of life. Someday, she'd told herself, he'd be the one to do the taxes or fix a loose chair leg instead of leaving it all up to her. Someday, she'd told herself, he would be so overcome with lust that he'd drag her into bed, strip her naked, and make love to her as if she were the most irresistible woman in the world.

But none of that would ever have happened. It wasn't his nature.

The waters of Poorhouse Creek frothed under the bridge as she crossed. She gazed toward the place where a fallen tree had formed a miniwaterfall. Ian was a new species to her. A man—full grown and mature—who didn't need coddling.

She reached the cabin and unlocked the back door. The curtains were drawn, exactly as she'd left them, but something was different. A pair of sneakers lay by the door. Sneakers that didn't belong to her. She took a cautious step inside.

Kelly Winchester lay sound asleep on the couch.

She was curled into a ball, fully dressed, a quilted jacket with a designer logo abandoned on the carpet. She'd pulled the old quilt Tess had tossed over the back of the couch up to her shoulders.

Tess's stomach churned at this violation of her privacy. And by Kelly Winchester, of all people. She thought of those small clues she'd overlooked—the tracked-in mud, the curtains she'd found open when they should have been closed. This wasn't the first time Kelly had come here. But why?

Kelly hadn't stirred. Tess started toward her only to stop. She thought for a moment, then backed out the same way she'd come in, making as little noise as she could. There was no sign of a car, so Kelly must have hiked up here. But why? There was nothing worth stealing, and if she'd intended to vandalize the place to get some kind of twisted revenge, she would have done it by now. Tess had so many unanswered questions.

She also had a weapon.

She'd witnessed something about the Winchesters that didn't fit. Instead of confronting Kelly, what if she let this play out a little longer? The Winchesters were a powerful financial and political force in Tempest. Kelly's animosity toward Tess was real, and Brad had a visible ruthless streak. They'd targeted Tess, and they held all the cards.

Except this one.

Tess now knew something that she couldn't imagine Kelly would want to become public. It was a flimsy weapon, and it might come to nothing, but Kelly wasn't doing any harm to the cabin, and Tess could confront her anytime she chose. Why not wait and see what unfolded?

As she hiked up the trail to return to the schoolhouse, she decided this was one more thing she wouldn't tell Ian. At least not yet. He wasn't a man who believed in subtlety, and he'd insist on an immediate confrontation. He could be right, but then again, he might not be.

He and Wren were both awake when she returned. He was sitting in one of the easy chairs in the living room feeding her. He'd crossed his ankle over his thigh with Wren perched on top. She must have soaked through her sleeper because she wore a fresh one. He glared at Tess. "She's the devil incarnate."

"True."

Tess hadn't imagined he'd noticed the morning bottle in the refrigerator, but apparently he had, and since it didn't look as though he'd replaced the formula with beer, she could relax. Except for the simple fact that she couldn't do that when he was wearing only an undershirt and jeans. An undershirt so old and worn she could see his skin through it. He hadn't shaved, his hair was sleep rumpled, and his hand looked massive around that small bottle.

She was staring. She quickly bent down to roll up the wet cuffs of her pajama bottoms. "Thanks for taking her last night."

"I must have been out of my mind."

"Still, it was a nice thing to do." As she hung his jacket, she remembered she wasn't wearing a bra under her T-shirt. He probably wouldn't notice.

He noticed. He gazed at her directly, making no attempt to be subtle about it. His gaze drifted from her breasts to her hips in a way that was technically offensive, but only technically. She hadn't even had breakfast, and she was already turned on.

Then a cold dash of reality. He was studying her body as an artist would, while she was looking at his body through the eyes of a man-hungry sex fiend. She shoved her sneakers out of the way. "Did you smell her head?

His gaze once again drifted to her breasts. "Hard not to."

"Pretty great, isn't it?"

"Better than what comes out the other end. I left a mess in the bathroom for you to clean up."

"You're a giver."

He smiled.

Instead of taking Wren from him, she went upstairs. She wrinkled her nose as she stepped into the bathroom. He hadn't exaggerated about the mess. She cleaned it up and took a shower. A cold one.

By the time she returned downstairs, he'd propped Wren in her nest on the kitchen counter. He was also frying eggs, which was unusual, since his normal breakfast consisted of black coffee. She stole a piece of bacon draining on a paper towel. "What's the occasion?"

He flipped two eggs onto a plate, added a slice of toast and more bacon, and passed it over to her. "No occasion."

"I can't eat all this. I mean, I *can* eat it, but I shouldn't."

"Why not?"

"Only a man who's never had to lie down to zip a pair of jeans would ask that question."

"What is it with beautiful women and weight? Do you ever look at yourself in a mirror?"

She was so hung up on the word *beautiful* that she stood there, plate in her hand, staring at him like a fool.

She could swear he curled his lip at her. "You women love to talk about how much more insightful you are than men, how much more emotionally mature. How men are basically unenlightened goons good for nothing more than burping and scratching our armpits."

"I never—"

"Well answer me this, smart one? If you females are so aware—so mature and so enlightened—why are so many of you"—he jabbed the spatula in her general direction—"so unhappy with your incredible bodies?"

"Incredible?" It came out as a croak.

"Never mind. Go eat."

"You . . . really like my body?" She sounded like she was fourteen. But when she considered how much time she spent cataloging her flaws—unruly hair, too-full breasts, total absence of thigh gap—she knew he had a point.

"Yeah, I like it," he drawled.

"Oh." She nudged the toast away from the rim of the plate. "You like it as an artist, right?"

"Yeah, as an artist." That cockeyed glint in his eye suggested he was messing with her. "What did you think I meant?"

Surrendering her dignity, she dug herself in deeper. "Because I look like one of those chubby women Renoir and his pals loved to paint?"

"Gain another twenty pounds and then you might— *might*—be in their league." He didn't quite smirk. A man like Ian North wouldn't smirk. But he did something with his mouth that told her he was thinking about it.

"My eggs are getting cold." Instead of the eggs on her plate, she thought about her internal eggs, the unused ones her ovaries kept diligently producing. But for how much longer?

Wren screwed up her face and let out one of her delightful little Wren-squeaks. Tess stood at the counter and dipped the corner of her toast into the yolk. "Aren't you eating?" she asked.

"I already did."

She couldn't put this off any longer. "Something happened that you should know about." She fidgeted with the toast. "Have you met Freddy Davis?"

He paused on his way to the sink. "Tempest's local law enforcement? I had the pleasure not long after I moved here. He heard about my line of work and told me not to get any ideas about bombing the town with gang tags."

She smiled. "Your teenage past still catching up with you."

"They were never gang tags, Tess." He pretended offense. "They were liberation tags."

"My mistake." Her laughter faded. "Freddy called me into the police station a couple of days ago. To interview me about Bianca's death."

He dumped the skillet in the sink and swore under his breath.

She gazed at him. "He said he'd been in touch with the coroner's office. They've finished the autopsy and listed her cause of death as inconclusive." She'd lost her appetite and set her plate on the counter. "There's been gossip in town about the two of us. About me moving in right after Bianca's death. I've made it clear that I'm only here to take care of Wren, but . . ."

Ian snatched up the dish towel. "I'm going to talk to him. Set him straight. You and I both spoke with the doctors. They said that the autopsy might not tell us much more then we already knew. What anyone else believes is immaterial."

"It's not immaterial to me." Wren cooed and kicked her legs. "I want to settle down here." For the first time, she said it aloud. Despite the fact that she only had one real friend here—one and a half if she counted Phish—these mountains had begun to feel as necessary to her as air and water. She wanted to stay. "How can I become part of the community with this shadow hanging over my head?"

"Don't you dare let those idiots get to you."

"Hi."

Eli stood in the kitchen doorway in a worn Titans T-shirt with brambles clinging to the leg of his jeans. "I brought you some eggs." He set them on the counter next to Wren. He didn't seem to be favoring one leg over the other, so he was healing well. "Your baby's really little."

"We're only taking care of her for now," Ian said. "And the next time you visit, you should knock first."

"I forgot." He peered at Wren. "Maybe you could take him to see Mom sometime. It might make her happy."

Tess doubted very much that seeing Wren would make Rebecca feel better about her miscarriage. "He's a she. Her name is Wren."

"It smells really good in here. Is that bacon? We don't have pigs but sometimes Dad trades stuff for it."

"Would you like some?" Ian asked.

Eli shuffled his feet and gazed toward the stove with the look of a kid who wanted bacon but had been instructed not to ask for anything.

"We have too much," Tess said. "It would be a shame to throw it out."

"I guess it would be all right then."

While Tess ate her now-cold eggs, Ian fried up the

rest of the bacon, and Eli demolished it in the way only an eight-year-old boy could, even one small for his age.

He and Ian chatted about a fox Ian had spotted in the woods and an upcoming display of synchronous fire-flies they were both excited about. "It's a phenomenon that only happens a few places in North America," Ian explained, "and East Tennessee is one of them. Thousands of fireflies all light up together."

She was once again amazed at how attuned a city slicker like Ian North was to the natural world.

"It's supposed to happen in the middle of June this year," Eli told her. "I think your baby would like it."

Her baby, she thought when Eli finally left. But Wren belonged to someone else.

"Jeff Denning called while you were in the shower." Ian put down the empty coffeepot in the sink. "They finally reached their son."

The toast stuck in her throat.

"Bianca neglected to let him know he was going to be a father. Jeff didn't come right out and say it, but it's clear her son's not exactly thrilled, because he gave his parents carte blanche. Told them to handle it however they want."

"It?"

Ian finally turned to face her. "They're coming to get Wren next week. In six days."

Six days. She grabbed Wren and fled the kitchen.

Ian wasn't exactly sure why he'd thought making breakfast would help soften the news. Losing Wren would be hard on Tess, but she'd known this would happen. She'd survived the loss of her husband. She was tough enough to survive this, too. And with Tess and Wren gone, he'd finally be able to pull himself out of this creative muck he was floundering in.

It had started to rain, but he needed to clear his head, and he grabbed his rain jacket. He didn't like having the forest sounds muffled, so he left the hood down, and by the time he got to the fire tower, the neck of his shirt was as wet as his jeans.

He climbed the slippery steps and ducked inside. Despite the smell of dust and damp, he liked coming here. It was quiet. Isolated. Nothing much had been left behind except an old four-burner stove that no longer worked, a rickety wooden table, and a couple of straight-back chairs. The windows were still intact and cleaner than his first visit, thanks to an old broom he'd used to sweep away the worst of the cobwebs. Today, the clouds hung so low there wasn't much of a view, but on a sunny day, he could see for miles.

He pulled up one of the chairs and propped his feet on the window ledge. He wanted Tess to pose for him again. Wanted to do another of those fussy, kitschy drawings that had no audacity, no grit, no call to arms—no point at all. He wanted to draw her nude. Every part of her. To capture her sensuality in pen and ink: the way she relished food, slipped her fingers into her hair, stroked the stem of her wineglass. The way she lifted her arms to stretch and tugged on her lower lip with her upper one. He'd watched her raise goose bumps on her own skin simply by stroking the inside of her wrist with the tips of her fingers, yet she seemed oblivious to this part of herself.

Now he needed to decided how far he was willing to go with this compulsion, because one thing was for certain. Capturing the luscious Widow Hartsong naked would only make the mess he was stuck in that much worse.

Chapter Twelve

Ian came back from one of his mystery walks dripping muddy water on the varnished wooden entryway in the same way she imagined generations of schoolkids had once done. He changed into dry clothes and took off in his car without telling her where he was going.

It was harder today for Tess to leave Wren with Heather. Tess wanted to curl up with the baby. Experiment with her little patch of hair and ponder whether her eyes would always be such a dark blue. She wanted to admire the way her cheeks were filling out and watch the play of that minikin mouth. To smell her head and treasure every moment she had left.

She made herself do the right thing—kiss Wren on her tiny cowlick and leave for the Broken Chimney.

Whenever she was at work now, she went on high alert, watching everyone who came in, trying to figure out who believed she'd caused Bianca's death and who was vandalizing her car. The women seemed especially hostile. So much for women sticking together.

Michelle had dark circles under her eyes and more frequent backaches as her pregnancy advanced. "You don't know what it's like to have precipitous labor like I had with Savannah," she told every customer who'd listen. "You can't imagine how scary it is."

Tess could imagine because she'd seen it. Precipitous labor occurred when the baby was born less than five hours after the first contraction, with some mothers delivering in less than three. Instead of feeling lucky at having such a short labor, they had no time to adjust to the violence of the contractions. Although their babies were healthy, some women ended up experiencing postpartum depression or even PTSD, while others were able to put it behind them. Michelle didn't seem to be one of them.

She confronted Tess, who was wiping down the doughnut case. "If I go into precipitous labor when you're around, promise me right now you won't lay a hand on me."

"Michelle, the last thing in the world I want to do

is deliver your baby." The last thing Tess wanted to do was deliver any baby. Even the thought of it made her light-headed. Something that had once given her so much joy and satisfaction was now twisted in the images of her nightmares.

Michelle emptied the knock box in the trash, spilling wet coffee grounds on the floor. "You find somebody to get me to the hospital as fast as they can. Don't wait for Dave." In several conversations with Michelle's husband, Tess had discovered that Dave Phisher's main goal in life seemed to be staying out of his wife's and daughter's tumultuous paths.

"I'll do that," Tess said.

Savannah piped up from across the shop, where she was enjoying a hazelnut latte. It was her day off, but she liked to watch them work. "I wouldn't put it past Tess to try to deliver your baby herself just to show off."

Tess slapped down the glass cleaner. "I swear to God if you weren't pregnant, I'd meet you in the back alley right now and take you out!"

Savannah sneered at her. "I used to be a gymnast."

"And I used to be a bitch. Wait a minute. I still am."

"That's true," Mr. Felder said from his customary table by the bookrack. "You tried to kick me out last week."

"Everybody shut up!" Michelle exclaimed. "If any of you had gone through precipitous labor like I have, you'd be more sensitive."

"If I hear one more word about you and your precipitous labor I am going to scream," Savannah countered.

Ignoring her daughter, Michelle pointed first to the mess she'd made on the floor and then to Tess. "Clean this up. It's too hard for me to bend over."

Tess grabbed the mop and beat the spilled coffee grounds to death.

While she was on her way to pick up Wren, the repairman called with the news that her furnace had arrived, and he could install it next week. She told him where to find her spare key and thought about also telling him to call Kelly Winchester if he had trouble getting in.

When she got to Heather's, she found her babysitter and Wren on the front porch. It had only been a few hours, but Tess could have sworn the baby had more strength in her neck and a few extra wisps of downy dark hair. Before long, Wren would be getting ready for prom.

And Tess wouldn't be there to see it.

"My life is too complicated right now for dating," she told Artie the next day, when he showed up at the counter to ask her out again. Coincidentally, less than an hour earlier, Tim Corbett, the local microbrewer, had asked her out, although he was smoother about it than Artie.

"You're hung up on that artist guy, aren't you?" Artie said. "That's what everybody's talking about. That maybe you didn't try hard enough to save his wife."

"Go to hell."

"Hey, I didn't say I was the one saying it. So do you want to go out or what?"

"No, I don't want to go out."

"You *are* hung up on him. I knew it."

"Do me a favor, Artie, and stop being a turd."

She and Wren came home that afternoon to the smell of fresh paint. Not artist's paint but house paint. She followed the smell to Bianca's room.

Drop cloths covered the floors, and a ladder sat in the corner. Ian was finishing the last wall. All the room's torturous twists and angles were disappearing, replaced by a fresh coat of the original pale gray paint. But Ian hadn't simply restored the decor. On top of the gray, he was applying a clear glaze embedded with tiny crystals. Only the section of wall between the windows remained unfinished.

She took it in with a sense of awe. "I feel like I stepped into a geode. Bianca would have loved this."

Ian stepped back to check his work. "Yeah, she would."

Tess turned Wren in her arms. Paint fumes or not, the baby needed to see this. "Wren, this is what your mother was like."

"On a good day," Ian added.

"But I think this is how her heart was all the time. Am I right?"

He set down his brush. "Yeah. Even if her sparkle was frequently misdirected."

"Why did you decide to do this now?"

"It was time, that's all."

Since she had been going through her own farewell for Trav, she understood.

The light shifted as the sun went under a cloud, but the room still glittered. "We missed a momentous occasion," she said. "Wren's birthday would have been two days ago, the day when she should have been born. We've decided to fix a real dinner tonight, and you're invited."

"I'm honored."

"You should be. Right, Wren?"

Wren yawned, bored with them both.

They'd just received a fresh grocery shipment, and while Wren slept, Tess made stuffed baked potatoes and fried chicken. The kitchen smelled heavenly.

"Why haven't you been cooking for me like this all along?" Ian said as the smells drew him to the kitchen.

Tess gave a final toss to the salad. "Because you don't eat."

"I eat."

"Frozen dinners at ten o'clock that taste like cat food."

"Now I know what I've been missing."

As they ate, they made conversation like normal people. Easy conversation, even after Wren woke up. They had similar opinions about politics, different taste in music, and a joint hatred of horror movies. Ian told her he was heading into town tomorrow and she should make sure the glazed doughnuts weren't sold out by the time he got there.

"I don't think it's a good idea for you to come into the Broken Chimney when I'm there," she said.

"What are you worried about?"

"Not exactly worried. I just don't see any reason to stir the gossip mill more than it's already stirred."

"The only way to deal with bullies is head on."

"You're an outlaw. That's the way you deal. But that's not my way."

"You'd rather hide?"

She bristled. "I'm hardly hiding working at the Broken Chimney."

"You're hiding when you don't want us to be seen in public together."

"I'm trying not to make any more waves. Work with me."

He didn't promise not to show up, but he stopped arguing with her.

Their dinner was long over, but other than getting a bottle for Wren, neither of them stirred. They began to talk about art. He described Paleolithic cave drawings as the original street art and Michelangelo as the first celebrity artist. He spoke of Daumier's lithographs, Seurat's dots, and the avant-garde modernists. She expected him to scoff at her passion for Mary Cassatt. Instead, he told her about Berthe Morisot, another female impressionist he thought she would appreciate.

The last spoonful of mango gelato had long ago melted in their bowls when he surprised her by mentioning his mother. "When I was little, she'd take me to the Metropolitan, the Whitney, the Guggenheim—whatever she was in the mood for."

"A nice memory."

"There weren't a lot of them." He leaned back in his chair, perfectly at ease. "She was a beautiful, alcoholic socialite who could barely take care of herself, let alone protect me from my father."

Tess's sense of justice flared. "From what I've read, your father should have been tossed in prison for child abuse. Why was he so horrible to you?"

"He was a prick. But also, I wasn't his kid."

Tess straightened in her chair. He'd delivered this bombshell as casually as someone giving a weather update. "He wasn't your father?"

"No. But he didn't find out about my mother's affair until I was around five. Too late to take back my name."

Tess moved Wren to her opposite shoulder. "Your biography doesn't mention this."

"I don't hide it, but I don't broadcast it, either. Misguided loyalty to my mother, I guess. She's in a long-term care facility now for dementia. She loved me, but she still looked the other way when the old man was slapping me around—letting me take the punishment for her affair. Her personality has changed with her disease. You couldn't meet anybody sweeter."

Tess's temper blazed. "I don't care how sweet she is now. She should have protected her child."

"All women aren't as fierce as you, Tess." He actually smiled. "She has no idea who I am when I visit, but she fusses over me the whole time—tries to give me cookies, worries that I'll catch a chill, takes me around and introduces me to everyone, even though she can't remember my name."

"Why didn't your father divorce her instead of abusing you?" One good thing Tess could say about her own father. He might have abandoned her, but he hadn't abused her.

"Divorce would have meant admitting he'd made a mistake. And Ian Hamilton North the Third could never make a mistake." His expression hardened. "Pride was everything to him. He treated the North family name as if it were a holy relic. You can imagine how it enraged him to see that name sprayed on trash bins and Porta-Potties."

"What about your biological father?"

"An actor. He made a couple of films in the eighties before his career crashed. We had an uncomfortable meeting about ten years ago, and neither of us has any desire to repeat the experience."

"What you went through as a child was horrible. But you're so dispassionate about it. How do you do that?"

"I'm not an emotional person, Tess. You know that. I'm pragmatic. I approach life analytically. That doesn't mean I'm unfeeling. It means I don't let those feelings rule me. A healthy degree of detachment makes life easier."

She'd seen the anger in his work, and she didn't buy his explanation, especially when she thought about his mother. The woman who'd purportedly loved him had never interceded to protect him from his father's horrors. Was it possible if, instead of feeling too little, he felt too much?

"Don't look so stricken," he said. "When I was seventeen, I got even. I beat the shit out of my father. He couldn't call the cops because it would have brought even more shame on the North family name than my arrests."

"Some people should never have been born." Wren let out a little wheeze. Tess cuddled her against her neck. "Not you, sweetheart. You should definitely have been born."

And the Dennings were coming in five days to take her away.

Tess couldn't do anything right at work. She mixed up orders, dropped a tray of mugs, and when Freddy Davis came in, burned herself on the espresso machine. She only wanted to be with Wren. But being with her was sometimes worse than being separated.

Taking in the little sounds she made—the squeaks and yawns, her baby snores. Her perfect deliciousness.

She and Ian didn't repeat their dinnertime coziness, but each day when she got back from the Broken Chimney, he took Wren from her and ordered her to rest.

She stayed home on the last day before she had to hand Wren over to the Dennings and kept her cradled to her body. At bedtime, she propped herself against the headboard and held Wren through the night. "It's going to be all right, my little one," she whispered. "They'll take good care of you. They will."

But who would take care of Tess?

Despite her best intentions, she'd fallen in love with this tiny creature. A ferocious, unconditional love more powerful than anything she could have imagined. She'd warned herself not to get attached, but it had happened. How could it not? She'd spent her days, her nights, her weeks with this tiny morsel pressed against her heart.

The baby slept better than she had in weeks, her breathing punctuated with noisy little goat grunts. As the dark hours ticked by, Tess absorbed the smell of her, kissed the flush of her cheeks, brushed her fingers over the soft fontanel. This baby was hers. She would give up her life for this child. She could not let her go.

But she had to.

By the time the first streaks of dawn crept into the room, she was nauseated. Wren, on the other hand, was wide-awake, ready to rock. Tess carried her downstairs and fed her, breathing in her milky smell. She took the bottle so much easier now than she had at the beginning. Her eyes focused on Tess's own. She curled her starfish fingers around Tess's.

Ian appeared from the back bedroom, his hair damp from his shower and the scar on his neck flushed from the warm water. He'd pulled on a pair of gray athletic shorts and a T-shirt. He was silent as he walked past her to make coffee.

Wren finished her bottle like a champ. Tess curved her hand around the baby's head as Ian brought her a mug. "She doesn't know I'm not her mother."

"She'll be well cared for."

If Tess hadn't been holding Wren, she would have launched herself at him. He was cold. Heartless. A man who didn't seem to understand any emotion except anger.

He was the one who got Wren's things together while Tess cuddled her in the geode bedroom. He was the one who packed up the bottles, the formula. He retrieved the stack of onesies from his dresser drawer and set the box of preemie diapers in the sleeping nest. He put the baby sling next to the diapers, but Tess couldn't imagine Diane or Jeff wearing it. Would they let Wren cry it out at night, alone and frantic in her bed?

Even the thought of it chilled her.

She heard the crunch of tires on gravel outside. "They're here," Ian said unnecessarily.

She nodded.

He went to greet them.

She broke out in a cold sweat. She was going to die. She couldn't do this. Couldn't hand her child over to strangers. Her stomach heaved. She raced for her jacket, for Wren's fleecy sleeper. Fumbling with the snaps, she pushed the baby inside.

The voices were coming closer. He was getting ready to bring them into the house. She ran from the room, through the kitchen, out the back door. She raced across the meadow, Wren clutched to her breast.

Ian's tree house had no walls yet. No place to hide. She dashed into the woods, her heart pounding so hard her ribs ached. She gasped for breath. Plunged off the path deeper into the trees. "It's all right, my angel girl . . . It's all right."

Her lungs burned. She couldn't go to the cabin. It was the first place he'd look. The old church . . . a ruin. She cut through the underbrush and ran toward the fire tower, not knowing what she'd find there, only knowing she had to keep running.

She climbed the rotting wooden steps with one arm around her child and one hand gripping the unstable railing. "Don't worry. I have you. Nobody's taking you from me. Nobody."

She got to the top. The door was stuck. She put her shoulder to it. It gave way. She shut the door behind her and leaned against it, drawing in great gulps of oxygen.

Wren gazed up at her, trusting. Not seeing a crazed woman.

Tears spilled over her lashes. She slid down the wall and sat on the dirty floor. Bending her knees, she tucked the baby against her. "We'll go to Wisconsin." Her words were garbled from her tears, but she kept on. "Or Arizona. I have friends there. Or Canada. Just the two of us. We'll stay someplace where no one will ever find us. . . ."

On and on she went. One insane, impossible scenario after another while Wren listened, content to be held.

She didn't know how much time passed before he found her. The door of the fire tower creaked open. He stepped inside and looked down at her crouched in the corner. "Tess . . ."

The way he said her name. So much sadness. He knew. He understood.

But he didn't. "Give her to me, Tess."

"No! You can't have her."

He knelt on one knee in front of her. "Don't do this."

"She's mine!"

He slipped his fingers in her hair, touched her temple with his thumb. "No. She's not."

She shook him off. "You don't care! You don't understand!"

The jerky movement, the shrillness of her voice, made Wren cry.

"I do understand," he said. "Let me have her."

Wren cried louder, her little chest spasming. "You can't. You can't take her."

"I have to."

She struggled against him, trying not to let go. . . .

"Tess . . . Tess, please . . ."

He peeled the crying baby from her arms.

"Don't." She staggered to her feet. "Don't do this!"

"It'll be all right." They were the same words she'd spoken to her child. But he was wrong. Nothing would ever be all right again.

"Give her back to me!"

The grooves around his mouth deepened. "Stay here," he said quietly. "It'll be easier for you."

272 · SUSAN ELIZABETH PHILLIPS

He opened the fire tower door, and with the sobbing baby tucked in his arms, disappeared.

"No!" She ran toward the door, stumbled, and fell to her knees. "No!" And then, from the depths of her soul, she howled.

As long as he lived, Ian would never forget that feral sound. He cupped the side of the baby's head to keep her from hearing Tess Hartsong's heart breaking.

He kept the baby in his arms as he lied to the Dennings. "Wren was fussy, and Tess took her for a walk."

The Dennings weren't suspicious by nature, and they accepted his explanation at face value. "Where is she?" Jeff said. "We need to thank her."

"She's staying away. She's gotten attached to Wren, and it'll be easier for her."

Diane pressed her hand to her heart. "Of course. We understand. And we can never thank either of you enough for what you've done."

It didn't take a trained observer to see they were both nervous. Diane kept licking her lips. Jeff fidgeted with his shirt collar. "We've had a lot to do to get ready for the baby," he said. "I don't remember Simon being this much work."

"We were younger then." Diane pulled at her bottom

lip with her teeth. "I prayed to be a grandmother, but I confess I never imagined it exactly like this."

"It's funny how life can change with a single phone call," Jeff said. "One day you're peacefully retired with nothing to do except plan your next cruise. The next day, you get a phone call from a famous artist telling you you're grandparents."

Diane fidgeted with her silver pendant. "We're willing to make any sacrifice so Wren will know she's being raised by two people who love her."

They were good people, but Wren didn't know them, not the way she knew Tess or even himself. He was the one who'd written down Wren's schedule that morning—how often she ate, how much formula to give her, where her medical records were—everything Tess should have written down but hadn't. He was surprised how much he'd absorbed without realizing it. But when he'd tried to double-check his notes with Tess, she wasn't talking.

The Dennings had been nervous about taking a preemie on a plane, so they'd driven down from New Jersey. Ian continued to hold the baby while he and Jeff had a brief discussion about legalities and exchanged contact information for their attorneys. Tess was right about the smell of Wren's head.

When their discussion ended, Diane and Jeff began carrying Wren's things out to their Lexus. Jeff returned from his last trip to the car and gazed at the baby. "There's mischief in those eyes."

Ian knew Wren well enough to suspect it was more likely gas.

The time had come. Ian carried Wren out to the car. Under the palm of his hand, he felt her release a long, satisfied fart. He'd been right about the gas.

The idiot baby chose that moment to lock eyes with him, and he could swear she had a satisfied look on her face. He couldn't believe he'd ever thought she looked like a squirrel.

"You have my number," he said. "Call if you have questions. Anything at all. Night or day."

"We will."

Jeff opened the back door of their sedan. Ian leaned down to put Wren in the car seat. A flash of red out of the corner of his eyes distracted him.

Tess erupted from the woods.

Her face was flushed, but she didn't look wild-eyed or crazed, the way she had in the fire tower. She looked sane and very determined.

"Hold up!" She marched forward, hair streaming in dark, curly swirls, nose red, eyes flint-hard. "We need to talk."

"Tess?" Diane turned. Her forehead knit with concern. "Oh, dear, I know this is hard for you."

"You have no idea." Tess stopped in front of them, slightly out of breath but with her jaw set. "Here's the deal. Wren is mine. Your son was only a sperm donor. I've taken care of her from the day she was born, and I want her."

It was as if she'd leveled them with a stun gun. Nobody moved. She rushed on. "Look at her. She's thriving. Can't you see? I know her in a way nobody else does. I know what her cries mean—whether she's hungry, or sleepy, or mad at the world. I know how she likes to be held and—"

"Tess," Ian cut in. "This isn't fair to Diane and Jeff."

"I don't care about Diane and Jeff!"

Jeff's head came up, and Diane looked wounded.

Tess softened. "I don't mean that. It's obvious you're good people, and Wren couldn't have better grandparents. But you're grandparents!" The words poured out, a rush of need, love, and desperation. "She's mine! You can see her anytime you want, but she's mine. You can be the grandparents you've always wanted to be. I'll send her to you for holidays. For summer vacations. I'll sign anything you want to protect your rights. But she belongs with me."

"Oh, Tess." Tess's outburst had brought out Diane's

maternal concern. "We can see how hard this is for you. But Wren is ours."

Tess's lips thinned into a snarl. "Why? Because your son knocked up her mother?"

"Tess . . ." Ian said softly. "That's enough."

Jeff wasn't as compassionate as his wife, and his jaw tensed. "She's our flesh and blood."

"But I'm the only mother she knows!" Tess cried. "I'm a good person! A good citizen. I'm strong and healthy. I'm sane. Most of the time, anyway. I'm ethical, and— Ian, tell them. Tell them I'm a good, competent person."

"You're a great person, Tess, but—"

"You're only making this harder on yourself," Diane said.

"She needs a real mother!" Tess exclaimed. "Someone young. Someone who loves her unconditionally. Not that you don't, but—" Some of the steam went out of her. "She needs me."

"We can see how much she means to you," Jeff said, more calmly. "But being raised by a single mother isn't what we want for Wren. She deserves a family."

Diane reached out to touch Tess's arm, then seemed to think better of it. "Women raise children on their own all the time, and they seem to turn out fine, but that's not what we want for our granddaughter. We may only be grandparents, but there are two of us. Girls need a father. Or in this case, a grandfather, to tell them they're beautiful and they're loved. To show them how good men treat women." She twisted her hands. "Tess, I didn't have that. I was raised by a mother who was so tired and frazzled that she never had time for me. And there were boyfriends." Diane's grip on her hands tightened, and her face seemed to collapse. "I— I can't bear for Wren to go through what I did with them."

Jeff slipped his arm around his wife's shoulders.

Diane had been molested. This was the crux of it. Ian could see that, just as he could see Tess wouldn't accept it.

Her shoulders shot back. "Bianca would have been a single mother."

"If Wren's mother had lived, Simon would have done the right thing," his father said firmly. "You don't seem to have a stable lifestyle, and I'm guessing you're not secure financially. As we understand it, you're working in a coffee shop. Grandparents might be second best, but there are two of us, and there's only one of you."

Tess stared at him. Blinked. She'd reached the end. She had no more arguments. She turned to Ian, but there was nothing he could say to fix this, and he hated that. He also hated the way she was frowning at him, as if this were somehow his fault, which maybe it was, since he was the one who'd dragged her into this mess.

She looked directly at him and shook her head. "You didn't tell them."

He felt an unpleasant chill at the back of his neck.

She took a quick step toward him. "We'd planned to take our time. Tell our families first. But I can see that's not going to work."

"Tess . . ."

She ignored the warning note in his voice. Instead, she hooked her hand through his arm, speaking quickly. "We intended to wait until next year, but if it's that important to you, we can get married earlier. Look at us. We're upstanding people. Ian's at the top of his profession. His only criminal record is tied to his early career, and look how well that's served him. He's clean and sober. Richer than anyone deserves to be. More than that . . ." Her throat moved as she swallowed. "He loves Wren, and he'd never do anything to hurt her. You should see them together. It's like they're one person. He feeds her, takes her on walks. Her favorite place to sleep is on his chest. Sometimes I have to make him give her back to me."

He shook himself out of his paralysis. "Tess!"

She dead-eyed him. "I know we agreed not to tell anyone, but we don't have that choice now." She spun back to the Dennings. "Two parents. Two stable, loving, involved parents. Neither of whom is a deadbeat or a child molester. Isn't that what you want for her?"

To his horror, they hesitated, looking suddenly confused. Tess had plunged him into the most god-awful mess he could never have imagined, and while he was trying to sort through his options, she went in for the kill.

"What does another day matter?"

Another day for what?

She took a deep, unsteady breath. "Take her with you. For tonight. There's a bed and breakfast right up the highway. They always have room, and you'll be comfortable there." She plunged on. Not letting anyone get a word in. "You have her things. You'll be able to hold her as much as you want and think about what I've told you. You can look into your hearts and decide what's best for her. For her. Not for you."

She made this weird shooing motion with her hands, as if she were swatting away chickens. "Go on, you two. I'll call the Purple Periwinkle and tell them to have their best room ready for you." She grabbed Wren from him. "Be good to Grandma and Grandpa, sweetheart. Mommy loves you." She kissed Wren's head, ducked into the backseat of the Lexus, and buckled her in.

Her head popped back out. "I'll fix breakfast for all

of us tomorrow morning. Ian makes the best coffee, and my eggs Benedict are to die for. Let's say ten o'clock. That way you can all sleep in. There! That's decided."

Jeff and Diane both had a deer-in-headlights look, and Ian could only imagine his own expression. But Tess was so forceful, so competent, so *commanding*— the fools did exactly as she said.

Jeff inched toward the driver's side. "Well, if you're sure . . ."

"Of course. Easy peasy," the woman known as Tess Hartsong chirped. She opened the passenger-side door for Diane with one hand and pushed her in with the other. "Go on, now. Enjoy her."

The next thing Ian knew, Tess was waving like a fool at the Dennings' Lexus as it disappeared down the road.

He grabbed her by the shoulders. "You! Inside! Now."

Chapter Thirteen

Tess wanted to race after the car. Grab it by the bumper like Supergirl and bring it to a screeching halt. What if Wren decided not to cry her little heart out from four in the afternoon until six? What if she didn't wake up three times tonight? Or neglected to have one of her explosive poops? What if she didn't test them?

Tess had taken the risk of a lifetime.

"Did you *hear* what I said?"

It was the voice of doom. He loomed over her, even larger and more ferocious than he'd been at their inauspicious first meeting. This time, an actual vein bulged at his temple.

"What possessed you?" His hand flew out, jabbing the air. "Have you lost your mind? What can you possibly hope to gain by lying like that? And not just any lie! Oh, no. This is the Grand Canyon of lies!" On and on he went, his words so scathing her skin should have blistered. He grabbed her elbow and perp-marched her toward the front door only to come to a dead stop and start yelling at her again. "How exactly do you expect this to play out? In what dim corner of your brain did you decide this would work?"

She answered honestly. "It was the only thing I could think of."

"Think? You weren't thinking at all!"

She grabbed his flailing arm. "You wrote down everything for them, right? You told them she has to sleep on her back and to be patient with her feedings. And— What if something goes wrong? What if they try to call us when we don't have a signal? Did you give them the doctor's phone number?" She moaned. "What did I do?"

"Wren is going to be fine," he said. "You, on the other hand, are not!"

She couldn't deal with him right now, not while Wren might be crying her heart out. She had to get away. Someplace. Anyplace. She snatched up her phone—her only lifeline to her baby—and fled, leaving Ian fuming behind her. "Come back here!"

She raced for the cabin, the only refuge she could

think of. *Please, Wren. Be your worst today. You can do it! You have to!*

But what if she didn't?

A cobweb broke across her face, and a deer ran across the trail. Her feet hit the bridge so hard the boards should have snapped. He wasn't following her—either because he was afraid he'd kill her or because he knew she needed some time. She let herself into the cabin. It was blessedly empty.

As her heartbeat steadied, she called Fiona Lester at the B and B and learned the Dennings were getting settled. Fiona was understandably curious about the baby with them. "Friends of the family," Tess stammered, and hung up before Fiona could ask more questions.

Knowing the Dennings hadn't taken off for New Jersey with Wren didn't ease her anxiety. They could change their minds at any time. She threw back the curtains, grabbed a broom, and abandoned it. She should crawl into bed and sleep, but she was too agitated. She found a rag and took a couple of swipes at the dust that had accumulated in the last month, but she could only think about Wren and how to deal with the rickety house of cards she'd built for herself with Ian.

She spotted her Bluetooth speaker and carried it outside. Fallen branches and storm-scattered leaves cluttered the yard. She set the speaker on the splintered picnic table, discarded her jacket, and pulled up her music.

Justin Timberlake.

She let the song sink into her bones. *Come on, dude. Do your job. Take me into your feel-good jam. You do the work, Justin, because I'm all done in.*

It had been so long since she'd tried to dance away her feelings. She tilted her head. Her hair curled down her back. The trees spun above her as she turned. She breathed in the smell of skunk, pine, and creosote. The cool air slithered through the weight of her hair to brush her scalp.

I will fear no evil, J.T. For thou art with me.

Beyoncé took command next. Glorious Beyoncé. *You're a mother, Bey. You understand. Watch over my baby, will you?*

Her movements grew more random, more disjointed. Her knee hurt. But she didn't stop.

"Are you deaf?"

The words came from her past. From the first time she'd seen him.

She stopped. Sucked in more oxygen. Let her hands

fall to her sides and tried to catch her breath. She'd known he wouldn't leave her alone for long. She was surprised he'd given her this much time to pull herself together.

He stood in the exact same place as that first morning. Instead of his red-and-black flannel shirt, he wore a white T-shirt that molded to his body. His hair was just as unruly—thick and dark, curling at his neck. He no longer looked as though he intended to strangle her, but he didn't look friendly, either. He switched off her speaker, the same as he'd done the first time, silencing Mother Bey.

"You realize that tomorrow morning when they show up—if they show up—you have to tell them the truth."

"They *will* show up!" she exclaimed. "They have to."

He was unrelenting. "You have to tell them you fabricated this whole marriage thing."

She sank onto the surviving picnic bench and studied the crumbling brick by her feet. She poked at it with her toes. "Would it be so awful?" she said quietly. "Getting married?"

"Are you serious?" Leaves pulverized beneath his boots as he stomped toward her. "You don't believe for a moment that I'll go along with your insanity, do you?"

"Maybe." She looked up at him. "All you need to do

is tell them we're getting married. After that, we can stall them."

"They intend to be part of Wren's life! Exactly how long do you think that would work?"

She braced her hands on her thighs and started talking faster, words tumbling over one another, trying to work it out as she spoke. "Let's say we have to get married. What's the big deal? What does marriage even mean anymore? Especially to the two of us. Who really cares, other than the Dennings? We're good at staying out of each other's way, and it's not like we'd live together. You could have your precious solitude, and I— Well, I don't know exactly what I'm going to do, but it won't be with you. I'll sign any kind of prenup you want to protect that money you don't care about. It won't make any *difference*!"

"I want to *draw* you, not marry you!"

She blinked. "If we're married, you'd be able to draw me whenever you want. It's— It's a package deal."

"I'm not buying." He turned away.

She came to her feet. As insane as this was, she couldn't give up. "Have you ever read about these incredible people who make grand gestures? Gestures that change lives forever? Like . . . donating a kidney. Or building a school. Or . . . lifting a car off somebody. That's what this would be. Your grand gesture."

He spun on her. "You need a kidney? I'll think about it. But I am *not* marrying you."

She dug her fingernails into her palms. "You'd have to do so little, and it would make all the difference in her life."

"You call getting married 'so little'?"

"Don't you want to keep her? Even a little bit?"

"That has nothing to do with it."

"It has everything to do with it! And marriage to me wouldn't be nearly as terrible as you think." Even she didn't believe that, so she tried to convince them both. "We're kind of friends, if you define a friend as someone you can be yourself with. Someone you don't need to impress or hide your flaws from. We've pretty much seen the worst of each other. At least I hope it's your worst, because you've seen mine. And any day now, Wren and I'll move down here to the cabin. You'd barely know we were around. Don't you see? Nothing would change."

"Except I'd be married, something that was never part of my life plan."

"Only until the ink is dry on the paperwork. When I know for sure that she's mine forever—we can split." She searched for something—anything—that would convince him. "Until then . . . you could have as much sex as you want."

One of those dark eyebrows shot up. "You mean *you* could have as much sex as *you* want."

"Tomato. To-mah-to." She rushed on. "It's only fair to tell you . . . I—" She swallowed. "I'm well trained in the art of seduction." Much better trained than she wanted to be.

"You sound like an eighteenth-century courtesan."

"But with better hygiene." Although she wasn't entirely certain she'd brushed her teeth that morning. "Of course, I'll need to know you aren't carrying around any STDs. Because I'm not."

"Neither am I, and this is crazy." He plowed his hand through his hair.

Was she finally wearing him down? Her exhausted heart raced. What could she say that would seal the deal? She licked her lips. "How about a test run?"

"A . . . ?"

Her dreams of being seduced vanished, but this was about Wren, not about sex. "A test run. On the condition that you'll seriously consider this?"

His silence was worse than a dismissal. He picked up her Bluetooth speaker and examined it, as if he were inspecting for design flaws. Finally he looked up at her. "Here's a counteroffer. Pose for me tonight. Nude."

She swallowed. "If I agree, will you tell them we're planning to get married? Just planning?"

"No."

"Then I won't do it."

He transferred the speaker from one hand to the other. "How about I agree not to tell them you're lying through your teeth. But—"

"I accept," she said quickly.

"*But . . .* Only if they don't ask me directly. Unlike you, I'm not going to lie."

It wasn't what she wanted, but it was better than nothing. "Deal. Now please leave so I can cry in peace."

He couldn't get away fast enough.

She was too agitated to nap, and the cabin felt claustrophobic, so she washed her face, ran a brush through her hair, and found her spare set of car keys. She hiked back up to the schoolhouse for her car and drove into town.

She roamed the aisles of the Dollar General without taking anything in, then sat on the bench outside and tried to calm herself down. When that didn't work, she got up, only to discover she'd sat in something sticky. She cleaned off her jeans as best she could before the fear that had brought her to town overwhelmed her. She had to make certain the Dennings were still at Fiona's Purple Periwinkle Bed and Breakfast.

She drove past Brad Winchester's rec center and the

Angels of Fire Apostolic Church. Around the bend, the Purple Periwinkle sat off to her left. She slowed to a crawl.

The Dennings' Lexus was there, but that didn't reassure her. Wren was too fragile to be around a lot of people. What if there were other guests? Unvaccinated children?

It took all her willpower to drive back to town. She made it as far as the rec center before she had to pull over. She leaned her forehead against the steering wheel as one awful image after another flooded her brain. Wren crying so hard her face broke out in splotches. Wren vomiting into her car seat. Wren with one of her explosive diarrhea attacks. Tess had wanted Wren to behave her worst for them, but knowing the baby might be doing exactly that without Tess to comfort her was more than she could bear.

She forced herself to go back to the cabin. The throw rug inside her front door was askew, and a manual lay on the kitchen table, but this time Kelly Winchester wasn't to blame. The furnace installer had been here. Now that it no longer mattered, she had heat.

With her phone curled in her hand, she dragged herself upstairs, crawled under the covers, and fell into an uneasy sleep.

The ding of her phone woke her before the nightmare could take hold. She fumbled through the covers to retrieve it.

It was a text from Ian. *Where are you?*

She squinted and poked at the keypad. *Beach house in Bora Bora.*

Book a return ticket. Dinner here in an hour. I'm cooking.

Not hungry. Her stomach growled in protest.

Doesn't matter. We have a deal.

The nude drawing. As if she could forget.

She glanced at the time. Almost seven o'clock. Her head ached and her mouth tasted like dirty socks. She dragged herself into the warm bathroom, filled the old claw-foot tub, pulled off her dirty clothes, and sank in.

We have a deal. As she lay back in the water, she imagined herself lying naked on that purple velvet couch. And for what purpose? Did she really think her dubious sexual allure would convince him to go along with the harebrained story she'd concocted on the fly?

She needed to prepare herself for whatever happened tonight, but shaving her legs was all that came to mind.

The water cooled. She towel-dried her hair and combed through it with her fingers. Her jeans were too dirty to put back on, and she'd perspired through her shirt, but with nearly all her things at the schoolhouse, she didn't have much left to choose from.

She rejected the black sheath she'd worn to Trav's funeral and the bright pink leopard-print jumpsuit her fellow midwives had once bought her as a joke. That left the full-skirted, off-the-shoulder crimson cocktail dress that was her staple for holiday parties.

Something about that red dress . . . She needed armor, and it felt brave, like a battle flag. She slipped it over her head and shivered as the chilly fabric slithered over her naked body. The skirt was full, letting plenty of air creep up her legs and beyond. As soon as she got to the schoolhouse, she'd put on some underwear.

Gathering her dirty clothes, she glanced at herself in the mirror. With no makeup, finger-combed hair, and the bright red cocktail dress, she looked like a hungover party girl creeping home at dawn from a long night snorting coke with an indie film director.

She slipped into the scuffed silver ballet flats she kept by the back door and got in her car. Much too quickly, she arrived at the schoolhouse.

Inside, she could smell something cooking.

"In here," he called from the kitchen.

She followed the sound of his voice. He stood at the kitchen counter in jeans and a navy FIFA World Cup

T-shirt, the detritus of salad-making in front of him, along with a wine bottle and two full glasses. He gave her an admiring once-over. "Very nice."

"I'm changing."

"Later." He held out one of the wine goblets. "This is a very good cabernet."

She slugged down the entire glass and held it back out for a refill.

"I anticipated that," he said.

"What?"

"Your pressing need to abuse alcohol." He refilled her glass. "I like the way you dressed up for me."

"My clothes were dirty, and I'm changing as soon as I eat." Between the wine and the sumptuous smells coming from the oven, she was suddenly hungry. Hungry enough to almost forget she wasn't wearing underwear.

"Lasagna for dinner."

"Frozen?"

He looked offended. "You underestimate my culinary skills."

"Definitely frozen."

His mouth twitched. "Grab some plates."

She looked like the wanton fourth wife of a dissolute Greek shipping magnate. The red dress and bare feet.

That extravagant chaos of inky hair against her olive skin. A woman too confident to bother with makeup. And those breasts . . . He'd seen a lot of breasts, but these were exceptional. He'd long suspected they weren't entirely symmetrical, which made them even more perfect.

She cleaned up the mess he'd made of the salad and transferred the remainder into bowls, the skirt of her dress swishing around her bare legs. He took the lasagna from the oven. "I lit the stove. Let's eat in front of the fire."

She shrugged and carried the salads into the living area. He tossed a wool throw on the floor in front of the potbelly stove and brought out the rest of the food. The table might be more comfortable, but he wouldn't have had such a captivating view. First, she sat cross-legged, the skirt of her dress tucked between her thighs, her calves and bare feet exposed. Later, she shifted her legs off to one side so the swirl of her skirt crept to midthigh. She was a ballet of decadent crimson and earthy cream.

And worry. Easy to see how upset she was. He'd also been thinking about Wren more today than he wanted to. He refilled Tess's wineglass, but left his alone, neither of them saying much. Finally, he gave up attempting to eat and did what he'd been contemplating all day. He picked up his sketch pad.

She stiffened, remembering her promise to let him draw her nude. He took his time picking out a 3B graphite pencil as the internal war between his compulsion to draw her and his contempt for what he would produce raged all over again. This wasn't art. These hackneyed drawings were a distraction keeping him from doing what he should be doing, except he didn't know what that was. How could he with all this mess?

The fire glowed through the stove's window. She'd been staring at it, but now she looked at him. "I don't get it. I don't understand why you want to draw me."

And he had no intention of explaining it. "Inspiration strikes in strange ways." He looked up from his sketch pad. "Today it's you. Tomorrow it'll be some big ass toadstool I spot in the woods."

She laughed, the first one he'd heard from her in a while. "A flattering comparison. It's a good thing I don't give a rat's ass what you think of me."

"Not the best attitude toward someone you're trying to convince to marry you."

He could have kicked himself for bringing that up, because all the laughter faded from her eyes. She glanced down at her skirt. "Is this the part where I have to strip?"

That pissed him off, which it shouldn't have, because he was the one who'd baited her. "You don't have to do a damn thing you don't want to."

"I don't want to." She set her wineglass on the coffee table next to her. "But I will." She reached behind her back to lower the zipper of her dress.

"Stop right there." As much as he wanted to see more, he wouldn't see it like this. Not with that stricken look on her face, which made him feel as if he'd turned her into a ten-dollar hooker.

"I need you on my side tomorrow," she said.

His grip tightened on his pencil. "I'm aware of that. Stay the way you are."

And so, instead of sketching her lying naked on the purple couch in his studio, she posed for him as she was. Legs drawn to her side, skirt ruffled around her thighs, head tilted. He was furious with himself.

Tess told herself she should be relieved by how detached he was. The idea of lying naked and passive in front of him, of letting him study her as if she were an insect mounted with pins, was beyond disturbing. But instead of relief, she felt like some sort of sexual pity case. She wanted more than that, so why didn't he?

Always the seductress. Never the seduced.

She sat up. "Have you seen enough for tonight?"

"Are you getting tired?"

"Yes." A lie. Her nap had refreshed her.

His pencil abruptly stopped moving. "I can't believe you tried to buy me with sex."

He hadn't been angry at the time, so why was he upset now? She brought her knees under her. "I didn't have anything else to barter with."

He came to his feet in one abrupt movement. "You had your . . . your character. Your intelligence. Your . . ." He struggled for words. "You can cook!"

His reaction mystified her. "Why didn't I think of that? Go along with my nefarious marital scheme, and I'll make you meat loaf."

He came closer, looming over her. "When we go to bed together, it's going to be because we both want to be there. Not because you're sacrificing yourself like some kind of vestal virgin."

"Did you say *when* we go to bed . . ."

"I did."

"But—"

"Don't pretend not to understand. A woman like you who oozes sex . . ."

She blinked. "You think I ooze sex?"

"You know exactly what I mean. Those eyes. That hair. Your body."

She swallowed. "I can go along with the eyes, and I guess my hair is personal preference, but the body?"

"That's enough. More than enough."

He whipped his T-shirt over his head.

Chapter Fourteen

He loomed above her, the flames from the potbelly stove licking his bare chest. He held out his hand, and she gave him hers. That simplicity of his big hand folding around her smaller one felt more intimate than anything they'd ever shared.

He drew her to her feet. She gazed into those dark, silver-sluiced eyes. How had she ever thought they were cold? He pressed his thumb into her palm and drew a delicious circle there. "I need to make sure we both understand. . . . This has nothing to do with tomorrow."

It has everything to do with tomorrow.

He circled her palm again. "Let me hear you say it."

If that's what he needed to hear . . . "This has nothing to do with tomorrow."

"And everything to do with tonight."

If he picked up his sketch pad, she would never forgive him. "I'm not on the pill."

"No problem. Those condoms you love so much . . ." He touched the pocket of his jeans. "I don't go anywhere without them, not when you're around."

She smiled. "Flattering."

His big hands slid down her back. Her skin hummed. Maybe tonight could be a singular point of time for them, disconnected from the rest of their lives. He paused at her waist. "You're killing me," he groaned. "All I want to do is strip you naked and take you right here. But . . ."

No buts!

". . . this could screw up everything between us in a hundred ways."

"For a man of few words, I've heard enough." She took over. She clasped her arms around his neck, went up on her toes, and parted her lips. Her fingers played with the thick, crisp hair on the back of his head. She caught his bottom lip between her own. Lingered there. Enticed.

Always the seducer. Never the seduced.

His body pressed hard against hers. She tilted her hips and rubbed against him like a cat, but kept her tongue tucked away where it belonged. Trav wasn't big on tongues.

His palms cupped her rear with only the thin layer of crimson fabric separating her skin from his. She waited for him to reach under.

He didn't.

Instead, he stole the kiss. Took it over. One moment she was in charge. The next moment she was spine-against-the-wall, her face cupped between his big, skillful hands. He angled her head ever so slightly and lifted her chin. His thumb brushed the pillowy center of her bottom lip, easing it away from her top one.

He slid his hands to her shoulders, dipped his head, and she felt his tongue. At first only a tease and then slipping inside. Exploring.

It was like being kissed for the first time. In an entirely new way. She was a stranger caught up in an exotic land. Did she really like being kissed like this?

She did.

His mouth-play didn't stop. How many ways could he kiss? He flattened his palms against the wall on each side of her head, his chest to her breasts. She fluttered her eyes open. His were half-closed. He was going to devour her. Her skin pebbled.

He clasped her wrists at her sides. She'd always been

slightly claustrophobic, and he'd trapped her with his body. She had no compulsion to pull away, nor did she feel completely safe.

The smell of woodsmoke. Of him. It was all so enticing.

He released her. Lowered his hands until they came to rest on the sides of her hips.

Reach under. Reach under my dress. . . . She silently urged him, but he didn't follow orders. Instead, he pulled back. His gaze searching hers. Forehead furrowed.

He wanted her. She could feel how much.

"God, Tess . . ."

She slipped away from the wall and knelt on the blanket. The bed would be more comfortable, but it was too far. He knelt beside her, the glowing flames from the woodstove painting their bare arms in gold and umber.

They lay back together.

He groaned. "You're every man's fantasy."

She fought the urge to argue with him.

He kissed her again. And again. Deep, thorough kisses so arousing she became drunk with them. His chest was bare, but he still wore his jeans. Her legs were bare, but she still wore her dress. His hand found the inside of her knee. Finally. But even then, he took his time, moving slowly. He located her collarbone. Kissed the hollow of her throat. Paused when he realized she wore no underwear.

She was wet. Embarrassingly so. But he didn't seem to mind. She arched her neck. Her thighs parted.

He touched her. The very center of her. Only the lightest caress. Then deeper. Firmer. Faster. She fell apart.

He barely gave her time to recover before he touched her again. Her breath quivered and once more she shattered.

She needed all of him. Had to have him. She splayed her hands against his chest and rolled him off her. Reached for the zipper of his jeans. Felt what was there. Thick and turgid.

He stopped her hands before she could unzip. She looked at him in shock and saw the troubled downturn taking over the corners of his mouth. With her heightened senses, she could read his thoughts. "This has nothing to do with tomorrow," she whispered.

"I wish to God it didn't." He thrust himself up from the floor and stalked toward the front door.

"Where are you going?"

"Outside."

"Why?"

"Guess."

"Oh . . ." She wanted to tell him he didn't need to. That she'd take care of it. Take care of him. But the door had already closed. Still bare-chested, he stalked out into the cold April night.

She couldn't bear the awkwardness of seeing him when he returned, so she cowered in her room. What could she say when she knew he was right? How could tonight not be connected to whatever would happen tomorrow? Despite his rough exterior, he was a man of honor. Right now she hated that about him.

She heard him return as she was taking off the badly crumpled dress she'd never wear again. The faint sound of running water came from the downstairs bathroom. He'd made her forget about Wren for a little while, but that magical flight from reality had ended. The Dennings hadn't called for advice. They hadn't begged her to come take a screaming baby off their hands. Jeff and Diane Denning had fallen in love with Wren the moment they'd seen her. It was something Tess understood too well.

The next morning, she showered, dressed, and even put on makeup to armor herself against the day. It was barely seven o'clock when she finished, and the Dennings weren't due until ten. She made her way downstairs. The door to the geode bedroom stood slightly ajar. Without glancing inside, she knew it was empty. The energy that charged the house when he was present had gone missing.

She glanced at the schoolhouse clock. What would she do with herself for the next three hours? She was too agitated to read, and she'd go crazy if she stayed inside, so she put on her sneakers, added a windbreaker, and went out.

She needed to dance away the tumult rumbling inside her, and she started to head for the cabin only to turn around and walk in the opposite direction. That last time she'd climbed toward the ruined church, she'd been carrying Wren. This time she walked alone.

He was there, standing in the misty meadow. She slipped into the trees. The power in his stance mesmerized her. His arms extended in measured thrusts, then his legs came into play. He wore only a T-shirt and a pair of gray shorts. Even from her hiding place, she could see the musculature of his calves, the power in his thighs.

She was spying on him like a fifteen-year-old lurking in the shrubbery in hopes of catching sight of her teenage crush. Enough of that. She stuffed her hands in the pocket of her windbreaker and walked out into the sunshine.

He was so engrossed in his practice that it took a few moments before he noticed her. She selected the flattest tree stump as a viewing place. He lost his rhythm. Picked it up again. But he didn't continue for long. Wiping his forehead on the sleeve of his T-shirt, he approached her.

She was a full-grown woman, and playing the blushing virgin didn't suit her. "Very nice, Mr. North. You should charge admission."

"What do you want?" He didn't say it rudely. More warily.

"Just avoiding that awful morning-after awkwardness. Not that we're really having a morning after. Since somebody chickened out." She hadn't planned to be so brash, but it felt exactly right.

"I did not chicken out!"

"Could have fooled me."

One dark eyebrow arched. "You don't have to look so proud of yourself."

"Unlike you, I got what I wanted." Her brazenness made her feel as though she was unearthing the woman she was meant to be all along.

Unfortunately, he didn't share her high regard. "I must have been crazy."

"Playing the man of honor is a real drag, right?"

"Jesus, Tess . . ."

"Speaking of Jesus. And since we're practically in church . . . I know I should forgive you for not sharing your goodies." She pretended to think it over. "But no. It's not happening."

He grinned. "You are one of a kind, Tess Hartsong."

That grin melted her. This is how he would have looked if he'd been raised in a different kind of family, free from all the childhood baggage he seemed to believe he'd left behind but that he still carried around like a sleeping elephant. The father who'd abused him, but even worse . . . The mother who hadn't loved him enough to keep him safe.

"How long have you been doing whatever it is you do up here?"

"Mainly tae kwon do. About ten years. I also practice in a backwater dojo over in Valley City."

"So that's where you disappear." Valley City was about fifteen miles away, and only marginally larger than Tempest. She nodded toward his backpack. "Do you have your sketchbook with you?"

"Of course."

"Draw something for me. Something that's not me." She pointed. "That window. The one with the vines growing around it."

He looked at the place she'd indicated, a narrow side window capped with a pointed arch. The glass was gone, and the remaining wooden grille pieces hung at odd angles.

He shrugged and walked over to fetch his sketchbook.

"Don't forget to sign it when you're done," she called after him.

"Still working on your sales strategy for eBay?"

"A woman's got to plan for retirement some way."

He snorted and headed back toward her. "Give me your tree stump."

She rose and stepped away to let him work. As he drew, she circled the church through the weeds and wandered toward the creek that ran behind the building. Much of the church's once-white paint had chipped away to reveal the weathered wood beneath. She imagined the voices of the Pentecostals speaking in tongues from behind these walls. The believers wading into the burbling headwaters of Poorhouse Creek to get baptized in the Holy Spirit.

She considered their absolute certainty that every word in the Bible was true. Their ability to dismiss the centuries of oral tradition that had existed before a word of scripture was transcribed. It would be comforting to have a belief that strong, but she preferred a more encompassing brand of Christianity. Still, she felt a kinship with these Pentecostals. Didn't they believe in spontaneous dancing?

She found a clump of tall grass and made a braid. As she tried to fasten it around her wrist, Ian called out from the tree stump. "All done."

She dropped the braid and went over to see. "Oh, my . . ."

She wasn't sure what she'd expected, but it wasn't this exquisite rendering. The window and the vines were executed in such impeccable detail they could have been a medieval engraving. But standing tall inside the window . . .

"That's a *rabbit*!"

"A very fine rabbit."

"A cartoon rabbit! What the hell, Ian?"

He practically smirked. "I thought you wanted an investment piece. That's what this is."

"How do you figure?"

He regarded her with exaggerated condescension. "You obviously know nothing about contemporary art. Mystery adds value."

"Aha."

"The art world will go crazy trying to figure out the significance of that rabbit. Your eBay auction will shoot right through the roof."

"And what *is* the significance of that rabbit?"

"I loved Bugs Bunny when I was a kid."

She smiled.

"I'd better give it a title." He took the sketchbook back from her, thought for a moment, and then wrote something. He returned it to her. Above his name and the date were the words *Composition in Pencil and Rabbit Pellets.*

"You didn't!"

"Unfortunately, I couldn't find any rabbit pellets. But with that title, you just made another grand."

She burst into laughter.

He grinned right back at her, looking exactly like the kid who'd once loved Bugs Bunny.

They returned to the house together. He pointed out bear scat on the trail and a set of coyote tracks. He showed her how the thickest stands of spring beauties and hepaticas grew beneath trees that hadn't yet leafed out.

"You're a city guy," she said. "I keep wondering how you know so much?"

"I've spent a lot of time outdoors over the years. Hiking, camping, canoeing. And artists tend to be close observers."

How much had he observed about her?

The tension that had temporarily eased reappeared when they reached the schoolhouse. "I need to get cleaned up," he said. "Don't fall apart while I'm gone."

"I'm not in the habit of falling apart." Blatantly untrue, since she'd been regularly falling apart.

As he disappeared into the geode bedroom, she went to the kitchen. Would he give her away when the Dennings arrived? He'd been clear that he wouldn't go along with her marriage story, but he'd also said he wouldn't expose her lie. Unless they asked directly.

She gazed around the kitchen, trying to recall why she'd come in here. Because she'd foolishly promised them eggs Benedict. She tried to clear her head enough to assemble the ingredients. There was no Canadian bacon on hand, so she'd have to use regular bacon. She'd also have to make a hollandaise sauce, something she'd only done once before.

Predictably, the sauce broke, butter and egg yolks separating into a grainy, watery mess. She started over only to have it break again. She went outside to search for a cell phone signal and found one by standing on her front right car bumper, where she watched a YouTube video that told her how to fix the sauce. By the time she'd made the repair, Ian had retreated into his studio, and her stomach was a churning mess. It was ten o'clock. Where were they?

Fifteen anxiety-ridden minutes later, she heard a car. She raced to the window and saw the Dennings' Lexus come to a stop in front of the schoolhouse. She gripped her stomach and made herself take three deep breaths before she ran outside.

Even with the car sealed shut, she could hear Wren crying. She yanked the back door open. Wren had wedged herself into the corner of the car seat, her eyes puffy, mouth wide, and potato chip tongue aquiver between her pink, toothless gums.

Tess fumbled with the seat buckles, pulled the baby out, and curled her against her body. Wren immediately quieted. Tess wanted to run into the woods again, hide in the fire tower. Make a little home for the two of them, with the mountains at their feet and the stars as their night-lights.

She cradled the baby, murmuring soothing shhhhs. Yearning to beg her forgiveness for abandoning her. She heard the low buzz of male conversation. Gradually, Wren's body grew lax.

"You have the magic touch," Diane said.

Only then did Tess turn. Jeff looked his normal natty self, but Diane didn't seem to have remembered to comb her hair. Her lipstick was in place, but not her eye makeup, and instead of a chunky silver necklace, her black sweater displayed a milky stain.

"Wren's like her father," Jeff declared proudly. "Simon could kick up a fuss, too."

Diane reached out to cup Wren's head. "We were younger then."

"She can be exhausting," Tess managed to say.

Diane offered a tired smile. "I've definitely had better nights."

Tess's spirits soared. Maybe her plan had worked. Maybe the reality of dealing with a cranky newborn had made them realize they didn't want to do it full-time. Maybe seeing how quickly Wren had quieted for Tess would open their hearts.

Diane immediately crushed her hopes. "She's so precious. Worth every moment of lost sleep. How could anyone not love this little creature?"

"I smelled bacon inside," Ian said. "Let's see what Tess has made for us."

"Everything's better with bacon," Jeff declared, the epitome of a cheery grandpa.

Tess straightened Wren's cap. The baby didn't smell like herself. Instead, she smelled of Diane's perfume and Jeff's aftershave.

Ian poured coffee.

"Wren smiled at me last night," Jeff announced.

"She didn't smile for me." Diane's curtness once again raised Tess's spirits only to—once again—torpedo them. "But I haven't forgotten how to burp a baby, and I do love the way she curled her hand around my finger."

Wren had fallen asleep. In order to finish making breakfast, Tess would have to set her down. Or hand her back to her grandparents. Neither was acceptable. Nor was carrying her in the sling around a hot stove.

She slipped the baby into Ian's arms. Mercifully, he didn't protest, although he didn't exactly look happy.

Her hollandaise was excellent, but the poached eggs were overcooked, and she'd charred the edges of the English muffins. Jeff was the only one who ate everything.

Tess barely touched her food. She was holding Wren again, treasuring her. Diane pushed her plate back from the edge of the table. "You probably think we're hopelessly old-fashioned by insisting Wren be raised in a stable family, but I can't bear thinking about her carrying around the same kind of scars I have."

Tess chose her words carefully. "I'm not sure it's fair to equate your experience with the experiences of other children of single mothers."

"You're right. Except . . . My mother had the best intentions, and I guarantee those intentions didn't include falling under the influence of abusive men."

"One thing I do know for certain," Jeff said, "is that

we all want what's best for Wren. The legalities could take a while, but I think we can agree that it's not in her best interest for us to wait until every *t* is crossed. She's only a month old. We need to act quickly. Settle everything before she gets too attached."

Tess started to tell them Wren was already attached, but Jeff wasn't done. "Diane and I understand the adjustments we'll have to make to raise a child at our age, but we're more than willing to do it. It's fortunate we can afford to hire help."

"Help?" Tess straightened in her chair so abruptly that Wren offered up a mew of protest. "Are you talking about a nanny?"

"Not necessarily, but—"

Tess came out of her chair. "You think it's best to rip Wren away from the only mother she's known and give her to a nanny?"

Diane's jaw set. "That's not our intention, Tess. And maybe you should turn that question on yourself. Do you think it's best for Wren to be raised by a struggling woman who, right now, seems to be jobless and whose plans for marriage are more than a little vague?"

"Your business, of course," Jeff added hastily. "Diane and I aren't judging your choices, except as they affect Wren."

Tess spoke as firmly as she could manage. "The only

reason our plans are vague is because we had no reason to hurry. Until now, that is." She couldn't look at Ian. Was this the moment he'd give her away?

Jeff turned to him. "I've done some more digging since your initial phone call. Your bio indicates you kicked up your heels quite a bit in your twenties."

"It was more than kicking up," Ian said flatly. "My family had disowned me. I was drinking too much, doing drugs, and living on the streets. I couldn't hold a job, and I didn't care about anything except leaving my mark on whatever flat surface drew my attention."

"Your family wasn't a family!" Tess declared. "You were lucky to get away from them."

Jeff hadn't blinked at Ian's self-assessment. "I admire a man who faces up to his mistakes. And you've certainly made up for it, not only with your career, but with your charity work."

What charity work? Tess wondered.

Ian was having none of it. "There's no work about it. Writing checks is easy, hardly a mark of strong character."

"You're too modest," Jeff said. "What about the time—not to mention money—you spend at those community art centers?"

One more thing she hadn't known.

Ian frowned. "Whenever there are budget cuts, the

arts are always the first target. More than a little short-sighted when they can be the only savior for kids in crisis."

"That's all commendable, but the Internet can't tell us what's most important." Diane gazed toward her granddaughter, asleep in Tess's arms. "We know how Tess feels about Wren, but what about you?"

"Ian loves Wren," Tess asserted. "He'd do anything for her. He's just more private about expressing his feelings." She turned to him, silently pleading. "You couldn't find a better father."

His eyes met her own. This was it. He couldn't side-step any longer. Sure enough, he rose from the table and went upstairs. Abandoning her. Abandoning Wren.

It was over. He'd had enough. She blinked her eyes. Swallowed. She put Wren to her shoulder, not looking at Diane or at Jeff.

She heard the clank of metal as Diane set her silverware on her plate. Jeff cleared his throat. Wren squeaked in her sleep. And then footsteps on the stair treads as Ian returned.

He'd brought one of his sketchbooks. He set it on the table in front of them and opened it to a pencil drawing of Wren asleep in Tess's arms. He flipped to the next page. Wren howling. Another page. Wren yawning. There was a study of her cockleshell ears and her orchid-petal mouth with its puffy top lip. One drawing after another—each daintier, more ethereal than the last, and none of which could have been executed with a spray can or paint roller.

Tess felt the sting of tears. She had no idea he'd been doing this.

"Oh, my . . ." Diane's hand flew to her cheek, and her voice caught in her throat. "These are . . . They're lovely."

For once, Jeff seemed at a loss for words, and it took him a few moments to recover. "I guess this answers Diane's question."

Diane's hand lingered on a page that showed the feathery whirl of Wren's cowlick. She gazed up at them, clearly troubled. "People can stay engaged for years. It happens all the time. We—*I* need to know you're committed for the long haul. That Wren will have parents."

"We sound like a couple of old fuddy-duddies, don't we?" Jeff said.

Diane rejected her husband's conciliatory chuckle. "I'm not apologizing, and I'm not going to spend the rest of my life worrying that Tess will end up with a revolving door of abusive boyfriends."

Tess raised her chin. "I'm not in the habit of surrounding myself with abusive men!"

"All it takes is one," Diane said. "May he rot in hell."

"What about Ian?" Tess exclaimed. "How do you know he's not slapping me around in private, or . . . harboring a sick obsession for little girls?"

"Is he?"

Tess had no right to be offended, since she was the one who had brought it up. "Of course not!"

"I didn't think so," Diane said. "I have exceptionally good radar when it comes to pigs. Even the most respectable."

"She does," Jeff said. "A local judge. One of the most important men in town, but Diane knew, and she's the one who brought him down."

She waved him off. "That's neither here nor there. I need to know the two of you are solid."

Ian tucked the sketchbook under his arm. "This is between Tess and me," he said firmly.

"Ian's telling us to butt out," Jeff said.

But the Tiger grandmother was having none of it. "And I'm telling them both . . . I'll make sure Simon won't relinquish his parental rights until I know for certain my granddaughter has real security."

Tess pulled Wren closer. "I'd give up my life for her."

Diane lowered her eyes to her lap. "I'm sure my mother thought the same thing."

"What you're demanding is unnecessary," Tess retorted.

"Unfair, yes," Diane said. "Unnecessary, no."

Tess had lost. Not only the battle but the war. "I can't do this."

"Then we have our answer," Diane said quietly.

"Hold up." Jeff slipped his arm around her shoulders. "Diane, we've been wanting to visit Asheville, and it's only a couple of hours away. Let's leave them alone for a day or so to talk things over." He looked at Tess. "I promise you, we'll make the transition as easy on Wren as we possibly can."

Diane touched the back of her husband's hand and gazed at her granddaughter. "You're not the only one who'd give up her life for her, Tess."

They were offering Tess a short reprieve. Ian, predictably, stomped off into the woods as soon as they drove away, muttering something about peace and quiet as he left. Tess fed Wren, changed her, trying not to think—not to feel—but it was impossible. Diane and Jeff were two of the most decent, well-intentioned people she'd ever met, and it wasn't right to hate them the way she did right now. As for Ian . . . He'd behaved honorably—more than honorably. What she was asking of him was beyond unreasonable, and she had no right to blame him for refusing. No right to blame any of them. But she did.

Ian was gone when she came downstairs the next morning, but his Land Cruiser sat outside, so at least he hadn't fled to Manhattan. As she finished feeding Wren, she heard a knock at the door. Were the Dennings back already? Or more teenagers? She couldn't deal with either, but her conscience wouldn't let her ignore the knocking. She tucked Wren in the sling and went to answer.

A broomstick-thin woman with lank, gray-threaded hair stood on the other side. Her age could have been anywhere from forty to sixty. She had the coarse, weather-beaten complexion of someone who'd earned her wrinkles outside. Unlike Rebecca Eldridge, this woman appeared to have been part of these mountains for generations.

"Sorry to bother you, missus. I'm Sarah Childers, and my husband, Duke—he's out in the truck—he cut his hand real bad on the posthole digger this morning. I heard you helped out the Eldridges when their little boy cut his leg, and I'd be mighty grateful if you'd take a look at Duke."

Tess started to say everything she needed to say—that she wasn't a doctor, she had virtually no medical supplies, and she wasn't certified to practice any kind of medicine in Tennessee, but the woman had already

322 • SUSAN ELIZABETH PHILLIPS

zeroed in on Wren. "God bless America, but isn't she a little sweetie pie?" She pressed a sun-spotted hand to her cheek. "Duke's mad as a hornet at me because I wouldn't sew up his hand myself."

Making it highly unlikely Sarah Childers could get her husband to a doctor.

Tess stepped back from the door. "I'll take a look at it, Mrs. Childers, but if the wound is serious, he has to see a doctor."

"Duke don't believe in doctors. And last time I sewed him up, God bless America, I ended up fainting right on the floor and had a headache that lasted all week."

"Concussions will do that to you," Tess muttered as Mrs. Childers went to the truck to retrieve her husband.

Duke Childers was even more grizzled than his wife, with big ears, an unkempt mustache, and wires of gray hair sticking out from beneath a work-worn hat of indeterminate color. A none-too-clean towel wrapped his hand. "Jes sew it up. I got work to do," he said, by way of a greeting.

"There's no need to be talkin' to missus like that." Sarah chided him as Tess fetched the first aid kit. "I apologize for my husband. He doesn't take well to bein' hurt."

"If you'd a done what I told you . . ." he grumbled.

"I'm not stitchin' you up again, Duke Childers!"

Tess directed him toward the dining table, which seemed to be turning into her general surgery table. "Have a seat, Mr. Childers."

"Name's Duke," he said. "I been settin' fence posts all my life. Damn fool thing to do."

The gash ran deep in his palm near his thumb and gushed fresh blood as Tess unwrapped it. Even if she'd had more of the same wound dressing she'd used on Eli, she wouldn't have been able to use it at that location. "This needs stitches," she said.

"God bless America, but that's why we're here," Sarah said, as if Tess had missed the point.

Tess pressed a clean gauze pad over the wound. "I'm not a doctor. I don't have any anesthesia to numb the area, and you need antibiotics."

Duke drew back his lips over crooked yellowed teeth. "It's not hard to see you ain't from around here. Up here in the mountains, we help each other out. Let's go, Sarah."

Tess knew when she was beaten, and she stopped him with a hand on his shoulder as he began to rise from the table. "This is going to hurt like hell."

He shrugged. "'Many are the afflictions of the righteous: but the Lord delivereth him out of them all.' Psalm thirty-four."

"Well, all right then." Tess reached around the sleeping baby to clean and stitch up Duke's hand. It was like sewing shoe leather, but he barely flinched.

Ian came in as she was finishing. She was irrationally angry with him for being out on one of his nature rambles while she had to deal with medical emergencies.

"You the artist fellow?" Duke said as Ian sat on the bench and pulled off his hiking boots.

Ian set his boots aside. "Ian North."

"I heard you helped out Pete Miller with his beehives."

Ian rose from the bench. "I mainly got in his way."

"Yeah, that's what he told me." Duke held his hand steady as Tess put in another stitch. "Your woman here's pretty good at doctorin', is she?"

Ian came close enough to look over Tess's shoulder. "I guess you'll be able to answer that for yourself." He must have seen enough because he quickly backed off. "I wouldn't trust her, though, if you need open heart surgery."

A good point.

Tess put in the last stitch and wrapped the wound

as Wren began to stir against her chest. "Even if you keep this clean, there's a good chance it's going to get infected without antibiotics." She stroked Wren's back. "Have you ever seen gangrene? Maybe in one of your dogs? That's what your hand's going to look like. And if you think even for a minute you can come running back here and order me to cut it off, you'd better think again, because I'll tell you to go straight to hell. Got it?"

Duke didn't seem offended. "Yes, ma'am."

Ian smiled.

Tess made Duke give her his word of honor that he'd come back in a few days to have the wound checked.

Ian regarded him sagely. "I strongly suggest you don't make her come after you. She has a mean streak."

"Mos' women do."

After Duke and Sarah left, Tess gazed down at the crumpled ten-dollar bill he'd thrust at her on their way out the door. "God bless America," she muttered.

Ian helped her clean up the mess. "If you're going to stay in Tempest long-term, you'd better either keep the door permanently locked or make yourself legal, because I have a feeling this is only going to get worse."

"It's not right! The pregnant women look at me like I'm going to hex their babies, and these people treat me like I'm the local emergency clinic. I don't want to be the village healer!"

"Then you shouldn't be so good at taking care of people. Now go get dressed. Heather's taking Wren so we can get out of here for a while."

"Taking Wren? I don't want to leave her. And going where?"

"Civilization." His gaze cut over her jeans and spit-up–stained sweater. "It's up to you, but you might want to change clothes."

She argued with him about leaving Wren, but he held firm. She begrudgingly changed into slacks, a silky white T, and a fitted blazer. Before long, they were on their way to Knoxville.

"Why there?"

"Why not?"

He was being deliberately obtuse, and they fell into silence. With each mile, the atmosphere in the car grew heavier. If it had been a normal day and they were two normal people, he would have told her where they were going, but he resisted all her attempts at conversation, and nothing about this felt normal.

By the time they'd reached a downtown parking garage, she was bitterly regretting the trip. She followed him out into the afternoon sunshine. He was walking fast, and she lengthened her stride to keep up with him, but no matter how quickly she walked, he stayed a few steps ahead.

He eventually stopped in front of an imposing redbrick building. His face was set in stone—furrowed brow, narrowed eyes, grim mouth. She read the sign.

KNOXVILLE COUNTY COURTHOUSE

"This is it, Tess." It was more a hiss than a sentence. "This is my grand gesture."

He might know what he was talking about, but she didn't. "I don't understand. What—"

He strode into the building ahead of her. She hurried after him. "Ian! Will you stop? What's this about? Why—"

"No questions!" He spun on her. "Let's get this over with so we can pretend it never happened."

"Get what over with?"

His eyes bored into her. Unflinching. She stared at him. Seconds ticked by. She didn't understand.

And then she did.

She felt as if the breath had been knocked out of her body. "Oh, Ian . . ." She grasped for air. "This— Are you sure?"

"Hell, no, I'm not sure! Do you have any other stupid questions?"

Her tongue was stuck to the roof of her mouth. She shook her head.

————

The paperwork took forever. *Birthplace. Parents. Education.* She paused as she reached the questions about marital history.

*Last Marriage Ended Date:*_____

*Last Marriage Ended Reason:*_____

Tess filled in the information with a knot in her stomach—not from the grief that had debilitated her for so long, but from the trepidation of someone stepping unprepared into the next stage of her life.

There was no waiting period, but advance appointments were required for an actual ceremony. Somehow Ian managed to coerce an officiant—possibly by threat, because he certainly didn't do it by charm—into performing the dirty deed.

The officiant was a cheery brunette who barely looked old enough to drive and who became decidedly less cheerful as the brief ceremony unfolded. Who could blame her? The grim-faced groom and robotic bride weren't exactly the embodiment of starry-eyed newlyweds. When it came time for Ian to give her a ring, he was momentarily baffled, then pulled a ballpoint pen from his pocket, picked up Tess's free hand, and drew a line around her ring finger.

As soon as it was over, Tess fled into the restroom, sealed herself in a stall, and tried to absorb the contradictions between the insanity of what they'd done, its looming complications, and the elation of knowing Wren could now be hers forever.

Unless the Dennings changed their minds.

When she came out, he was leaning against the wall, arms crossed, head down. A man defeated. She owed him everything, and all she could do was touch his arm. "What made you change your mind? Why did you do this?"

"Because you're that little demon's mother, and you're the best person to raise her, and this is for damn sure what Bianca would have wanted."

One more debt he believed he owed Bianca. A debt he'd long ago paid in full.

Chapter Fifteen

On the long, silent return trip, Tess stared at her ballpoint ink wedding ring. Her real wedding ring was sealed away in a box in her bottom dresser drawer. As she studied the smudged ink around her finger, she knew she had to stop drifting. Everything had changed. If the Dennings kept their word, Wren would be hers, and Tess would have to get her life in order. That meant finding a real job that would support the two of them, something the Broken Chimney couldn't offer.

The miles slipped by. As much as she wished otherwise, she could come up with only one solution. She had to go back to nursing. There was no other way she could provide a decent living for them.

The images from the nightmares swept through her

brain. *The blood. The helplessness.* Nursing, yes, but not midwifery. Never that. Geriatrics maybe, or dermatology. Anything that didn't involve coaxing another slippery, cone-headed, vernix-coated infant into the world. A job where she'd never again have to watch a young mother slip away.

By the time they picked up Wren at Heather's house, she'd resigned herself to the inevitable. She had no passion for either geriatrics or dermatology, but she'd do what she had to.

Heather opened the door, took one look at Tess's and Ian's stony faces, and grimaced. "Congratulations?"

Tess spun on Ian. "You told Heather what we were doing, but you didn't tell me?"

"Heather's like God," he retorted. "You can tell her anything."

Heather chided them as she handed Wren over. "Babies pick up on the energy around them. Be patient with each other."

Ian and Tess replied at the same time.

"Tell her, not me."

"I'm always patient."

Heather fingered her mala beads. "You could both benefit from a regular meditation practice."

"Especially him," Tess said.

Heather sighed.

At the schoolhouse, nothing had changed. Ian's boots still lay where he'd abandoned them. The morning's dishes remained in the sink. Tess carried Wren upstairs and managed to transfer her into the sleeping nest without waking her.

She sneaked into the bathroom. Her reflection stared back at her: dull skin, bloodshot eyes, tense jaw. She looked like hell. She tried to wash away her ballpoint wedding ring, but the ink was too stubborn.

She carried the monitor downstairs and found Ian slouched into the couch with a full tumbler of whiskey. He lifted it toward her in a mock toast. "This is it. You understand that, right? You and Wren are no longer my responsibility."

She felt an odd tenderness toward him. "Absolutely," she said. "You've done more than enough. I'll take it from here."

It was her turn to make a grand gesture. She sat next to him on the couch. *Always the seductress. Never the seduced.* She slipped one leg over his thighs and straddled him. He curled his palms around her waist. "This would be so much better if you'd stop frowning."

"I'm not frowning!" Crap. She was frowning. And he was hard. She forced her face to relax. "Better?"

"Marginally." One of his hands strayed to her hip. "But, Tess, this isn't a job."

A loud rap sounded at the door. She jumped, and he glowered. "What now?"

It was nearly ten o'clock. Too late for casual visitors. She gritted her teeth and extracted herself from his lap. "You answer and tell them I'm not a doctor!"

He stalked to the door and opened it.

"Is . . . Tess here?"

The voice was young and male. She looked over Ian's shoulder and saw four teenage boys standing on the other side. She recognized Ava's boyfriend, Connor, a good-looking, blond, athletic kid, and Imani's tall, bespectacled boyfriend, Anthony. The other two she vaguely remembered from the Broken Chimney, a slightly built kid named Noah and a redheaded giant everybody called Psycho.

Connor shoved his hand in his pockets. "Ava . . . She . . . like sent us."

Tonight? Tess had to do this tonight at the end of what was surely the longest day in history?

"It's late," Ian said.

"Could you come back maybe tomorrow?" Tess asked. "Or the next day?"

"Oh, sure . . . Yeah." They backed off so quickly she knew they'd never come back.

"Wait." They were already at the end of the walk.

Ian groaned. At the same time, he moved aside,

whispering in her ear as he let them in. "Worst idea yet."

They shuffled toward the two couches but jammed themselves into only one of them. The four of them were all gangly legs and arms they didn't seem to know what to do with. Ian was right. This would only bring her more trouble. "Do your parents know you're here? Never mind. Of course they don't."

Each of them developed a passionate interest in his feet.

She struggled between her duty and her sense of self-preservation. Duty won. Unlike the girls, this might be her only chance with these boys, and she needed a quick icebreaker. "Let's get this out of the way first. Stop worrying about your penis size, okay? Bigger isn't always better. Right, Ian?"

He came to a screeching halt in his stealthy journey toward the stairs. The grooves in his forehead grew into highway ditches. She must be punch-drunk from the day because she didn't have much trouble mustering her brightest, most chipper smile. "Bigger, smaller . . . Everyone's is different, and they all tend to work equally well, wouldn't you agree?"

"I wouldn't dream of contradicting you," he said, in a way that told he'd very much like to contradict her about a lot of things, especially her intention to draw him into this discussion.

"Could you find some paper and pencils for these guys."

"I can't think of anything I'd rather do." He didn't even try to rein in his sarcasm.

The boys would be more reticent to open up than the girls, and she needed an efficient way to cover the essentials and get them out of here. "Write down all your questions, no matter how stupid you think they might be. Disguise your handwriting if you want."

The giant who called himself Psycho snorted, but after Ian handed them paper from the kitchen grocery pad, they began scribbling. She picked up the monitor to check on Wren and heard the reassuring sound of baby snorts. She walked across the room and positioned herself between Ian and the stairs so he couldn't escape. He saw her game and bent down to whisper in her ear. "I have a couple of questions."

"I'll give you a copy of my pamphlet," she whispered back.

"That's nice of you, but . . . I was wondering . . ." His gaze was deliberately perverse. "How big is too big?"

He'd gotten the best of her, and she hurried over to collect the boys' questions.

What if your penis gets stuck?

How many inches really is too small? For real?

Is it bad if you fart when you're doing it?

How do lesbians have sex?

How many times can you jack off without being a pervert?

"Great questions, guys," she said with a straight face. "But too much for us to cover tonight, so let's start with the most important stuff." She sat on the couch across from them. "First. You don't have to do it just because you think you should or because you think everybody else is. Having sex before you're ready is a sign of immaturity. There are a thousand good reasons to wait."

"I'm ready," Connor boasted.

"Me, too," Psycho said.

"Really?" She pointed the slips of paper at them. "Then why haven't any of you asked about birth control? Or maybe you want to be teenage fathers."

That got their attention.

She began doling out the basics of birth control and STDs, along with bringing up some of the finer points the girls had mentioned including hot tubs, oral sex, and—without looking at Ian—anal sex.

Imani's Anthony leaned forward as she talked, his arms braced on his thighs. Ava's Connor slouched into the couch cushions looking sulky. Psycho seemed like he wanted to take notes, and Noah started chewing his nails.

She made another pitch for waiting to have sex, then went back to the basics. "If you ever tell a girl you don't want to use a condom because it doesn't feel good or tell her that she doesn't really love you if she makes you use one . . . If you do any of that it means you're a total asshole who only cares about himself."

With a cocky smirk, Connor splayed his arm across the back of the couch. She was developing a hearty dislike for Ava's good-looking boyfriend.

"There's something else none of you have asked me about," she said. "It's called consent."

She started to say more and then had a better idea. She turned to Ian. "Ian, maybe you could talk about this. From a man's perspective."

Instead of backing away, he came over and sat next to her. "That's easy." He shot them straight in the eyes. "'No' means 'no.' 'Maybe' also means 'no.' Let's say a girl is drunk . . . You back off. Because if she's drunk and you keep at it and she wakes up with regrets, you're going to feel like a real shit, and you also may end up in jail." Tess resisted the urge to applaud, but Ian wasn't done. "Some guys tell themselves a girl is playing hard to get, and that means they can get rough. That's called rape. Women aren't afraid to speak up, and here's the thing. . . . Walking away from a situation will make you more of a man than trying to fuck every woman you see."

Blunt and perfect.

She rose from the couch. "Would you all please talk to your parents? I know it's embarrassing, but try waiting until you're driving with them in the car. That way you won't have to look at them."

Only Psycho seemed to be considering the possibility.

As the boys unfolded from the couch, she glanced at Noah, still chewing fingernails already bitten to the quick. He alone hadn't spoken. "One more thing. We've only talked about girls tonight, but this can be a confusing time for teenagers. Maybe some of you or some of the guys you're friends with— Maybe they already know they like boys better than girls."

They hooted at that, the loudest hoot coming from Noah. Without making eye contact, she said, "Being gay or being trans isn't nearly as big a deal as it used to be, but it's still really hard for teens trying to figure everything out. If anybody wants to talk to me about it, I'm not that hard to find."

Ian poked her hard in the ribs and then shocked her by saying, "Me, either. I don't have much patience with intolerance. It makes life too small."

After she'd closed the door behind them, she sank

down on the piano stool. "All I ever wanted to do—or used to want to do—was deliver babies. Not keep them from getting born."

He picked up the slips of paper with the boys' questions and began thumbing through them. "You know there's going to be hell to pay for this, right?"

"I know."

He held up one of the paper slips and cocked his head at her. "Point of information. How many times *can* you jerk off without being a pervert?"

She laughed then rose from the piano stool as the baby monitor picked up Wren stirring. "I need to feed her."

"You do that."

The next morning, she put Wren in the sling and walked down to the cabin. After everything Ian had done, he deserved to have his privacy back, and she needed to get the cabin ready so she and Wren could move in.

The place was empty, the curtains still drawn. It was also warm. Too warm. She should send Kelly a note telling her to turn off the heat when she left.

Maybe she was making a mistake by letting this situation with Kelly go on, but right now, home invasion was the least of her problems. She was a lot more worried about her complicated relationship with Ian and her fears that the Dennings would still refuse to let Wren go. She gazed around the dim, depressing interior. No sparkling white beadboard walls and cornflower-blue paint, no shiny dark wooden floors and brimming bookshelves. Somehow she had to turn this into a real home.

She carried Wren upstairs to park her in the middle of the bed, away from the cleaning fumes, while Tess gave the bathroom a fresh scrub. But as she entered the bedroom, she froze. The bedspread was rumpled, one pillow dented, the other on the floor.

Goldilocks had been here, too.

"Damn it!" Tess stomped into the room. It was bad enough having Kelly sleeping on her couch. This was too much.

A board creaked behind her. She whirled around to see Kelly trying to sneak downstairs. "You could at least have made the bed!"

"I was . . . I was checking the property. The . . . roof used to leak." Kelly hurried down the stairs.

"Stop right there!"

Tess rushed after her, but Kelly kept moving. "This . . . this cabin has had problems over the years. It was built before World War II, so it's quite old." She hurried toward the front door, her rumpled silk blouse hanging loose from one side of her slacks. "The second floor was unfinished until—"

"I know you've been sneaking in here." Tess closed the distance between them.

Kelly faltered. "I haven't—"

"I've seen you. A week and a half ago. You were asleep on the couch."

Kelly had nearly reached the door. "I— Well, then . . . I apologize."

"I don't want an apology. I want to know why you keep showing up." She pushed in front of Kelly and saw what her intruder didn't want her to see. That she'd been crying. Her hair was flattened against the side of her head, her makeup had worn off, and her eyes were red-rimmed.

Kelly looked away. "This was my grandmother's place. I—I have happy memories of the time I spent here growing up. When I get stressed . . ." She curled her hands into fists at her sides. "It won't happen again."

Tess wrapped her arms protectively around Wren and thought of Ava and her worrisome boyfriend, Connor. Was that what had Kelly so worried, or could it be the pressure of being the wife of the town's most important citizen?

Kelly ducked around her. "I have to go."

"Wait. My shoulders are killing me. Hold Wren."

Tess took her baby from the sling and placed her in Kelly's arms. Tess's shoulders were fine, but something about the woman's vulnerability tugged at her.

Only the most callous could resist a newborn, and Kelly wasn't callous. Her arms instinctively closed around Wren, who didn't look happy with the transfer. Tess told herself this woman's pain wasn't her business—a woman she didn't even like—but butting into other people's lives seemed to be her obsession these days. Besides, it was easier to be clearheaded about other people's troubles than about her own. "I'll make some coffee. Or tea. Tea is supposed to make everything better. And I need some advice."

Kelly moved away from the door. "You want advice from me?"

Kelly would eventually hear about the boys' visit last night, so why not broach it now? Maybe it would mediate the fallout. She lifted the teapot from the stove and gestured toward the kitchen table. "You know the town a lot better than I do, and I seem to have stepped into it again."

"How?"

"Four teenagers showed up at the schoolhouse last night. Boys this time." The teakettle had a dusty film, and Tess rinsed it off at the sink. "And before you say anything—I told them to talk to their parents." One of the kitchen chairs squeaked on the floorboards as Kelly sat at the table. "They weren't having it."

"Who were they?"

"Local boys. Nice kids. Or at least three of them seemed that way." If she called out Connor by name, she'd be breaking the teens' trust. She set the teakettle on the stove and turned to the table.

Kelly held Wren to her shoulder. Tess couldn't see from here if Wren's eyes were open, but the baby didn't appear to be squirming. "If you'd been me," Tess said, "and you suspected at least one of the boys might be ready to have unprotected sex, what would you have done?"

Kelly's expression hardened. "I would have told them to stop. Teens shouldn't be having sex."

"I doubt that would have been effective." Tess couldn't keep the edge out of her voice, but Kelly was too wrapped up in her own misery to notice.

"They have no concept of how sex can ruin their lives." Kelly blinked, fighting tears. "They're too young. They think love will last forever. They don't understand the consequences. They think they know everything, but they know nothing." She lost her battle, and Tess watched the woman whom she'd disliked so thoroughly fall apart. "You have to make them understand how hard life can be. They think they're in love, but they have no concept of what love is. They don't see what a trap sex can be. How it can destroy their lives. You have to . . . They have to stop before that happens. You have to tell them."

Wren began to cry. Tess picked her up and tucked her back in the sling. Kelly buried her face in her hands, and Tess put it all together. "That's what happened to you."

"The town scandal," Kelly said bitterly.

"You were trapped."

"People still haven't forgotten. After all this time. All my charity work. The women's alliance. The school board. All of it."

"And yet you wouldn't give Ava back for anything."

Kelly swiped at her running nose with the back of her hand. "She's the most important thing in my life."

Tess handed her a tissue. Now she understood Kelly's strident support of abstinence sex education. She'd been a pregnant teenager. Tess did the math in her head. Ava was only fifteen, so Kelly was only a few years younger than Tess, although she looked older.

Kelly stared across the room. "I was the most popular girl in high school. I wasn't one of those mean girls, either. I was nice to everybody. I was happy. And then I wasn't." The mass of diamonds on her wedding band caught the light as she blew her nose. "I was home with a baby while Brad went to college. I don't want that life for my daughter. I want her to get an education and find a career so she learns how to be her own person."

"You want her to have the chances you didn't get."

Kelly's eyes clouded, as if she were far away. "I'm disappearing. Every day, I get smaller."

This wasn't what Tess had expected, but then she'd heard more than her share of strange confidences over the years.

Kelly twisted her wedding band. "Getting smaller and smaller until I'm afraid I'll wake up some morning, and I'll be so small that Brad won't even know I'm there." She pressed her fingers to her mouth and shot up from the table. "I have to go."

Despite the grief this woman had caused, Tess pitied her. "You can talk to me if you'd like. I'm the town pariah, remember? Your secrets are safe."

The teakettle whistled, and Kelly slumped back into her chair, as if she didn't have the energy to do anything else. "I don't have any secrets. Forget what I said. I'm being stupid."

"You don't sound stupid." Tess turned off the kettle and posed the question she'd been trained to ask. "Do you feel safe at home?"

"What do you mean?"

"Has your husband ever hurt you?"

Kelly's red-rimmed eyes widened. "Are you asking if Brad abuses me? God, no." She bit out the words. "Brad is perfect. I'm the one with the problem."

Tess dropped the tea bags in the mugs. "I doubt he's perfect. Not if you're afraid he'll squash you."

"I'm not afraid. I told you. I'm being stupid." She fell silent.

Tess brought the tea to the table one cup at a time, not pressing her.

Kelly gazed around the cabin. "Sometimes I imagine living here. There used to be an iron patio set in the back, a little table and two chairs. My grandmother and I had tea parties. She . . . She made me feel like the most important person in the world." Her eyes lost their focus, as if she'd drifted far away. "I imagine Ava coming to visit me here. And Brad . . . Brad standing outside the window. Not able to get in." Her hand flew to her mouth. "I—I can't believe I said that. I must be insane."

"Not insane. Just unhappy."

"I have no reason to be unhappy. I have everything I could ever want. Everything!" She crushed the damp tissue in her hand. "It's only that . . . He's so big. Everything about him. His voice. His appetite. His ambition. He sucks all the oxygen out of the house until I can't breathe!" Her eyes widened with alarm. "I don't know what I'm saying. He's a good husband. A good father. He gives me anything I want. He *loves* me."

Tess settled at the table, saying nothing.

Kelly curled her hands around the warm mug. "It's . . . exhausting."

"Have you thought about talking with someone?" Tess said gently.

"What do you mean?"

"You're dealing with a lot. A counselor might help."

"I don't need a therapist! God, no. Brad would be so hurt."

Tess cocked her head, speaking softly. "Then how are you going to fix this?"

"I don't need to fix anything! I'm fine. In a mood, that's all." She pushed the mug aside and rose. "I'm sorry you had to listen to this."

"It can help having someone to talk to." Tess hesitated, then gave in to her do-gooder instincts and found a scratch pad from the clinic where she'd worked. She wrote her name and cell number. "I can't always get a signal, so I don't know how useful this is." She held out the paper. "If you need to talk . . ."

"I'm sure I'll be fine," Kelly said, even as she stuck the note in her purse.

Tess didn't want to say it, but she had to. "You're welcome to use the cabin whenever you need to get away."

"Really? You'd let me do that?"

"Sure."

"Thank you." Kelly fiddled with the clasp on her purse. "If anybody found out what I've said . . . I'd appreciate it if you kept this conversation to yourself."

"Tell that to Wren. She's the blabbermouth."

Kelly managed her first smile. "Thanks."

Kelly had just left by the front door when the back door opened and Ian came in. So strong and steady. So decent. Beneath that hard-bitten exterior, the most honorable man she'd ever known. He gestured toward the front windows. "Is it my imagination or did I see Kelly Winchester heading down the trail toward town?"

"Not your imagination. She's my new bestie."

"How did that happen?"

"The magic of my personality."

"Why do I think there's more to the story?"

"Because you're more perceptive than you like to let on. What are you doing down here?"

"Checking up on you. The next time you decide to disappear, leave a note."

"Why?"

"Because you're hauling around a six-week-old baby!"

She was glad he didn't know about the nasty messages on her car.

As he wandered toward the fireplace and bent over to look up the flue, she curled her toes in her sneakers. She had something she needed to get out of the way before she let another hour pass. "Wren's asleep," she said. "Let's go upstairs and get this marriage thing off the ground."

Chapter Sixteen

Ian straightened from the fireplace and gave her his patented half-lidded glare. "I don't like your attitude."

"My attitude?"

"'Getting this marriage thing off the ground.' It makes it sound like a job on your To Do list."

Maybe it was. Once this was behind them, she might be able to relax again. "You want to be seduced? I can do that."

"And do it very well, I'm sure." He propped an elbow on the roughly hewn fireplace mantel. "As you've told me several times."

This wasn't going the way it should. She felt as clumsy as one of the teenagers who kept showing up at the door. "I'm not sure what you want."

"I know you aren't." He crossed his ankles, his smile bordering on smug.

He'd unbalanced her, and she didn't like it. "Do you want to do it or don't you?"

"There it is again. That vicious frown of yours."

"That's it!" She stomped toward the stairs. "I'm done with whatever game this is. If you want me, come get me. Otherwise, you can go to hell!"

He watched her—the luscious Widow Hartsong— storm upstairs. She was furious with him, and he was furious with himself. From the day they'd met, he'd wanted her. And here she was—all ready to give herself over, and what did he do? He put the brakes on. Not once, but *twice*! Any other man would have gone ahead with it, but not him. Why? Because he was an oversensitive asshole, that's why.

But he didn't want sex to be one more *responsibility* she had to undertake, like all the rest of the responsibilities she'd assumed. For Wren, for the teens, apparently for Kelly Winchester. And now for fucking him.

Overhead, he heard Wren start to wail. And wasn't that perfect? A howling baby, teenagers banging at the door, people bleeding all over his dining room table, and topping it off, he was now something he'd never remotely imagined. A married man. Tempest hadn't been a refuge for him. It had been a goddamn disaster!

He followed her upstairs and entered the closest of the two bedrooms. This one had a slanted ceiling, a pair of windows, peeling floral wallpaper, and minimal furniture: a bed, nightstand, and chest of drawers. Tess was walking Wren around the room. He spoke over the baby's wails. "The Dennings are stopping by soon. They want to set eyes on the happy newlyweds."

Tess's anger faded into worry. "You've talked to them?"

"Earlier this morning. Diane feels marginally guilty for pushing us to get married so quickly, but I think they're both relieved not to have full-time responsibility for Wren."

"They're really going to let me keep her?"

"It looks that way."

"What about Wren's father? He could change his mind."

Wren cried louder.

"They seem certain that won't happen. It'll take a while to make everything official, but as long as you guarantee them reasonable visitation privileges, I don't think they'll stand in your way."

While she was trying to absorb that, he dipped into his pocket and pulled something out. "You're going to need this." As he opened his palm she saw a ring. A little over a quarter of an inch wide, it was handmade from what looked like copper electrical wire. "I didn't have much to work with, but you need something to wear in front of them."

He'd looped and braided the wire, creating intricate spirals and unexpected twists. It was exquisite. The work of an artist.

"It's beautiful." She took it from him and only hesitated for a moment before she slipped it on the same finger where she'd once worn a thin platinum band. The ring was light on her hand, with every rough edge smoothed. "This is costing you a fortune."

"I found the wire in the toolshed out back."

"Not the ring." She shifted Wren in her arms, still trying to calm her. "The lawyers. Everything."

"Forget about it. Otherwise, you'll start tallying up how much more time you have to spend on your back servicing me."

Her eyes flashed thirteen different kinds of fireworks. "What am I supposed to do, Ian? Tell me. I owe you everything! How am I supposed to repay that?"

"First step . . . Stop being so annoying!" He strode toward her. "Now give me that baby. You're getting her all riled up again." He snatched the wailing little hellcat from her and headed for the stairs.

"Where are you going?" Tess cried as he reached the bottom step. "Wait for me!"

He looked down at Wren, who had abruptly stopped crying. "Your mother is only crazy part of the time. You'll probably be fine."

The meeting with the Dennings went better than Tess could have hoped. By the time they left, she and Diane were both in tears, and Tess had promised herself she'd make certain Wren had the relationship with them they all deserved. The baby was nearly hers.

She slipped her finger inside Wren's curled hand. The puffiness of the baby's eyelids had disappeared, and the tiny white milia around her nose were gone. The flood of love rushing through Tess was like a river whose current moved so swiftly it dislodged all the debris that had accumulated beneath its surface. Runaway Mountain had given her a new life. Despite the hostility of the town and the memory of the awful night she'd lost Bianca, she wanted to stay here. To watch Wren grow up in the mountain's sunlight and shade. The sweet weight of this child in her arms, the child she was now responsible for . . . This was her new life.

Ian had gone outside to work on his tree house studio, a project that seemed to be coming along more successfully than his artwork. Every fierce blow of his hammer echoed inside the house. She hoped he got rid of his aggression before she had to talk to him again.

She went to work that day with her copper wire wedding band tucked in her pocket. Savannah ignored her, and Tess resisted commenting on her co-worker's edema-swollen feet or the fact that she looked as though she'd been crying.

The after-school crowd arrived. Tess recognized Psycho, Jordan, and Noah. Ava was with Connor, and Tess hated the proprietary way he draped his arm across her shoulders, as if she were his personal coat rack. Noah and Psycho avoided looking at Tess, but Connor gave her a cocky smirk.

As soon as she had a break, she dashed into the back room and grabbed an old piece of poster board and a black marker. On the cleanest side of the poster board, she wrote her message:

COMMUNITY MEETING!

HOW TO TALK TO YOUR TEENAGER ABOUT SEX

She added a date the following week, noted the time beneath it—8:00 P.M.—and the location, the Broken Chimney.

Phish was stationed behind the ice cream freezer

when she came out. She marched past him and taped the poster by the front door.

"What the hey-ll, Tess?!" he exclaimed. "Take that down!"

She stalked over to him and leaned close enough so only he could hear. "Do not touch that sign. If it comes down, I'll tell the whole town that you're dealing weed out of the back room."

He looked hurt. "Sharing my stash with friends is not dealing."

"You heard me. I'm done playing nice." She stomped toward the door.

"You were never that nice to begin with!" he called after her.

She flipped him the bird and went to get her daughter.

Wren's bath the next morning wore her out, and Ian semivolunteered to watch her during Tess's short, two-hour work shift. "As long as you bring me doughnuts."

"Done."

Phish was in a foul mood. "Damn Internet squatters. They think one cup of coffee means they can hog my WiFi all day. And if they're not doin' that, they're yelling about politics or givin' me a hard time because I don't have any gol-damn gluten-free doughnuts. What the hey-ll, Tess?"

"Life sucks." She gave him a quick peck on the cheek to make up for yesterday.

Courtney Hoover came in right before Tess's shift ended. After she'd taken a selfie licking the rim of one of their coffee mugs, she wandered over to the counter. "What are you doing in town, Tess? I thought you'd be on your honeymoon."

Phish turned from the espresso machine. "What honeymoon?"

"Didn't you hear, Phish? Tess got married. To the artist. The one whose wife died in March having their baby."

Courtney's smugness made Tess see red. "Is your life really so small that you don't have anything better to do than gossip about mine?"

Courtney wasn't daunted. "It's amazing, Tess, how you can keep holdin' your head up."

"And without taking a single photo of myself doing it!" Tess stormed out.

Her husband and baby were both missing when she got back to the schoolhouse. Daffodils had poked through the weeds in the neglected front garden, and a robin carried a few blades of dried grass to the curve in the drainpipe where she was building a nest. Tess brushed off the bench and sat. Regardless of Courtney's spite, the community's suspicion, and her co-workers' bitchiness, Tess felt at home on Runaway Mountain. She imagined Wren racing through the trees with a bandaged knee and dirty face. She saw Wren's bedroom windowsill cluttered with rocks and dusty bird feathers. Wren coming out of the woods, riding on the shoulders of a father who could point out animal scat and—

She jerked herself upright. There would be no father.

As if she'd conjured him, Ian emerged from the trail. He should have looked ridiculous with Wren in the sling across his chest, but he wore it like a bandolier ammo belt. The baby was wide-awake and content as he approached Tess. "I had a helluva time keeping her from chomping on the poison ivy and petting the bears, but she's a good hiker."

If Tess didn't know how much he'd hate it, she would have thrown her arms around him and told him he was the best man she'd ever known. Instead, she straightened Wren's crooked cap. "I have bad news. I forgot your doughnuts."

"That's it! We need to have a serious conversation about gender roles. I'll bring home the animal carcass. You're supposed to bring home the doughnuts."

"Noted."

His eyes narrowed with suspicion. "It's not like Phish to run low on doughnuts."

She resumed fussing with Wren's cap. "I might have forgotten them when I stormed out."

"Let me guess. One of your many enemies."

"Savannah and Michelle practically make the sign of the cross in front of their pregnant bellies when I'm nearby, but this time it was Courtney Hoover broadcasting to the whole town that we're married. She made a point of reminding everyone that your *wife* died less than two months ago, implying that I might have murdered her."

He winced. "How did she find out we were married?"

"Not from Heather. The Dennings probably mentioned it to Fiona Lester at the Purple Periwinkle. Fiona has a reputation as the town gossip. One of many gossips, I might add."

"People need to mind their own damned business."

"Small towns don't seem to work that way."

She tried to make up for the missing doughnuts by baking a chocolate sheet cake while Wren dozed in the sling. After she put the cake in the oven, she went outside to dig in the garden and try to work up some enthusiasm for job hunting. The idea was so depressing that she lost track of time, and when she returned to the house, she was greeted with a burning stench and the sight of Ian's lean, jeans-clad butt bent over the open oven door.

"Maybe you should be the one bringing home the animal carcass," he said as he pulled out the charred sheet cake.

"Sorry."

"I saw the sign you put up in the Broken Chimney. That meeting you're planning. You can't seem to keep your opinions to yourself, can you?"

She thought of Connor's smirk and the way his fingers coiled around Ava's shoulders. "I'm doing what I have to."

He dumped the cake in the trash. "People are stirred up about you. Cancel the meeting, Tess, and give everybody time to find somebody else to gossip about." He set the dirty pan on top of the stove and regarded her with what looked like concern. "Tempest is an insular town. You know that. All they welcome from outsiders is our cash. It's not our job to barge in here and tell them how to live their lives."

"It's my job, and they need to listen." She sounded self-important and judgmental, but she didn't care.

He leaned against the counter. "I talked to Freddy Davis. He tried to give me the same crap he gave you."

"I'd like to have seen that."

"The point is, somebody's got it in for you."

She reached past him to carry the empty pan to the sink and turn on the water. "Brad Winchester leaps to mind."

"He leaps to my mind, too." He snagged his thumb in the waistband of his jeans. "You say you're thinking about staying here."

"I'm not thinking about it. I'm doing it." Wren wheezed in her sleep. "I'll have to get a nursing job. Dermatology, maybe. Or geriatrics."

He frowned. "You're a midwife, Tess. What are you talking about?"

"How can you say that?" She felt betrayed. "You, more than anyone, know why I can't deliver another baby!"

A series of demanding knocks at the door interrupted them. He stalked out of the kitchen. "We're putting a whole basket of condoms on that front porch right now. With a big sign that says, 'Take as many as you want and go away.'"

But instead of teenagers demanding entry, Eli stood outside the door. "It's my mom. I'm real worried, Tess. She won't get out of bed."

Ian refused to let her go by herself, but he stayed outside with Wren and Eli. Rebecca Eldridge lay curled on her side, knees drawn up, her long hair stringy on the pillow. There was no sign of Paul.

The bedroom was sparsely furnished: a mattress and box springs on the floor, a bare window, an old chest of drawers, and a straight-back chair with chipped green paint. Instead of a closet, a metal coatrack held their hanging clothes.

"Rebecca, it's Tess Hartsong." Tess pulled the chair to the side of the bed.

Rebecca's eyes fluttered. "Tess?"

"How are you feeling?"

"Tired." Rebecca rolled to her back. A few strands of hair stuck to her pillow-creased cheek, and she had the stale smell of someone who hadn't bathed in a few days. "What are you doing here?"

"Eli's worried about you."

"Did he bother you?" she said listlessly. "I told him not to bother you. I'm tired, that's all."

Tess touched her forehead. It was cool. "How long have you been in bed?"

"Not long. A day or two."

Three days according to Eli. "Have you had anything to eat?"

"I'm not hungry."

She smoothed Rebecca's hair back from her face. "Do you want to tell me about it?"

Rebecca managed a halfhearted shrug. "Women lose babies. Life happens." A tear trickled from the corner of her eye.

"I'm sorry." Tess knew too well how inadequate those words were.

"It was a girl. Paul says I couldn't know that, but I do. I know it was a girl."

"And you wanted her very much."

"More than anything. But Paul says it was meant to be. How does he know that?"

"He doesn't."

"It's my fault!"

"Rebecca, it wasn't your fault."

"You don't know that. Paul needed help clearing rocks in the field. I should have told him no, but you can't tell him anything. I shouldn't have done it. I should have been more careful."

"You didn't do anything wrong. The majority of miscarriages are the result of chromosomal problems. I'm sure your doctor told you that."

"I only saw him once." Rebecca turned her face into the pillow.

Tess wasn't a therapist, and she didn't know how to

help her, but Rebecca needed help. "Let me fix you something to eat."

"I'm not hungry."

"I understand. But I'll fix you something anyway."

She overcame Rebecca's weak protests and got her out of bed. Rubbing her back, she led her to the kitchen table. As she scrambled some eggs, she could see Eli through the window, showing off the chickens to Ian and Wren.

Rebecca had just taken a small forkful of eggs when Paul appeared. Half-moons of sweat stained the armpits of his long-sleeve work shirt, and dirt clung to the cuffs of his jeans. Ignoring his wife, he addressed Tess. "You didn't need to come up here. Eli and I are going to have a talk."

"It's no problem. Sometimes a woman needs another woman."

Paul pulled off his orange work gloves. "It's been three months now. She needs to get over it."

"That's what people kept telling me after my husband died." She remembered how Paul had shown up to help Ian with the tree house studio and wished she hadn't spoken quite so sharply. "Unfortunately, grief seems to have its own timetable. She needs to see a doctor."

"She needs to keep busy," he retorted, before he

turned to his wife. "'Becca, you stay out of that bed. You're worrying Eli, and it's not good for you."

More than Eli's worrying wasn't good for her. Rebecca needed follow-up care, something her husband refused to recognize.

When they got back to the schoolhouse, two strangers waited on the front step—Abby Winzler, who turned out to be a friend of Sarah Childers, had a broken finger, and her survivalist husband, Chet, was plagued with a bad headache that Tess immediately suspected came from a concussion. On Tess's orders, Ian strongarmed a belligerent Chet into his Land Cruiser and drove him to the hospital. Tess splinted Abby's finger as best as she could and received two quarts of last summer's peaches in return, along with a troubling list of Abby's other ailments, all of them untreated.

There were so many women around here like Abby and Rebecca. Too poor, too remote, or too suspicious of doctors to get decent medical care. They had no place to go for advice on menstrual problems or breast health, no one to talk to about depression, heart disease, osteoporosis. Prenatal and postnatal care seemed to be virtually nonexistent.

All the care she'd been trained to provide.

She couldn't do it. Not with Bianca's screams echoing in her head. Someone else would have to step up. This wasn't her responsibility.

Ian texted that the hospital was keeping Chet for overnight observation, and Ian intended to stay in Knoxville so he could bring Chet home tomorrow.

Her mood sank even lower. Something told her Ian's generosity had more to do with avoiding her than with transporting Chet.

Chapter Seventeen

When Tess got back to the schoolhouse the next evening from the cabin, she found Ian polishing off a beer. "The next time one of these old mountain goats shows up, you're on your own."

She eased Wren out of the sling. "I gather you and Chet didn't bond."

"He doesn't believe we put a man on the moon, and he thinks aircraft contrails are really poisonous toxins secretly spread by some kind of alien forces. Don't ask me why."

A car pulled up outside.

He regarded her accusingly. "I swear to God, I'm painting office hours on the front door."

But it was Heather, and she came bearing gifts. "I hope you haven't eaten yet, because I've brought take-out from The Rooster." Her long earrings brushed her cheeks as she set the bulging carryout sack on the floor. "Also, my very own homemade carob quinoa wedding cake with avocado frosting. Kidding! Sara Lee. It's a belated wedding present. I'm disorganized." She flipped her loose braid over her shoulder. "And that's not all. Pack up, Miss Contrary. You're having a sleepover at Auntie Heather's house."

"Heather, you don't have to. . . ."

"A wedding present. Now time's a wastin'. Wren's favorite male stripper is due to show up at my house any minute now."

Tess smiled, but the last thing she wanted was time alone with Ian. Heather, however, was an unstoppable force, and she soon had Wren and a bulging diaper bag loaded up.

"Grab a blanket," Ian said as Heather drove off. "I'll get the wine."

"Blanket?"

"I don't want to stay inside."

He had the tree house in mind. A sturdy platform with a skeleton frame stood about ten feet off the ground. He climbed the ladder first with the food and wine, then reached down to take the blanket from her. When she got to the top, she spread out the blanket and sat on it cross-legged, using the view as an excuse not to look at him.

It was the golden hour right before sunset. A wash of honeyed light glazed the trees and softened the edges of the rocky outcrops. He handed her wine in a plastic cup, poured some for himself, and sat next to her. His arm brushed hers.

"I like your tree house," she said.

"Studio," he clarified.

"Uhm."

He rested his wineglass on his thigh. "You don't think I'll work here?"

"Of course you will."

She'd replied too quickly, and he frowned. "I will. Once I have some peace and quiet."

"It won't be long." She gazed out at the land—the trees and crags, ridges and valleys. "Wren and I should be resettled at the cabin in the next day or two."

"Then what'll my excuse be?"

His brutal honesty touched her. "You're finding your way. Those beautiful drawings of Wren . . ."

"And of you," he said scornfully. "Sketches like that are a dime a dozen."

"You're the authority, so I suppose you're right. But I love them."

The sun slipped behind the hills. Straws of pastel light reached into clouds that looked as if they'd been splashed by Easter egg dyes. The back of his hand brushed her neck as he picked up a long lock of her hair. It curled around his finger, and gooseflesh pebbled her skin. She took in his fierce nose and graven jaw; the whittled lines of his cheekbones; those enigmatic eyes. This was a face that had learned at a painfully early age to obscure its emotions. The face of a man who would only give up his secrets with his artist's tools.

What was he seeing when he looked at her? Was he seeing the smudges under her eyes from worry and interrupted sleep? Was he seeing how ordinary she was?

He kissed her. The lightest brush of his lips on hers. He drew back and gazed into her eyes. "Say 'stop' whenever you need to."

"Go," she heard herself whisper.

"Don't let me rush you."

He couldn't rush something she'd been waiting so long to enjoy.

He kissed her again. A deeper kiss. His fingers eased into her hair. His tongue slipped through her parted lips. He explored, taking his time, sending her into a slow frenzy. His big hands moved to her shoulders, down her back, drew her closer until her breasts pressed into his chest. It was only a kiss. Just a kiss. And yet she thought she would expire from it.

She needed to take over. To do her job as she was meant to. To repay him. And she would. Any second now. As soon as this kiss ended. But for this moment, she would enjoy.

The moment ended as he rolled them both to the floor of the platform. He angled his body under hers and pulled her over him as if she weighed nothing. It was a position she knew all too well. Forever on top. She straddled him, ready to take charge. She owed him everything, and she had to do this right. What would he like the most?

He liked kissing. She could definitely do that.

Her hair made a private curtain around their faces as she leaned forward and touched her lips to his. He liked deep kisses, but she didn't have much practice using her tongue. Thank god she'd only had wine and no cheese. Cheese mouth would be disgusting.

How deep should she go? Not far, or she might choke him. But she didn't want it to feel like a dental exam, either.

Trying to do everything perfectly had cooled the fire that had been burning inside her to ash. She needed to stop thinking so much and rely on her instincts to restoke that fire. But her instincts wanted her to get off him, climb down the ladder, and hurry to the house in a haze of disappointment.

He spoke against her barely parted lips. "Where are you?"

She pulled her head back. "What do you mean? I'm right here."

"Are you?"

She reared back on his hips. "Are you going to critique me?"

He smiled, but she wanted to cry. She scrambled off him, determined to get to the ladder before she completely humiliated herself. He reached up and caught her by her wrist. "Hold on."

"Let go," she said.

He didn't.

"I told you to let go!"

He came to his knees, still clasping her wrist. "I will. I promise. But can you give me thirty seconds leeway?"

"To do what?"

"I don't know. Mess around. Tell a knock-knock joke. Do my Thomas Edison imitation." He released her wrist. "I need to think about it."

Her urge to cry disappeared, but she refused to let herself smile. "Nobody does a Thomas Edison imitation, and your thirty seconds are already up."

He looked offended. "It's my understanding that the timer doesn't start ticking until I'm done thinking."

The heaviness in her chest had disappeared, and she managed a surly growl. "I guess."

"Great." He sat back on the blanket, one leg extended, the other knee bent, and pretended to go into deep thought only to shake his head. "This isn't working. I need some inspiration. Would you mind taking off your shirt while I think? No harm in that, right?"

Where was the grim-faced stranger she knew so well? This man seemed to have given up hiding behind grunts and snarls. Was she going to play his game? She was.

"I s'pose not." She went to her knees at the edge of the blanket and crossed her arms over her chest. "You might want to prepare yourself. I'm not wearing my sexy bra." She pulled her shirt over her head to reveal a plain white underwire with an edge of limp lace spilling over the tops of her breasts.

He regarded her bra so uncritically. "That's a problem for sure. How am I supposed to get turned on when you're not wearing your sexy bra?" His gaze didn't wander from her breasts. "Before you answer that, I need to know— Are you wearing your sexy panties?"

"I don't remember which underpants I put on this morning," she said primly, "but I'm pretty sure they're not my sexy ones."

"See, that's the thing. Sexy is in the eye of the beholder."

"Is that so?"

"I'm surprised you don't know that," he said oh-so-earnestly. "What you have to do now is take off your jeans so I can give you my impartial opinion. Unless you think I might hurt your feelings."

Laughter and arousal formed a deliciously melting jumble inside her. She came to her feet. "I'll risk it." Her hands flicked open the snap on her jeans and went to the zipper tab.

"Hold on. You're not doing that right."

"I'm not unfastening my jeans right? You've got to be kidding me."

"I told you this might hurt your feelings, but I'm kind of shocked that an experienced nurse like yourself doesn't know about the injuries a person can get from a zipper."

"Really? I had no idea."

"I can see that. Medical professionals like yourself should know more of the basic safety rules."

"Such as?"

"Such as . . . It's better for men to take over unzipping. Our fingers are stronger."

Could this be happening? Could sex with Ian North be both hot and fun? She pretended to think it over. "I suppose you have a point."

"I'm very intelligent." He went to his knees in front of her, slipped the tips of his fingers inside her waistband, and tugged on the zipper tag. But he pulled it down only halfway before he paused to trace his fingers across the fleshy curve of her abdomen. She automatically tightened it and then thought *what-the-hell* and let it go.

He pressed his lips to the V of skin he'd exposed. His mouth trailed lower, right along with the zipper, until he arrived at the top edge of her underpants. He nuzzled there, his breath warm on her skin. "Now this," he whispered, "is what I call a good time."

And she'd done nothing. Nothing except stand here with knees that were starting to wobble.

He took her jeans lower. To her knees. His hands slipped around her thighs.

She'd lied about her underpants. These were a cheeky little lavender number a friend had given her in hopes of cheering her up. And by cheeky, she meant . . . exposed cheeks.

Which Ian North had already discovered. "You lied." He held her bare bottom in his palms. "These might be the most glorious pair of panties a man could ever hope to see."

He nuzzled again.

Her knees weren't going to hold her up much longer. Maybe he felt them tremble because he clasped her wrists and drew her to the blanket. Within seconds, her sandals were gone and so were her jeans. She lay before him in her serviceable bra and enticing underpants. He knelt above her, his head and shoulders outlined against a melted gummy bears sky.

Despite the ferocious bulge in the front of his jeans, he didn't seem in any hurry.

"Don't take this as a criticism," he said, "but it's a shame about that bra of yours. Maybe I should take it off."

She came up on one elbow. "I could do it. Or is that another safety hazard?"

"You're a fast learner. It's one of the qualities I most appreciate about you."

She was going to incinerate, and she wasn't even naked. "Dangerous bra clasps?"

"Sends women to the ER all the time." He nuzzled her shoulder with his lips as he reached around her back. "But not this woman." He unclasped the bra and freed her breasts.

He gazed at her. Took her in. Seeing the details. The shape of her nipples, the fact that one of her breasts was a bit larger than the other. He pressed gently on her shoulders, sending her back on the blanket. "It's a crime against humanity," he murmured, "to keep these covered up."

His words— His gaze— She'd never felt more abundant in her womanhood. He cupped her, his breath warm against her skin, taking in the slope of her breasts, their weight, celebrating her body. He brushed his jaw lightly over one nipple, gently chafing it. And then the other. Her back arched. She had to make him stop before she climaxed. "Get rid of the shirt."

He did. Taking all the time in the world. Acting as if undoing each button required all his concentration. But when she rose on her knees to make short work of what should have been an easy task, he stilled her hands.

And that's when she understood. She was being seduced.

She, Tess Hartsong, the Queen of Seduction, was now the object of an exquisite, calculated, over-the-top . . . seduction.

With his shirt finally off, his jeans unsnapped but still in place, he propped himself next to her and explored her body. He returned to her breasts. At first his hands and then his mouth. Doing the most delicious things to her, making her writhe beneath him even as her silly lavender underpants stayed firmly in place. She couldn't hold back her entreaties.

"Please . . . Please . . ."

He touched her stomach. Touched her through the lace of her underpants. The lightest brush. And that was enough.

Her neck arched. Her body went rigid. She soared, flew through the air, suspended in space, and finally shattered.

Seconds, hours, days passed before she could settle back to earth even as the sky spun above her. This was the second time he'd done this to her, and she hadn't done a thing to reciprocate.

He leaned back on his heels. "More wine?"

She shot up onto her elbows, nearly screaming at him. "What are you doing? How can you be so . . . *detached*?"

"Detached?" His eyes shot thunderbolts. "Ever since I met you, I've been living with a permanent hard-on. Watching you sashay around . . ."

"I don't sashay."

"Seeing those glorious breasts of yours. That beautiful ass. Even the back of your neck. And all the while, you've been oblivious. Now, babe," he said with a growl. "It's payback time."

"Payback?"

"Think of it as well-deserved retribution."

The way he said that word. The delicious menace thrilled her. "I'm sorry." She wasn't, but she loved how meek she sounded. No longer the seducer . . .

"You're going to be even sorrier." He jammed his hand in his jeans pocket, pulled out one of those condoms he carried around, and slapped it down on the platform in a way that told her exactly how serious he was. In one swift motion, his jeans came off along with the silky boxers she'd seen in his drawer. She was hardly a stranger to the male anatomy, but this . . . This was . . . "I don't think . . ." she said. "I'm ready for all that."

"Tough," he said, "because you're going to take it."

She shivered. This was a whole new game, and she was more than ready to play it. "I— I'm not ready." The world's biggest lie.

He lowered himself next to her. "I'll see about that." And he did.

He explored her. Delving. Testing. Her underpants gone. His expression fierce and his touch perfect. How did he know this was what she'd craved in her fever dreams?

She shattered again, even before he entered her, but it was his turn now. He thrust deep. She stretched. He arched. Drove. Again and again. Erupted.

Sated and smiling, she held him through the aftershocks, feeling his scars, wanting to kiss away each one. He finally rolled over. "That"—he groaned—"was a total failure."

"Very disappointing."

"There's only one thing to do."

"Try again?"

"I'm afraid so. But first . . ." He poured more wine.

They sipped, sitting naked on the blanket in the darkness, barely talking. Eventually, they fell back on the blanket, and this time it was even better.

Afterward, they lay on their backs. She stretched and said the only thing she could think of that made sense. "Can we eat now?"

"A woman after my own heart."

But she wasn't. No matter how satisfying this had been, his heart was safely entombed in the sturdy wall that had protected it for so very long.

The night had grown chilly, and they went back to the house. It seemed natural for him to return to his old bedroom, to lie down with her. Make love again. And then again.

Eventually, she heard the deep, even sound of his breathing, but she couldn't sleep. She was thirty-five years old, and until now, she'd been with only one man.

Ian didn't stir as she slipped from the bed and curled into the chair by the window. She stretched her feet onto the ottoman and tried to unknot her tangled thoughts. The intimacy of sleeping together made her feel exposed and defenseless, but defenseless against what?

Against this surge of emotion . . . This swelling in her heart . . . This yearning for more than sex. For . . .

Stop! She couldn't go there. Ian's emotional boundaries were set in stone, and she needed to be equally firm with her own. Love had almost destroyed her once. That would never happen again.

She awakened at dawn with a stiff neck and a few other sore places that had nothing to do with spending the night in the chair. She sneaked into the bathroom for a shower. When she came out wrapped in a towel, he was still in bed, but awake. The hair on one side of his head stood up in crisp peaks, and the snowy white pillows deepened his tan. "You're up early."

"I want to see Wren before I go to work."

"Missing her?"

"I can't help it." Wren was perfectly safe with Heather. Sending her off last night hadn't been anything like the night the Dennings had taken her. But Tess's arms felt empty.

He cocked his elbow behind his head, exposing the white scar on his arm, and giving her a scruffy, sexy, half-lidded once-over. "How 'bout dropping that towel."

She was tempted. Too tempted. "I would, but then you'll think I'm easy."

He laughed, got out of bed, and walked naked across the room. His body was strong and rangy, with long ligaments instead of bulky muscles. He was lean where she was curved. His scars were dramatic, while hers came from nothing more notable than a childhood tumble off her skateboard.

He knew she was looking at him, but he merely smiled and disappeared into the bathroom, leaving her alone with the messy stew of her thoughts.

He stepped into the shower before it warmed up. He needed the shock of cold water. Otherwise, he'd go right back in the bedroom and change her mind, something he doubted would take much work.

He'd never been with a woman like her. A lover so over-the-top sexy, so imaginative, so raunchy and seductive. As the water grew hot, he used his index finger to draw a naked silhouette in the steam on the shower door. The curve of a thigh, the bow of a breast.

He wiped out what he'd drawn and turned his face into the spray. He wouldn't hurt her for the world. He'd give her the sex they both craved. The fun and smut of it. But he'd also guard her in a way she wouldn't guard herself. For all her toughness, Tess Hartsong was a woman who offered her heart too freely. The worst thing she could do would be to give it away to a man who couldn't treasure it.

He intended to make very sure that didn't happen.

Chapter Eighteen

When her afternoon shift was over, Tess Face-Timed the Dennings from Heather's house, where the signal was stronger. She held Wren up so they could see her. "See. Her neck is already stronger."

"It is! Look, Jeff. She's getting so big!"

They admired Wren from all angles and applauded when Wren showed off her cutest sneeze. As the call ended, Tess thought about how these people who had been such threatening strangers only a few weeks ago would now be an ongoing part of her life. She was surprised at how right that felt.

She transferred a few more of their things down to the cabin. Even though she'd freshened up the place, it still felt musty and cramped. She'd miss the state-of-the-art kitchen appliances, the comfortable furniture, and those big, uncurtained windows.

"I promise, sweetheart"—she kissed the top of Wren's downy head—"I'll have this place fixed up for us in no time."

As dusk fell, she fed Wren and made a sandwich for herself with food she'd taken from the schoolhouse. Without the home deliveries Ian paid for, grocery shopping was going to be difficult and expensive.

Ian came through the back door. He took in the laundry basket she'd packed with some of Wren's disposable diapers, formula, and other supplies. "I can't believe you're moving down here. Look at this place."

"Nothing a little paint won't fix." She gestured toward the dingy walls. "You're welcome to have at it. Maybe a creamy off-white."

"I'm a famous artist. You can't afford me."

She started to make a crack about offering a sex discount, but stopped herself. She should pay him. "You need your space back."

"This isn't the city. It's too isolated up here."

"If you get scared in the dark, pull the bell rope. Wren and I'll come running."

"Not funny."

She peered down at Wren. "We think we're pretty funny, don't we, love?"

Wren huffed and batted an arm.

"I'm serious, Tess. This place is a shack. And Wren is too young for you to stay here on your own."

"I'm going to fix it up."

"I don't see what the rush is."

"I'll buy you an air horn."

"Give me that kid! You're bouncing her around like she's a tennis ball." Before she could protest, he had Wren out of her sling and cradled in his arms. "If you want her back, come and get her!"

He stormed out the door with her child and some serious attitude.

She turned on all the lights and went upstairs to put away some of Wren's things. The cabin creaked in an unfamiliar way. Had it always made these sounds? All she could remember from her first weeks here was her misery. She gazed around the bedroom at the peeling wallpaper and dim corners. She was no more isolated here than at the schoolhouse, but she was uneasy in a way she hadn't been. Not exactly spooked—the cabin windows had curtains—but jittery in a way she didn't like.

She should enjoy these moments of respite before she retrieved her daughter, but she was too restless to read and in no mood for more chores. A few months ago, she would have turned on her music and danced, but she'd lost the desire. What she wanted to do now was talk to Ian over a glass of wine. Or—who was she kidding?—make love with him again. She shivered at the reminder of what had happened in the tree house.

It wasn't so much the schoolhouse she would miss as it was simply being with Ian. She stepped out on the front porch, bringing a fog of depression along for companionship. The evening was cool, and she needed a jacket, but she didn't bother going back inside to get one. A moth banged futilely against the single light-bulb screwed into the cracked porcelain wall base. She wanted a real light fixture and a porch swing where she and Wren could talk. A pair of comfy couches and a cozy reading chair. A spruced-up kitchen . . . and a room painted like the inside of a geode.

She jumped as something large moved in the woods. A stick splintered, and a man came out of the shadows. She took an instinctive step backward and bumped against the log wall.

"Alone for a change?" he said.

She'd forgotten how big and bulky Brad Winchester was. Wide chest, thick waist, heavy arms . . . "What do you want?"

He moved into the edges of the dim, yellow porch

light. He wore a lightweight jacket, dark slacks, and a threatening air. Moments before, she'd been chilly, but now her palms were clammy in a way they wouldn't have been if he'd driven to her front door instead of skulking out of the woods.

As he stepped uninvited onto the porch, the single bulb cast an eerie phosphorescence on his prematurely gray hair. He took in the log posts and the overhanging porch roof. "Kelly's grandmother grew up here. Kelly loves the place. I should have bought it when it came back on the market. It would have saved us all a lot of trouble."

"But you didn't."

He came nearer. "I don't tolerate anyone upsetting my wife."

She forced herself to move away from the cabin's front wall. "You need to leave."

"I found this in my wife's things." He pulled something from his jacket pocket and held it out so she could see.

It was Tess's phone number written on the notepaper with her old clinic's letterhead.

He wadded the paper in his fist. "Kelly should have told me right away you were harassing her, but she didn't want to bother me."

"Harassing her?"

He dropped the crumpled paper to the porch floor. "The way you've been trying to get her to meet with you so you can badger her with more of your propaganda."

Tess put the pieces together and didn't like what she saw. Brad had found Tess's phone number, and Kelly had lied about why she had it.

He moved closer, using his size to intimidate her. "My wife and I think alike. Do you really believe you can make her change her mind? She never interferes with politics."

"Politics?" Tess shoved her thumb in the waistband of her jeans. "I thought this was about what's best for kids."

A pair of headlights swept across the clearing. They both turned to see a silver Lexus stop in front of the cabin. The engine shut off, the door opened, and Kelly sprang out.

She stood at the side of the car, her gaze darting nervously between Tess and her husband, clearly worried about what Tess might have told him. She moved toward them. "Is something wrong, Brad? I saw your car parked down the road. You weren't supposed to be back from Nashville until tomorrow."

"We finished early. Where have you been?"

"Margie Wexler's mother's sick. I sat with her for a while."

"That was good of you." He stepped off the porch and stretched his arm toward his wife. Not going to Kelly but making her come to him. She hesitated for only a moment before she complied.

The possessive way he wrapped his beefy arm around her slender shoulders reminded Tess of the way Connor had entrapped Ava. "I needed some exercise," he said, "and I also needed to talk to Tess here. I know you didn't want me to interfere, but you're too easy on people. Tess needs to understand that she's not ever to bother you again."

Kelly's stricken eyes flashed to Tess and then to her husband. Brad chucked her under the chin as if she were a child. "You're not the only one she's been bothering. Connor's mother called me today. It turns out Tess has been meeting with some of our teenage boys. Helene's not happy about it."

Kelly fixed her gaze on her husband. "Of course she's upset."

"Nothing like sneaking behind our backs to teach a bunch of randy boys how to have sex." He released his wife to turn on Tess. "You keep sticking your nose in where it's not wanted."

It was Tess's turn to be belligerent. "You seem to be spending a lot of time poking your nose into my life, so let's call it a fair exchange."

His chest puffed up like a hot marshmallow. "You're not to harass my wife or anyone else in this community. We aren't interested in your opinions. Isn't that right, Kelly?"

Kelly dipped her head and muttered something inaudible. Tess hated this woman's timidity. Where was her backbone?

He wasn't satisfied with his wife's muffled response. "Kelly?"

Her head came up. "You should listen to Brad, Tess," she said stiffly.

Any warm feelings Tess had experienced for her vanished in the face of her cowardice. "I only listen to people I respect, and right now, you've both fallen off my list."

"Is that so?" He released his wife. "Go on home, baby. I'll walk back to my car."

Kelly regarded them hesitantly—still afraid Tess would expose her lie. Tess could have given her some kind of reassuring gesture, but she wasn't that nice a person.

Kelly walked slowly to her car. Tess didn't want to be alone with him, but she couldn't make herself run inside. Brad called after his wife. "I'd love to have a drink waiting when I get there. Three olives this time. Those good ones you stuff with blue cheese."

The confident woman who'd first confronted Tess at the Broken Chimney over the condom display had disappeared. Kelly gave a short, jerky nod and drove off.

Tess regarded Brad with disgust. "They don't make men like you anymore."

"I'm old-school," he retorted, "and I won't apologize for it. I protect my family."

"Yeah, I'm a big threat, all right."

He jabbed his finger at her. "Leave my wife alone. My daughter, too."

"Here's a thought. Why don't you do them both a favor and let them speak for themselves?"

"Do you seriously think you can challenge me? You're nobody."

She mustered all the bravado she could. "And you're a big deal. The undisputed king of Tempest, Tennessee. I get that. I just don't care."

"You will." He turned away and disappeared into the woods.

Tess went back inside and locked the door. Brad Winchester was narrow-minded, pretentious, and combative—the worst kind of bully. But was he also violent?

Kelly had denied that he was physically abusive, but was that the truth? Winchester's hostility seemed out of proportion to what Tess had done. Maybe his antipathy had more to do with his need to be in charge than it had to do with the town's sex education curriculum. He was a man used to having his own way in everything, and he didn't intend to let anyone, especially a woman and an outsider, challenge him.

When she returned to the schoolhouse, Wren was asleep in her nest in the upstairs bedroom. As Ian approached, baby monitor in hand, she decided not to tell him about Brad Winchester's lurking. It would only strengthen his concern about the move to the cabin, and Tess needed to get back to living on her own again. Without him. And soon.

He gave her a lazy once-over. "This time I'm going to paint you for real."

She shook off the aftereffects of her disagreeable encounter at the cabin. "I've heard that before. You tend to get distracted."

"It's all about mental discipline. I didn't concentrate enough last time."

"And this time will be different?"

"Absolutely." He drew her into the studio where the rolling metal cart, loaded with tubes, pots, and squeeze bottles of paint, already sat in the middle of the room.

"Feel free to take off your clothes," he said. "I won't look." He turned his back, unnecessarily studying the supplies he'd already organized.

"Do we have to do this?" she said. "I'm feeling self-conscious."

He braced a hand on his hip. "Are we back to all your body-image crap again?"

"I'm allowed to have body-image issues. It's my body."

"And God couldn't have created a more perfect one. Come on, Tess. Inspire me."

"Damn it!" She pulled her sweater over her head, grumbling the whole time. "You could hire the most beautiful figure models in the world, but do you do that? No." She kicked off her shoes. "Here's what I think. I think you're just cheap." She tugged off her jeans and unfastened her bra. "You don't want to pay for a professional. Instead, you take advantage of a defenseless widow. . . ."

He snorted.

She tossed aside her bra. "And I'm leaving my underpants on!"

He crossed his arms over his chest with an annoying

smugness. "A little late, considering I've seen everything underneath. And I mean everything."

She loved this new, playful side of him. And she loved not knowing exactly what would happen next. "I'm cold," she said semipetulantly.

"Now there's where you're wrong. You are hot, babe. So damned hot."

She suppressed a smile. "Says you." Wearing nothing but a skimpy pair of bikini underpants scattered with flamingos, she faced him. "No photos. I don't want my cellulite plastered all over the Internet the next time you get pissed at me. Which you know you will."

"Your cellulite is safe from my petty revenge."

He unrolled a long sheet of what looked like white butcher paper, laid it out on the floor, and drew her over to stand on it.

She practiced a pout. "How come you get to keep your clothes on?"

"Discipline, remember?" He sank his hands into her hair and spread it out until she must look like a wild woman. "Perfect." He reached for one of the paint pots. "Don't be concerned. It's nontoxic."

"Why should I be con— Hey!" She gave an involuntary yelp as he touched her nipple, leaving a curl of bright blue behind. "What are you *doing*?"

"I'm a renegade, remember? Used to working with all kinds of surfaces." He swirled the color around the tip.

That's when she understood. When he said he wanted to paint her, he'd meant it literally.

She stood motionlessly and let him turn her breast into an elaborate medallion of blue, crimson, maroon, and gold, with feathery edges drifting over her ribs. The warmth of the paint and the sensuous touch of his fingers grew into an exquisite torture. Her bones began to melt as he cupped the weight of her breast in one hand and used the little finger of the other to swirl the pigment.

He selected a square of thin canvas from the fabric pile on the cart. Gently, meticulously, he molded it to her breast, transferring the image from her skin to the small canvas. Using her body as a pliable stamp.

She stood before him, weak-kneed and ferociously aroused. He set the canvas aside and painted her other breast into an intricate, multicolored pattern of airy lace. Her palms grew damp as he tormented the nipple with ochre, lemon, and maroon. Sweat began to pool at the base of his throat.

Once again, he pressed the canvas to her breast, made his stamp, set it aside, and moved on to her naval. His hair had fallen over his forehead; his brow furrowed with the intensity of his concentration.

Her skin was alive, every inch of it stimulated by his sensuous touch. He surrounded the oval of her naval with a mosaic of rolling waves. Pressed a new canvas to her. Set it aside.

Paint dripped onto her underpants. He shrugged out of his sweat-damp shirt and went to his knees. She fisted her hands to keep them from sinking into his hair. His breath fell hot on her skin. He moved behind her. He pushed the rear waistband of her underpants down and caught the fabric on one side in the crack of her buttocks, exposing a single cheek.

She couldn't see him, only felt his hands on her skin and imagined what they were creating. The room was too hot, the sensations too intense. He molded the canvas to her bottom, his finger straying.

Now he was in front of her again. Paint smeared his bicep and stippled his hair. Her underpants were in his way. He pulled them off and spread her legs. He worked carefully, painting the tiniest design high on her thigh. The back of his hand brushed her intimately as he worked there until she lost her balance and sank to her knees in front of him.

Their eyes met and held. A spatter of white paint clung to the stubble at his jawline. A dab of green hovered at the corner of his mouth. Keeping her eyes locked with his, she cupped her breasts and rubbed the paint that remained there on her hands.

"Now you," she whispered.

He groaned as she splayed her palms on his collarbones and dragged them down his chest to his waist.

When he felt her fingers opening the snap of his jeans, pulling out the condom, he lost the last of the control he'd so rigidly clung to and pulled her to the floor on top of him. He tunneled his paint-streaked hands into her hair and kissed her, inhaled her. They rolled over, mouths together, both of them struggling with the barrier of his jeans, their breathing heavy, their movements clumsy. An elbow here, a knee there, the wayward scrape of a fingernail—no graceful choreography. Bodies slick with paint and sweat.

He turned her. Under him. Over him. The slip-slide of pigment between their bodies. On her knees. Cupping her from behind, smearing what was left of the patterns he'd made.

Turning her again.

The paint pots tipped, and pigment spilled onto the floor. They rolled in it. The two of them, out of control, out of their minds.

And then he was inside her. Part of her. This lush, giving body. This woman with glazed, violet-blue eyes and midnight hair wreathed in a chaotic corona around her head.

The sweat poured from his body as he held himself back. Waited for the arch. The cry. Her arch. Never— never so much restraint.

He drove deeper. Holding her. Riding her through her torrent. Through his own. Into an explosion of the spectrum.

When he came back to himself, he saw they'd turned his careful work into mayhem, a beautiful nightmare of smeared paint on olive skin. She picked up one of the untouched canvas squares from the cart and pressed it to a smudge of paint on his side. She pressed another to his chest. Her hair tumbled forward, shrouding her face, the strands streaked with ultramarine and cinnabar. She stamped his thigh. His groin. One place after another.

He lay still and watched her work even as panic began to grow inside him, beating harder and faster. He hid it behind a smile and a quip. Hid it as they showered together, unearthing paint from all the secret crevices. Hid it as they took each other again.

When the sound of crying came through the baby monitor, Tess grabbed a robe and disappeared, her wet feet leaving imprints on the floor. He went back into the studio and set each of the canvas squares out to dry before he cleaned up the mess they'd made. Still, the panic wouldn't leave him.

He had to get away from this place. From her.

Not even Tess's belligerent co-workers could spoil her mood the next day. She picked up Wren at Heather's and drove to the schoolhouse, still thinking about the crazy insanity of last night. When she reached the schoolhouse, a Nissan Ultima was parked crookedly in front, and a man she'd never seen stood on the porch ready to knock. As she got out of the car, he turned to look at her.

He appeared to be in his late twenties, unshaven, with rumpled light-brown hair and clothes he might have been wearing a few days too long: wrinkled chinos, a long-sleeved tan shirt turned at the cuffs, and an old khaki safari vest with multiple pockets.

Leaving Wren in the backseat, she walked up the path. "Can I help you with something?"

"Are you Tess Hartsong?"

"Yes. And you're—"

"I'm Simon Denning."

Chapter Nineteen

Tess stalled for time. She opened the front door and invited him inside then returned to the car to get Wren. As she reached in, she banged her head on the doorframe. She grabbed the car roof to steady herself and blinked her eyes hard against a sudden urge to cry, not from the bump but from the feeling that the world was once again poised to crash in on her.

Wren was wide-awake, her eyes the deep navy of a Van Gogh sky, her fist on an erratic course toward her mouth. Tess picked her up and tucked her into the curve of her neck. The pulse beneath the baby's fontanel tapped against her cheek. She kissed the downy softness and turned to face the new demon who'd invaded their lives.

He stood in the hallway exactly where she'd left him. With her free hand, she flipped the light switch on the schoolhouse globes.

"Is that the baby?" he asked unnecessarily.

"This is Wren. Yes. My daughter."

He shoved a hand in the pocket of his chinos. "You wouldn't happen to have a beer handy? And a bathroom. I've been traveling for most of two days."

She directed him toward Bianca's old room. He stopped on the threshold and gazed at the geode interior. "Damn. I've never seen anything like this."

"Yes, it's unusual."

"Incredible."

She held Wren close as she retrieved a beer from the refrigerator. She moved robotically, trying to convince herself this man was a nomad with no desire to raise a child. But if he didn't want Wren, why had he traveled all this way to see her? And where was Ian? She wanted him here, by her side, even as she knew this was her hurdle to cross alone.

Denning brought the faint smell of soap with him as he emerged from the bedroom. She set the beer at one end of the dining table and walked with Wren to the other end, as far away as she could get. He picked up the bottle but didn't sit. Neither did she. The table stretched between them, loaded with land mines. "Your parents said you were in Afghanistan."

"I was."

"Have you seen them?"

"I'm going there after I leave here."

Wren sucked at her collarbone. She waited.

He tilted the bottle to his lips and took a long slug before he spoke again. "I don't know what Bianca told you, but that's not my baby."

A long, ragged sound escaped from somewhere inside her.

"I did the math," he said. "The numbers don't add up."

Wren's wet fingers touched her cheek. She grasped the baby's hand. "But . . . You talked with your parents. You said . . ."

"I know what I said." He took another long drag of beer. "I was out near the Korengal Valley, and the connection kept breaking up. It wasn't until two days ago when I was back in Kabul that I could sort out all the dates. I was due for a vacation, so I took the next flight out—first to see you and then to talk to them." He finally sat at the table, the beer still curled in his palm. "Look, I'm sorry you've had to go through all this. That's why I knew I had to come here and tell you in person. Tell them."

The front door opened and Ian walked in. He stopped when he saw their visitor. "Another injury in the neighborhood?"

She backed away from the table. "Ian, this is Simon Denning."

Ian was a master at hiding his emotions, and she witnessed his skill in a whole new way. "Is that right?"

"He says he's not Wren's father."

"I'm not." Denning drained his beer and set the bottle down with a *thunk*.

Ian came closer, not looking at her, only at him. "Maybe you'd better tell us the whole story."

Denning outlined his brief fling with Bianca, beginning with their meeting in an East Village bar. "A couple of guys were hitting on her, and she obviously wasn't happy about it, so I stepped in and acted like we had a date. She was fun, crazy, wild. I'd never met anyone like her. She was into me, but I was only going to be in town for a week, so it was never serious. Still, it was intense while it lasted."

He went on, offering up dates, where they'd gone, who'd they'd seen. He was so forthcoming that Tess knew he was telling the truth even before he pulled out his phone and flipped through a series of dated photos of the two of them together. Bianca's stomach was flat, but a quick mental calculation suggested she was about six weeks pregnant.

Simon rubbed his scruffy jaw. "I didn't think anything about it at the time, but I never saw her drink, not even the night we met at that bar. Now it makes sense. She was already pregnant."

"You'll take a DNA test?" Ian said.

"As long as you're paying for it."

"This is my fault," Ian muttered when Simon left. "She told me Denning had gotten her pregnant, and I bought it, even though I know better than anyone how careless Bianca could be with the facts."

Why wouldn't Ian look at her? "You had no reason to suspect she'd lied to you."

"I knew her." He rubbed the back of his neck. "I should have investigated, but she'd told a couple of acquaintances the same thing."

She bit her bottom lip. "Maybe this is for the best."

"You know it isn't."

He was right. Tess couldn't imagine enduring months—years—waiting for another man to show up and claim her child.

"I'm going to Manhattan," Ian said. "I'll talk to everyone who knew her. I'll get to the bottom of this."

"It's my responsibility."

"Why?"

"Because Wren is mine. You're her . . . her fairy godfather."

He finally looked at her, but there was a distance about him, as if they'd only recently met.

"You know what I mean," she said.

"About many things, yes. But not about this."

"I can handle it alone."

"I'm sure you can, but why should you?"

Because that's how she would be raising Wren. Alone.

Ian surprised her by setting off a few hours later. Something about his manner—an aloofness that hadn't been there a few days ago—made her uneasy. She told herself to ignore it. She needed to stop trying to read his thoughts and focus on her own life. That meant moving into the cabin permanently.

It didn't take long to transfer the rest of their belongings. She worked on her notes for tomorrow night's community meeting, but mainly she held her tiny, cranky baby and tried not to think about the uncertainty that lay before them.

Even with the drapes shut that night, she imagined Brad Winchester peering through the windows, and she hated that he'd made her so skittish. As she lay in bed, she missed Ian, and not only for their sex life. She missed talking to him, being with him.

Wren didn't seem to like the cabin any better than Tess—or maybe she missed Ian, too—because she fussed on and off all night.

In the morning, Tess mainlined two cups of strong coffee and worried about whether anybody would show up for tonight's meeting. Or maybe everyone would show up with hot tar and a bucket of feathers ready to run her out of town for corrupting their youth. She told herself that wouldn't happen. Yes, the town had its share of reactionary diehards, but it also had sensible people . . . although more than a few of them might have bought into the idea that she was responsible for Bianca's death.

The Tempest Women's Alliance was meeting at the Broken Chimney that morning, making the place too busy for Tess to contemplate what she would do if she couldn't get past this latest roadblock. Michelle, who was due to deliver at any time, had quit the week before. Savannah was still working, but moving so slowly that she was useless. Since Tess was a sucker for pregnant women—even ones she'd grown to heartily dislike—she didn't complain, not even about Savannah's current drawn-out rest break.

Michelle came in as a customer and took a seat at a four-top below Phish's most recent poster:

WIFI SQUATTERS

PAY UP OR GET UP!

Michelle sat well back from the table, knees splayed, hands clasping her abdomen. Savannah used her mother's appearance as an excuse to extend her rest break even longer.

A few weeks earlier, Savannah had shaved the bottom half of her head and dyed the longer top green, so it looked as if she'd sprouted a patch of garden chives on her head. As soon as she moved to a seat opposite her mother, she began grousing about her best friend, Taylor. "She doesn't understand. She acts like I should still want to go out to The Rooster every night."

Michelle fanned herself with a napkin. "Taylor's immature. I don't like to say, 'I told you so,' but—"

"Then don't!" Savannah shot back. "I can't say anything about anybody without you getting all up in my face and criticizing."

"I'm not criticizing. Whatever I say is for your own good. Taylor is lazy, and you need a better class of friends." Michelle tugged at the last open button on her black-and-white-check maternity blouse and blew into her generous cleavage to cool herself off. "Stop glaring at me like that. You need to be more considerate of my condition."

"Your condition? What about my condition?"

"It's completely different." Michelle went in for the slam dunk. "You're not forty-two with a history of precipitous labor."

"If you don't stop talking about your precipitous labor, I swear I am tippin' this table right over in your big, fat lap."

Tess plunked Michelle's lemonade in front of her. "Could you two tone it down? You're driving away the customers."

"What do you care?" Savannah retorted. "It's Phish's place, not yours."

Tess pressed her hands to her heart. "This is what I love most about working here. The deep bonds of friendship I share with my beloved co-workers." She glared at Savannah. "I'm being sarcastic in case you can't figure that out."

Michelle heaved herself to her feet. "You have no right to talk to my daughter that way."

"Okay, I'll leave it up to you since—"

Michelle gave a sudden cry of pain and doubled over. "Oh, my god! Sweet Jesus!"

Tess grabbed her to keep her from falling.

"Call . . . call your father!" Michelle gasped.

Savannah leaped to her feet and rushed for her phone faster than she'd moved all day. As the contraction ended, Michelle gazed at Tess with big, frightened eyes. "It's happening again! I'm going to have this baby right now! I knew this would happen!"

Tess felt the room beginning to spin. Her heart raced as Michelle fell back into the chair. "This is exactly the way it happened last time!" Michelle cried. "You are not delivering this baby. I have to get to the hospital right now!"

"Dad isn't answering!" Savannah cried.

"Asshole!" Michelle barred her teeth. "I told him not to go anywhere without his phone."

Michelle was hysterical, and Tess couldn't deal with it. Bianca's pleas and cries, the agony of those final minutes had become part of Tess's DNA. Everything she had to escape. She wanted to run, but Michelle had a death grip on her hands.

"Get the car!" Michelle shrieked at her daughter. "I had Savannah in two and a half hours. The pain was so bad, and it hit so fast. The doctors wouldn't believe me. They wanted to send me home."

Tess forced her mouth to move. "Your . . . your doctor knows your history."

"I'm forty-two! I'm too old to have a baby." Michelle

moaned and carried on as three minutes passed, then four, then five, accompanied by a long stream of grievances but not another contraction.

"I want my pie!" Mr. Felder shouted from the counter, with his usual lack of sensitivity.

"Where's Savannah?" Michelle cried. "Where's the car? I have to get to the hospital now! She's lazy. She's always been lazy. The only time she ever moved fast was the day she was born."

At six minutes, another contraction hit. Michelle yelled and crushed Tess's fingers in her grip.

Tess tried to talk herself down. Michelle's water hadn't broken, and with so much time between contractions, it was unlikely she'd deliver nearly as quickly as she expected. Unlikely, but not impossible.

Savannah raced through the door, clutching her own belly. "I've got the car."

"It's about time!" Michelle staggered up from the chair. "Let's go. We have to go."

"I want my pie!" Mr. Felder croaked.

"Get it yourself, you old buzzard!" Michelle screamed. "I'm goin' to have this baby in the car. I know it!" She clawed at Tess. "You're coming with me."

"No! No, I can't. You have plenty of time. You'll be fine."

Her grip tightened. "You're supposed to help people."

"Yes, but . . . you hate me, remember?"

"I never said that."

"You told me not to touch you. You made me promise not to lay a hand on you. Your exact words."

"I didn't say anything like that!" Michelle started to cry.

"Stop being such a bitch, Tess!" Savannah exclaimed from the door. "If she dies, it'll be on your conscience."

Michelle wasn't going to die. Not like Bianca. Michelle's contractions were six minutes apart. It was more likely she'd be sent home from the hospital for arriving too early. But all the self-talk in the world didn't keep Tess from wanting to cry right along with Michelle.

Savannah splayed her legs, balancing her weight on her heels. "You don't have any heart."

Tess was used to Savannah's bitchiness, but Michelle's frightened tears defeated her. Somehow she managed to help Michelle up from the chair, although she wasn't certain who was supporting whom.

"Call Phish!" Savannah shouted at Mr. Felder on their way out the door. "You're in charge until he gets here. And you'd better not let anybody steal anything."

Even though Savannah could barely fit behind the steering wheel, Michelle insisted she drive so Tess could stay with her in the backseat. She sank her claws into Tess's arm. "We'll never make it."

"I'm not going to behave like this when I have my baby," Savannah growled as she pulled out onto the highway.

"That's what you say now!" Michelle dug deeper into Tess's arm.

"It's your fault for getting pregnant," Savannah countered.

"And it's your fault for getting knocked up, so stop throwing this in my face."

Tess had calmed dozens of irrational women over the course of her career. She was an expert at creating a tranquil atmosphere. But all the skill she'd acquired had vanished. She was paralyzed, helpless. Incapable of doing more than pray that Michelle's contractions would hold steady at six minutes. She thought of the meeting she had scheduled for tonight. How could she believe she had anything to share with other people when she was such a mess herself?

Fifty minutes later, they pulled up to the hospital emergency entrance. Michelle hit the button on the rear window and stuck her head out. "Get me a wheel-chair!"

An aide extracted Michelle from the car. When the

door closed, Tess sagged back into the seat, shut her eyes, and rubbed the crescent-shaped fingernail marks on her arm. She was done. She had no more responsibility. She should be relieved, but she felt broken instead.

The car began to move only to stop a few moments later as Savannah pulled into a parking place. "Let's go."

"I'll wait for you in the lobby."

"Bullshit! What if she gets some idiot nurse who doesn't know what she's doing? How do you expect me to deal with that?"

"She's not going to get an idiot nurse."

"You don't know that. God, stop being so selfish."

Tess had to get out of the car, not because of Savannah's bullying but because she was suffocating under an avalanche of ugly memories. She gripped the top of the car door, trying to talk herself down. *You'll be all right. You're not in charge. You don't have to do anything.*

Savannah clasped her hands under her abdomen. "God, you'd think you're the one having the baby."

Tess followed Savannah to the labor and delivery ward. Instead of calming her, the familiar sights and sounds made Tess want to flee.

Savannah tried to barge into the triage room, and

when she was rebuffed, she did her best to push Tess in. "She's a trained midwife. You have to let her in!"

Tess shook her head, the motion barely detectable, but the nurse got the message. "You'll both have to wait outside until we've examined her."

"That bitch," Savannah muttered.

Tess finally had a target for her self-disgust. "You can abuse me all you want, but don't disrespect the staff."

Savannah ducked her head, momentarily cowed. "I didn't say anything that bad."

"Don't say anything at all!"

"God, you're so unreasonable," she muttered.

The nurse eventually appeared with the news that Michelle's labor was progressing normally, and she was asking for them both. But as Savannah followed the woman toward the birthing room, Tess darted down the opposite hallway.

For a while, she hung out by the nursery. She gazed through the window at the wizened newborns. Wren already looked different—plumper, more observant. Tess needed her baby.

She took the elevator to cardiology and drank a cup of hospital coffee in the waiting room. The soothing squeak of sneakers on the tile floors, the soft hum of conversation, the familiar smell of disinfectant did nothing to relax her. She'd be okay. She'd be safe in another field where she wouldn't have to fear hemorrhaging mothers. It would work out. It had to.

Her community meeting was at eight. She should never have put up that sign. Tempest's sex education curriculum wasn't her battle to fight. She'd call Phish. Make him take down the sign and tell everyone she was sick. And then she'd—

Run away again? Wasn't that what she'd been doing? She'd tried to run away from her grief by moving here. She'd run away from her profession by working at the Broken Chimney. She'd even been running away from admitting to herself that she'd fallen in love with Ian North.

It was true. She loved this difficult damaged man who wanted only solitude. Instead of confronting her feelings head on, she had focused on Wren, on her job, on the teenagers—anything that would let her keep running away from the painful reality that she'd fallen in love with a man who would never love her back.

That was over now. Losing Trav had been unexpected, but losing Ian . . . ? She'd never had him to begin with. From now on, she'd be clear-eyed. No more running away, not even from tonight's meeting.

She left cardiology and found Savannah holed up in the labor and delivery waiting room. "Mom was stressing me out," Savannah explained.

"I need to borrow your car. You can ride back with your dad when he gets here."

"You want to leave?"

"Your mother's in good hands, and I have to get back."

"You can't go yet," Savannah said, in her customary belligerent fashion. "What if something happens?"

Tess's nerves shredded. "If something happens, nobody is going to come running to me. I'm a *murderer*, remember?"

The word hung in the air between them. Savannah dropped her gaze. "I never said that."

Tess stared out the window at the parking lot below.

Savannah spoke softly. "I can't get hold of Dad. Somebody has to stay with me."

Her disagreeable co-worker's neediness got to her, and Tess settled in to wait.

The baby, a seven-pound, eight-ounce healthy boy, wasn't born until dinnertime, less than half an hour after Michelle's husband, Dave, arrived. Savannah dragged Tess with her to meet her new brother. Tess said all the right things, and then quickly excused herself. If she left now, she'd have just enough time to pull herself together and get changed before the meeting. She reiterated her request for Savannah's car keys.

"I'm not hanging around here," Savannah said. "We can go back together."

"I need to hurry."

Savannah dug the heel of her hand into her back and rolled her eyes. "Oh, yeah. You've got your big meeting tonight. Good luck with that."

If Tess had thought Savannah's brief show of vulnerability would change anything, she'd been proven wrong.

Savannah took so long talking to her father, badgering her exhausted mother, and waddling to the parking garage that Tess thought they'd never get to the car. Forget having a chance to decompress, let alone take a shower. She'd be lucky to throw on clean clothes.

She grabbed the keys. "I'll drive. You need to rest."

They were barely past the hospital entrance before they hit a construction delay. Savannah stretched in the passenger seat to ease her back. "I can't believe how crazy Mom was. I mean, I know she's crazy, but I didn't expect her to be that crazy."

"She was afraid."

"I'd die before I acted like that. I have my pride."

"Women labor in different ways." Tess drummed

her fingers on the steering wheel as the traffic inched forward. Forget changing her clothes. At this rate, the best she could hope for was getting to the meeting on time. If she didn't, everyone in town would think she'd lost her courage.

They arrived at the Broken Chimney three minutes after eight. Tess's hopes that no one would attend were squashed when she saw that all the parking spaces in front were taken. She pulled up and got out, leaving Savannah to fend for herself.

The place was packed, with the overflow standing wherever there was floor space. She recognized many of the coffee shop regulars, along with the parents of a few of the high school kids. Not unexpectedly, Brad and Kelly had taken over a table toward the middle of the room. Imani's and Jordan's families were there. Old Mr. Felder had shown up. So had Artie. Courtney was pouting into her phone's camera, looking for the best angle, and Phish was behind the counter, dishing up ice cream and pie as fast as he could manage. Tess spotted some of the retirees in the crowd, all of whom should be long past worrying about teenagers getting pregnant. This had turned into a circus, and she was the primary exhibit.

The crowd gradually quieted as they spotted her. Instead of feeling professional and authoritative, she was out of breath, disheveled, and rattled in her oldest jeans and a coffee-stained T-shirt. The brush of makeup she'd applied that morning had worn off, and her hair was a rat's nest. She looked around for Ian but didn't see him anywhere. She swallowed her disappointment.

Phish jerked his head toward the scarred wooden barstool he'd retrieved from the backroom. As she edged toward it, she remembered the information sheets still sitting on the kitchen table in the cabin.

Savannah came in through the front door, along with Quincy, the bartender at The Rooster. Tess cleared her throat. No matter how unnerved she was, she had to project confidence. But her voice wouldn't cooperate. "Th-Thank you all for showing up."

"Can't hear you!" somebody shouted.

She spoke louder. "Let me . . . Let me start with a question. Does anybody here . . . Do any of you think it's a good idea for young teens to be parents?" Fortunately, no one raised a hand. "Great. We're all in agreement so far."

"Doubt that'll last long," Phish called out from behind the counter.

The general laughter that followed eased a few of the knots in her stomach. She took a deep breath. "Parents have a big role in making these years healthy ones for their kids."

"Tell your girls to keep their legs crossed," Mr. Felder called out.

"How about telling the boys to keep their damn pants zipped?" Mrs. Watkins countered.

Tess raised her voice to speak above them. "I hope we all know it's not so simple."

Reverend Peoples stepped forward, full of disapproval. She hurried on before he could speak. "Let's go back to Biology 101." They mercifully quieted enough for her to offer a brief lecture on the physiology of puberty and development of the teenage brain. "Our brains don't fully develop until late teens or even early twenties. This means teens have an immature prefrontal cortex—the exact part of the brain that assesses risk." She slid off the stool. "This is the part of the brain that goes missing in action when a kid decides it'd be super fun to steal a six-pack and go joyriding. It's also the part of the brain that's likely to ignore sex education lectures that begin and end with abstinence."

"Go ahead and tell the kids how to screw around instead!" A fierce-looking woman with a big blond bouffant rose from her chair.

Tess fought against losing her temper. "You can

talk to your teens about the emotional consequences of having sex before they're ready *and* give them the information they need to stay safe."

"That's what I did." Mrs. Watkins fingered the crucifix at her neck. "Y'all need to listen to her."

Emboldened by this small show of support, Tess said, "Some of your teens are struggling in ways you may not realize. Gay and transgender kids, for example—"

"We don't have those kinds here!" a man she didn't know shouted.

"Shut up, Frank," Phish called out.

"I don't know what world you're living in," Jordan's mother said to Tess, "but the last thing my daughter wants to talk to me about is sex."

"That's why they need another trustworthy source of information."

"Now she gets to her real agenda. Our schools." Brad Winchester ambled forward, commanding the room. "Ever since Miss Hartsong got here, she's been determined to ignore our values. She's gone behind our backs, talked to our children without our permission, saying only God knows what. She sees us as a bunch of country hicks who aren't capable of deciding what's best for our own families. She wants our schools to do a parent's job."

Everything Tess yearned to say pushed at her tongue—

that their school policy had less to do with a teenager's well-being and more to do with parental anxiety—but the bouffant blonde was back on her feet. "I don't want my kids getting an instruction book on all the ways to have sex!"

"Then you'd better keep them away from Miss Hart-song," Winchester replied, "because that is the *exact* kind of information she's handing out."

A hoarse moan cut through the commotion as Savannah grabbed the wall and looked down at the floor in disbelief. "My water broke!"

Chapter Twenty

Savannah doubled over, clutching her abdomen as her mother had done earlier in this very same place. Kelly rushed to her side, where she was quickly joined by four other women. They crowded around Savannah, standing too close.

Just then, Ian came through the door. He looked travel-mussed and harried. Ignoring the disruption surrounding Savannah, he searched the crowd for Tess. His pace quickened as he spotted her. "I tried to get back earlier, but—"

"I want my mother!" Savannah cried from the doorway.

He turned toward the commotion. "What's happening?"

"Savannah's water broke."

He took in the cluster of women. Looked down at Tess. Rubbed the stubble on his chin. "Shouldn't you . . . Check on her?"

"No reason to." Plenty of people were around to get Savannah to the hospital. This time, Tess was in the clear.

Savannah howled with another contraction. Tess didn't have to look at her watch to know that barely two minutes had passed since the previous one. "She'll be fine."

He nodded slowly. "Maybe somebody should tell her that."

"It's her first," Tess said firmly. "First babies take forever."

Savannah cried out.

"Are you sure about that?" he asked.

"The night's clear. The roads are dry. She can be at the hospital in no time."

"You're the authority."

Tess carefully returned the stool to the back room. The crowd around Savannah had grown. Savannah cried out again. Ian returned to Tess's side. She licked her dry lips and focused on the bridge of his nose. "Some women vocalize more than others."

"That's a lot of vocalization," he said.

Savannah's next outburst was the shriek of a woman

in terrible pain. The intense pain a woman might experience if she were in precipitous labor.

Tess winced.

Ian regarded her quizzically. "This isn't normal, is it?"

She managed a jerky shake of her head.

"Is there time to get her to the hospital?"

Before she could answer, Savannah screamed again. This time with a specific purpose. *"Tess!"*

Kelly spun around. "Tess, where are you?"

Panicked, Tess gazed up at Ian. "I can't do this."

"Sure you can," he said.

"No! You don't understand."

"I do understand."

"Then you know why."

He looked into her eyes, taking his time, seeing everything, and then he nodded. "Okay. Tell me what to do."

She looked away. "I can't tell you what to do!"

"Sure you can." But even as he said it, he was guiding her forward, a gentle hand in the small of her back. "I'm right here."

"Let Tess in," Kelly exclaimed.

His soothing, encouraging hand sifted up her spine, settled lightly on her shoulder, eased her through the women clustered around Savannah.

Savannah lay on the floor, her black knit maternity pants soaked, her face blotchy with pain and fear. Tess remembered how Savannah had kept pressing on the small of her back throughout the day. She'd been in labor and hadn't known it.

Savannah's breath came in short, hoarse gasps. "I didn't want to be like Mom. Making a scene every time she had a cramp. I thought it was false labor."

"If you'd a kept your legs crossed, you wouldn't be in this fix," Mr. Felder said.

"Out!" Ian ordered. "Everybody out of here!"

Artie grabbed Mr. Felder by the neck. "Let's me and you have a little talk outside, Orland."

Tess reached blindly for the hand of the woman standing closest to her. "You stay." Only as the woman knelt beside her did she realize it was Kelly Winchester.

"It hurts so bad!" Savannah cried, looking younger than her nineteen years. "You didn't tell me it would hurt this bad."

Tess couldn't control her own trembling. "Somebody call an ambulance."

"Already on it," Phish said.

The closest emergency service was in Valley City, fifteen miles away. Not that far.

Savannah gazed up at her from under her green spray of hair. "I'm scared."

"You're going to be fine." The same words Tess had uttered to Bianca.

"What do you want me to do?" Kelly asked.

Tess searched her mind and couldn't come up with a thing. She simply stood there, frozen and stupid.

"Phish, do you have a plastic tablecloth we can put under her?" Ian said. "And cover up the windows so she can have some privacy. Mrs. Winchester, find some clean dish towels, string, and scissors."

Ian remembered what Tess couldn't.

"The fire department's on its way," Phish said.

Only fifteen miles. They'd get here in time. They had to. Because Tess absolutely could not do this.

"Do something, Tess!" Savannah pleaded. "Make it stop hurting so bad."

Tess stood there unmoving. Not speaking. Watching Bianca's life drain away in a sea of blood.

A familiar male voice whispered in her ear. "Don't make me slap you, sweetheart. I'm an artist, not a fighter." And then he pinched her rear. Hard.

Tess's head came up. She sucked in a fresh stream of air. "I . . . need to wash up."

Ian turned her toward the sink behind the counter. She moved. One step at a time. She passed Kelly carrying a stack of clean dish towels. She unlocked her jaw and heard her own tremulous voice. "Get Savannah's pants off."

She began scrubbing up at the sink. Phish was at the windows, closing off the view of the crowd who'd gathered outside as Ian spread a plastic tablecloth on the floor. Tess stared at a box of disposable food preparation gloves, and then picked them up. After all Michelle's talk of precipitous labor, it was her daughter who'd fallen victim.

Kelly had Savannah's pants off. Swallowing hard, Tess knelt between her legs. Savannah's water had broken. A vaginal exam in these conditions would risk infection, but without it, she couldn't know how far Savannah's labor had progressed. In the old days, she would have relied on instinct, but her instincts were shot, and she was paralyzed.

"Tess! Help me! Why aren't you helping me?"

Swallowing her nausea, she rubbed Savannah's arm. "Can you get on your hands and knees? Would that feel better?"

Savannah managed a nod. Kelly helped her roll over and get into a more comfortable position, a position where she was less likely to tear. Savannah cried out. Tess responded automatically, unsteadily. "You can handle it. Your body knows what to do."

Bianca's body didn't. It betrayed her.

Tess's T-shirt stuck to her chest. Ian was right behind her, his hands warm against her shoulders. She was used to the sights and smells of childbirth: the poop and pee, the bulging perineum, the leak of amniotic fluid—but he wasn't. She should tell him to leave, but she couldn't. She needed him.

The contractions were coming more quickly and with greater force. Savannah had no time to adjust to their strength, and Tess could feel her mounting panic, right along with Tess's own. "We're going to . . . going to breathe together. Breathe with me, Savannah." But as Tess tried to inhale, the air stuck in her windpipe.

Her hands twitched. The breathing pattern was as familiar to her as the sound of her own voice. *Pant, pant, blow . . . Pant, pant, blow . . .* She'd led countless women through the sequence of those two quick pants followed by that short puff of air, but her lungs had constricted. The room started to spin. She couldn't find any oxygen.

Ian's mouth brushed her ear in a whisper. "Chicken shit."

The air rushed into her lungs, and the room settled. She inhaled again, her body steadied, and she began the breathing pattern.

The minutes ticked by. Kelly wiped the hair from

Savannah's damp face. Savannah fell into the rhythm of the contractions as they gained more intensity.

The front door burst open, and three of Valley City's volunteer firefighters rushed in. Ian shot up and positioned himself in front of them. "It's under control."

No, it wasn't under control!

"She's a nurse midwife," Ian said. "She's handling it."

"Get them out of here!" Savannah gasped. "Don't let them touch me."

"Stay by the door," Ian told the men. "She'll let you know if she needs you."

She. He meant Tess, not Savannah.

The firefighters were trained to give way to anyone with a higher degree of experience, and they did as he directed, even as Tess started to order them to take over. But she could see the top of the baby's head.

Savannah emitted the unmistakable guttural sound of a woman who needed to push.

"Don't push! Pant." Tess couldn't let her tear. She acted automatically, massaging Savannah's perineum to help it stretch naturally. Ian moved to the side to give her room. He held steady before all the muck of childbirth, and she'd never loved him more.

"Keep panting," she told Savannah. "We're taking it slow. That's it. Good."

The baby's head began to move. "Slow now. Slow."

The top of the baby's head emerged, and the contraction eased. "Good job. You're doing great."

Savannah dropped her own head on her folded arms to rest, her hips still high in the air. The beautiful indignity of giving birth.

"Keep panting," Tess said. "You're almost there."

With a deep grunt, Savannah was back up on all fours.

"Easy! Don't push. Pant." More of the wet, wrinkled head appeared. Tess kept the baby's head supported. In the background she heard Phish's contribution. The baby would enter the world to the muted sounds of the Grateful Dead singing "Ripple."

"That's the way. You're almost done." Another contraction. A tiny shoulder. The baby slipped into Tess's palms. "It's a boy."

Savannah collapsed onto her back. Tess wrapped the messy, blue-skinned baby in one of the dish towels Ian handed her. The infant gave a tiny mew followed by a lusty cry. Tess had no stethoscope but she went through the rest of the steps automatically: the cry, the flexation, chest moving. The baby was pinking up. All good.

She set the baby on Savannah's chest and covered them both with the coat Ian handed her. She leaned back on her heels, heart racing, listening to "Ripple," and waiting for the placenta. She delivered it into a plastic mixing bowl that she suspected Phish would never use again.

Savannah lay still, the baby to her chest. And now . . .

The screams . . . The gush of blood . . .

Tess swallowed hard.

But unlike Bianca, Savannah wasn't dying. She was too busy admiring her baby. "He's so much cuter than Mom's."

Tess had never heard more welcome words. She had a healthy mother. A healthy baby. She wanted to weep from gratitude.

Ian's complexion, however, had a faint green tint. "Good job," he said. "And I'm never having sex again."

At first Savannah, being Savannah, refused to go to the hospital with the firefighters. "Why should I? You said me and the baby are doing good, right?" She paused to gaze at her newborn, her features softened from an abundance of oxytocin and maternal love.

"Yes, but you both need to be checked."

"You already checked us."

"I'm not a doctor," Tess protested.

"Half the time you act like one."

The same old Savannah.

Savannah stunned her with a smile that transformed

her sulky nineteen-year-old expression into the face of a Madonna. "Zoro."

"Excuse me?"

"His name is Zoro. With one *r*. I don't want him to have the same name as every other kid."

"No worries. You and . . . Zoro . . . are going to the hospital whether you want to or not. Every newborn needs an immediate vitamin K shot."

Fortunately, Savannah had heard about the importance of the shot and agreed, but not until Tess promised to personally drive her and baby Zoro back home from the hospital the next day—and not until she lambasted Tess for not having a supply of vitamin K on hand. "If you're going to keep on delivering babies, you need to stay on top of this shit," she said as the firefighters approached with the stretcher.

"I'm not going to keep delivering babies."

"Why not?"

"Because I don't want to."

"That's totally selfish." Savannah kept talking as the firefighters transferred her and the baby to the stretcher. "Anybody can grind coffee, but not anybody can do what you did. Don't tell me you're seriously still hung up on what happened with Ian North's wife?"

"She wasn't his—"

"Jeez, Tess, what's wrong with you? That wasn't your fault. It could have happened to anybody." She lifted her head as the firefighters wheeled her toward the door. "I know for sure if I ever have another baby, which I am seriously not ever going to do, but if I did, I wouldn't let anybody deliver it but you. Get over yourself, okay? People need you."

And she was gone.

Ian approached Tess from behind. "Out of the mouths of bitches."

"Don't you start on me, too."

"No need. You already know what you have to do."

Ian left the Broken Chimney to retrieve Wren from Heather's while Tess drove home. She pulled in to the cabin instead of the schoolhouse where she wanted to be. It squatted in the clearing, gloomy and unwelcoming, no light on to greet her. She tried to get out of the car, but she couldn't face this place, not on a night when so much had happened. She backed out and drove up to the schoolhouse. Only for this one last night. And only with a clear head.

The white clapboard walls and old wooden floors embraced her. She was dirty, dog-tired, yet too full of energy to sleep. She lit a fire in the potbelly stove and poured herself a glass of wine. But she'd barely settled before the door burst open and a distraught Ava Winchester rushed in.

"Tess!" Ava raced across the room and threw herself into Tess's arms so suddenly that Tess nearly upended her wineglass.

"Oh, honey . . ."

Ava sobbed against her shoulder, her words running so closely together that it was impossible to make out what she was saying. Tess stroked her the same way she stroked Wren. She thought about how the people of this town had woven themselves into the fabric of her life. How this new life with all its warts and uncertainties felt so right.

Ava wept with the desperation of a teenager who believed her life was over. When she finally lifted her head, her cheeks were blotchy from crying, and her words came out as hiccups. ". . . awful, and . . . can't go back . . . pocket . . . kill me . . . stay here . . ."

"Shhh, sweetheart. Give yourself a minute. It's okay."

"It's not!" Her chest convulsed. "My dad is going to . . . he's going to kill me! He found . . . Connor—"

Tess jumped as a fist thundered at the door. Ava gasped and sprang up from the couch. The door flew open, and Brad Winchester stormed inside. "Ava! Come here right now!"

Kelly appeared in the doorway behind him, ashen-faced and trembling, still wearing the same clothes she'd worn at the Broken Chimney. Ava cowered. Tess wrapped her arms around the teen and confronted Winchester. "Stay where you are."

"Don't tell me what to do! You're responsible for this!" He opened his fist and revealed a pair of wrapped condoms. "I found these when I came home from that meeting of yours. They fell out of her coat pocket. My daughter!" His eyebrows drew together like silver lightning bolts. "Do you know what the penalty is for giving birth control to a minor without the parents' permission?"

She managed to sound calmer than she felt. "There is no penalty, Mr. Winchester, and I suggest you settle down before I throw you out."

You and what army? He didn't say it, but that's what she heard in her head because he was so intimidating.

He pointed his finger at his daughter. "I don't know what this woman's told you, but this is not how you were raised. You're going home right now. If I have to ground you for the rest of your life, I'll do it. I hope to God it's not too late."

"Dad!"

"I know what's best for you, and I don't want to hear another word." His eyes locked onto Tess even as he spoke to his daughter. "Go with your mother right now."

Kelly rushed forward. Ava sank into her mother's arms. "Mom . . ."

"Get to the car!" He pointed his finger at Tess. "And you . . . You've ignored my warnings right from the beginning, and now this. Do you have any idea how difficult I can make your life?"

"Brad, don't," Kelly said.

"Go to the car. Both of you."

Kelly clutched her daughter tighter but didn't move. He spoke coldly, methodically. "You hardly pay any property taxes on that place of yours. I think the county assessor needs to take a fresh look."

"Brad!" Kelly exclaimed.

"And the road up here. If the county falls down on the job, it'll be nearly impossible to get a car through. As for your job—"

"Brad, stop."

"This doesn't concern you, Kelly." He raised his chin. "That woman who died having the baby you're so attached to—"

"That's enough!" Kelly said.

"Maybe it's time somebody other than Freddy Davis took a closer look into the—"

"I gave Ava the condoms!" Kelly cried.

Brad barely seemed to have heard. "What?"

She released her daughter. "I'm the one who gave Ava the condoms."

He shook his head, confusion replacing his smugness. "You? You're the one who gave our baby—"

"Yes, me! Because she looks at Connor the same way I used to look at you. Because I don't want her to end up trapped the way I've been!"

"Trapped?" He tried to find his bluster. "You're hardly trapped."

"I feel trapped! Kelly do this. Kelly do that. You never ask. You demand. And I'm sick of it. Sick of you!"

"Stop talking like that. Saying things you don't mean."

"I mean every word."

Ava started to cry again. Tess hurried forward. This was a conversation Kelly and Brad needed to have alone. "I'm calling a time-out. Right now."

"You can't—"

"Yes, I can."

"Yes, she can!" Kelly exclaimed.

"I have to talk to Tess!" Ava wailed.

Tess touched Kelly's shoulder. "You and Ava go to the cabin. Stay there tonight and get some rest."

"Don't listen to her," Brad said. "Everybody has to calm down. We're going home—"

Ignoring him, Tess nudged Kelly. "Go on."

Without a glance at her husband, Kelly grabbed her daughter and rushed out.

Brad looked at Tess, bewilderment replacing his anger. "What have you done?"

"Given your family some breathing room."

Ian came in, Wren on his shoulder, and took in the scene in front of him. "Damn. Why does all the fun happen when I'm gone?"

"Go home," she told Winchester. "Or sleep in your car. In a tent. I don't care. But if you take one step toward that cabin tonight, you'll regret it."

"Don't you threaten me!"

"Why not? You've made it clear that I have nothing to lose. You, on the other hand, have everything."

"Winchester, just do whatever the hell she tells you," Ian said. "She's had a hard day, and she could be mentally unstable."

Tess gave Ian a weary smile and reclaimed her baby. Her heart-meltingly beautiful, sound-asleep little squid.

Brad Winchester collapsed on the couch and dropped his forehead into his hand.

Tomorrow, she'd apologize to Ian for abandoning him, but she couldn't take any more of Winchester or even of Kelly and Ava. She cradled her baby to her breast, climbed the steps to the bedroom, and shut them all away.

Chapter Twenty-One

Ian studied the man slumped on his couch, as unwelcome as a carbon monoxide leak. "Tess is impulsive, but she has good instincts. And the heart of a lion. If she says you need to stay away from the cabin tonight, I suggest you stay away."

Winchester rubbed his face in his palms. "My Ava . . . She's the most important thing in the world to me."

"Jesus, Winchester . . . Tell a therapist, not me."

"And Kelly . . . I've never loved another woman."

"Seriously. I'm not the one you want to confess your troubles to."

Winchester's head finally came up, the thick gray hair he was so vain about hanging lank over his forehead. "Yeah. You're right. Sorry."

Ian regarded him with disgust. "Leave or sleep in your car. I don't care. But stay the fuck away from the cabin."

Ian gazed toward the stairs, hesitated, and turned away to the geode bedroom.

Wren awakened Tess before six after a rotten night's sleep. Tess changed her diaper, slipped into sweats, and carried her downstairs, where she found Brad Winchester snoring on the couch, an empty bottle of Ian's scotch lying on the floor next to him. It was more than any mortal woman should have to face.

Ian was either still asleep or out on his morning ramble. She collected Wren's bottle, bundled her up, and made her way down the trail to the cabin.

Birdcalls whistled through the woods, and the redbud outside the back window showed the tiniest hint of pink. Someday she'd be able to appreciate it all.

She went upstairs and found Ava and Kelly asleep together in the small back bedroom. By now, Kelly would have seen enough of Tess's things in the cabin to know Tess was no longer living at the schoolhouse.

Careful not to wake them, she returned downstairs to give Wren her bottle. Wren's eyes were fixated on her. "You are the smartest, bravest, most mathematically gifted little girl in the universe," she told her.

No sense in passing on her own math aversion to her child.

Her child. The old unwelcome pit had resettled in her stomach. There was no three of them, only Tess and Wren, with Ian forever on the outside.

Wren burped, a big sound from such a little body. Tess patted her bottom and thought about the previous day: the trip to the hospital, her aborted community meeting, delivering Savannah's baby, and the final explosive encounter with the Winchesters. Looming over it all, the identity of Wren's father. She wanted to run away from it all, but that was no longer an option.

Kelly eventually stumbled downstairs, followed by Ava. They wore the same rumpled clothes from the night before, although Ava's jeans and sweater had held up better than her mother's blouse. Kelly looked past Tess and ran a hand through her unkempt hair. Ava poked at a floorboard with a black and gray argyle sock. Neither of them seemed to know what to say. Tess offered up Wren as an ice breaker. "One of you hold her, will you? I'll make coffee. And how about toast? I'm afraid I don't have anything more to offer."

"You have a lot to offer, Tess." Kelly finally met her eyes. "I'm sorry we put you through all that last night. Sorry about the way Brad treated you. The way I treated you." She picked up her purse from the table next to the couch. "We have to go. We've imposed on you long enough."

"If you need to stay for a while, you're welcome to."

Kelly bit her bottom lip. "I'll have to face him sooner or later."

"Mom." Ava's head came up, her customary sparkle extinguished. "Mom, I have to talk to Tess. Alone."

Kelly's face fell. "Oh . . ." Her fingers constricted around the strap of her purse. "Only her?"

"Please? I need to."

Kelly's internal struggle in the face of her daughter's rejection was heartbreaking to watch. "I see." Her shoulders slumped. "All right. Maybe I could—" She struggled for something to say, somewhere to go. "I— I can wait on the porch."

Tess couldn't bear it. "Ava, your mother will always be there for you. You can count on her in ways you won't be able to count on me. Can we talk together? All three of us?"

Wren squawked. "Sorry, Wren," Tess amended. "All four of us."

That elicited the wobbliest of smiles from Ava, a smile that quickly faded. "It's bad, Mom. It's really bad."

Kelly's hand flew to her mouth. "You're pregnant!"

"No! Ohmygod, no!"

Kelly rushed to her side. "He raped you."

"No!" Ava drew away from her mother and collapsed on the couch, where she started to cry. "I almost . . . I don't wish he had. I mean, that's awful. But, it's . . . If he had, I wouldn't feel so guilty. It wouldn't be my fault."

Tess carried Wren toward the window so Kelly and Ava could have this time together. Kelly sank onto the cushion beside her. "Baby, this has nothing to do with fault. Not a single thing."

Ava raised her head, looked at her mother. "But we did it, Mom. Last night. While you and dad were at the meeting. I told Connor I wouldn't do it unless he like wore a condom, and he didn't want to, but he did. But it hurt. I didn't like it. I told him I didn't want to do it again, not for a long time. And he laughed at me, Mom. He laughed at me and told me I was a big baby."

Tess gritted her teeth, unable to stay quiet. "I am going to take that boy *out!*"

But Kelly's entire focus was on her daughter. She stroked her tangled hair and cupped her cheek. "You spoke up for yourself, baby. I'm so proud of you."

"But I spoke up too late," Ava sobbed. "And . . . I wanted to do it. But now . . . I hate Connor! Everybody thinks he's so fine, but he's not. And now you and Dad are going to get a divorce, and it's all because of me."

"No!" Kelly gripped Ava's hands and shook them between her own. "Don't even think that. If your dad and I get a divorce, it'll be because of me. Because I don't have the same kind of courage you have. I never speak up. I let Dad make all the decisions for us. Yours and mine. I let him order me around. But worst of all, I've let him tell me who I am instead of figuring it out for myself."

Ava's lower lip trembled, like the child she still was. "Do you . . . Do you love him anymore?"

"I love you. We both love you."

"But . . . Do you still love him?"

Kelly looked away from her and then back. "I want to say that I do, so I won't scare you. But that's how I've behaved my whole life. Saying what other people want me to say instead of what I feel. And right now . . . Right now, I don't . . . I don't think I do."

Ava started to cry again. Kelly stroked her hair, but she didn't take back what she'd said. Tess observed it all and silently promised Wren that she'd do her best to keep things honest between them.

She made coffee and laced a cup of mint tea with honey for Ava so they could have some breathing room before they went home. Relinquishing their secrets to each other seemed to have brought them closer. They both held Wren, and Tess found herself telling them about Trav. It was nice being able to share that part of her past with them, even nicer to talk about Trav as she might speak of a once beloved childhood friend who'd moved far away.

When they'd had enough time to regain their equilibrium, she offered them her car to drive home, but they decided to walk. She carried Wren upstairs. The bed looked so inviting that she curled up with her, and they both fell asleep.

She awakened to the sound of footsteps on the stairs. She opened her eyes as Ian walked in. He gazed down at her, taking her in from her toes to out-of-control hair. "You're a sight, Tess Hartsong."

She yawned. "And good morning to you." She slid her legs over the edge of the bed. Wren performed her best baby stretch, and Ian came over to pick her up.

"I kicked Winchester out, but now he's come back. He says he has to talk to you."

She moaned. "Do I look like I'm awake enough to endure another character assassination?"

"You do not." He tucked Wren in the crook of his elbow. "He says he won't leave until he talks to you. I'm aching to throw his ass out, but I don't want him coming down here while you're alone."

"Thoughtful."

"Knowing you, I also suspect there's an off chance you actually want to talk to the son of a bitch, something I highly recommend you forgo."

"Look! Wren's smiling at you!"

"Yeah, she does that every once in a while."

"It's like she's flirting."

"Little girls and their—" He stopped and brushed his thumb along the edge of Wren's blanket. When he looked up, he regarded Tess with disgust. "You're going to do it, aren't you? Talk to him."

"It's a sickness." She grabbed a brush from the dresser and ran it through her tangles.

"If he expects me to leave you alone with him, he'll have to rethink."

She tugged at a tangle. "For a man who hates messy emotions, you can't seem to get out of the sludge pond."

"I almost feel sorry for the son of a bitch. You should see him. He's so used to everything going his way that he doesn't know how to cope when it doesn't."

She could see what Ian meant. Winchester's skin was ashen, his manicured gray hair disheveled enough to reveal a newly balding patch at the crown. One side of his dress shirt hung out of his wrinkled trousers, and his bare ankles indicated he'd forgotten to put his socks back on before he'd shoved his feet into his formal black wingtips.

He heaved himself from the couch and regarded her with his customary belligerence. "Since you seem to know everything, explain my wife's insane behavior."

"It's not insane," Tess said.

"Everything was fine until you came here."

Ian handed Wren over to her, a muscle in the corner of his jaw ticking. "Here's a thought, Winchester. Maybe if you stopped blaming Tess for your problems and looked at yourself, you could figure this out."

"Kelly didn't start sneaking off to the cabin until she got here."

"Possibly because Tess made the cabin habitable again," Ian retorted. "You have a broken family, man. The family you're so proud of. Your wife is suffocating and your daughter is afraid of you, and all you want to do is blame Tess."

Brad's belligerence collapsed like a parachute hitting the ground. He dropped to the couch and sank his head in his hands. "When did I turn into the bad guy? I love my wife. And since when is it a sin to want to keep your daughter safe and innocent? To protect her."

"You love your daughter," Ian said. "I'll buy that. But your wife? Do you love her or do you only love the way she does everything you tell her?" He leaned against the wall by the piano. "Here's why I think you have such a vendetta against Tess. Because you can't control her. She doesn't care that you're the big man around here, and she's missed the memo that says everybody's supposed to suck up to you."

"That's not true." It sounded more like a question than a statement. "She . . . We have our values. We . . ." He made a helpless, halfhearted gesture. "I've had plenty of chances, but I've never once screwed around on Kelly. All these years. I've given her everything she could possibly want."

Ian wouldn't back off. "Just a wild guess, but did you think of asking her what she wanted or did you only tell her? You're a bully, Winchester. You've bought into the bullshit about your own self-importance. You're the guy with the money and the connections. But now somebody you care about has pushed back, and you can't hack it." Winchester flinched, but Ian wasn't done. "Man up, dude. Take some fucking responsibility."

The town's most prominent citizen collapsed in on himself. "All I want is my wife back. How am I sup-posed to do that?"

"Hell if I know," Ian said. "You'll have to ask Kelly."

Winchester rose unsteadily from the couch. Without a backward look at either of them, he stumbled out.

And Tess had barely said a word.

"That," she told Ian, "was awesome."

He smiled. "More awesomeness awaits."

"What do you mean?"

He gazed at the baby in her arms. "Wren, do you want to see my tree house?" He bent close to her face, as if he were listening. "Yep. She does."

And so they climbed to the tree house together, the three of them, Wren in Ian's arms. Tess sat on the edge, her legs dangling. Ian settled next to her. Wren was all big eyes, fascinated by the play of sunlight through the frail spring leaves beginning to open above her.

Tess braced herself to ask the question that had been tormenting her ever since Ian had left. "Tell me what you found out."

"None of Bianca's friends and ex-friends knew any more than we do, so I drove out to Queens. I'd had her things shipped to a storage facility until I figured out what to do with them, and I decided to take another look."

"You found something."

He nodded. "Inside an old makeup case from her modeling years. I almost missed it."

"What was it?"

"The Holy Grail."

Wren sneezed.

"I found paperwork," he said. "From a sperm bank."

It took her a moment to comprehend. "Are you telling me . . . ?"

"Wren is a sperm donor baby."

Tess's hand flew to her mouth.

"I took the documents right to my attorney. Everything is legal. For once in her life, Bianca did it all right."

"Oh, Ian . . ." Her heart stretched so wide in her chest that it squeezed out everything else. Bianca had no family, and Ian's name was on Wren's birth certificate. Her child's eyes sprang open as a tear landed on the baby's cheek. Tess sniffed and swiped the back of her hand over her own eyes. "Is it really over? Is she really mine?"

He nodded. "You have everything you want. Not only Wren. After last night, I think you have your career back."

It was true. Tess had safely delivered a healthy baby under difficult circumstances without losing the mother, but was that enough to break through her paralysis, or was she going to keep running away?

Never again. Bianca's death would always be with her. She couldn't imagine delivering a child without experiencing that tug of fear. But she'd do it. She'd worked through it last night, and she'd work through it every time. She was a midwife. That was her identity.

A bird fluttered in the branches over her head. She'd have it all. Her career. Her child. The mountain that had become her home, and the town that both embraced and challenged her. Everything except Ian North.

She gazed out at the treetops. "Now we don't have to stay married."

He shifted next to her. "There's no rush, but . . ." He rubbed his hand over his jaw. "I've gotten an offer for the schoolhouse."

She swallowed. Looked straight ahead. "Are you going to sell?"

"I don't know."

She made herself say the obvious. "It isn't as though life here has worked out for you."

"No, it hasn't."

She rose from the edge of the platform. "I need to pick up Savannah at the hospital."

"The ladder's steep. Give Wren to me."

"I can handle her."

"I know you can, but . . ."

She was already maneuvering down the rungs. At the bottom, she hesitated. He stood above her at the top of the ladder. She needed to say something, and she needed to say it now while she had her clothes on and was thinking clearly. "I think you should take the offer."

"Why's that?" He came halfway down the ladder before he swung himself to the ground.

"You should know better than anyone. You haven't been able to produce anything you like since you got here, and you've been roped into a marriage you don't want, along with taking responsibility for a child who's not yours."

"Nobody made me do anything," he said stubbornly.

"Ian, you have to cut free. For yourself and for Wren." Tess knew she had to be clear about this, even if it broke her heart. "If you stay at the schoolhouse, you'll seem permanent to Wren, and she'll want more than you can be expected to give. I don't want her attaching daddy fantasies to you. It's not fair to either of you."

"Jesus, Tess, she's only seven weeks old. There's plenty of time."

"She already goes to you as easily as she comes to me."

"She's a newborn! There's no rush."

"Just do it, Ian. There's no reason to wait." She strode toward the schoolhouse, leaving him behind.

Ian didn't like anything about their conversation, especially her implication that he posed some kind of danger to Wren. Tess was crazy. And yet . . .

That edginess he'd been dealing with since the night he'd painted her body—the uneasiness that was screwing up his sleep—wasn't quite as sharp. Not only had she given him permission to reclaim his life, she'd practically ordered him to do it.

Tess was at the hospital waiting for Savannah to be released when Kelly called. "Brad came back to the house this morning, but I'm not ready to talk to him. I know you're living at the cabin now, but would it be a terrible imposition if I took the other bedroom? Just for a bit. I shouldn't ask, but—"

"Of course, you can." Kelly didn't inquire why Tess was living there now, but she had to be curious.

It rained on the trip back to Tempest. Savannah rode in the backseat along with Zoro and Wren. She spent the first few miles gloating over being discharged less than twenty-four hours after she'd arrived at the hospital while her mother couldn't leave until later today. For once, Tess welcomed Savannah's chatter, since it almost kept her from thinking about Ian.

"Are you even listening to me?" Savannah said from behind her.

"I'm listening."

"Promise you'll tell me if I'm doing anything wrong. I'm not screwing up Zoro like Mom screwed me up."

"Savannah, since when have you ever listened to my advice?"

Savannah cracked her chewing gum. "I've changed. I'm a mother now."

"How have you changed? Not even twenty minutes ago, you told me my jeans were too baggy and I should dye my hair because it's boring."

"That doesn't have anything to do with the baby! That's for your own good."

Tess raised her eyes to the roof of the car. "Dear Lord, don't let me dump her on the side of the road no matter how tempting."

Savannah grinned. "I did great yesterday, didn't I?"

"You did great," Tess acknowledged.

"A lot better than mom."

"I'm pleading the Fifth."

"I don't know what that means, but all I'm saying is that I didn't go batshit like she did." Another crack of her gum. "Because of you."

"I'm glad it was a good experience." More glad than Savannah could ever know.

"You were so calm through the whole thing. You knew exactly what to do."

"If you give me any more compliments, I'm going to have you checked for a head injury."

"I'll make Phish clear out the back room so Mom

and I can set up a nursery there for Zoro and John. What kind of a lame-ass name is John? All the kids'll make fun of him."

There were so many responses Tess could make, but she took the high road. "It's nice they'll grow up together."

"Wren'll grow up with them, too."

"I hope so."

In the rearview mirror, Tess saw Savannah drape her arm over her son's car seat. "You need to open a doctor practice, Tess. You really do."

"I'm not a doctor."

"You know what I mean. Being a midwife. A lot of women around here don't like doctors, but they'd go to you. Remember that empty building Phish owns down from the Broken Chimney? You could rent it from him. Have some kind of office there."

"You're going too fast for me."

"Somebody has to push you. It's like you have to take forever to make up your mind about anything."

"Don't forget how many people still think I murdered Wren's mother."

"Nobody really thinks that, Tess. It's just that a lot of people—like a lot of women—are kind of threatened by you."

"Threatened?" The windshield wipers squeaked against the glass. "Why would anybody be threatened by me?"

"Oh, come on. Like you don't know."

"I don't know!" Tess exclaimed.

"Keep your eyes on the road. You've got babies back here."

"This coming from the worst driver in the world."

"I s'pose you're clueless enough not to know. It's because of the way their guys look at you," Savannah said with exaggerated patience. "Not like all of them. But like a lot. Even guys who don't screw around, like my dad. It drives Mom crazy. The wives and girlfriends don't like it."

"You're exaggerating."

"For a medical person, you should be more observant."

Tess remembered that silly thing Ian had called her. *A luscious widow.* She stomped on the accelerator. "Ridiculous."

After she'd settled Savannah and Zoro, Tess stopped at the cabin to check on Kelly and was greeted with the smell of fresh baking. "I know this is an imposition," Kelly said from the couch, where she and Ava were each eating a sugar cookie as they watched the rain tap on the windows. "I'm sorry. I'm not sure where else to go right now."

"Mom, you said you were going to stop apologizing all the time."

"Yes, but . . . We've taken over Tess's home."

Tess hung up her jacket and transferred Wren into the sling. "You're welcome as long as I can have a cookie. Did those really come from my oven?"

"I hope you don't mind."

"I'm glad to know it works."

Tess sat in the armchair across from the couch with Wren curled against her and took the cookie Kelly offered.

"This is only temporary," Kelly said. "Staying here."

There was nothing like a warm cookie to help stave off sadness, and Tess took another bite. "If you keep baking like this, I don't care how long you stay."

Kelly resettled next to her daughter and gazed out the window. "I'm thinking about going to college."

"Really, Mom?"

"I've wanted to do it for years." She looked over at Tess. "Whenever I brought it up to Brad, he'd tell me I already had everything I wanted, and I didn't need a degree."

"He's weird," Ava said. "He's always telling me how important it is to go to college. He wants me to be a lawyer."

"What do you want?" Tess said.

"Well . . ." Ava looked embarrassed. "I kind of want to be a lawyer."

Kelly laughed, which made Ava defensive. "So I'm better prepared to go into politics. I think more women need to be in government, don't you?"

"Definitely," Tess said.

Ava pulled her legs out from under her. "Mom, I remember the things Dad told you whenever you talked about going back to school."

"It doesn't matter."

"He said it was a stupid idea. He said you weren't a good enough student in high school to go to college."

"I never studied. It's why I'm so strict about you doing your homework."

"You're a lot better in math than I am." Ava looked at Tess. "Dad told Mom she didn't need another degree because she already had her M.R.S. Isn't that like something old people used to say back in like the sixties or something?"

"Don't look at me," Tess said. "I wasn't born then."

Ava set aside what was left of her third cookie and

studied her socks. "Dad pulled me out of last period algebra today."

Kelly frowned. "He shouldn't have done that."

"It was okay. We sat in his car and talked. Or I guess he talked. He said he's sorry and that he wants things to be different between us." She rubbed the toe of her socks against the rug. "He said I can tell him anything, and he won't get mad at me. Like I'd really do that." She twisted a lock of her hair. "I think he thinks I didn't like have sex, and I didn't tell him I did. But . . . He didn't look good, Mom. I'm so mad at him, but I kind of feel sorry for him, too."

"Your father is a grown man. You're not responsible for him."

"I know that, but . . . I told him I was sorry I'd disappointed him. I tried not to cry, but I cried a little, and do you know what he said? He said I could never disappoint him in a million years. He told me I was perfect."

Kelly smiled. "You're not. But I love that he thinks so."

"He asked me to come back home tonight."

"What did you say?"

"I told him I'd give it due consideration."

Kelly laughed. "Did you really say that? 'Due consideration'?"

Ava nodded. "He also tried to tell me some things

he wanted me to tell you, but I told him I wouldn't do that. He had to talk to you himself."

"Good girl."

"So what I'm thinking is . . . While you figure out what you're going to do, I might sometimes stay here with you and sometimes stay with him. Is that okay?"

"Of course it is. Your father loves you, and you love him. Nothing will ever change that."

Ava left not long after, kissing her mother and refusing to take any cookies home to her father.

Tess needed to tell Kelly she'd be staying at the cabin instead of the schoolhouse. She could lie, say she didn't want to distract Ian from his work, but Kelly had been honest with her, and she deserved honesty in return. She cuddled Wren and told her the truth. Or most of it, anyway. She didn't tell her how deeply she'd fallen in love with Ian, and she definitely didn't mention their astonishing sex life. When she finished, Kelly regarded her sympathetically. "Well, aren't we a pair?"

"That we are."

With both Michelle and Savannah on leave, Tess had promised Phish she'd work that night. As she went upstairs to get ready, Kelly asked her about Wren.

"I'm taking her to Heather's."

"Why don't you leave her with me? I'd love to watch her."

"You don't mind?"

"Not at all." Kelly smiled fondly at Tess's sleeping daughter. "It'll be like the old days."

Tess received a hero's welcome at the Broken Chimney. It was as though she'd never been the town pariah. Everyone wanted to hear about last night, and she had her hands full talking and filling orders at the same time. Two hours elapsed before she realized she'd left her phone in her car. If Kelly had an emergency, she couldn't reach her.

She abandoned a half-made salted-caramel hot chocolate and raced out the back door.

The rain had stopped, but the security light spread a rancid yellow phosphorescence across the alley. A shadow moved behind her car. A shadow that shouldn't have been there.

Tess took a quick step to the side and saw Courtney Hoover. Her hand was frozen in midair—a hand that held a tube of lipstick. Smeared across the rear window of Tess's SUV were seven letters and part of the eighth: MURDEREI

Tess charged forward. "You're the one!" she exclaimed.

Hostility radiated from Courtney like toxic waste. "Everybody in there is kissing your fat ass!"

Tess grabbed the lipstick from her. "I wouldn't call it fat. I'd call it ample."

Courtney wailed like a petulant kindergartner. "I work out every day. It's not fair!"

"My ass?"

"Artie! It's your fault that we broke up!"

"Artie?"

"We were doing fine until you showed up."

Slowly, the pieces came together. Tess remembered how many times Artie had arrived at the Broken Chimney only to have Courtney appear, too.

"We were going to get back together. We always got back together. Then you started coming on to him."

"That's right," Tess retorted. "I'm married to the sexiest man in Tempest, Tennessee, but secretly lusting after Artie Thompson."

"You're always talking to him!"

"I talk to everybody. If you and Artie broke up, it doesn't have anything to do with me, and you know it."

"We always got back together. Right until you and your fat ass—"

Tess shoved Courtney and her pristine white jacket against the lipstick-smeared rear window. "That was one 'fat ass' too many."

All of Courtney's exercising was no match for Tess's anger, and she fended her off well enough to dive into

Courtney's pocket, pull out her phone, and hold it up to her overly made-up face to unlock it. "Smile."

Courtney lunged at her, but not before Tess snapped a photo.

"Give me that!"

"Not yet!" With a sharp jab of her elbow, Tess sent Courtney back against the car. Tess examined the photo. It couldn't have been better. Shadows from the security light had turned the Instagram Queen's eye sockets into sulfurous holes and formed wrinkles where there were none. "Not your best shot."

And then she texted it to herself.

With a cry, Courtney once again grabbed for her phone. This time, Tess let her have it. "Just so you know, that's going straight to the cloud, where it'll stay. Unless . . ."

Courtney whimpered.

"Unless you piss me off again." Tess retrieved her own phone from the car. As she shut the door, she pointed to the rear window. "Clean up that mess. And don't even think about coming back to the Broken Chimney until you can act like a decent human being."

The canvas squares from four nights ago were dry now. Ian studied the multicolored images he'd transferred from Tess's body. Maybe he'd hoped they'd somehow unlock the secret of what he needed to do next. Something spectacular. Something important. But nothing came to him. The ideas that used to tumble through his head so quickly he could barely catch them were nowhere to be found. He'd lost his identity, and so he did nothing.

He carried a sketchbook over to the window and flipped through it. Page after page of fine-line drawings as detailed as a Dürer engraving: Wren's eyes, Tess's mouth; Wren's curled hands, Tess's bare foot; Tess's bristly hairbrush, Wren's silky one; a sneaker, a bootie. He tossed the sketchbook aside. He should slam a stencil against the biggest building he could find and create something that made sense to him. A monster cat with all the world's people falling like mice from its gaping mouth. A tree crawling with twisted animals groping for the world's last food resources.

But those images were nothing but regurgitated crap.

The front door banged open downstairs, and a woman cried out, "Ian! Ian, are you here?"

He hurried from the studio.

A frantic Kelly Winchester stood at the bottom of the stairs. "It's Wren! She's gone!"

Chapter Twenty-Two

I an burst into the cabin, his heart battering his ribs. Wren's sleeping nest sat empty except for her pink blanket. He broke out in a cold sweat.

Kelly rushed through the door behind him. "I only went upstairs for a few minutes! She was asleep!"

He snatched up the baby monitor. "Did you take this with you when you went upstairs? Did you hear anything?"

"No!" she cried. "No, I didn't even think of it. Why didn't I think of it?"

"What about a car? Did you hear a car outside?"

"No. Nothing."

He checked the front door. "This is locked. What about the back door? Was it locked?"

"I don't know. I can't remember. I—" She pressed the heels of her hands to her temples. "I— No. When I ran out to get you, it wasn't locked. I didn't lock it after Tess left. I should have done that!"

"How long were you upstairs?"

"I don't— Maybe five minutes? Ten? I shouldn't have left her!"

"Did you hear anything unusual? See anything?"

"No, nothing. Ava and Tess were here today, but nobody else. Tess got a bottle ready for me before she left. I gave it to Wren, and she fell asleep. I held her for a while." Kelly started to cry. "She was so sweet. Lying in my arms. Those little fingers . . . I put her down so I could unpack."

He thought of all the scrapes he'd been in as a kid. Ducking his father's fists. Running from the police. Even Bianca's death. None of it had given him this mind-numbing fear. "Call Freddy Davis and the county sheriff. You stay here." He set his teeth. "I'm going after your husband."

"No!" Kelly grabbed his arm. "No, Ian. Brad would never do anything like this. Never!"

"Like hell. He's had Tess in his crosshairs from the beginning."

"That's his ego." She swiped at her runny nose with

her sleeve. "You have to trust me. Brad can be an ass, but he wouldn't kidnap a child. If you waste time with him, whoever did this will only get farther away." She shoved her keys at him. "Take my car. I'll call Freddy and the sheriff. Go!"

The person who stole Wren could be miles from here by now, but doing nothing was unthinkable. He ran outside but stopped before he reached Kelly's car. He had to think. To push aside the nightmare images of Wren tossed on the floor of a strange car, no blanket, her tiny arms and legs flailing. He didn't trust Kelly's assessment of Brad's innocence, but what if she was right?

The rain had left muddy craters in the cabin's sad excuse for a driveway. Kelly said she hadn't heard a car, but she could have missed it. If he backed out her car, he'd be driving over any tracks that might have been left. He switched on his cell phone's flashlight and swept it over the ground. He might not know anything about tracking, but he knew a hell of a lot about patterns.

It was easy to match the tread on Kelly's tires with one set of tracks. He circled the light until he found a different tread. Had it come from Tess's car or the kidnappers? He looked more closely. He could see lots of footprints but no other tread marks. Only two cars

had driven in here—Kelly's and Tess's. Someone could
have left a car down on the road.

The longer he stood here playing boy detective, the
farther away the kidnapper might be. The horrific
images of Wren screaming . . . abandoned . . . cold . . .
swarmed his brain. He refocused on the muddy footprints: Tess's, his own, Kelly's. She'd said Ava was
here, so her prints were probably also somewhere in
this mess.

Sweat drenched his T-shirt, and his hands started
to shake. His life had shifted into slow motion. *Focus!*
A footprint was nothing more than a pattern, and patterns were his life's blood. *Look closer.*

Prints pointed toward the cabin's back door. Prints
pointed away. Impossible to sort them all out. He had
to. They were only forms and shapes. An everyday part
of his world.

He sorted them in his head. Cataloged them. His
large shoe print was easiest to find. Next to Kelly's car,
he spotted a diamond tread and a flat imprint, each
small enough to suggest a woman's shoe. Kelly and
Ava. He squatted down closer to examine a fourth pair.
This one was slightly longer than the other two, and
narrower, with a waffle print at the toe heel, but no
visible instep. He'd drawn Tess's foot enough to know

that she had a high instep, but did that mean her sneakers had the same?

He shoved his hand through his hair. Blinked to clear his vision. And then he saw it.

A fifth footprint.

He examined it. Spotted its mate.

There.

And there.

He swept the flashlight in a wider arc to the perimeter of the muddy area. Over there. And there.

He followed his gut into the woods.

Brush clawed at his jeans, and wet branches slapped his bare arms. He hadn't thought to grab a jacket, and it was cold. Too cold for a vulnerable infant. He found more footprints. The moon was out, but it didn't offer enough light to penetrate the forest canopy. How much charge did he have left in his phone? If it died, he'd have no light at all.

His breath grated in his ears. He stopped looking for footprints and began to run. If he was wrong . . .

At the top of the ridge, the dogs heard him coming and unleashed a ferocious barking. The front door flew open, and Paul Eldridge stood silhouetted against the light, his rifle pointed. "Who's there?"

"It's Ian North." The gate was padlocked. Ian vaulted over it, cutting his hand on the way.

"Buck! Deke!" Paul called off the dogs. They snarled at Ian's ankles but didn't attack.

Ian covered the uneven ground in long, quick strides, images of those small sneaker prints burned in his mind. "Where's Eli?"

"Eli? He's in his room. What's going on?"

If Ian was wrong, he'd have wasted time he could never get back, but if he was right . . . "I need to see him."

Paul, visibly confused, stepped back from the door to let him in.

Rebecca sat curled up on the couch in a dirty nightgown, greasy hair hanging around her face. She gazed at Ian with empty eyes as her husband disappeared through the curtained doorway, calling out for his son. "Eli!"

Within seconds, Paul burst back through the curtain. "He's not here! What's going on? Where's my kid?"

Ian braced his bloody hand against the doorframe. "Eli has my daughter."

"The baby? What the hell are you talking about? Why would he have a baby?"

"Later. For now, we have to find him." Ian snatched up one of the flashlights they kept by the door and raced outside.

The dogs snarled but didn't attack. Ian ran toward the outbuildings, stopping at Paul's truck to whip upon the driver's door. No one was inside.

"I'll take the barn," Paul shouted from behind him.

They searched the property together, calling Eli's name. Each fruitless, passing second lasted forever. Paul asked no questions, either because he didn't want to slow the search or because he'd figured it out for himself. "I'm going up to the knob," he said.

"I'll head the other way. And, Paul . . . she's only seven weeks old."

Paul gave an abrupt nod and took off. Ian headed the other way, working hard not to let his fear slow him down. There was only one reason for Eli to have taken Wren. His eight-year-old brain must have decided to give Wren to his mother so she'd get better. But why hadn't he made it back here? And where was he?

Every possibility was worse than the last. All the accidents that could befall a child carrying a newborn through the forest at night hammered through his brain. Where would he go if he were a kid in the biggest trouble of his life?

To the basement storage area of his condo. That's where he'd hidden from his father, but Eli didn't have that option.

Ian veered off the main trail onto a smaller, barely

accessible path. He barely noticed the scratches on his arm or the stinging in his injured hand as he imagined Eli taking Wren by the creek. He'd seen what rainfall could do to that water. He ran faster.

The abandoned still squatted in the distance, shards of moonlight spattering the rusted ruins. He heard the gush of the swollen creek water . . . and the animal sound of an infant's inconsolable cries.

His heart exploded in his chest. She was alive.

Ian raced across the clearing, dropping the flashlight and whipping off his T-shirt as he ran. Eli crouched against the rusted oil drum with Wren screaming and squirming precariously on his skinny knees. Her blanket was gone, leaving her in nothing but a thin cotton one-piece.

Ian picked her up, wrapping her clumsily as he curled her quaking body against him.

Her ear-piercing animal wail filled the clearing. He willed his body's heat into her, murmured to her, silly words, comfort words. He pressed his lips to her forehead. "You're all right. . . . I have you. . . . I have you. You're all right. Shh . . ."

Eli came to his feet sobbing. "I was gonna take her back! I was! She got heavy! *I'm sorry!*"

Ian snatched up the flashlight, not trusting himself to look at him. "Go home!"

Cradling his precious cargo, he strode toward the trail, ignoring the throbbing in his bloody hand, focusing only on warming her. Eli was still crying behind him. Let Paul deal with him.

As if it had happened yesterday, he felt his father's fist . . . *"You worthless piece of shit!"*

Paul Eldridge was a hard man. What if . . . Ian slowed and did what he least wanted to do. Forced himself to turn around.

Eli crouched on the ground, his hands over his head in exactly the way Ian used to crouch to avoid his father's blows.

Ian's jaw tightened. "You're coming with me."

Eli's head came up. "But—"

"You heard what I said. Get going."

"I'm sorry!"

"Shut up and start walking."

Eli regarded him fearfully but did as he was told.

Wren had finally quieted, either from the warmth of his body or the rhythm of his stride. They made their way down the ridge accompanied only by the sound of their footsteps and Eli's snuffles.

Red lights from a police cruiser flashed over the cabin. Tess's car was parked next to Kelly's. He knew exactly how Tess was feeling right now, and he quickened his stride, even as Eli lagged farther behind.

Freddy Davis stood by the fireplace, scribbling something in a field notebook, Kelly sat on the couch, her head in her hands, and Tess stood in the middle of the room as if she didn't know what else to do with herself. She was the first to see him coming through the back door. She let out a guttural howl that stunned him. Only when he looked down did he see what she did.

Wren, wrapped in a T-shirt splattered with blood.

Tess lips parted, frozen in terror.

"It's my blood!" he exclaimed. "I cut my hand. It's my blood."

Tess sank to the floor. His warrior woman brought to her knees.

He rushed to her side and knelt. "Look at her. She's not hurt, just asleep."

He didn't know she wasn't hurt. He knew she wasn't bleeding, but she'd also been exposed to the cold and jostled, maybe dropped. She could end up with pneumonia or a head injury, or—

With a sob, Tess took her from him.

Kelly had come off the couch, and Freddy Davis was using his shoulder microphone. Ian finally remembered Eli. With a last glance at Wren, he went back outside.

He thought the boy might have run off, but he was huddled against the side of the cabin. "Come inside, Eli."

Eli raised his dirty, tear-streaked face. "My mom . . . She's always crying, and she won't eat anymore, and I think she might die. I thought if maybe she had a baby. . . . Or maybe if she could even hold a baby for a while . . ." He hiccupped on a sob. "I was gonna talk to Tess about it, but she wasn't here, and I saw Wren, and I was really, really careful. But then she started to cry really hard, and I tripped and almost fell. And I knew I'd done a really bad thing and even if my mom dies, I knew I had to bring Wren back."

Ian spoke as calmly as he could manage. "Tell me the truth. I promise I won't get mad. Did you drop Wren? Did she fall?"

"No! That's why I had to stop. My arms were hurting, and she was screaming and wiggling, and I was afraid I was gonna drop her. I was gonna bring her back. I promise!"

"Stay here."

Ian went back inside. Tess had Wren wrapped in a blanket. He was still bare-chested and freezing his ass off. The black-and-red flannel shirt he'd given her weeks ago hung on a hook by the door. As he pulled it on, he gave Freddy a brief outline of what had happened. "The Eldridges don't have a phone, and I need to get Eli home. You can talk to him tomorrow if you need to."

"You'd better do something about that hand first," Freddy said.

"Later." He grabbed Tess's car keys.

Freddy followed him outside and hovered over the frightened eight-year-old. "If you were my kid, you wouldn't sit down for a month."

Exactly what Ian was afraid of.

Paul came running from the field as he spotted Ian's headlights. "Eli!" He pulled open the car door and reached in to grab his son. "Eli! Where have you been? What the hell did you do?" He glanced over at Ian. "Is the baby all right?"

Ian nodded. "Yes. We need to talk."

"Damn straight we're going to talk." He jerked his son from the car and toward the front door. Ian followed.

Rebecca stood with one hand curled over the back of the couch to support herself. "Eli!"

Eli ran to her, crying and apologizing, his words muffling as he buried his face against her.

Paul stood watching them. His clothes were worn, his hands dirty. The deep, sun-etched lines in his face made him look older than he was. Ian touched his shoulder. "Outside. We have some things to discuss."

Paul didn't protest. He was a man comfortable with hard work, not emotional displays, something Ian understood all too well.

The dogs sniffed at Ian's feet as they went into the yard. Paul pulled a pack of cigarettes from his shirt pocket. "I'll make this up to you," he said stiffly.

"There's only one thing I want."

"What is it?"

Ian gazed toward the ramshackle barn. "I grew up with an old man who beat the shit out of me. I want your word that won't happen to Eli."

Paul's jaw tightened. "He's going to be punished, that's for damn sure."

"Think long and hard about what that punishment is going to be." Ian set his uninjured hand against one of the barn's rough posts. "I'll give it to you straight. What Eli did is on you."

"What are you talking about?"

"Tess told you a week ago that your wife needs help. Hell, anybody could see that. But you haven't done a damn thing about it, have you?"

"We take care of ourselves," Paul said stubbornly.

Ian met his glare dead-on. "How's that working out for you?"

Paul looked away. "She'll get over it."

"When? Eli believes his mother's dying, and from the look of things, I can't blame him. What he did was scary as hell, but it was the only way he could think of to help his mother. How does that feel, Eldridge? A kid trying to do what you won't do."

"You think I don't love my kid? That I don't love my wife? That's why we're here. So I can keep them safe from all the shit out there!"

"But what's keeping them safe from you?" Ian said quietly.

Paul stared at him.

"You're pigheaded and stubborn. Your wife needs counseling, medication—hell, I don't know. All I know is that telling her to get over it isn't working, and because of that, you put my family in jeopardy. You did it. Not your kid."

Ian half-expected Paul to take a swing at him, but he didn't. Instead, he ground out his cigarette and stalked back to his house.

Tess looked up at him as he came in. She was curled in the chair by the cabin window, her face pale and Wren asleep in her arms. She gave him a wobbly smile, a smile that quickly turned to concern. "Your hand . . ."

"It's not that bad."

"Bad enough." Her forehead wrinkled. "The first aid kit is at the schoolhouse."

He hated all her back-and-forth from the cabin to the schoolhouse. He needed her to stay put. With him. Where she belonged. "We're going up there." He pretended not to notice her hesitation and grabbed the diaper bag and Wren's nest. "We're leaving."

Maybe she wanted to get away from the cabin as much as he did because she didn't argue.

When they reached the schoolhouse, she made him check all the doors and windows, something he suspected she'd be doing for a long time. He retrieved the first aid kit and set it on the table, then washed his hands at the sink. It stung like hell. The wound wasn't long, but it was deep, and it started to bleed again.

She couldn't tend to him and hold the baby at the same time, but she couldn't seem to put her down. He understood and took Wren from her. The baby stirred, opened her eyes, saw him, and closed them again.

He sat at the table, Wren in his free arm, and while Tess bandaged him up, he filled her in on everything that had happened. She inspected the final dressing. "I want to kill Eli, but . . ."

"I know."

"Do you think Paul will hurt him?"

Ian considered how his survivalist neighbor was both different and similar to himself. "No. He loves his kid and his wife. He's just stubborn and paranoid."

"I'll check on them tomorrow."

"Of course, you will. I'm also sure you'll be checking on Savannah and her baby. Then there's Kelly and Ava. I wouldn't be half-surprised if you went to see Winchester, too, just to lecture him."

"The busybody of Tempest, Tennessee."

"You've got a big heart, Tess Hartsong."

Even as he said it, the uneasiness he couldn't shake made him turn away.

She and Ian slept together that night, with Wren next to the bed, neither of them willing to let her out of sight. Wren didn't awaken until a little after five. Tess pried her eyes open far enough to see that Ian had slipped away. As always.

She pulled the baby and her leaky diaper out of the sleeper and curled her to her chest. Wren didn't seem to have suffered from yesterday's episode, but Tess couldn't say the same. "I'm glad you're perky," she told her, "because I'm a wreck."

Wren was unusually alert that morning. After her feeding she looked at Tess as if to ask what Mom had planned for their entertainment that day. Tess dressed them both, put Wren into her sling, and stepped into a beautiful mountain morning.

She found Ian at the abandoned church. Ignoring his injured hand, he was using the lintel over the doorway to perform a series of punishing pull-ups. His T-shirt lay on the ground next to him. The man couldn't seem to keep his clothes on.

She watched the contraction of muscles across his shoulders, the long extension in his spine. His legs stayed straight and strong as he raised and lowered himself. Judging by his sweaty back, he'd been working out for a while. She wanted to remember him like this. Rumpled and sweaty, strong and decent, in the wild where he belonged.

Wren was beginning to experiment with her voice, and she screeched. He dropped to the ground. "Ladies."

She watched as he picked up the T-shirt and rubbed it across his damp chest. "Thank you," she said.

"For?"

"I could have lost her yesterday."

"We could have lost her."

"Of course, but—"

"She's mine, too, Tess. You keep forgetting that."

"No, I—"

"You keep forgetting a lot of things." He yanked his T-shirt so roughly over his head it should have ripped.

"What put you in such a foul mood?"

"All these plans you have. These plans for yourself and for Wren."

"I have to plan. I don't see what—"

"Have you consulted me about any of these plans? Asked me how I feel about them? Whether I have plans of my own? Or have you just told me?"

Where had all this anger come from? "Whatever it is you're trying to say, say it, because I don't know what you're talking about."

He came toward her. "I never hear the word *we* in your plans. I only hear *I*."

"There isn't a *we*."

"We're married, Tess." The way he said it . . . With an unhappy twist at the corner of his mouth. "That might be old hat to you, but it's not to me."

"We're not really married. You know that as well as I do."

"The state of Tennessee begs to differ." The wind caught his hair, blowing it back from the harsh bones of his face. "Do you have any idea what last night was like for me? Wandering around the woods with no idea where she was or who had her? She's not only yours, Tess. I've been with her since the second she was born. You don't have a monopoly on her."

He'd never talked about Wren this way, but the way

he said it—his antagonism—didn't sit well with her. "Be careful. Those are lots of big emotions."

"So what?"

"You said you were selling the schoolhouse."

"I said I had an offer."

She couldn't have this conversation now. "We can talk about it when you've had coffee because you're not making sense."

He cut in front of her. "We'll talk about it now because no amount of coffee is going to change anything. I love you, Tess. I love you, and I love Wren."

She stared at him. These were words she yearned to hear. Words she'd never imagined a man so averse to messy emotions would ever speak. She should have been joyous, but the joy wasn't there. He looked like a man who'd lost everything.

She drew Wren closer to her heart. "You'll get over it."

"Did you really say that?"

She blinked hard. "Being in love is supposed to be a happy thing, but I've never seen you look more miserable."

"I'm not miserable!"

"You're not happy."

"I am happy! I'm—" He dragged his hand through his hair. "It's taking me by surprise. Not the part about loving you. I've loved you for a long time. But I put other names to it."

"Like . . . ?"

"Inspiration. Admiration. Lust. But last night . . . Last night it all came crashing in on me. A crisis has a way of sorting out what's really important."

Her bottom lip began to tremble. She caught it between her teeth, knowing she had to do the right thing for both of them. All three of them. She spoke carefully. "Exactly how do you see us moving forward?"

"What do you mean? I see us together."

The harsh way he tossed out the words told her everything. "What about your work?"

"What about it?"

"You're an honorable man, Ian, but you're not a domestic one." She formed the words she needed to say. "Your work is who you are, and I've gotten in the way of that."

He leaned down and picked up a rough-edged stone. "You haven't."

"Since the day we met, I've brought you nothing but complications. You came here to find direction, but what you've found is pandemonium. I haven't been an inspiration to you, Ian. I've been a blockade."

He palmed the stone. "Don't say that."

"Tell me one thing you've produced since we've been together that's satisfied you. One piece that's made you happy."

"I have a sketchbook full of drawings."

"They're beautiful. But you hate every one of them."

He rolled the stone in his hand. "I don't hate them."

"You can't even look at them without curling your lip."

"I don't do that!"

She blinked away tears. "It's not going to work, Ian. You're an artist trying to find himself. Wren and I are standing in the way of that happening."

He clutched the stone in his fist. "You don't know what you're talking about."

"All those messy emotions . . . You talk about your father's abuse, but I think it's your mother who's left the deepest scars. A woman who supposedly loved you but was never strong enough to protect you as a mother should. I understand why all this cripples you—me, Wren. Everything we bring with us."

"I'm not crippled."

She'd never heard him speak with less certainty. "Look at yourself. The idea of being in love, of having a family . . . It makes you angry, not happy." Her voice caught. "You know it's not right for you. How could we have a good life with you working so hard to hide your resentment of all the complications, all the disruptions Wren and I bring along?"

"Don't make me sound so cold-blooded."

"You're exactly the opposite." Wren began to cry. Tess moved her to her shoulder. "You feel everything. That's why you can't be the husband I want or the father she needs."

"You act like reimagining a career happens overnight. It doesn't. These things take time."

"We're not only talking about reimagining a career. This is reimagining your life. Go back to Manhattan, Ian, and stop running away from yourself. It's not good for you here. And it's not good for me to want what you can't deliver."

His shoulders dropped. He looked out toward the horizon. He had no counterargument, and he didn't even try to come up with one. Instead, he drew back his arm and flung the stone as far as he could. "Have it your way."

She left the clearing, silently begging him to stay away until she didn't love him anymore.

Chapter Twenty-Three

Tess gazed out the back window at the tree house and imagined it gradually rotting away, forever unfinished. Ian was gone, taking all his clothes with him, and she'd hauled her things back to the schoolhouse, but only temporarily. As soon as it was officially up for sale, she'd move out, but for now, she'd leave the cabin to Kelly.

Letting Ian go had been the right thing to do, no matter how sick she felt inside. One look at his unhappy face had proven that. She wanted him desperately, but she only wanted him whole and happy, free to love with an open heart. And that was something she couldn't have.

She pulled herself away from the window before she

fell into a full-on pity party. She needed to attend to something, and now was as good a time as any.

The schoolhouse's WiFi was working for a change. She settled on the couch with Wren asleep in the sling and pulled up FaceTime to make the call she'd been thinking about for days.

"Tess?" Diane looked awful. She wore no makeup, and her blond bob lay flat against her head. It seemed as though a lifetime had passed since Simon had shown up at the schoolhouse, but it had been only four days.

Diane sneezed and pressed a tissue to her nose. "Sorry. Simon left this morning, and I have a cold."

"If this isn't a good time—"

"No, it's fine. I don't have anything else to do except feel sorry for myself."

Tess knew exactly how that felt. "I should have called you earlier, but I didn't know what to say."

"It was a shock." Diane's voice began to tremble. "When I think about Wren . . . About all we put you through . . . And for what? For nothing."

"Diane, this is awkward."

"I have another word for it." She dabbed at her eyes. "It was lovely having a grandchild, even for a few weeks."

"That's what I want to talk to you about."

"Wren? How is she? Is she all right?"

"Yes. She's fine. She's asleep right here. But I was wondering . . . I know it's a lot to ask, and I don't want to put you on the spot, so promise me you'll say no if you think this is a stupid idea. I was wondering if . . ." The words came out in a rush. "Would you and Jeff consider being Wren's grandparents?"

"Her . . . ?"

"I know it's a lot to ask, but—"

"*Yes!*"

"Really?"

"Oh, yes! I never dreamed you'd want us to do this."

"There's nothing I want more for her." She told Diane what they'd learned about Wren's conception and then reminded her of a complication. "Simon's still young. Regardless of what he says now, you could end up with real grandchildren."

"Don't say that! Wren is our real grandchild. We took her into our hearts. That's why we've been so upset."

"But if Simon has children . . ."

"Do we seem like the kind of people who'd couldn't love more than one grandchild?"

Tess's heart lifted for the first time all morning. "No, you don't."

"Oh, Tess . . . Let me see her. *Jeff! Jeff!* Tess is on the phone with Wren. Our granddaughter!"

Paul and Rebecca brought Eli to the schoolhouse that afternoon. The boy burst into tears when he saw Tess. She wanted to cry, too, although not for the same reason.

Eli was so distraught that she didn't have the heart to lecture him. Besides, what would she say that he didn't already know? She gave him a hug. "I think Wren understands, and she forgives you."

Rebecca's lips were dry and cracked. "I didn't mean for this to happen. I have to pull myself together. I know I do."

"You've done your best," Paul said with rough kindness. And then, to Tess, "We've found a doctor. A woman."

"That's wonderful."

"She's supposed to specialize in this kind of thing." He wrapped his arm around his wife's shoulders. "We're going to see her tomorrow."

Before they left, Eli personally apologized to Wren. "I'm really, really, really, really, a hundred *really*s sorry I scared you last night."

Wren had a short memory, and she gifted him with a yawn that he interpreted as a smile.

"I think she doesn't hate me anymore."

"I'm sure she doesn't," Tess said.

As the Eldridges left, Tess decided to make herself follow through on an idea she'd had. Maybe trying to help Rebecca would take her mind off the help she needed for herself.

Ian was furious. He couldn't get the image out of his head—Tess walking away from him, the wind whipping her hair into a midnight dervish. And taking his child with her. Did she have any idea how much courage he'd needed to muster to tell her he loved her? He'd opened his veins. Bled all over. And what had she done? She'd thrown it right back in his face.

He took a long pull on his drink and looked out toward the Hudson River from the top floor of the five-story Tribeca building he owned. He'd chosen the furnishings here himself, including the uncomfortable Italian leather sofa where he was sitting. He'd even designed some of the pieces: the cantilevered chairs made of tubular steel and black mesh, the kidney-shaped coffee table balanced on a heavy ball of sandblasted glass, the thermoplastic wall sconces. His studio was on the other side of the wall, a cavernous loft three times the size of the schoolhouse studio and the place where he'd once done some of his best work.

Years ago, he'd divided the rest of the building into rent-free studios for emerging artists—his attempt to do for them what Bianca had once done for him. He didn't regret giving them work space, but being around so many young creatives brimming with ideas was what had driven him from Manhattan to Runaway Mountain. They all wanted his advice, his encouragement, his blessing. Being around them made him feel like a fraud.

And so he'd run. For all the good it had done him.

Tess's rejection shouldn't hurt so much. Hell, this was the way he'd grown up. He was used to getting slapped around by the people he was closest to. He'd just never expected it from her.

And he'd never expected being alone to feel so suffocating.

Tess should have been—if not happy—at least reasonably content. One week rolled into the next. By the beginning of May, Wren had grown out of her newborn clothes, Diane and Jeff had scheduled a visit for after their river cruise, and the nightmares had disappeared. The people of Tempest were also no longer treating Tess as a menace to society. Artie taught her how to change the headlamp on her car when it burned out, and Kelly was instructing her in bread baking. Tess had been invited to join the local Women's Alliance and discovered that its president, Mrs. Watkins, was an excellent herbalist, eager to share her knowledge. Fiona Lester had volunteered to show Tess how to make her own natural skin-care products, and Michelle was intent on helping Tess start a compost pile. Even Mr. Felder had stepped up by giving her a reading list about Tennessee history. "If you're goin' to stay here, you need to stop bein' so damn ignorant."

The community had so much to teach her, and Tess was eager to learn. Still, the ache in her heart wouldn't ease. She was the one who'd kicked Ian out of his own house, and now she was left with a gaping hole in her life that she'd dug for herself. Who was she to tell Ian Hamilton North IV what he needed?

She was the woman who loved him and understood him better than he understood himself.

She yearned to call him to see how his work was progressing. If he was happy. But she didn't call. Didn't want to hear the relief he wouldn't be able to hide that he'd escaped Tess's messiness and finally had the space he needed. She touched the copper wedding ring she hadn't gotten around to taking off and scheduled her second meeting with the director of the county health department.

Her career was falling into place, if not the rest of her life.

The health director had invited two Knoxville physicians to the meeting, both of whom were concerned about the lack of medical care for rural women. They were impressed with Tess's background and eager to discuss a plan to move forward. Tess's head was spinning by the time the meeting was over. It was all happening so fast.

Kelly, Tess had discovered, had a talent for finance. Thanks to carefully investing a small inheritance from her parents, she had money of her own and could easily afford better accommodations. But she loved the cabin far more than Tess did, and for now, Tess was happy to accommodate her, especially as Kelly had painted the walls and brought in pottery vases of fresh flowers.

Sometimes Ava stayed with her mother, other times with her father. Either way, Brad was a frequent visitor—at both the cabin and, unfortunately, the schoolhouse. Tess never offered him coffee, but that didn't stop him from pouring his own.

"She's like a whole new person," he complained as he made himself at home in her kitchen.

"She's the same person she's always been. You

weren't paying attention." Seeing him standing by the counter, in the exact place Ian used to stand, made her testier with him than usual. "The problem is, you've been a dick for so long it's hard for you to change course."

He stiffened. "I don't know why I keeping coming here only to get abused."

"Because I've seen the worst of you, and I'm not married to you, which makes this the one place where you don't have to put on your public face." She'd looked into Brad's political record and been surprised to discover he wasn't quite the reactionary she'd imagined, especially when it came to environmental issues. She pointed her cereal spoon at him. "You also come here because you think I can fix your marriage. I can't."

"Kelly listens to you. She respects your opinion."

"You still believe you can win me over enough so I'll persuade Kelly to kneel before you and beg forgiveness."

"I'm not that unrealistic."

"But that's exactly what you want from me. Admit it."

He shrugged. Neither admitting nor denying.

He was a lost soul, and she had to restrain herself from dumping all her frustration and all her sadness on him. Why did she have to have so many difficult people in her life? Ian, Brad, Savannah—although Savannah had declared Tess her best friend in the world. Which was a trial all its own.

"Best friends tell each other everything," Savannah had said yesterday as she'd sat on her front porch nursing Zoro. "So tell me all about you and Ian North. He left you, didn't he? I hate him."

"He didn't leave me," Tess had lied. "He's in Manhattan working."

Ian, the most difficult person of all. His continuing silence proved that sending him away was the right thing to do, and one day she'd make peace with it. Today was not that day.

She forced her attention back to Winchester. Despite the way she groused at him, she felt a stab of sympathy for the state senator. He loved the old Kelly, but he didn't handle change well, and the new one baffled him.

"Now she wants to go to college. And study finance of all things!"

"As I understand it, she's been handling your finances since you got married. And doing a good job of it." She was also helping Tess understand her own finances better.

He sulked. "Only because I didn't have time."

She threw up her hands. "Out! I've reached my Brad

Winchester limit for the day."

He stormed off, but she knew he'd be back. She'd become his therapist, whether she liked it or not.

Reinvention, my ass! He'd show her. She thought he was emotionally paralyzed. Unreliable. An unfit father! Screw that! He'd take his work in a brilliant new direction and throw the results at her.

Ian hauled three canvases from his studio into the alley and used a propane torch to scorch them. He threw paint at them, cut them with X-Acto blades, cut them again. He assaulted them with hydrochloric acid and ran them over with his car. When he was done, he stacked them against the wall of his studio, stood back, and assessed this new work.

It was bullshit. A thirty-six-year-old man impersonating a rebellious art school grad. He was a fucking poser pretending to give the finger to the system that had made him rich.

He destroyed it all and made himself more miserable by laying out the small canvas squares with the imprints from Tess's body. The memory of that night, the beauty of it, was more than he could handle. He shut the door on the studio and didn't go back inside for days.

He hated ultimatums. Despite the traffic and police sirens, this place was too quiet. He should drive to Tempest right now so he could hold his child, finish his tree house, and tell Tess they were going to do things his way.

So why didn't he?

Because he couldn't.

He was lost, besieged by loneliness and uncertainty—by the smell of diesel and the stench of rotting garbage from the trash bags piled at the curb. Would Wren even remember him when she saw him again? It had been only a few weeks, but he knew how quickly she changed, and he was missing all of it.

His anger with Tess butted straight up against his longing to be with her. Life without her was as pointless as soda that had lost its fizz. She'd opened him to new experiences, new emotions, to becoming part of a community that existed beyond the boundaries of studios and galleries. She'd shown him what it was like to make love with a woman who held nothing back. Life with her had unfolded in every hue of the rainbow.

Then she'd ruined it by rejecting him. How could she think he was a threat to Wren when that baby belonged to him as much as to her? All that bullshit about him not being domestic. If that was true, why was the schoolhouse and their life on the mountain all he could think about? She'd even had the gall to accuse him of looking miserable when he told her he loved her. What the hell kind of thing was that to say?

His head ached. Maybe he was running a fever. He should go out to the drugstore and get something to take, but if he opened the door, they'd be waiting for him.

"Ian, I don't want to bother you, but could you take a look at—"

"Ian, I'm not sure it has anything to say . . ."

They were great kids, talented, and deserving of the studio space he was happy to give them. He just didn't want to talk to them right now. He didn't want to talk to anyone. Yet now that he was back in Manhattan, his phone wouldn't stop ringing. He turned it off, then turned it right back on again. What if there was an emergency with Wren? What if Tess finally realized how unreasonable she was being and called to apologize?

He replayed their last conversation a thousand times in his head, but no matter how hard he tried, he couldn't remember her ever once saying she loved him.

He was up at dawn. He should go train, but his dojo here didn't smell of pine and leaf mold. No weeds brushed his calves. No birdsong mingled with the sound of his own breath.

He forced himself back into the studio. It was more functional than his schoolhouse studio, but its cement floor; high, open ceiling; and cold, industrial walls weren't nearly as welcoming. And why, with all the noise around him, was it so quiet here?

He flipped through those small canvas squares. What he really wanted to do was sketch—a squirrel scuttling through the underbrush, early wildflowers in the meadow. Tess. Wren. Sketching calmed him, but therapy wasn't art.

In a fit of frustration, he grabbed a canvas he'd abandoned months ago, a big, insipid, tonal composition. He turned it upside down and set it on the easel hard enough to make the frame shake. He snatched up the closest tube of paint and squeezed all of it into his hand. Primary yellow. Good enough. He rubbed the thick paint between his palms and smeared it over the canvas without caring where it went or how it looked. He picked up another random tube, squeezed it out, and did the same. He found another and then another— edges bleeding, no regard for line or form, shape or value.

He glued the canvas imprints from Tess's body on top and pulled a random can of Krylon from the shelf. He shook it and spattered it in short, choppy bursts without attempting a pattern. He found another can and did the same. And then another. He was breathing hard as he finally spelled out IHN4.

He dropped back, drained.

It was a madman's mess, lumpy, disjointed and non-sensical. It could have been done by anyone or anything. One of those elephants who'd been given a brush and a bucket of paint. He set his pigment-smeared hands to his knees, trying to catch his breath. He looked again. The chaos in front of him had no purpose, no reason for being.

Like him.

He needed order, some kind of structure and sanity. He rubbed his palms on the legs of his jeans and reached for the one thing in the studio that held the order he craved: his sketchbook. He opened it without looking and tore off a random page.

Tess's profile.

He taped the drawing to the top corner of the messy canvas and stepped away. Rubbing his hand over the back of his neck, he first studied the small sketch and then the canvas. He turned the easel to better cap-ture the midday light and grabbed a black illustration marker with an extra fine point. He went to work, re-capturing a miniature of Tess's profile on a dry speck of the canvas.

When he was finally satisfied, he put aside that sketch, taped up another, and began again. He worked through the rest of the day, through the night, and into the next morning, moving from the second sketch to a third.

It was dawn before he finally stumbled to bed, but he slept for only a few hours before he got back up, made a pot of coffee, and returned to the studio.

He lost all reference to time. The shadows moved across his studio floor, disappeared, reappeared. He changed the angle of an eyelash here, the length of a fingernail there. He slept for a few hours, made more coffee, and began again, hiding each of the minuscule, detailed drawings in the chaos of his random streaks of color. He didn't shower. Didn't eat. His stomach burned from the endless cups of coffee he drank out of a paint-spattered mug.

Sometime in the midhours of the third night, he left the studio and shut the door behind him. Reeking of sweat and paint, he fell into bed.

When he finally awakened, he took a long shower, shaved, and made himself a decent breakfast. Only after he'd done all that did he let himself go back into the studio to look at what he'd created.

From a distance, only the chaos was evident. But up close . . . Up close, visible only to those who wouldn't pass by too quickly—those with the patience to stop and see—were the tiny, hidden drawings: Tess's profile, her spine, her nose, all of it executed with exact, precise detail. There was Wren's foot, caught in a ribbon of dioxazine purple, her dimple captured in a stroke of gold. In this canvas, he saw it all—the violent, rebellious kid who only cared about destruction and the grown man who'd lost his heart to a single-minded widow and an orphaned child.

This.

This was who he was.

The punk and the artist. The insurgent and the peacemaker.

The man who'd been trying so hard to fit into a single identity that he'd run away from himself.

He loved what he'd created. Loved it so much that all he wanted to do was race outside with his cans of Krylon, his rollers, his lawlessness. Find a wall, scale a ladder, and turn his joy into a vision of something new and beautiful.

In the month since Ian had left, May had unfolded with all her showy lace and earthy perfume. As June approached, hepatica and trillium gave way to wild geranium and bleeding heart, while rhododendron, azalea, and mountain laurel spread their joy. Runaway Mountain had never been more beautiful, but Ian wasn't here to share it.

Her almost three-month-old baby batted her hands and cooed at her feet. Tess swallowed the lump in her throat. "It's only you and me, buttercup," she whispered.

Wren, insensitive to Tess's sadness, craned her neck to look around the schoolhouse kitchen. She'd done this so many times lately that Tess could swear she was looking for him. It was one thing for him to leave her, but how could he abandon Wren?

Because Tess had ordered him to leave.

The sound of hammering echoed from the backyard. She didn't need to look through the window to know Paul Eldridge was outside. He'd raised the final wall in the tree house.

Paul kept showing up, even though Tess had told him it wasn't necessary, but he was a proud man. Eli usually came with him, and the two of them worked side by side, Paul stopping occasionally to rumple Eli's hair or help him with a stubborn nail.

She stroked one of Wren's baby sideburns. Yesterday evening, she'd followed through on something that had been on her mind for weeks. She'd hosted the first gathering of a miscarriage support group here at the schoolhouse. Michelle had volunteered to put the group of eight together. Some of the women, like Michelle, had miscarried a decade ago; others had newer wounds. Rebecca wasn't the only one who'd cried, but thanks to a combination of therapy and medication, they were healthy tears. The women had made plans to meet again, and, of all people, Rebecca had volunteered to host.

Today was Tess's last day working for Phish. The paperwork was nearly complete, and tomorrow she would begin setting up her own practice. Thanks to Brad Winchester, she'd be working rent-free out of a room in the rec center. With the backing of the Knoxville physicians, she'd be able to offer prenatal and postnatal care, well-baby checkups, vaccinations, and reproductive counseling. She'd also be delivering babies.

Tess picked up Wren's diaper bag. She had people to care for, a child to raise, and she couldn't let this wrenching sadness get the best of her.

Word about her new practice had gotten out at the Broken Chimney, and the locals were already jumping the gun.

"Gimme some pills for my bursitis," Mr. Felder demanded as she finished her last day behind the counter. "Damn fool doctor told me I had to get phys'cal therapy when all I need are some pills."

Tess shoved his pie at him. "I'm only going to be practicing women's reproductive health care." She spoke loudly enough for everyone to hear, even though she knew this community well enough by now to suspect restricting her practice would never be that straightforward. "Do what your doctor tells you."

"Women's reproductive health? What the hell kind of bull is that?" Mr. Felder railed. "I'll sue you for discrimination!"

"Oh, I wouldn't want that," she replied with fake-concern. "Let's compromise. As soon as you finish your physical therapy, I'll be happy to prescribe additional medication. Or arsenic, depending on my mood."

"Did y'all hear what she said?" Mr. Felder shouted. "That's malpractice! She threatened to poison me!"

"Will you shut the heck—the *hell* up, Orland?" The Broken Chimney's newest employee shook an ice cream scoop at him. It was difficult for Kelly Winchester to curse, but she'd been working hard at it. As she'd explained to Tess, "I need to figure out who I am, and the only way I can do that is by trying different things, even if they make me uncomfortable."

This new, experimental Kelly was turning into a force

to be reckoned with. For example, Ava's ex-boyfriend, Connor Bowman, had disappeared. Kelly refused to tell Tess what she'd done. All Tess knew was that the boy had abruptly left town to finish what remained of his senior year in Nashville, where he'd be his grandmother's problem.

With Tess quitting and neither Michelle nor Savannah back at work full-time, Phish was delighted to have Kelly on board. Brad, however, was not. Last week, when he'd heard the news, he'd barged into the cabin where Kelly was sharing a meal with Tess and Wren.

"It's unthinkable!" he'd roared. "You're the wife of a state senator! You don't need to do this!"

"I'm pushing my boundaries," Kelly had said calmly.

"How is working in a third-rate coffee shop pushing your boundaries?"

"Watch your language." Tess felt duty bound to protest on behalf of the Broken Chimney.

Brad paced the cabin floor as he launched into one of his lectures about the importance of image, but Kelly wouldn't back down. "I want to see what it's like to have a real job. And the work schedule gives me plenty of time to study."

"Study what?"

Kelly was as patient with him as she was unbending.

"I'm taking some refresher courses this summer so I'll be ready to go to school full-time in the fall."

Since Kelly had her own money, Brad was smart enough not to debate her decision to go to college, but not smart enough to back off entirely. "I understand that this college thing is important to you, but you need to be back home where you belong instead of living here in this—this—" He waved a hand around the cabin.

"Hovel?" Tess helpfully provided.

Brad had tried to cover his gaffe in his typical clumsy way. "I'm only saying, without you there, who's going to look after the house?"

Tess rolled her eyes. "And it gets better and better."

"I'm not concerned about the house, Brad," Kelly had said firmly. "I realize this is difficult for you to understand, but I'm evolving. I don't know who I'm going to be. You're free to go your own way or wait and see what unfolds."

He had no intention of going his own way, and he'd looked for a new angle of attack. "I— I like your hair." He was obviously lying, but Tess gave him props for trying.

Kelly touched one of the blue streaks Ava had added around her mother's face. "I'm not sure it's me, but then I'm not sure it's not me, either."

In addition to the new blue streaks, Kelly had taken to distressed jeans, Ava's cast-off T-shirts, and a pair of cherry-red Chuck Taylors. Each change unsettled Brad more than the last. "You'll be comfortable at home. I'll—I'll sleep in the guest room. Tell her, Tess."

"I'm not telling her anything," Tess retorted. "I'm scared of her."

Wren thought that was funny, but Brad didn't. "What do I have to do to get you to come home, Kelly? I can change, too. Tell me what you want?"

"Right now? I want you to lobby your friends for broader sex education in all our schools. Tess has been right about that from the beginning, and you know it."

Brad stared at his feet. "It's not that easy. They're a bunch of stubborn bastards."

"You are, too," Tess pointed out, "so you know exactly how to talk to them."

Kelly gently reprimanded her. "That's not nice, Tess. Brad has a lot to deal with."

Tess maintained a straight face. "You're right. Apologies, Senator. You're not nearly as much of a bastard as you used to be."

"Tess!" Kelly exclaimed.

Tess made a zipping motion across her lips. She was falling in love with Kelly Winchester, and thanks to his offer of rent-free space, she'd also grown a lot fonder of her blustering husband.

A pounding on the schoolhouse door awakened Tess early the next morning. She stumbled downstairs in her pajama bottoms with Ian's red-and-black flannel shirt on top. Mercifully, the knocking hadn't awakened Wren.

Tess expected to see someone who needed medical help on the other side of the door. Instead, Freddy Davis stood there.

"Your phone's not working," he said accusingly.

She shoved her hair out of her eyes. "Big surprise."

"You need to come down to the police station."

"What have I done now?

"Not you. It's your husband?"

"My husband?"

"He's in jail."

Chapter Twenty-Four

Tess nearly rear-ended a Jeep Wrangler when she saw what Ian had done.

He'd painted the town.

Color was everywhere: the front of the Broken Chimney, above the sign for The Rooster, the side wall of the Angels of Fire Apostolic Church, and the western half of the Brad Winchester Recreational Center. Then there were the painted streetlamp posts and utility boxes.

She parked her car, strapped Wren to her chest, and got out. She didn't know where to look first. At the animals on the rec center—a luminous bird with dissolving wings, a cartoon mouse, a house fly? What about the zeppelin on The Rooster or the faith symbols embedded in the streams of color on the church?

Beautiful, funny, grotesque, and thought provoking . . . It was all here. Most of it had been done with stencils, but regardless, no man could have achieved all this in a single night. He'd had help.

She turned, taking it in again. But as she absorbed more of what lay in front of her, she grew increasingly puzzled. She'd seen dozens of photographs of Ian's street art. The concepts were his, but something about the execution didn't seem familiar.

Except at the Broken Chimney.

She could have picked out his work from a thousand artists. His use of color, his precision, the scale.

Wrapped around the front of the Broken Chimney was a stenciled rendering of a woman. A woman who was most definitely not Tess. This was a wind-whipped amazon with ropes of blond hair and the muscles of a warrior. She was strong. Beautiful. Determined. The personification of a tempest. Near her foot, in small letters, was his tag, *IHN4.*

Mesmerized, Tess absorbed the work in its entirety and then section by section. The eyes and nose. The strength of the jaw. The twisting locks of hair. The—

Her gaze shot to a muscular calf. To a knee. An elbow. An earlobe.

Surely she was mistaken.

Her gaze flew from one part of the figure to another.

There. Over there. And . . . THERE!

Dear God . . .

Tess's own body parts had been carefully drawn on the amazon's body! Her toes in the elbow, her nose in an earlobe, and her breast— Her breast in a knee. She was everywhere!

She clutched Wren and took a step backward as she spotted . . . in front of her . . . right in the amazon's shoulder blade . . .

No! Even he wouldn't . . .

But he had. Tucked in the shadow of the amazon's waist were her own *labia.*

Bastard!

She wasn't going to bail him out of jail. She was going to kill him!

Freddy shot up from his chair as she stormed into the police station.

"Let me at him!" she exclaimed.

"I gotta search you before you go in there."

"Like hell!"

He apparently decided a woman, however furious, couldn't do too much harm with a baby strapped to her chest because he opened his desk drawer, drew out the keys, and led her through the doorway.

The only jail cell held a stainless steel toilet and a cot

with a blue polyurethane mattress where Ian lay sound asleep. Freddy unlocked the barred door for her. "Call me if it gets out of hand."

"I'll do that," Ian said, in a sleep-rasped voice.

"Not you," Freddy said. "Her."

"Just shows what you know."

As Freddy left, a pair of leather, paint-crackled boots hit the floor of the cell. Ian stood up. He'd never been scruffier. His hair hadn't been cut since she'd last seen him, and he displayed at least a week's worth of beard stubble. But instead of looking at Tess, he only had eyes for Wren. "Hey, sweetheart, remember me?"

Wren kicked at the sound of his voice. He walked over to Tess and pulled Wren out of the sling. "Look at you. . . . You've grown a foot."

Wren gazed up at him with her shiny, navy-blue eyes, taking in every detail. She smiled. A big, gummy, drooly smile. He tucked her against his neck, turned his back on Tess—*turned his back!*—and carried Wren to the other end of the cell, crooning to her the whole time. ". . . missed you so much. . . . My big girl. . . . My little sweetheart . . ."

Tess waited.

". . . Disneyland . . . and the circus. We'll pitch a tent and read books . . ."

Tess crossed her arms over her chest.

". . . shoot baskets and paint."

Tess tapped her foot.

". . . ride bikes." He finally turned to look at Tess. "We'll dance together."

Her heart did a flip-flop. She set her teeth against it. "You put my *vagina* on the wall of the Broken Chimney!"

He smiled. "You know that, and I know that. Are you planning to tell anyone else?"

She started to give him the smackdown of his life and then paused. Her body parts were all there, depicted in miniature on the amazon. And yet . . . If she hadn't known what the two of them had done that night in the studio, would she have recognized those small details for what they were? Surely someone would spot a breast or a navel, but it wasn't as if he'd labeled the parts with her name.

She regarded him quizzically.

Wren studied him with googly eyes, but now he had his full attention on Tess. "You put me through hell. I was furious with you, but it turns out you were right."

She tilted her head She needed to hear more, even as she was afraid of what he'd say.

Wren kept staring into his face as he spoke. "I had to find a new direction, but I couldn't. I was stuck."

"And now you've found that new direction?" Her legs were giving her trouble, and she sank down on the edge of the cot.

"I painted it all over the Broken Chimney," he said, with the trace of a smile.

"My body parts?"

"What I've been missing." He moved toward the cell bars. "Last year, I blamed my problems on all the distractions in Manhattan. Then, when I came to Tempest and still couldn't work, I blamed Bianca. Finally, I blamed you. But all the blame was on my own shoulders. I didn't need peace or quiet. What I needed was to remember the most basic precept of street art. It's about freedom."

"Art for the people, not only the elite, right?"

"Exactly. A great street artist's work shouldn't fit into a single box. It's not supposed to. But I had pigeonholed myself, and it paralyzed me. Then you came along."

"Me?"

"You got in my head with all your messes and your complications." He wrapped his hand around a bar in the cell door. "I tried to back off, but all I wanted to do was sketch you. It was a compulsion. Sketching you, then Wren, then a rock that caught my attention or the curve of a blade of grass."

"You hated all of those sketches."

"Every one. I was already on shaky ground creatively. They were trite, ordinary."

"Beautiful."

"But they didn't have anything to say that hadn't been said a thousand times before by a thousand other artists. They scared the hell out of me, yet I couldn't stop." He moved away from the cell door. "Then you kicked me out."

She pressed her hands together in her lap. "You make me sound heartless."

"I was furious with you," he said gently. "Who were you to tell me what I needed?" Wren's eyelids were growing heavy. He tucked her closer. "I wallowed in self-pity and thought about those sketches. How they didn't belong. How much I hated them. And then, one night, I didn't."

"You didn't hate them?"

"I finally understood why I was obsessed with them. How they were pivotal to what I want to create now."

"The warrior?"

"She's the past. Her size, her boldness. That's who I used to be as an artist—who I'm proud to be. But the hidden details—the images from the sketches that are right there to be seen or not seen—that's what's new, what I'd been missing. Those small, hidden images show the subtleties in life, the parts you have to search for to see. Hiding those subtleties, those details inside big concepts—it makes my heart sing."

She smiled. "I'm glad."

"I have so many ideas. What you saw today . . . That's just the beginning."

"Quite a beginning. And you didn't do it alone."

"Some young artists owed me a favor."

She gestured toward the cell. "They seem to have gotten away in time, but you're in jail."

"I'm not too worried about it." He propped his foot on the rim of the toilet. "It won't take long for people to figure out that I've made this town a bucketload of money."

She was still working that through in her head when he went on.

"Tempest, Tennessee, has the biggest Ian North art installation in the world." He dropped his foot. "It still needs a lot of work, and it's going to be a bitch to maintain, but it'll be worth it."

She understood. "You've turned the town into a major tourist attraction."

"I'm only getting started. It'll be a mecca for art lovers, and a nice boost to the local economy. But,

Tess . . ." Wren startled in her sleep. He set his hand lightly on her chest. "It was also the only way I could think of to send you a big enough message."

She cocked her head.

"You understood what I couldn't. You saw all the old baggage I was still carrying around, the crap I'd told myself I'd left behind years ago. But I hadn't, and you knew that."

"Childhood scars like those run deep."

"A lot deeper than I wanted to admit. Being away from you and Wren, going back to my life the way it used to be . . . It became so clear even I couldn't miss how much fear I was carrying around."

"A big emotion."

"Big and ugly." He moved closer. "You were right. I wasn't happy when I told you I loved you. I was afraid. You saw that. My cowardice."

"You aren't a coward. You were a kid living with a brute of a father, but worse than that, you were living with a mother you loved who looked the other way while you were being abused. How could you trust anyone after that, including yourself?"

He gave her a wan smile. "I understand it now— maybe watching you with Wren. I don't know. Anyway, I'm done with it." He gazed at his sleeping child. "I need to tell you up front that I won't give her up. You're her mother. I'd never let anyone challenge that. But she's mine, too, and since you have an innate sense of fairness, I know we can work out the logistics, no matter how complicated they are."

Once again he'd confused her. "You're talking about . . . ?"

"It'll be messy. I understand that. But we'll figure out what's best for her. For the three of us."

"You hate messy."

He gave a dry, unhappy laugh. "That's what's so ironic. Trying to hide from the mess ended up crippling me—as an artist and as a man. Life will never fit into some perfect geometric composition. Of all people, I should have accepted that years ago. Life will always slither over the borders of the frame. It's going to splash on the floor and spill into the streets. It's going to feel good and hurt bad. That's what being alive, being creative, what loving someone, means."

"So what you said before you left . . . ? About us staying married . . . ?"

"I'm a selfish bastard, but I'm not selfish enough to keep you trapped," he said grimly. "I know I'm a lot to deal with, and I can't do that to you. But I'm not giving up Wren, too, and that means joint custody."

She shot up off the cot. "Are you really trying to weasel out of this marriage? Is that part of your great artistic epiphany?"

"Weasel? I'm trying to do the right thing here."

"By ditching me?"

"Ditching? I love you! I love you more than I've ever loved anyone. You're smart and funny and decent, and god knows you're persistent. You understand me in a way no one else ever has. And don't get me started about the sex. You've turned everything in my life upside down. You set my heart on the course I've been searching for as long as I can remember. Tess, you're an unshakable force."

"Then why do you want to get rid of me?"

"I don't want to get rid of you!" he exclaimed. "You're the one who doesn't want me."

She was stunned. "Why would you say something like that?"

"Why wouldn't I? You like the sex, I get that. You like me. I appreciate that. But you're not in love with me."

"I'm *what*?"

He turned away from her. "I'm not saying it twice."

She darted in front of him. "You've inhaled too many paint fumes."

"Have I?" His familiar belligerence was back, but this time it had an overlay of pain. "In all our arguments, all our conversations, all our over-the-top sex, you've never said you love me."

"Of course I have."

"Not even once."

"You're delusional."

"Not one single time."

"But . . ."

"Never."

"Are you sure?"

"Believe me. I'm absolutely sure."

"Oh." She swallowed. He was right. Of course, he was right.

He waited. She collapsed on the side of the cot and rubbed her temples. "Now who's the coward?" she said.

The smallest kick of a smile caught the corners of his mouth. "I'm sure you have your reasons."

She sprang back up and laced her hands around the back of his neck. "Ian Hamilton North the Fourth, I love you. I love you with my whole heart. I will never stop loving you even when I'm mad at you or you're mad at me or Wren's mad at both of us, and people are pounding on the door. You're kind and fascinating and scary-smart. You're ambitious, which I know is a weird thing to say, but after Trav, it means a lot to me. And the thing with Trav . . ." Her voice caught. "He would love me loving you." She smiled as she saw a glaze of tears in his eyes. "You're mine. Is that good enough?"

"That is most definitely good enough." He kissed her long and hard until Wren, who was squeezed between them, squawked.

Ian brushed the baby's silky hair, slipped his free arm around Tess, and gave her a crooked grin. "Of all the places to find a muse, I never expected to find mine dancing in her underwear on top of Runaway Mountain."

"Am I really your muse?"

"Who else would it be?"

Wren squeaked.

Ian smiled down at her. "You're second place, sweetheart."

Right then, an image flashed through her head of the three of them— Ian, Wren, and herself . . . All of them . . . All three . . . In front of the tree house. Dancing together.

But as it turned out, she'd miscalculated the number.

Epilogue

Hi, Grandma Dee! Hi, Papa Jeff! It's me, Wren! But I guess you can see that. I know you're still on your safari, and you won't have WiFi for a while, but I'm making this video with Dad's phone so it'll be waiting for you when you do get WiFi. You always miss us so much when you go on your trips, and Mom and Dad agreed this would make it easier on you being separated.

As you can see, I'm in the tree house. Honestly, I had to get away from the house. The twins are running all over the place playing ninjas, and that's making Snuffles go crazy, so he's barking his head off, and Dad is yelling at him to stop barking, and Mom's throwing up again the way she did in her first trimester with the twins. It better be a girl this time! Dad says we don't have a family. We have a menagerie.

Oh, and the carpenters are here, working on the new addition. Dad says if the schoolhouse gets any bigger, it's going to be a university.

I know you've been worried about Mom working so hard, but the new midwives at the clinic are helping a lot. And Eli's mom has taken over all the talking-to-teenagers stuff, so Mom has a lot more time off.

And remember I told you that Savannah said I could be in the room when she had her new baby? It happened two days ago. Zoro didn't want to go in there, but I did, and I got to help Mom. It was so gross and cool! I think I want to be a midwife when I grow up. Or maybe a doctor. Or a forest ranger. I do not want to be an artist like Dad. Painting doesn't make my heart sing the way he says his heart does when he finishes a new canvas or mural or one of his big light installations.

I can't tell him this other thing because it might make him worry, but I kind of wish he wasn't so famous. Like when we go to New York, sometimes people ask me what it's like to be his daughter, which is super embarrassing. He's just my dad.

Another thing that's getting annoying . . . You know how Mom and Dad like to talk to me about Bianca, my birth mother, so I don't forget her. They're always saying how much she wanted me, and how artistic she was, and all that kind of stuff, blah blah blah. But I'm not stupid, and I can sort of tell she might have been kind of a loser, too. Maybe you could find out more about that next time you're here. Still, I definitely hope I look like her someday!

What else do I want to tell you? Me and Zoro and John are going to hike up to Eli's today. He said he'd help us look for salamanders, but I had to promise him I'd stop asking so many questions about the time he kidnapped me. Even though he's a teenager, it gets him upset. But I like to hear the details. It's kind of cool how brave he was.

Heather invited just me for a sleepover tomorrow night. We always do fun crafts and yoga stuff together, but I have to be careful when I eat dinner there because you never know what she's going to feed you.

Phish is going on dates with this lady Miss Kelly introduced him to, but she doesn't like The Dead so much, so nobody thinks it'll last.

Miss Kelly opened a bigger office in Knoxville, but she still comes home to Tempest almost every weekend to stay with Mr. Brad. People at the Broken Chimney are always talking about how they're married but not really married, so I asked Ava about it the last time she was home from Atlanta, and she said her dad is crazy in love with her mom, but her mom likes her independence. That kind of worried me, so I talked to my mom about it last night, like why she doesn't want her independence like Miss Kelly does, and she said because Dad makes her heart sing. Dad heard her say that, and he lifted her right off her feet and started kissing her, and the twins started running around them, and Snuffles started barking, and then Mom flipped on the music, and you've been here when that happens, so you know exactly what we had to do next. Even though it was raining! We all had to run outside and start dancing.

Bye, now. I can't wait till you get back.

Oh, one more thing. I hope nobody ever sees us dancing like that because it's super embarrassing.

Dear Readers,

I appreciate you in more ways than you can imagine for your willingness to accompany me on my creative journeys—whether to Texas for the Wynette books, to Chicago where our Chicago Stars take the football field, or—as in *Dance Away with Me* and the rest of my stand-alone books—to the newest place, with the most recent characters who have captured my imagination. I've been able to get to know so many of you personally through Facebook and Instagram, and I treasure the relationships we've developed.

I couldn't have written *Dance Away with Me* without the invaluable input of my personal team of medical advisors. No babies in an NICU unit could have more dedicated nurses than my niece, Lisa Barrera

Phillips, and her delightful co-worker Rachel Russell. Thank you both. Thanks also to Dr. Claire Smith and Dr. Neil Smith, neither of whom saw the final manuscript, so please don't tell them if you come across any mistakes I made.

My editor extraordinaire, Carrie Feron, and my uber-agent, Steven Axelrod, have been with me forever, and I could not have two more decent people in both my personal and professional lives. I have the most amazing publishing team behind me at William Morrow and Avon Books: Superhero Liate Stehlik and my dear friend Pamela Spengler-Jaffee, along with Jennifer Hart, Tavia Kowalchuk, Kaitlin Harri, and the saintly Asanté Simons. Thanks to the wise and enthusiastic digital, audio, sales, marketing, and production teams: Angela Craft, Caitlin Garing, Kathy Gordon, Brian Grogan, Andy LeCount, Rachel Levenberg, Andrea Molitor, Jessica Rozler, Carla Parker, Dale Schmidt, and Donna Waitkus. The entire art department is filled with so many creatives, and I cheer you all on. I love Virginia Stanley's hugs, and Shelly Perron, I promise I'll get better with all those compound and "un-compound" words. As for mega-assistant Sharon Mitchell . . . The books simply don't get written without you.

My international team of publishers, editors, and

agents have given me a great gift—a sense of belonging to your countries. I've grown especially close to my friends at Blanvalet in Munich—Nicola Bartels, Berit Bohm, Anna-Lisa Hollerbach, and my beloved "voice," Angela Spizig. *Herzlichen Dank.* A long overdue thank you to Lori Antonson and Camilla Ferrier for making these relationships possible.

Every writer needs a tribe. Mine includes some of the smartest, kindest, most perceptive women in the world: Nicki Anderson, Robyn Carr, Christina Dodd, Kristin Hannah, Kristan Higgins, Vicky Joseph, Jayne Ann Krentz, Margaret Watson, Dawn Struxness, and Suzette Vandewiele. Then there's Lindsay Longford, who throws me a lifeline when I need it most.

Family is everything to me: Mr. Bill, Lil Sis, my three sons, my three daughters-in-law, my four amazing grandchildren. And my favorite next-door neighbors!

And, finally, to any pregnant women reading this book: an amniotic fluid embolism is extremely rare, so please don't stress about it. I hope you're able to labor in whatever way makes you most comfortable and that all of your beautiful babies grow into passionate readers.

With my deepest affection,
Susan Elizabeth Phillips
SusanElizabethPhillips.com

HARPER LARGE PRINT

We hope you enjoyed reading
our new, comfortable print size and found it
an experience you would like to repeat.

Well – you're in luck!

Harper Large Print offers the finest in
fiction and nonfiction books in this same larger
print size and paperback format. Light and easy to read,
Harper Large Print paperbacks are for the book lovers
who want to see what they are reading without strain.

For a full listing of titles and
new releases to come, please visit our website:
www.hc.com

HARPER LARGE PRINT

SEEING IS BELIEVING!